MW00563527

THE HOLIDAY BRIDES COLLECTION

Books 1 - 4

Ginny Baird

THE HOLIDAY BRIDES COLLECTION
Books 1 – 4

Published by
Winter Wedding Press

Copyright © 2014
Ginny Baird
Trade Paperback
ISBN 978-1-942058-04-5

About the Author

From the time that she could talk, romance author Ginny Baird was making up stories, much to the delight – and consternation – of her family and friends. By grade school, she'd turned that inclination into a talent, whereby her teacher allowed her to write and produce plays, rather than write boring book reports. Ginny continued writing throughout college, where she contributed articles to her literary campus weekly, then later pursued a career managing international projects with the US State Department.

Ginny's held an assortment of jobs, including school teacher, freelance fashion model, and greeting card writer, and has published more than twenty works of fiction and optioned ten screenplays. She's additionally published short stories, nonfiction and poetry, and admits to being a true romantic at heart.

Ginny is a *New York Times* and *USA Today* bestselling author of several books, including novellas in her *Holiday Brides Series*. She's a member of Romance Writers of America (RWA), the RWA Published Authors Network (PAN), and the RWA Published Authors Special Interest Chapter (PASIC).

When she's not writing, Ginny enjoys cooking, biking and spending time with her family in Tidewater, Virginia. She loves hearing from her readers by email at GinnyBairdRomance@gmail.com and welcome visitors to her website http://www.ginnybairdromance.com.

Books by Ginny Baird

Holiday Brides Series
The Christmas Catch
The Holiday Bride
Mistletoe in Maine
Beach Blanket Santa
Baby, Be Mine

Summer Grooms Series
Must-Have Husband
My Lucky Groom
The Wedding Wish
The Getaway Groom

A Haunted Holidays Special Edition
The Ghost Next Door
(A Love Story)

Other Titles
Real Romance
The Sometime Bride
Santa Fe Fortune
How to Marry a Matador
Counterfeit Cowboy

Books by Ginny Baird

Holiday Brides Series
The Christmas Catch
The Holiday Bride
Mistletoe in Maine
Beach Blanket Santa
Baby, Be Mine

Summer Grooms Series
Must-Have Husband
My Lucky Groom
The Wedding Wish
The Getaway Groom

A Haunted Holidays Special Edition
The Ghost Next Door
(A Love Story)

Other Titles
Real Romance
The Sometime Bride
Santa Fe Fortune
How to Marry a Matador
Counterfeit Cowboy

About the Author

From the time that she could talk, romance author Ginny Baird was making up stories, much to the delight – and consternation – of her family and friends. By grade school, she'd turned that inclination into a talent, whereby her teacher allowed her to write and produce plays, rather than write boring book reports. Ginny continued writing throughout college, where she contributed articles to her literary campus weekly, then later pursued a career managing international projects with the US State Department.

Ginny's held an assortment of jobs, including school teacher, freelance fashion model, and greeting card writer, and has published more than twenty works of fiction and optioned ten screenplays. She's additionally published short stories, nonfiction and poetry, and admits to being a true romantic at heart.

Ginny is a *New York Times* and *USA Today* bestselling author of several books, including novellas in her *Holiday Brides Series*. She's a member of Romance Writers of America (RWA), the RWA Published Authors Network (PAN), and the RWA Published Authors Special Interest Chapter (PASIC).

When she's not writing, Ginny enjoys cooking, biking and spending time with her family in Tidewater, Virginia. She loves hearing from her readers by email at GinnyBairdRomance@gmail.com and welcome visitors to her website http://www.ginnybairdromance.com.

Bundles
Real Romance and The Sometime Bride
(Gemini Edition)
Santa Fe Fortune and How to Marry a Matador
(Gemini Edition)
The Holiday Brides Collection
(Books 1—4)
A Summer Grooms Selection
(Books 1—3)
Wedding Bells Bundle

Short Stories
The Right Medicine
(Short Story & Novel Sampler)
Special Delivery
(A Valentine's Short Story)

Ginny Baird's

THE HOLIDAY BRIDES COLLECTION

Books 1 - 4

Holiday Brides Book 1

THE CHRISTMAS CATCH

The Christmas Catch

John turned his attention on Tyler, waiting eagerly nearby.

"Ever been on a toboggan, young man?"

Tyler shook his head.

"Well then, you're in for a treat. Hop on!" he instructed, positioning Tyler right behind Mason. Tyler promptly wrapped his arms around the dog, who leaned back to lick his face.

"Will he be all right?" Christine asked with concern.

"Sure. You'll be right behind him, holding on."

"And where will you be?"

"I'll be hanging on to you." John grinned and her heart melted.

Christine warned herself not to get carried away. It was just an outing in the country. But when John settled in behind her and snuggled her and little Tyler securely in his arms, she couldn't help but blush in his embrace. He was so strong and capable. Though the steep slope ahead looked formidable, Christine had no qualms about her and Tyler heading down it with John.

"Ready?" he asked, as Christine gripped Tyler.

"What about Mason?"

"That old daredevil?" John asked with a laugh. "He'll be fine!"

Then they were off, gliding at lightning speed down the snowy white slope.

"Whee!" Tyler shouted. "Whoohoo!"

Christine laughed with giddy delight, feeling like

a child again herself.

"What do you think of Vermont?" John asked with a husky whisper.

The truth was that she loved it. Loved it even more than she could have imagined.

"It's perfect," she said with a happy sigh.

John hugged them a little tighter and settled his chin on her shoulder.

"I'm glad."

Chapter One

Christine sat at her drafting table and focused intently on her sketch. In the background, cheery Christmas music played from her high-end system. Dan had bought it three years before as a Christmas gift for her. Christine tightened her lips in concentration, ignoring the familiar ache in her heart. She couldn't quite get the angle of the sleigh. Perhaps if she brought it down closer to the rooftop...

"Mommy, it's almost—"

Christine startled at the tug on her sleeve, nearly upsetting her coffee. She gripped the mug to steady it. "Tyler! How many times have I told you not to—?"

Saucerlike eyes brimmed with tears. "But I'm late for school," he said, flagging his tyke-size cell in her direction. He clutched his big, black teddy bear, the one with the tattered ear. Christine's cheeks sagged as her baby boy stood before the snowy window. Flakes beat down harder outside, but work—and preschool—would go on. This was Chicago, after all.

She drew Tyler into her arms, awash with shame. How many times had she snapped at him this week already? And it was only Tuesday. "Mommy loves you very much," she said into his charcoal curls. "I'm so sorry."

"I love you, too, Mommy," his tiny, muffled voice returned.

Christine hugged him tighter, her gaze caught by a framed photo of Dan in his military fatigues standing with his new bride. He'd been so handsome and hopeful at the time. When Tyler smiled, he looked just like him. Christine thought back to the happy, carefree brunette Dan had fallen in love with, wondering what he might think of her now. Her role as a single parent clearly didn't allow her to be carefree, but she wouldn't trade being a mother for the world. Dan had left her with a host of happy memories, but the best gift he'd supplied snuggled up against her here.

Ellen was right in urging them to get away. Apart from being Christine's boss at the greeting card company where she worked, Ellen was also her best friend. Ellen had noted the toll these last two years had taken on Christine and declared Christine was becoming ragged around the edges. Not only that, she was losing touch with her growing son. Christine denied it at first, but she could see it was true. A single tear slid down her cheek as she took in the Christmas decorations around them. Perhaps getting away would be good for her and Tyler, both.

"Mommy?" Tyler said.

"Yes, baby?"

"You're holding me so tight I can't breathe."

Christine released him and thumbed his nose.

"You really are the best little boy a mom could hope for. You know that?"

"And you're the best mom," he said with deeply sincere eyes.

Children can be so wonderfully forgiving, Christine thought with a tender sigh.

"It's snowing awfully hard out there," she said, her voice brightening.

Tyler raised his brow. "Yeah?"

"Yeah." Christine shot him an impish smile. "So,

how's about you and me taking a little detour on our way into town?"

Tyler bounced on his heels. "Oh boy! You mean—?"

"I don't think Auntie Ellen would fault me too much for running an hour behind on such a snowy day."

"Can I get the Happy Stack?"

Christine ruffled her fingers through his hair, her heart brimming with affection. "You, little man, may order anything that you want."

He beamed from ear to ear, a pint-size image of his dad.

"And while we're there," Christine continued. "I'll tell you all about our upcoming trip to Vermont."

Tyler scrunched up his face. "Vermont? What's that?"

"It's a state, sweetheart. Just a little ways away."

He paused, considering this, then held his teddy up to his ear. "Jasper wants to know if there'll be snow there."

"At least as much as we've got here."

Tyler listened to his teddy again. "Will we be there for Christmas?"

"You bet!"

Tyler hung his head, drawing Jasper into his chest.

Christine reached out a hand and gently raised his chin. "What's wrong, honey?"

Tyler glanced at his Christmas stocking, then swallowed hard.

"Jasper doesn't think Santa will be able to find us."

"Trust me on this," Christine said with a knowing

air. "Santa will *always* be able to find us. Don't you know he has his magical ways?"

Tyler twisted his lips in thought. "You mean like a GPS?"

A chuckle escaped her, in spite of herself.

"Something like that," she said, steering Tyler toward the door. "Come on, let's grab our coats. The Pancake Palace awaits!"

Christine sat in Ellen's office in a glitzy skyscraper, a hazy view of the river just visible through the pounding snow.

"I'm glad you're taking me up on this," Ellen said, handing the plane tickets and a house key across her desk.

"It's not exactly like I had a choice," Christine said, accepting them.

Ellen shifted in her expensive leather chair. She was good at what she did and ran this department without a hitch. Christine only wished Ellen would give her a chance to prove herself as something more than a copywriter. Apart from having a knack for turning a phrase, Christine had artistic talent, too. She was certain she could put her own line together, given the opportunity. She'd fleshed out several concepts already, but Ellen wouldn't even take a look. Ellen said she was burning out, that she needed to get away and recharge her batteries. No sense branching off into something new when Christine could barely keep up with the day-to-day, as it was.

Ellen centered her snazzy red frames on her nose, then said with assurance, "You'll love it up there. Nice and peaceful, the perfect getaway for you and your boy. Give you two a chance to reconnect."

"Plus, I'm doing you a favor," Christine reminded her.

Ellen laughed heartily, tossing her chin-length auburn hair. "All right, already. You're doing me a favor."

Ellen's book editor cousin was vacationing in Europe and needed a house sitter. Ellen, who generally accepted the holiday task, was jetting down to Mexico with some hot new number. Christine admired Ellen's chutzpah in sticking with the dating scene year after year. Disappointments never seemed to faze her, and she remained hopeful—one boyfriend after the next—that this guy was finally the one.

"So, when do you go on vacation?" Christine asked.

"Day after tomorrow. Same day as you."

"Guess you'll be packing more lightly."

"If you're asking whether I'm taking the string bikini, the answer is yes."

Christine was impressed with her older friend. Ellen was fifty but still had the figure of a woman in her thirties. Of course, Ellen and her Stairmaster worked at it. Christine got her workouts chasing after Tyler.

"How old is this guy?" Christine asked, betting he was several years younger.

Ellen furiously fanned her face with some desk papers. "Of age," she said slyly. Suddenly, her face lit up. "Say! Maybe you'll meet someone in New England?"

Christine stood, gathering her things. "You're forgetting one very important fact. I'm not looking."

"Pays to keep your eyes open," Ellen said with a smile.

Chapter Two

"Mommy! Look out!" Tyler yelped from the backseat. Christine gripped the steering wheel of the huge SUV, wrenching them off to the side of the road and out of the path of the oncoming pickup. Her heart beat furiously as she brought the car to a halt and cursed the driving snow. This wasn't some idyllic New England snowfall; they were caught up in a blizzard, one as blinding as they come.

"Tyler, baby," she asked, reaching back and laying a hand on his leg. "Are you all right?"

She caught his big-eyed gaze in the rearview mirror. "That was cool! Can we do it again?"

"No," Christine answered, breathing heavily. "We most certainly can't do it again."

Just then something knocked at her driver's side window. Christine glanced quickly at Tyler, then cautiously lowered the glass.

A handsome man with a rugged face and stunning blue eyes peered into her vehicle.

"Everyone okay in there?" He wore a deep blue parka, jeans, and sturdy boots. A large golden retriever bounded up behind him, leaping against the side of the SUV and perching its paws on Christine's windowsill.

"Doggie!" Tyler cried happily.

"Well hey there, little fellow," the man said kindly before sternly commanding his dog. "Mason, get back in the truck."

The dog immediately obeyed, springing inside the truck that sat across the road with its driver's door

ajar. The man turned his gaze on Christine and she
unexpectedly felt her heart skip a beat. She judged
him to be in his thirties, maybe five or six years older
than she was.

"Yes, yes. We're fine."

"Good to hear," the man said. "You nearly ran
me off the road back there."

"I nearly—?"

He shared a warming smile. "It's not that I mind.
It's how it all comes out in the end that matters."

She stared at him dumbfounded, lost in his blue
gaze. He probably thought she was some sort of
inexperienced city slicker. And he was right.
Christine didn't even own a car in Chicago and it had
been some time since she'd driven one. She'd never
been in anything with four-wheel drive, particularly
anything this big.

"Where you folks headed?"

Christine lifted a map from the front console and
handed it to him. The GPS had gotten them so lost,
she'd turned if off over an hour ago. "Are we even
going the right way?"

He studied the name of the village she'd circled,
as the wind picked up around him. "Only if you want
to take the long way there."

"Oh, no."

"You need to stay on this road for about five
more miles then turn right at the fork. From there, you
can follow the signs toward town. You got enough
gas to help you along?"

Christine nodded, feeling her tension ease.
Things would be all right, wouldn't they? It hadn't
even been snowing when she'd picked up the SUV.
Surely they were caught up in a sudden burst of storm

that would abate in a short while.

The man stepped back and surveyed her vehicle with a shrill whistle.

"Looks like that front tire's wedged in pretty deep."

Her previous panic regained steam. "We're stuck here, aren't we?"

"Not for long," he said with a grin. "Lucky for you, I carry a chain in my truck."

Christine blinked hard, trying to gather her thoughts. She didn't even know this guy, but still, when he looked at her, her silly heart went all a-flutter. Ellen was right. She'd been out of the scene so long she'd lost her ability to cope. She apparently couldn't even make casual conversation with an attractive man without assessing his age and availability. Not that she was in the market, or anything like that. For all she knew, Mr. Good Samaritan and his trusty dog were taken. Though it was impossible to know about a wedding band, given the sensible gloves on his hands. Christine gasped when she realized that she'd been checking.

"Just hold it nice and steady!" he called through the howling winds. "I'm going to pull up ahead of you. Then, once you get going, I'll let the chain drop. Whatever you do, keep your eyes on the road—and don't stop!"

Christine's heart hammered against her chest as she gripped the wheel. How nutty could she be? She was here to rebuild things with Tyler, not to find some fly-by-night romance for herself. She didn't even believe in romance anymore. She'd already had the romance of a lifetime with Tyler's dad, and he'd left her with responsibilities. At the moment, her number one priority lay in getting her son to safety.

"Get ready now!" the man shouted. "On three! One... Two..."

"Mommy, I gotta pee," Tyler interjected.

"Not now, baby. Just hold it."

"Three!"

At once, the front of their vehicle was airborne and Christine feared they'd career off the road. Then the pickup moved ahead at a gradual pace until her fishtailing SUV centered itself on the road. Sweat beaded her brow as Christine muttered prayers under her breath. Finally, they were moving forward, going straight as an arrow down the narrow road. The pickup slowed, pulling onto the shoulder to let her pass. The heavy chain dropped to the snowy lane. Christine glanced in her rearview mirror as the man scurried out of his truck to scoop it off the road, his tail-wagging dog behind him.

"Who was that?" Tyler asked, as the pickup faded from sight.

Christine heaved a grateful sigh. "Our guardian angel."

John sat in his truck with Mason, watching the beautiful woman and her son disappear through the snowdrifts. The kid was cute enough, but it was the mom who'd held his attention. What with those big, dark eyes and that long brown hair that fell in waves to her shoulders, it would be impossible for a man not to notice. Still, it was nonsensical that he'd paid attention to her looks. It wasn't like he'd consider dating someone that homicidal behind the wheel. Besides, where there was a boy, there was bound to be a father. John was nowhere near interested in getting tangled up in that. He had his fair share of picks in Burlington, and had always steered clear of single mothers. He wasn't even sure he had room for a woman in his life. At this point in his career, a full-blown family was a nonstarter. If she was still married to the boy's dad, that was even worse. John wouldn't be touching that with a twenty-foot pole.

John pushed back his parka hood and shook his head, attempting to clear it. Maybe the December air had gotten to him, because here he was, thinking all sorts of crazy thoughts about a woman he didn't even know. From the way she'd been totally thrown by the landscape and the tags on the rental SUV, she wasn't a local resident anyhow, just someone passing through. Chances of seeing her around were minimal. But what did that matter to him? The most important thing was that she and her son got to where they were going without running themselves—or anyone else— off the road again.

"What did you think, old boy?" he asked, patting the retriever's head.

The dog barked loudly.

"Yeah, they seemed like city slickers to me, too."

Christine pulled the SUV to the side of the road and double-checked the address. Just ahead of them sat a classic farmhouse nestled in a snowy field behind a split-rail fence. She stepped into the biting cold to wipe the snow off of the sign dangling from a post at the head of the drive. WINTERHAVEN appeared in stenciled lettering. Winds whipped up as Christine battled her way back to the SUV, shielding her face with her coat sleeve. She clambered into the driver's seat with a shiver and cranked up the heat another notch.

"Looks like we're home," she said softly to Tyler, who snoozed in his car seat. They'd paused for a potty break ten miles earlier then he'd promptly passed out from exhaustion. Not even the chill of the wind on his face woke him up as she carried him toward the house.

Moments later, Christine carted her sleeping boy over the threshold of the old-style structure. The great room was cozy yet elegant, with exposed wood beams and a large stone hearth. A fire had been laid for them in advance, a neat stack of logs and extra kindling sticks piled in a box nearby.

"Nice," Christine said to herself.

She decided to let Tyler rest on the sofa while she settled in. After laying him down and covering him with a handy throw blanket, she perused the rest of the place. The kitchen was expansive and well equipped, and the three bedrooms upstairs were every bit as comfortable, with four-poster beds and huge down comforters. From each window, visions of a winter wonderland beckoned her to run outside and play. Christine felt her inner child delight in the thought of making snowmen and snow angels, then racing indoors to hot cocoa and homemade cookies. Maybe Ellen was more right about this trip than she knew. A fresh change in scenery and limited interruptions could set just the right stage for quality Mommy and Tyler time.

A little while later, Christine sat at the large farm table near the front of the great room sipping her coffee and studying directions to the local market.

Tyler stirred, then sat up and rubbed his eyes, yawning.

"Where are we?" he asked, clutching Jasper.

"Winterhaven."

"Huh?"

"It's where we're staying, baby. What do you think?"

He looked around, still a little dazed.

"Where's the TV?"

"I don't think there is one."

His small lips pulled into a pout.

"What's there to do?"

"Plenty! There are puzzles over there in the cupboard. Legos, Lincoln Logs..."

"Lincoln who?" he asked, astounded.

"I'll show you, honey. It's fun."

Unconvinced, Tyler scooped his little backpack off the floor and extracted a portable video game. Next, he dug out its charger, settling back on the sofa to survey the surrounding lamps. "Least there's 'lectricity."

Christine studied her son, thinking he was a tad too modern for his own good. She had to admit, though, that even she'd forgotten about old-fashioned fun stuff like roasting marshmallows until she'd walked in here. "You hungry?" she queried, thinking he must be.

Dark eyes lit up. "Deep-dish Chicago pizza?"

"Not here."

"Oh," he said, disappointed.

Christine folded the map in her hands, noting the snow had stopped outside. It was likely a temporarily lull in the weather. Best to take advantage while they could.

"I was just reading about the local market. I'm not sure if they'll have pizza, but they're bound to have provisions. How about you and I head over there and check it out?"

Chapter Three

Christine halted her brimming shopping cart in the aisle as Tyler dropped in a huge bag of marshmallows. They were at Mac's Market, the sole grocers in the tiny village on the outskirts of Burlington. Already they had chocolate bars and graham crackers. Their list was nearly complete. "Can't forget the cocoa," she said, smiling at her son. She reached for it but it was high on a shelf, all the way to the back.

"Here, let me help with that," a familiar masculine voice said over her shoulder.

Christine heard a happy bark and turned to find the man from the road behind her. He wore winter boots, jeans, and a gray college sweatshirt beneath his open parka. Up close and personal, he looked even better than he had outdoors, his short dark hair and ruddy complexion a heady complement to his eyes.

"Well, hello," he said with a smile. Mason wriggled on his haunches beside him, wagging his tail. Tyler stared up at the guy and his jaw dropped.

"Are you really an angel?"

"Beg pardon?"

"Mommy says you're an angel."

Christine felt her face flush. "Oh no, I think he misunderstood. I was just… What I mean is…" She glanced down at Mason, then up at him, amazed. "They let dogs in here?"

The man leaned forward with a confidential whisper. "He doesn't know he's a dog. He thinks he's a college student."

Why did the mention of college spark some vague recognition? Christine's eyes locked on his sweatshirt. "Carolina?" she asked with surprise.

"The University of North Carolina at Chapel Hill," he said with pride.

"No way."

"Way."

"You went there?"

"Most certainly did."

"Small world."

"And you?"

She looked at him and smiled. "I know why the sky's Carolina blue."

"God's a Tar Heel," he said with a laugh.

Tyler studied him with awe. "I thought you might know God."

The man eyed Tyler curiously. "Here," he said to Christine, "let me help you with that cocoa." He reached for it and easily took it from the shelf, handing it to her. She accepted it, inexplicably spellbound as his blue eyes crinkled at the corners.

"You know, I never got the chance to thank you for our daring rescue."

"Oh, it wasn't so daring," he said.

"We could have been stuck there for hours."

"How's the SUV holding up?"

"As long as I stay on the road it works like a charm."

They shared a bout of companionable laughter, then stood there staring at each other as if each wanted to speak but neither could think up anything to say.

"Well, I guess that's it, then," Christine offered awkwardly. "We'd best finish up. It's been a long day."

"Of course."

John thoughtfully watched them walk away, feeling an unfamiliar tug in his chest. She was just some girl from Carolina. So what if she'd wound up in Vermont? That didn't mean she'd be interested, and certainly didn't indicate she was available. Mason stood beside him, itching to follow after the woman and her son. How come his dog always knew things he didn't?

"You know I was thinking," John called out.

She turned on her heels, her cheeks flushed.

"I was just thinking the same thing."

"You were?"

"I mean, I meant to tell you... wanted to say, it was really great running into you."

Boy, was she a looker with those big, dark eyes and neatly compact figure. She was even prettier than he'd given her credit for in the SUV.

"Yeah, you too. But, you know, I was wondering…" Mason interjected a happy bark, not wanting to be left out. "My dog and I were wondering… what's a Carolina girl like you doing all the way up here?"

"I'm a Chicago girl now," she said, taking her son's hand.

"The question stands."

"We're house-sitting for a friend," she said with a sweet smile. "And you?"

John shifted on his feet, feeling as if she were assessing him. He'd probably forgotten to shave or something. "I teach over at the college." He mentally kicked himself for the one little detail that had slipped his mind. "My apologies," he said extending his hand.

"I never introduced myself. I'm John Steadman."

She stepped forward to accept his grip and John caught a whiff of her perfume. She smelled all sweet and womanly, like a field full of wildflowers in summertime.

"Christine White. Nice to meet you."

Soulful dark eyes met his and John felt the back of his neck flash hot. There was a tug at his sleeve and John looked down.

"I'm Tyler!" the little boy said, bouncing on his heels.

John kneeled to greet him at eye level, man to man.

"Good to know ya, little fellow," he said, firmly shaking Tyler's hand. "You taking good care of your mom?"

Tyler nodded solemnly and John chuckled.

"Well, keep up the good work!"

Mason held up a paw in Tyler's direction. John glanced at Christine for her approval, got it, then looked at the boy. "Seems like Mason wants to shake hands, too."

Ten minutes later, they stood in the snow outside the rental SUV where John had helped load groceries in the back. While it had been fun running into them, John didn't have the nerve to suggest seeing them again. What kind of sense would that make? Christine and Tyler were bound to have made their own vacation plans, and John had plenty to take care of too.

"You and Tyler take care, Christine," John said, waving good-bye.

"Thanks, you too," she said through her open

window. Tyler raised a mitten and called good-bye to the dog as they backed out and slowly pulled away.

John watched their taillights fade as Mason stood by with a sullen expression.

"Don't look so down, fellow," John told him, stroking his head. "Santa's coming soon."

The dog gave him a sideways glance like he'd just made the biggest mistake of his life. Okay, so maybe he'd noticed she wasn't wearing a wedding ring, but that didn't mean he had to act on it.

"And none of that nonsense about how I should have gotten her number," John scolded, adjusting his parka. "I have a very occupied life."

But Mason just ignored him and loped through the snow toward their truck.

Chapter Four

Christine whisked about the kitchen, talking on her cell while she fixed dinner. A pot of chili simmered on the stove as she mixed a cornbread batter. The snow had started up again outside, beating down harder than ever, but they were snug inside their getaway. "Hang on, Ellen," she said into the receiver. "Just let me check on Ty a sec." She peered through the swinging door to find him happily engaged in a game of Legos by the fire.

"So?" Ellen asked as Christine popped the cornbread pan in the oven. "Is it as lovely as I said?"

"Just beautiful," Christine answered, gazing out the window. "And very, very cold."

"I wish I could sympathize…" Christine heard a low murmuring in the background. It was Ellen's voice, soft and sultry. "A little more on the shoulders, honey?"

"I'm sorry. I didn't get that."

"I was just saying I'm enjoying the warmth down here." She giggled and Christine could have sworn she heard the tinkling of a tropical drink in her hand. She even bet it held a little paper umbrella. She could just see Ellen in that tiny bikini wearing a big straw hat and gigantic dark glasses. "Cancun's been incredibly welcoming."

The man Ellen was with was bound to be scorching hot. It wasn't like Christine hadn't met her own share of hunks, as well. "I know what you mean," she said in a mysterious tone. "Vermont's been friendly, too."

There was a subtle slurping, then a startled cough. "Don't tell me the confirmed bachelorette has met someone?"

"I didn't say that... exactly."

"You've been there all of eight hours! Good girl!" Christine could tell Ellen was pleased with her, probably beaming like the Cheshire cat from ear to ear.

"It's not like that at all. My SUV got stuck in a snowstorm."

"And Prince Charming rescued you? Ooh, I'm just loving it! Come now, dish to the woman who made it all possible. What's his name?"

"John Steadman."

"Sounds promising. What's he do?"

"He's a college professor."

"I'll Google him!" Then Christine heard her whisper to her boy toy. "Hand me my iPad, baby."

"That's stalkerish!"

"You're just jealous because you didn't do it first. Let's see S... T... Is it just an 'e' or an 'ea' in Steadman?"

"How should I know?"

"Yep. It's 'ea.' Here he is. Mister... Whoops! Make that *Doctor* John Steadman. Um-hum... Burlington, Vermont. My oh my oh my. Is he a hottie!"

"Ellen!"

"What? I'm terribly proud of you. *So,* when are the two of you going out?"

"That's what I've been trying to tell you. We're not."

"Why not?"

"He didn't ask."

"Then you ask him."

"We're only here for two weeks."

"And I'm only here for one," she purred. "That doesn't mean I'm letting *my* vacation go to waste." Christine feared she heard kissing and hoped Ellen wasn't making out on the other end of the line.

"I'm not like you, Ellen. This is different. I'm—"

"Chicken."

"No. Out of practice."

"That's the whole point, Christine. It's been over two years. Don't you think it's time?"

Christine opened her laptop and set it on the counter. Of all the nerve! Ellen went and Googled her guy before she'd had a chance to. Christine felt a rash of embarrassment for thinking of John Steadman as hers. She hadn't laid claim to him, for heaven's sake. They barely even knew each other and had only met a couple of times. By accident. Literally.

Suddenly a smoke alarm sounded and Christine looked up to find chili bubbling over on the cooktop and black smoke curling from the oven. "Oh no!" she cried, leaping from the barstool.

Tyler rushed into the room, hollering, "Something's on fire!"

She grabbed two potholders and pulled the charred cornbread from the oven. Quickly opening the kitchen door, she tossed the seared pan out in the snow, then dashed back inside to wave a towel beneath the blaring smoke detector.

Tyler clambered up on the kitchen stool to watch the show as the air cleared and the wailing instrument finally quieted.

"Whew!" Christine breathed, dabbing her

forehead with the dishtowel.

Tyler slowly spun his stool toward the counter, then cried with delight.

"Mommy, Mommy! Look! It's our angel!"

Christine crossed to the counter and shut her laptop.

"John's not an angel, baby. I already explained that to you."

"But, when he helped us you said—"

"It was a figure of speech. Something someone says when they mean something else."

"But that doesn't make any sense."

"That's how people talk sometimes."

"Why don't they just say what they mean?"

"I guess that would be too easy." She reached for her son and helped him off of the stool. "Come on, let's get ready to eat. You hungry for dinner?"

Tyler wrinkled his nose. "Can I skip the cornbread?"

An hour later, Christine and Tyler were constructing a fortress out of Lincoln Logs. Tyler crowned the final turret with a tiny toy flag. "Tadahh!" he proclaimed proudly. "It's done!"

Christine's heart swelled with pride. She was so honored to call this charming young man her son. "It's awesome, Ty. World's best."

Tyler beamed.

"You see," Christine told him, "playing the old-fashioned way isn't really so rotten."

"It's all right, I guess." Tyler yawned and rubbed his eyes.

Christine checked the mantel clock, seeing it was after nine.

"Oh gosh, look at the time. It's up to bed with you."

"But mom—" he protested, even as he picked up Jasper.

"No buts about it. There will be more time for play tomorrow."

"You mean it?"

Christine nodded as he headed up the stairs dragging his teddy beside him. Slowly, thoughtfully, he turned toward his mom. "I like Vermont," he said.

"Yeah, buddy," she answered, smiling softly, "I like it, too."

Chapter Five

With Tyler tucked in, Christine sat at the dining room table to work on her drafts. Her first task was reworking her earlier sketch of Santa's sleigh over a rooftop by using Winterhaven as a model for the scene. After a while, tired from her labors, she stood for a stretch and walked to the window, surveying the already buried-in-snow SUV. *Guardian Angel,* she thought with a chuckle, casting her gaze up the stairs to where Tyler lay sleeping.

Nabbing her laptop off of an end table, she carried it with her to the sofa and perched it on her knees. Within seconds, a computerized voice told her she had mail. Curious, Christine opened her messages to find a new e-mail in her inbox from, of all things, the University of North Carolina Alumni Association. She thought of John, but then realized she was being ridiculous to take this sheer coincidence as any sort of sign. Even if they had gone to the same school, she reasoned, they probably hadn't been there at the same time. He had to be in his mid to late thirties at least, and she had just turned thirty-one. Still, she couldn't keep herself from clicking over to his Web page, which she'd bookmarked earlier, to review its details one more time.

Department Chair John Steadman is a full professor of business and economics. Steadman holds a BA from the University of North Carolina at Chapel Hill and a PhD from the Massachusetts Institute of Technology. Before coming to Vermont, Professor Steadman served as an associate and then full

*professor at Tulane University in New Orleans, where
he was instrumental in developing innovative
business models.*

Below his bio and an extremely flattering
professional photo, a link directed the reader to
Contact Professor Steadman. Christine could just bet
that a number of coeds had the hots for the steamy
professor. Lots of girls got crushes on their teachers,
and John's easygoing nature and gentle charm would
make him easy to fall for. His ruggedly handsome
face and that built, athletic body didn't hurt much
either... But Christine was no college kid. She was a
full-grown woman and a mother besides. She was
way too mature to go crushing on people, particularly
people she didn't know that well.

Christine pondered the prospect of getting to
know John. Perhaps Ellen was right. Christine hadn't
gone out for so much as coffee with a man since Dan
died. She couldn't sequester herself forever. What
was the harm in a casual connection anyway? Maybe
being in Vermont for a limited time made it all the
better, less risky somehow. She could take a chance
on seeing someone on a friendship basis, where
circumstance clearly dictated that a friendship was all
it could be. She wasn't ready for full-scale dating.
Plus, she had Tyler to consider. Though he was too
young to remember a lot about his dad, he'd already
lost a father once. Christine didn't want to put him in
the position of forming an attachment that might not
pan out. Truth be told, she didn't want to put herself
in that situation either.

And yet, *getting back out there,* as Ellen called it,
didn't have to be such a scary proposition. Christine
could take it in little, bitty, baby steps. That's right,

one thing at a time. This Christmas, maybe she'd brave a coffee date in Vermont. Next year, who knew? She might work her way up to lunch with someone. By the time Tyler was eighteen, she might even find herself ready for sleepovers... A flash of heat tore through her as she suddenly imagined herself going to bed with John. But that was a ridiculous thing to consider. Plain crazy. She wasn't interested in anything like that right now. She'd already thought the whole thing through.

Christine gingerly guided the mouse over the e-mail link, wondering if she could really do it. She'd been raised so traditionally that she didn't totally feel comfortable making the first move. Then again, if it was a simple move toward friendship, what was the big deal? A vision of John sweeping her into his arms raced through her mind, and she slapped her laptop shut, losing her nerve. She stood and skittishly began to pace the room. "On the one hand," she said out loud. "It's no harm, no foul. I just write and say, thanks again. That's innocent enough. I don't have to be the one to suggest going out. I'll leave that to him. And, well... if he doesn't, there's nothing lost."

Feeling her courage surge, Christine sat on the sofa again and reopened her laptop. She slapped it shut two seconds later. "On the other hand, what does that say? That I can't get him off my mind? He'd clearly know I looked him up! What kind of woman does that? A desperate one, obviously..."

She set her laptop on a sofa cushion and strode to the bar, thinking some merlot might help. Either to grant her the wherewithal to go through with it, or realize what a cockeyed idea it was. She poured herself a glass, still musing aloud. "Then again, I am a fellow Tar Heel, and we Carolina types are always friendly with each other." She took a long swallow, draining her glass. She was worse off than she thought. Talking to herself and swigging down wine! Something had to be done, and fast!

Christine sat back down with fire in her belly and determination in her soul. If Ellen could do this, then so could she, damn it. It wasn't like she was proposing marriage. She was only writing to establish contact. She clicked the link and a dialogue box opened. Now, if she could just think of the perfect thing to say.

John opened his e-mail the next morning and was pleased to find a message from Christine White. "Who says it's not an equal opportunity world?" he asked Mason, who was scarfing down his breakfast. "Hey," he said to the dog, who just kept eating. "Hey!"

Mason stopped chomping and looked up.

"Yeah, I'm talking to you," John said with a grin. "Guess what, buddy? I think we've got a date."

Mason cocked his head sideways, waiting.

"No, I haven't asked her yet. But that doesn't mean I'm not going to."

John took a sip of his coffee, devising a plan. The truth was that he was inordinately happy to hear from Christine. She hadn't said much, just *Thanks again for the 'absolutely daring' rescue* or some such, but it was what was written between the lines that counted. She'd looked him up! Had actually taken the time to track him down, despite the fact that she couldn't be in town for more than just a few days. John reasoned there wasn't much harm in taking her and her boy out for coffee and cocoa. Show them a bit of genuine New England hospitality. Heck, it was lonely up here in wintertime. Besides, maybe his best friend Carlos was right. Spending all his time trapped indoors with a dog was getting to him. Sooner or later, he was going to start hearing Mason talk back.

It wasn't like John didn't have his lady friends. But honestly, none of them were as good as Mason to talk to. It happened every time. Just when John thought things were going really well, someone had to bring up the marriage talk, that someone not being him. It wasn't that John was opposed to marriage in theory. It was extra good for the economy, in fact. Just not for him personally at the moment, not with his big promotion coming up and his professional papers due. Maybe one day he'd settle down, but it didn't need to be any day soon. Fortunately, that was neither here nor there. That sweet Carolina girl was only here for a little while, so there was no harm in being friendly and making a connection. All in the spirit of the General Alumni Association of course, John thought, beginning to type.

Christine sat up in bed and flipped open her laptop. Yes. There was a message from John Steadman! *Coffee and cocoa this afternoon? I know a place that you and Tyler might enjoy.*

Christine grinned broadly and quickly typed back *Yes*.

"Yes, yes, *yes!*" she hollered, merrily kicking her feet under the covers. He'd done it. The handsome professor hottie had actually gone and done it! Asked Christine and Tyler out on a date! Okay, so maybe it wasn't a date, technically. An outing then, yes. That's

what it was, an outing. Just the three of them. Four,
counting Mason. She was sure that he would come
along. Tyler was bound to love that. *"Yes!"*

Christine brought her hands to her flaming
cheeks as Tyler pressed his way in the room.
"Mommy?" he asked groggily. "What is it? Is it time
to get up?"

"I'm sorry if I woke you, honey. I was just
making plans. How does having cocoa with John
sound?"

He looked at her uncertainly. "It sounds all
right."

Christine deposited her computer on the floor.
"Come here, you," she said, giving her little boy and
his teddy a hug. She was still grinning in spite of
herself, as gleeful and nervous as a teenager.

Tyler peered up at her with big, dark eyes. "Are
you happy, Mommy?"

She pulled him up onto the bed and nestled him
firmly in her arms. "Yeah, I suppose I am."

"I like it when you're happy," he said, snuggling
up against her. "You're not like that much."

The simple declaration hit her like a sucker
punch. "Oh baby, I'm so sorry," she said, hearing her
voice crack. "Sorry that Mommy's been such a
crank."

"It's not your fault," his little voice said.

"What do you mean?"

"I know you need friends too."

She jostled him in her arms.

"I've got Auntie Ellen."

"That's not enough."

"No?"

"Billy's mommy has a friend."

"Oh?"

"Sometimes he sleeps over."

Christine swallowed hard. "We don't need to worry about that."

"I wouldn't mind."

"But Mommy would. She's... I'm... not ready."

"Well, I think John's nice. Even if he's not an angel."

"I bet you like Mason too," she said, kissing him on the head.

Tyler grinned. "I like Mason best!"

Chapter Six

Christine, Tyler, and John sat in the small café housed in a country cottage. A real wood fire blazed in the fireplace nearby, its mantel crowned with Christmas decorations. A sign on the opposite wall read *Kiddy Korner.* Below it children played with old style blocks, puzzles, and a handcrafted circus train, stocked with various animals. Tyler set down his hot chocolate and pointed across the room.

"Can I go over there?"

Christine dabbed his upper lip with a napkin. "Sure baby, go right ahead." She turned to John. "This place is great."

He grinned at her, blue eyes crinkling. "I thought you and Tyler might like it." At his feet, Mason lazily lifted his head. John patted him lightly and he went back to sleep.

"You're pretty good with kids," Christine told him. "Got any of your own?"

"Me? Oh no. I mean, not yet. Never married. I've got two nieces and a nephew, though."

"Are they close by?"

"I wish, but no. They're with their mom in Baltimore. That's where I grew up."

He shifted awkwardly. "And you and Tyler? Are you all on your own in Chicago? Any family there?"

"It's just the two of us," she said. "My husband, Dan, Tyler's dad, passed away a few years ago."

"I'm sorry, Christine. I had no—"

"It's all right. It's good for me to talk about it."

"Was it an illness?" he asked tentatively.

"Afghanistan."

John was quiet a moment. When he spoke his voice was tinged with compassion. "Things must be hard, getting by on your own with a young son."

"Ty and I manage," she said, sounding braver than she felt. The truth was that she hadn't been managing well at all lately.

"You seem to do a great job..." His lips creased in a subtle smile. "...except for when you're driving in snowstorms."

"Hey!" she cried in mock offense, but secretly she appreciated his effort to lighten the moment. Mason awakened, startled by her shout of surprise. John slipped him biscotti under the table to quell his interest. The dog took it and gnawed contentedly.

"So tell me," John said, changing the subject. "What do you do in Chicago?"

"I'm a copywriter for a major greeting card company."

"That sounds interesting."

"Not as interesting as I'd like."

"What do you mean?"

"I basically write the words, but it's always been my dream to illustrate too. You know, develop my own line—soup to nuts."

"Why not go for it?"

"It's not as easy as all that," she said with a frown. "Company politics."

"So? Start your own company."

"What?"

"What's stopping you?" John leaned forward with his challenge.

Christine sat back. "Oh, about a million things. First, I'd have to raise the capital, find investors. I couldn't front even a small operation like that on my own. Then, I'd need to locate a printer, contract distributors…"

"None of that sounds impossible."

"Impossible, no. It's just nothing I've ever considered."

"With the Internet these days, there are bound to be new opportunities."

"Sure."

John took a slow sip of coffee, surveying her over the rim of his cup. After a beat, he surprised her by raising his cup to hers. "The future is long," he said with an enigmatic smile.

"Yes. Yes, it is," she answered thoughtfully. "Very long indeed."

She returned his toast, mulling over his proposition. *I mean, it would be a really big dream. Totally cool,* she thought. Just no way could it happen now. Maybe someday, when things were more settled…

Their eyes locked for a moment and Christine's cheeks flamed. All John had to do was look at her and old embers leapt into brushfires, igniting sensations all over her body. Christine hadn't felt those smoldering sensations in quite a while. In fact, she hadn't been sure they still existed. But they did and here they were, raging out of control. So much so that Christine nabbed some ice from her water glass and dumped it in her coffee. Drinking something hot at the moment seemed positively contrary when Christine clearly needed to cool down.

John swallowed hard and followed suit, likewise chilling his java. "It *is* a little warm in here," he said, his face coloring as well. She couldn't tell if it was from the warmth of the fire or from the way that she'd looked at him. In any case, his chiseled face was exceptionally handsome in the subtle glow.

He studied their water glasses, then stumbled slightly with the words. "In present day, we seem to be all out of ice. Should I get us some more?"

"That would be great, thanks."

When John returned, the conversation turned to something thankfully less personal, the topics of courses he taught at the business school. While Christine wasn't familiar with all the nuances, it was refreshing to talk to someone so enthusiastic about his work. Before she knew it, two hours had flown by and they were standing at the door ready to make their departure. Christine had nearly forgotten how good it felt to talk comfortably with a man. Maybe there'd been a few peaks and valleys during their dialogue, but overall they'd gotten on reasonably well. So well, in fact, that she couldn't help but feel slightly depressed that the outing was over.

"Come on, Ty," she told her son as he said good-bye to his newfound friends. "Let's get on your hat and gloves. It's awfully cold outside." Mason watched them with ears drooping, not wanting them to go.

"I'm really glad that you could make it," John said, helping Christine on with her coat.

"Thanks for asking us," she said, holding his gaze.

Just then, a middle-aged man barreled through the door carrying a blast of frigid air with him. Mason excitedly bounded for him, covering him with doggie kisses.

"Mason, down!" John said. This time Christine was sure he'd flushed red, from his neck to the tips of his ears. The dog slunk to the floor, looking embarrassed.

"Don't be so hard on the pooch," the man said. "Some days it's the only loving I get!" He unwrapped his broad scarf, exposing a handsome older face and a graying beard. He shot John a merry grin.

"Steadman! How's it going? Surviving sabbatical?"

John affectionately pumped his hand. "Good to see you, Carlos."

Carlos sent a quick glance at Tyler then gave Christine an appreciative once-over.

"Hello…" he said to Christine, his voice lilting with a light Spanish accent. "And you must be?"

"Christine White," she said, extending her hand.

"Carlos Dominguez. It's a pleasure." He turned his gaze on Ty. "And you, young man?"

John smiled. "This is Christine's son, Tyler."

Carlos eyed them all, apparently pleased with the situation.

"Well, well… Isn't this delightful? Where are you two from?"

"We're here from Chicago," Christine said.

"It's a permanent move, I hope?"

"Just a vacation," she told him.

"I didn't think my colleague had that much luck."

"Weren't you on your way somewhere?" John asked Carlos, clearly trying to get rid of him.

"Fine, fine," Carlos said, shaking his head. "I can see when I'm not wanted." He smiled warmly at Christine before taking his leave. "Christine, hope to have the opportunity again."

"I'll bet you do, you old dog," John said under his breath. Mason nuzzled his hand, but John waved him away.

"He seemed nice," Christine said as Carlos made his way to the coffee bar and ordered.

"We've been friends for a long time. Knew him down in New Orleans, in fact."

"At Tulane?" Christine queried before she could stop herself.

John dissected her with piercing blue eyes and her cheeks caught fire. Now he'd know she'd been stalking him. Not only had she looked up his e-mail address, she'd practically memorized his bio!

John cocked his head sideways and studied her with amazement. "That's right."

Christine slid on her gloves, anxious to extract herself from the humiliating moment. "Tyler and I should head back."

"That's not a bad thought," John said, peering out the door beside them. "It's starting to flurry out there."

"Does it ever stop snowing in Vermont?" Christine asked with a laugh.

"A few months out of the year," he answered.

Christine finished bundling up Tyler and pulled on her winter hat.

"You know," John said. "The snow may be a pain for driving, but it makes for awfully good sledding."

"Sledding? Yahoo!" Tyler crowed, springing up and down.

Christine stared at John, her heart hopeful. Oh to be in a winter wonderland with this handsome man, gliding down snow-covered hills. Christine brought her hand to her mouth, hoping she'd just thought that, not said it. By the way John's eyes crinkled at the corners, she wasn't sure.

"I was thinking," he said as a smile spread across his lips, "that maybe the three of us could go for a ride?"

"He knows where all the best hills are!" Carlos shouted from across the room.

Christine turned, to spy Carlos seated in the corner, apparently eavesdropping from behind his splayed newspaper.

John spouted back, feigning irritation. "Could you mind your own business for one fraction of a second... please?"

Carlos shrugged and rattled his paper, making Christine giggle out loud. Tyler stared up at her with joy in his eyes. "Can we Mommy? *Puhleeze?*"

John met her gaze and said firmly, "I do know where all the best hills are."

"Sledding sounds great," Christine said with a happy grin. "Only I don't think there's a sled at the house."

"No worries. I'll supply one. Where are you staying?"

"Winterhaven. Do you know it?"

"Know it?" John lowered his voice. "Carlos used to date the woman who lives there."

"Oh," Christine whispered back, intrigued. "What happened?"

"She's a very nice person," John replied quietly. "Just didn't share Carlos's sense of... adventure."

Christine's cell rang, startling her out of the moment.

"I'm sorry," she told John. She checked and saw

the call was from Ellen. "I think I'd better take this."

"I hope you're having half as much fun as I am," Ellen chirped. Her voice wavered, almost as if it were windblown. "I'm about to go airborne!"

"What?" Christine shrieked, before getting herself under control and turning politely away from John and the other interested coffee patrons. She found herself facing Carlos, who pointedly lowered his paper. "Ellen, what on earth is going on?"

"Parasailing, Christine. My gorgeous man Emilio and I are setting our sights for the sun!"

"Be careful. That sounds dangerous."

"Dangerous, ha! It's a blast! This is our second time up!"

"Well, seeing as how you survived the first time, do you think I could call you back? I'm kind of busy with something."

"Just as long at that *something* spells his name S... T... E... A..."

Christine pressed End Call and whirled on her heels, finding herself nearly in John's arms. She backed away from his broad chest seconds before crashing into it.

"Everything all right?" he asked, steadying her by the elbows. Even through her layers of winter clothing, the electricity from his touch tore up her arms and sent tiny shivers racing down her spine. Christine's stomach flip-flopped. She wondered if she was getting sick or was just nervous. John's stare dove into her and she felt faint from his perusal. Had to be the nerves. Yeah, those combined with the coffee.

"Oh yes. Everything's fine." She affected a laugh. "That was just my best friend Ellen. Senior editor, too, but we're friends as well. Anyhow…" She drew a deep breath. "What time were you thinking about for sledding?"

He released her with a heartwarming grin. "How's two o'clock tomorrow sound?"

"Two o'clock sounds good." She smiled feebly in return, wondering if she looked as smitten as she suddenly felt. Oh God, was she crushing on the professor just like some silly coed? And right in front of the entire town's tiny population, including his inquisitive best friend?

Christine took Tyler's hand and raced out into the weather, hoping the frigid wind would drive some sense into her. She was only here on vacation, not poised to spend the rest of her life! What was she doing letting her emotions get the best of her?

"See you tomorrow!" she called, as she and Tyler headed for the SUV. "And thanks again!"

"Mommy?" Tyler asked as she snapped him into his car seat. "Is John your friend now?"

She smiled at him and answered uncertainly. "I think so, sweetie."

"It's about time!" he declared.

Chapter Seven

John couldn't believe he was doing this, taking Christine and her young son sledding. If he didn't know better, he'd swear he'd already tumbled headlong down a hill and taken a knock on the noggin. John wasn't even interested in getting involved. With that potential promotion looming, he had to make work his priority. When John made Associate Dean, *then* he could entertain thoughts of a personal life. Even if his advancement came off, he'd want to keep things clean and simple while he took to his new task. What he'd been doing up until now worked fine. Occasional outings with certain lady friends, no fuss and no strings attached. That was what he wanted, wasn't it?

John recalled that moment in the café when he'd been trapped in the heat of Christine's gaze. Hell, it had been more than one moment. There were several times, in fact, when he'd felt his pulse pounding and his reason racing into overdrive. It wasn't just that she was pretty; there was something else about her too. She was obviously smart and could hold her own in a conversation. And when she'd nearly landed in his arms, it was all John could do not to imagine bringing his mouth to hers. Seriously, it wasn't like she'd been graced with those lips for no reason. Clearly that reason had to do with her needing a good kissing now and again.

John strode toward his truck and deposited the handcrafted toboggan in its bed, determined to put these cockamamie notions out his head. The heavy snow had abated to a light sprinkle. It was the perfect afternoon for the occasion. What was so wrong with a toboggan ride anyhow? It wasn't exactly romantic, with the little boy coming along. It was more like a family outing. John swallowed hard at that last thought, feeling like he'd bitten off more than he could chew. Was it really so wrong to take them out, knowing they'd be gone in just a little while? Perhaps that was John's best form of protection. It was likely Christine's too. Surely she wouldn't want to become entangled with someone living so far away. Her life was complicated enough as it was. Mason barked and John looked down to see him furiously wagging his tail, apparently ready to get on with it. At least *he* wasn't conflicted.

John's cell rang and he tucked a hand inside his coat to pull it out.

"Your timing's rotten," he told Carlos.

"No, what's rotten is your holding out on me. Ten years together and you didn't breathe a word!"

"That's because there's nothing to talk about."

"Aha! I knew it. This one's really gotten to you, hasn't she?"

"Nobody gets to me, Carlos. You know that."

Carlos chuckled. "Not until now, amigo. Not until now. Not that I disapprove. Christine seems different somehow. Not quite so… eager."

"Please."

"You know what I mean. With the others, I could practically hear those talons springing out to catch you."

"You, my friend, have an overblown sense of the dramatic."

"I, compadre, have a total connection to the

truth."

John opened the door of his truck and Mason sprang inside. "I'd love to chat all day," he said. "But the truth is I've got someplace to be."

"You're seeing her, aren't you? Probably her and that cute kid too."

John stared at Mason and shook his head before replying in a singsongy voice. "Good-bye, Carlos!"

Snow fell lightly as John lifted the toboggan from his truck. They were on a scenic hill, the splendor of the snowcapped countryside around them. Christine ran a gloved hand down the side of the toboggan, admiring the sheen of its wood.

"She's a beauty," she said to John. "Almost like a work of art."

He gave her a smile that swept the chill from the bitter wind. "Thanks. I appreciate that."

"Hang on…" she said with surprise. "Are you saying you made this?"

"Some time ago. It was one of my first pieces."

Christine was impressed. She'd never met a man who'd made a toboggan—or much of anything else— before. "You've made others?"

John positioned the toboggan on the hilltop and looked up. Mason immediately jumped on. "Toboggans, no," he said. "I figured one was all I needed. But I've built other things: bookshelves, tables, and the like."

"Tables? Really?"

"My dining room table in fact." He studied her thoughtfully. "I'll have to show it to you sometime."

Christine's cheeks warmed as she dropped her eyes. "I'd like that."

John turned his attention on Tyler, waiting eagerly nearby.

"Ever been on a toboggan, young man?"

Tyler shook his head.

"Well then, you're in for a treat. Hop on!" he instructed, positioning Tyler right behind Mason. Tyler promptly wrapped his arms around the dog, who leaned back to lick his face.

"Will he be all right?" Christine asked with concern.

"Sure. You'll be right behind him, holding on."

"And where will you be?"

"I'll be hanging on to you." John grinned and her heart melted.

Christine warned herself not to get carried away. It was just an outing in the country. But when John settled in behind her and snuggled her and little Tyler securely in his arms, she couldn't help but blush in his embrace. He was so strong and capable. Though the steep slope ahead looked formidable, Christine had no qualms about her and Tyler heading down it with John.

"Ready?" he asked, as Christine gripped Tyler.

"What about Mason?"

"That old daredevil?" John asked with a laugh. "He'll be fine!"

Then they were off, gliding at lightning speed down the snowy white slope.

"Whee!" Tyler shouted. "Whoohoo!"

Christine laughed with giddy delight, feeling like a child again herself.

"What do you think of Vermont?" John asked with a husky whisper.

The truth was that she loved it. Loved it even

more than she could have imagined.

"It's perfect," she said with a happy sigh.

John hugged them a little tighter and settled his chin on her shoulder.

"I'm glad."

Chapter Eight

A week later, John pulled a blazing marshmallow from the fireplace. Blowing it out, he laid it on a graham cracker held by Christine and loaded with chocolate. She grinned, first at him and then at Tyler. "This will have to be your last," she said to her son before handing him the squishy treat.

The boy's face was liberally dotted with sticky mess. "But, Mom!"

"She's right, you know," John said, backing up Christine. "We wouldn't want you getting a bellyache. Not so soon before Christmas."

Tyler eagerly dug into his s'more while Mason ate his—complete with paper plate, but minus the chocolate—in the corner. John took in the cheery scene, acknowledging he hadn't had this much fun in months. Heck, maybe even in years. The afternoon spent outdoors with Christine and Tyler had been filled with happy hill rides and gleeful shouts. On the way back to the truck they'd had an impromptu snowball fight, and John had been mightily impressed by Christine's strong throwing arm. She'd invited him over for lunch the next day to compensate for whipping his tail in the competition. The next few days were lost in a blur of chats over coffee and prolonged Lego games with Tyler.

Now, here they were, all huddled up indoors beside a roaring fire and after a dinner of homemade stew. *It's like stepping into a greeting card,* John thought, his eyes lingering on Christine. She was beautiful in the firelight and the more he was around her, the more he wanted to be with her. She was captivating and sincere, and she had a sense of humor he appreciated. They could talk about everything in the world or nothing at all, just sitting in companionable silence. She was just as much fun as Carlos to be around, though John was betting she was a better kisser. Not that he'd be comparing the two, it was just odd for John to consider that a person could appeal to him in a womanly way and also act like a best friend. John was longing to get more than friendly with Christine. During their few moments alone, he'd actually considered making a move, but he'd stopped himself, weighing the impact on Tyler.

If things deepened between him and Christine, what would that mean? He clearly couldn't lead her on by engaging in some casual fling, when the outcome might be devastating for them all. Christine was loving yet firm with Tyler, and naturally a very protective mom. She wouldn't want to expose the boy to any fallout from a short-term affair any more than John would.

"When does Santa come again?" Tyler asked, still munching.

"Not until you're fast asleep," Christine answered.

"Did you ask for something special?" John asked the boy.

"Mommy says it's best to let life surprise you."

"Does she now?"

Christine blushed mightily under John's appreciative perusal. She really was lovely that way. It seemed to embarrass her that any man might cast an admiring eye her way. John wasn't sure how any guy in his right mind could stop himself.

Christine stood, collecting cooking supplies. "Ty, you'd best head upstairs and wash up. It's getting late and tomorrow is a big day." She turned to John. "Will you excuse me a minute while I tuck him in?"

"Maybe I should get going," John said, standing as well.

"No, don't." Her expression softened. "What I mean is, please stay. I won't be but a minute."

"Well, all right. Just for a bit."

Tyler twisted his lips and surveyed them both.

"Is John sleeping over?" he asked his mom.

John felt heat scorch the back of his neck as Christine flushed red.

"Oh no, honey," she sputtered quickly. "That's not what I meant."

Tyler stuck out his bottom lip. "Why can't he sleep over? He can stay in my room."

John smiled kindly at the child. "Maybe some other time, little buddy. Okay?"

"Promise?" Tyler asked, his face lighting up.

"We'll talk about it later," Christine said firmly, herding him toward the stairs. "Now come on, up to bed with you!"

Tyler turned with disappointment and slowly climbed each step.

Mason slunk out of the corner and stealthily followed after him.

"Mason, get back down here," John ordered.

The dog turned his head with a petitioning look.

"Please?" Tyler pleaded. "Just for a little while?"

When Christine came back downstairs she found the great room spotless. She entered the kitchen to find John drying the last of the dinner dishes.

"How nice," she exclaimed with surprise. "You really didn't have to."

"I have a skill set," he said. "Just because I'm a male that doesn't mean I don't know my way around the kitchen."

John didn't have to remind Christine what sex he was. Every time he centered his blue gaze on hers, she remembered through and through. He was so capable at so many things it sent her heart awhirl. She just bet the women were after him in this tiny town, probably in all of greater Burlington too. Not just the coeds, either. Adult women, single ones, widows, and divorcees. John was intelligent, handsome, and kind. Just the sort of man it was easy to envision spending more time with.

This past week had been like a dream. Christine hated the thought that her vacation would soon be over and that this wonderful existence would end. But that's what getaways were for, stepping back from your normal routine. She couldn't hope to have anyone as wonderful as John in her life for the long term. She'd found her Prince Charming once and real life didn't grant a lot of second chances. So she'd determined to enjoy this moment while she could. Being around John felt good, so relaxed and natural. Who knew? Maybe they could keep up after this trip, sort of like long-distance friends? Christine frowned at the thought of leaving John behind for another woman to snap up as a boyfriend, but she had no doubt that it would happen over time.

"My cooking's not that bad," John said with a laugh.

She met his eyes, realizing he'd been expounding on his culinary talents, and she'd missed every word.

"I'm sure it's delicious, every bite."

"Really?" he said with a grin. "I never figured you for Cajun food. I'll have to make something for you sometime."

The way he said it was almost like he was in denial that she was leaving too. Would they just go on like this, then? Carrying on like congenial neighbors until it was time for her and Ty to board their plane? What else could Christine expect? Getting involved with John romantically would prove a mess. It would be bad for Tyler to become attached if things were not to work out. Christine felt a twisting in her gut, worrying that she'd already done the wrong thing in having them spend so much time with John. But, as long as Tyler understood the truth, that they were merely friends, would that ultimately matter? It was good to have friends in the world. Isn't that what she always told Ty? The more the merrier?

"Would you like me to open some wine?" John asked, looking and sounding a little puzzled.

Christine shook off her reverie, embarrassed at having been so consumed by her own thoughts. "That would be terrific," she said, feeling as if having a drink was a fine idea. She was getting overwrought, making too much out of nothing. Perhaps a glass of wine might calm her nerves enough to help her enjoy the rest of the pleasant evening with a terrific guy. "I'll grab a bottle from the bar in the great room," she said. "Would you like red or white?"

"What are you in the mood for?"

Christine knew he didn't mean it as a double entendre, but she felt herself blushing just the same. If circumstances were different and she and John starting an actual courtship, she could envision herself being in the mood for all sorts of things, not the least of which might involve John bringing his mouth to hers. She envisioned running her hands across his broad, muscular chest and slowly unbuttoning his shirt, hearing him moan. Christine gulped. "I'm partial to reds," she said with a squeak. She walked over to the built-in wine rack and rummaged clumsily through the bottles, reading labels and finding two varieties. "What sounds best? A cabernet sauvignon or merlot?"

"Let's have the merlot," he said, approaching from the kitchen.

"Do you think you can grab a corkscrew from the drawer by the sink?" she asked, needing an extra moment to collect herself. Christine smoothed out her hair and adjusted her sweater, hoping the five pounds she'd gained these past two years wouldn't put him off. Not that she was interested in turning him on. God, she was a mess.

He returned seconds later as Christine made for the kitchen, wine bottle in hand. They surprised each other on the threshold, nearly colliding.

"Whoops!" Christine exclaimed, almost dropping the bottle.

John steadied her shoulders in his strong hands. "Are you okay?"

Christine stared into brilliant blue eyes, then looked heavenward toward the mistletoe dangling above them. She met his gaze again, her cheeks, neck, and chest on fire. If she hadn't just been thinking about it, perhaps she wouldn't feel so much like a kid caught with her hand in the cookie jar. The only cookie here was about six feet tall and stood right in front of her. She found herself longing to take a bite.

"Christine?" he questioned uncertainly. Slowly, his eyes traveled north. He released her, stepping back.

"It's just a silly old tradition," she said, affecting a laugh.

John tilted his chin. "Not so silly, really."

"No," Christine said, swallowing hard. What had she been about to do? Tackle him to the floor? Maybe that wouldn't have been necessary. She could have stripped his jeans off right here, and...

"Shall I pour?" he asked, his complexion crimson from the neck up.

"Please." she said, catching her breath on the word. She had to get a grip. She would absolutely die if John had a clue about what she'd been thinking. He obviously wasn't interested in becoming physical. This week had provided ample opportunity for John to make a move after Ty had been tucked in bed, yet he hadn't acted on it. And it was a good thing, too. *Keeping things at arm's length is precisely what I want,* she thought, forcing a smile.

John poured them each a glass of wine and set the bottle on the dining room table. "Say," he said, noting her sketches, "are these yours?"

Christine had been so intent on serving their big bowls of stew by the fire, she'd completely forgotten she'd left these out from earlier in the afternoon. "They're just a couple of rough drafts. Something I'm working on."

"Well, I think they're fantastic" he said admiringly. "Really, Christine. When you said you wanted to start your own line, I had no idea. You've got serious talent."

"Thanks. I'd like to think so. At least enough to get something of my own going someday."

"I don't doubt it for a moment." He raised his wineglass to hers. "I have faith in you. Faith that you can pretty much accomplish anything you want to."

She clinked his glass, her heart light. John was so kind and accepting. His encouraging words meant the world to her. She was finally starting to recover from her earlier urge to ravage him. She must have been tipsy, thinking unclearly. When it was clear he meant to be only on platonic terms.

He lifted one of her drawings and studied it closely. "You know what you need?" he asked, looking up. "A business plan."

"A what?"

"A business plan," he said firmly. "A way to plot how to get from point A to point Z."

Christine hesitated. Of course she wanted to do it... eventually. Ever since John had first suggested starting her own company, she'd been considering her options. But it was a far-off dream, some nebulous fantasy. Nothing she could work on concretely at the moment. Starting her own line as a writer was ambitious enough. "I don't know," she began, "that involves a lot of time and effort. And right now, things are complicated. There's my present job... There's Ty..."

He eyed her astutely. "Hmm, yes. I see."

"What do you see?"

"Just that you're not ready, but that's okay. When you're ready, you'll know it."

Everyone needed long-term goals and this one was fun to think about. It didn't have to be this year, or even next... *Christine White Originals,* yes, that had a ring to it. Christine met John's gaze. "The future is long."

"It is indeed," he said with a grin.

Chapter Nine

As they sat by the fire enjoying their wine, John noted a CD on an end table. He picked it up with pleased surprise. "*A James Taylor Christmas*. Hey, is this yours?"

"In my mind I'm going to Carolina," she said with a smile that made him want to drop everything and go there with her. John liked James Taylor, but probably hadn't listened to his music in years.

"Mind if I put it on?" he asked.

"Sure. The stereo's right over there," she said, pointing to a cabinet near the bar.

"What's Christmas Eve without music?"

"You're right," she agreed. "We should have thought of it sooner."

John inserted the CD and a sappy yet sexy rendition of *Baby It's Cold Outside* began to play. "An oldie but goodie," he said.

"With a new twist."

Rich dark waves spilled to her shoulders as her cheeks took on a gentle glow. She was gorgeous in that pretty white sweater and jeans, her deep brown eyes sparkling in the soft light. Outside the windows, snow fell lightly, gently streaking the darkness. It was John's best Christmas Eve in recent memory. Maybe ever.

"You look really nice tonight," he said, his voice growing raspy. "Beautiful."

"Thanks," she said, her eyes locked on his. "I was just thinking that you look great too."

John sensed inside that he shouldn't do it, but an

even louder inner voice said he'd be a fool to stop himself. Here he was, alone with a gorgeous woman on Christmas Eve, and John could think of only one thing he wanted—to close the distance between them. He'd been longing to hold her all week, and now he had the perfect excuse. He approached her and set down his wine. "Care to dance?"

John held out his hand and she took it, letting him guide her off the sofa and into his arms. She was so warm and feminine against him, the light scent of her wildflower perfume in the air. Firelight cast shadows on the wall as they gently swayed to the music. John pulled her close and she sighed softly, while his heart beat like big kettledrum. He had the feeling he was falling, sinking into depths he'd never known. As long as she went there with him, he didn't care if they ever came back.

At last, the CD ended and she looked up. There was a longing in her eyes, deeply beautiful. John led her to the threshold separating the great room from the kitchen. His voice was husky with desire as he spoke below the mistletoe.

"It's not such a silly tradition."

"No..." she said, tilting up her chin.

John brought his mouth to hers and kissed her sweetly at first, and then with the all-consuming passion he'd restrained these past several days. He wrapped her in his embrace and she moaned, molding into him. That was all the encouragement he needed to cradle her head in his hands and deepen his kisses, his hands eager to explore her body. She was all woman, and she was all his. He ached to carry her to the sofa and drive home that point, making her cry out with pleasure and delight.

"Mommy!" a small voice called.

Tyler bounded down the steps, Mason barking loudly and following after him.

John and Christine broke their embrace as John hitched his belt and Christine quickly straightened her sweater. Tyler sensed their interaction and halted his descent. "Oh," he said, absorbing the scene.

"Ty!" Christine said, flushed. "What are you doing up?"

"I heard something outside."

"It was probably just the wind," Christine told him.

"No," Ty protested. "I think it was Santa and his reindeer!"

John and Christine exchanged glances.

"We'd better go and check," he said.

Christine and John leaned out the bedroom window, spying nothing but a craggy old tree scraping the shutter.

"It was just an old oak, little fellow," John said reassuring Tyler. "I'm sure he didn't mean any harm." Christine's heart warmed at how natural it seemed for John to interact with her boy. He really was very good with children, with Ty in particular.

Tyler's face fell with disappointment. "Are you sure it wasn't Santa?"

"Santa hasn't gotten here yet," Christine said.

"And he might not come," John said, forcing a stern look, "if you don't go back to sleep."

Tyler snuggled down under the covers, pulling them up to his chin.

"I'd probably better hit the road," John told Christine.

"Are you sure?" She desperately didn't want him to go, but knew deep inside that he should. She couldn't exactly ask him to stay the night, not with Ty in the house. It wouldn't be right. Maybe it wouldn't even be right for her. They were leaving in less than a week. As wonderful as John's kisses were—and they'd been knee-melting terrific—it was likely better for Christine to not get in any deeper. If he kissed her again the way he'd done under the mistletoe, they might not be able to stop things there.

Blue eyes sparkled with understanding. "I think my leaving's for the best, don't you?"

She knew he was right, so she didn't argue. John mussed Tyler's hair and told him good night before heading for the door.

"We still on for tomorrow at five?" he asked Christine. "Christmas dinner at my place?"

"We wouldn't miss it for the world," she said with a happy smile.

Chapter Ten

The bright sun beat a path through the windows as wrapping paper littered the floor. Christine sat on the colorful hooked rug by the fire, helping Ty construct his Lincoln Log tower. He'd been as happy as a clam to learn Santa had brought him his own set, one he could take back to Chicago. He'd gotten a huge assortment of Legos too. That Santa really knew his stuff. Christine's cell rang and she nabbed it off the coffee table.

"Still snowing up there?" It was Ellen's voice on the other end of the line.

"Not at the moment," Christine answered cheerily. She was having the best New England Christmas. "But it never stops for long."

"That's good," Ellen said, "because I need somewhere to cool off."

"What?"

"A truly wicked sunburn," she continued in a pitiful tone.

"Oh my gosh! How did that happen?"

"Let's just say Emilio and I spent some time at the beach." She lowered her voice and spoke with a mysterious edge. "A... very... private... beach."

"Didn't you use protection?" Christine asked in shock.

"Of course we did! But not sunscreen."

Christine blinked at Tyler, opting to take her conversation to a more confidential locale. She stood, walking out of his earshot, then whispered into the phone. "Ellen, oh my God. You're burnt *everywhere?*"

"Some parts more than others," she quipped. "But that's neither here nor there. I'm calling to tell you my time in the sun is done."

"What do you mean?"

"Emilio and I weren't as compatible as I thought. He had a much harder time taking a tanning. And that says a lot, considering I didn't do so well... In any case, I'm calling to tell you the happy news! I'm coming up to relieve you in Vermont!"

Christine swallowed hard, staring at Tyler. They were finally settling in. Now clearly wasn't the time to walk away. They had three more days on their agenda. Besides, they had Christmas dinner plans. "Ellen, I really don't think that's necessary. Ty and I are doing just great holding down the fort."

"Of course, I don't mean to push you out completely. You can go home any time you want. Just make room for one more!"

Christine sighed and ran her fingers through her hair. "When were you thinking of arriving?" she asked weakly.

"At four. I'm calling from the airport, as a matter of fact."

"Four *today*?" Christine spouted in a panic. She'd been looking forward to an intimate evening at John's place. She hadn't planned on bringing along her brash best friend.

"I don't eat that much," Ellen said, affronted. "Frankly, Christine, I'm surprised at you. I didn't think you and Ty would... Wait a minute! Hold the phone!" she cried, her tone brightening. "Is this about the sexy professor?"

"Ellen!"

"I knew it! You finally went out, didn't you?"

"Actually, we stayed in."

"That sounds even better! So... out with it! Is he some kind of dynamite kisser?"

"Ellen!"

"Hmm, I see. No time for that yet. Well, no matter, sweetheart. Goodness knows I want you to have a love life way more than the next gal. I won't get in your way."

John laid three elegant place settings on the sturdy handmade table while Carlos heckled him from nearby. "I can't believe you'd disinvite your best friend on earth from his favorite holiday meal."

John wryly twisted his lips. "But you've always criticized my Indian pudding."

"That's because it's a little lumpy."

"Is not!"

"Is too. Although the Cornish hens always come out well," Carlos added thoughtfully.

"Thanks, Carlos. You're a pal." Mason followed him excitedly, repeatedly knocking his legs with a huge rawhide bone that sported a large red ribbon on at one end. "Mason, please. Will you just *sit*?" The dog sat immediately and John nearly tumbled over him.

Carlos smirked and got back to business. "So? Does she have any friends?"

"You mean, mature female friends?"

"No, I mean ones her age."

"Keep dreaming."

"What? Women find me attractive."

"That, my friend, is one of life's great mysteries."

"You're just jealous because you can't grow one of these," Carlos said stroking his beard.

"Could too. If I wanted to look like an old billy goat."

"Hey!"

John's cell rang and he held up a hand.

"Christine," he said cheerfully. "Well, hello. Uh huh... Uh huh... I see."

He stared at Carlos, who eyed him suspiciously.

"No, I don't think that would be a problem," John continued into the receiver. "In fact, it will work out fine!"

He pressed End Call and Carlos implored, palms up, "What gives?"

John shot him an enigmatic grin. "Let's just say it's your lucky day."

Chapter Eleven

A few hours later, John opened his front door to greet the trio, with Carlos and Mason at his side. Dusk had settled outdoors and it was snowing once more. Christine entered first, radiantly beautiful in a red Christmas scarf. "Welcome! Welcome to all of you," John said, greeting Christine with a hug. He patted Tyler on the shoulder and turned toward Christine's slightly senior friend. The attractive redhead was slender and fit, with a russet glow about her. "You must be Ellen," John said, extending his hand.

"Professor John Steadman!" she exclaimed, pulling him into a bear hug. She winced, the moment they made contact, her skin seemingly bruising in the embrace. "I feel like we're old friends." John raised his brow at Carlos, who repressed a grin. "Let me introduce you to Carlos Dominguez," he said, pulling back.

Carlos took her hand, turning on his Old World charm. *"Encantado,"* he said, laying his accent on thick.

Ellen preened like a peacock. *"Igualmente,"* she returned in nearly flawless Spanish.

Carlos addressed Christine next. "Great to see you again. You're looking well."

"Thanks, Carlos. You too. Merry Christmas," she said with a smile.

"Well, come on in! Come on in, everybody. In— and out of the cold."

The happy group strode toward the living room,

Tyler with a bundle of packages in hand. "Can I put these under the tree?" he asked, Mason tagging along beside him.

"Under the tree's just fine," John said.

Before long, they were enjoying a scrumptious dinner John had cooked completely from scratch. *Is there no end to his talents?* Christine wondered. The ranch-style house was tastefully decorated for a bachelor pad, with upscale artwork hung on the walls. It was nicely done up for the holidays. A tall balsam fir nestled by the bay window, adorned with twinkling lights and a smattering of simple, yet elegant, ornaments. Carlos was in the midst of regaling them with business school stories.

"And that's when I said to Santa, 'That wasn't a signature line, it was an escape clause!'"

Ellen giggled with delight. Christine swore the evening had taken a decade off of her already youthful complexion, or perhaps it was the bright red hue on her cheeks inspired by an overexposure to the sun. "Carlos, what a great story. Have you ever thought of becoming a writer?"

"Oh, I'd say the folks at the business school find me verbose enough."

"It's true," John deadpanned. "We don't want to encourage him."

John stood to clear the dishes and Christine got to her feet as well.

"Let me help," she said with a soft smile.

Ellen and Carlos exchanged glances. "We'll come too," Ellen said, as they both made an effort to stand.

"No, please," John replied. "You two stay here

and keep Tyler company. You all done with your food?" he asked the boy.

"Yeah, thanks! I've never eaten a whole chicken before."

Adults chuckled all around as John and Christine slipped into the kitchen.

Christine deposited dishes in the sink, thinking how much fun she was having. John wasn't only good in the kitchen, he was a great host too. "It was a wonderful dinner. You're some kind of cook."

"I've a few years to practice," he said, carrying a platter over.

Suddenly, they were face-to-face in the small space.

Christine froze, trapped in his gaze. He was a marvelous man. Gracious too. "It was really nice of you to include Ellen so last-minute."

"She and Carlos seem to be hitting it off."

"Boy, do they ever."

"I think it's cute."

"And so unexpected."

"You certainly weren't expecting Ellen to show up."

"No."

Christine searched his eyes. "Sometimes life delivers things we don't plan."

"I like to think of them as pleasant surprises." John stepped closer, taking her in his arms just as Carlos and Ellen entered the kitchen.

"Oops!" Ellen said.

"We were just hoping to help serve dessert," explained Carlos. He massaged his beard as Tyler and Mason also entered the kitchen.

"What's going on?" Tyler asked, contorting his lips. "More *kissing*?"

Ellen and Carlos stared at each other while Christine and John flushed.

"Actually, Tyler," Carlos said to the child. "We were all just thinking it'd be a good idea for some of us to go and look at that Christmas tree."

"Yeah, right," Ellen piped in. "I believe there's a package or two with your name on it."

Tyler's face lit up. "Really? Whoohoo!"

As they departed, Christine heaved a sigh. "Great friends."

"World's best."

"What were we saying?"

"I don't know," he said, drawing closer. "Something about life's surprises?"

And boy, hadn't life surprised her with John. She hadn't realized until last night how much she cared about him. Judging by the way he'd kissed her under the mistletoe, he had feelings for her too.

"Sometimes what we least expect is the best, don't you think?" she said, looking up at him. "What I mean to say is…" Christine stood a bit straighter, gathering her courage. "John, this holiday has been great, the best ever. I could never have imagined it happening to me, but it has."

"What has?"

Heat swept from her temples to her toes as she locked on his gaze. "This… us, being here with you. Having you fit in so well with me and Tyler. And, you know what? I'm happy, really happy, for the first time since I don't know when."

John swallowed hard and stared at her blankly. This was just what he had worried might happen. She was growing attached, more attached than he was ready for. John had seen the signs before and they'd always sent him running for the hills. He liked Christine, cared about her of course, but this was sounding really heavy. He'd made a hell of a mistake with that kiss when he would have done better to control himself. Now, she thought... Hell, he didn't even know what she thought. He only knew he didn't want to think about it. "Yes, well," he said after a pause. "It's been pretty terrific getting to know you all too."

There was an awkward silence during which they heard Ellen's melodious laughter from the next room. John lifted a bottle of wine from the counter. "I'm going to see if anyone needs a refill," he said, sounding like he might need one himself.

Christine quickly followed after him, thinking she could use a drink, too.

While the rest of the group seemed oblivious, Christine felt unsettled. She'd practically spilled her guts to John, and he'd basically said—nothing. Even now, he sat apart from her as if something were amiss. Maybe she was letting her insecurities get the best of her. She hadn't felt close to a man in forever, and hadn't even kissed anyone since Dan. And now, here she'd gone acting like some giddy teenager engaged in her first crush. She'd probably frightened John a little with her admission, but why wouldn't he feel good that he'd helped make her happy? She studied him, hands clasped at his knees as he leaned forward with a congenial smile, watching Tyler opening his gifts. Was he avoiding meeting her eyes, or was she imagining it?

Tyler dug into another package, Mason snoozing contentedly at his side. "Nintendo! Oh boy! Thanks, Auntie Ellen. Mommy said I couldn't have one."

Ellen shot Christine a look. "Sorry."

"It's fine," Christine said, wishing everything really was okay.

Carlos wrapped his arm around Ellen's shoulder. "That's what Aunties are for," he whispered gruffly, but not quietly enough so the others didn't hear him.

Ellen grimaced at Christine, but Christine couldn't tell if it was in apology or because Carlos's embrace hurt her.

Carlos studied Ellen with concern. "Are you all right?" he asked, lifting his arm. "Is this bothering—?"

"Not much," she said, snuggling against him in encouragement. "Just a touch of sunburn."

"Maybe I can help with some cold cream later?" he said softly in her ear.

"Oh!" Ellen responded with delighted surprise. She locked on Carlos's gaze and blinked. "That would be nice, very nice indeed."

John leaned forward, lifting a small box from an end table. "Wait," he told Tyler, who was organizing his gifts. "There's one more." He glanced at Christine, his complexion ruddy. "This one's for the two of you."

"Thanks," she said, accepting the package. She felt bad that she hadn't brought anything for him other than a bottle of wine. But, in light of how skittish he was acting, maybe her omission was for the best. "Ty? You want to do the honors?"

The child grinned and slid the silky ribbon from the gift, peeling back the wrapping. He dug in the box and extracted a tiny toboggan tree ornament. "Look Mommy," Tyler proclaimed. "It's a sled! Just like we went on!"

"Just a little something for you to remember Vermont by."

"Oh how cute," Ellen chimed in.

Emotion welled in Christine's throat. Of all the moments they'd shared with John, that was one she'd never forget. "It's wonderful," she said softly. "Thank you."

"John took me and Mommy sledding!" Tyler informed the others.

"So I *heard*," Ellen said with a knowing look.

"Does this mean we'll get a real Christmas tree next year?" Tyler asked.

"Christine doesn't believe in Christmas trees," Ellen told Carlos.

"Really?" Carlos asked with surprise.

"That's not true," Christine protested. "I just haven't gone to the trouble these past..." Now, it was her turn to avoid John's gaze. "... few years."

"Well..." John clapped his hands together and glanced around. "Maybe next year things will be different."

The room was silent as all eyes fell on him. John stared first at Carlos and Ellen, then at Tyler and Mason by the tree. Finally, he looked at Christine. "For you, Christine. I meant, for you," he said, his voice cracking. He stood suddenly, sweat beads dotting his brow. "I'm going to grab some water. Anybody else want a glass?"

"I'll come help," Carlos said, getting to his feet.

John leaned into the counter and took a long

drink.

"What is it, amigo," Carlos asked. "What's wrong?"

"Suddenly, I don't feel so hot."

"No joke. You look like you've seen a ghost."

John gradually met his gaze. "I have, Carlos. The Ghost of Christmas Future, and it's too much. It's all too much."

"What's too much?"

"*This.* Old home week. Christine… Tyler… I just can't do it."

"Nobody's asked you to do anything, other than have them to dinner. As I recall, it was your invitation."

"Her best friend's here. You know they've been talking about me."

"That's what best girlfriends do!" Carlos reassured him. "They even weigh the merits of the UPS man, from what I hear."

John looked Carlos in the eye. "I heard from Mary Stewart."

"On the personnel committee?"

John nodded. "If I want it, the position's mine."

"That's awesome news. Congratulations."

"You know what this means. Long hours… extra meetings… Honestly, it's a good thing Christine and Tyler are going home."

Carlos cocked his chin. "Sometimes distance doesn't matter."

"And sometimes it's an excellent deterrent," John said firmly. "Just the right thing, at just the right time, before anyone's in too deep."

Carlos shook his head with a disapproving look. "And I thought the only chickens in this house were the ones you served for dinner."

Chapter Twelve

Christine and Ellen rode in the front of the SUV while Tyler slept soundly in his car seat in back. It had been a full and joyful day for her little boy; Christine was grateful for that at least. She kept her eyes on the road, trying not to think too hard about John's parting statement. Could she really have made such colossal mistakes that he didn't ever want to see her or Tyler again?

Ellen checked her lipstick in the driver's side mirror and fluffed her hair, lost in her own world. "I think the sexy professor's sweet on you," she said settling back in her seat. "*Maybe next year things will be different...?* That sounded promising!"

"You totally misread that, Ellen. I doubt that's what John meant at all."

"He's got the love bug for you, sister," Ellen stated authoritatively. "The love bug and it shows. That man wants you in his future."

"That man, as you call him, was only making conversation. Think about it Ellen. I'm in Chicago, he's in Vermont... Just how is that supposed to work?"

"I used to date a guy in New York."

"*Used to* being the operative phrase."

Ellen folded her arms across her chest. "As a girl who's got a date tomorrow, I don't appreciate your pessimism."

Christine turned toward her, pleased. "Carlos?"

"Isn't he gorgeous," Ellen asked with a sigh.

"I guess he's got a certain appeal," Christine said

noncommittally. "So, where are you two going?"

"Snowmobiling!"

"Seriously?"

"What? It's not like bungee jumping. Though I'd be up for that too... What do you think? Too much to suggest for a second date?"

"How long are you planning on staying?"

"For the rest of the holiday, and you?"

"Our return flight's on the twenty-eighth. You know that, you arranged it."

"Oh right, right. Sorry. I forgot." Ellen fiddled with her purse, sneaking out her cell to check for messages. "Do you think Carlos has been married before?"

"From what I hear, twice."

"Third time's the charm," Ellen quipped merrily.

"You two just met!"

"I know, I know... Don't take me so seriously. Heavens!" She frowned, tucking away her cell. "So... When are you seeing John again?"

Christine's lips took a downward turn as she fought the burn in her heart. "I'm not."

Ellen reached out and touched her arm. "What happened?"

Christine felt a tear escape her and she stealthily stroked it back, hoping Ellen hadn't seen. "I should never have gotten involved. I knew from the beginning where things would end."

"Did John say something to you?" Ellen asked with concern. "When we were leaving, I mean?"

Christine pressed her lips together steeling her emotions.

"Have a nice flight," she said, battling the sting of her tears.

"Oh Christine, I'm so sorry. I had no idea, hon. Honestly, none. John seemed like such a nice guy. I was hopeful, really hopeful—for the first time in a long while—that you were finally getting your life back."

Christine collected herself, wiping her cheeks with her coat sleeve. "My life's in Chicago," she said with more resolve than she felt.

"I know, and mine is too." Ellen set her jaw, weighing her own insecurities. "I'm not fooling myself with Carlos. The two of us are old enough to know what the score is. That doesn't mean we can't enjoy a little fun while we've both got some life left."

Christine forced a smile. "Oh Ellen, I'd say you've got plenty of life left. Maybe even more than Carlos can handle."

Ellen laughed, the tension in the air lightening. "Thanks," she said. "I try."

Later that night, Christine locked herself away in her room, her heart breaking. All night long she'd held it in. Fear started as a gentle roll, cresting the wave of her emotions, the moment John gave her that deer-in-the-headlights look in the kitchen. By the time they were saying good-bye, hope had sunk in the well of silence between them. It wasn't that they didn't talk. Discomfort sprung instead from all that went unsaid. There was no discourse on keeping in touch, or John seeing them off to the airport. The holiday had come, then—boom—it was done, just as suddenly as fireworks exploding on the Fourth of July. But here it was Christmas… *Christmas*… and all its twinkling lights had faded for her, it seemed.

There'd been a time when the whole world had

looked promising. She'd had a handsome young officer on her arm and they'd been expecting their first child. Dan had sworn he'd never leave her, but, due to the cruelty of fate, he had. She'd never believed she'd love again, or even meet another guy who'd catch her eye. Now here she was more painfully aware of being alone than she'd ever been.

Christine sank to the carpet, her back to the door, arms folded around her knees. "Oh Dan," she said, doubling forward with her sobs. "I miss you so much."

A light rapping came at the door. "Everything okay in there?" It was Ellen from the other side, her voice tinged with worry.

Christine sucked in a breath, her throat raw. "Yes, Ellen!" she called back. "Just fine. Merry Christmas."

Ellen hesitated before replying, concern clear in her voice. "Merry Christmas. Sleep tight."

Christine listened to her footsteps fade away, then folded her face in her hands. She'd been acting like a fool. Crushing on a man who lived hundreds of miles away and clearly had no interest in falling in love, much less having a family. She'd been crazy to believe there could be more to her relationship with John than just a simple two-week affair. Maybe it was good that she was heading back to Chicago, where she could put her real world in order and ensure it all made sense. In the meantime, she'd need to put on a brave face for these last few days and make the most of this vacation for little Ty. He was the main reason she came here after all, not to create delusional fantasies about her achieving a *happily ever after*.

Christine dropped her forehead to her knees and

let the tears come quietly, as winds beat against the storm shutters. It was snowing harder now, almost as fiercely as it had on the day they arrived. But nothing could match the chill that settled deep in her soul to ravage her aching heart.

Chapter Thirteen

John fixed his brow in concentration, spreadsheets strewn across the tabletop around him. His printer spewed out more papers as he typed busily at his laptop, ignoring the doorbell the first time it chimed. It rang again and Mason barked. John looked up with a start to find sun streaming in through the windows. He stood wearily and walked to the door. Pulling it open he spied Carlos dressed for the cold. Beyond him, Ellen smiled and waved from a truck loaded with winter fishing gear.

"Carlos!" John said with surprise. "I thought you had a date."

"I do." Carlos grinned broadly. "We're just stopping by to be sure that you won't join us."

Mason tried to spring out the door, but John stopped him. "Not today, buddy," he said to his dog.

"Come on now," Carlos prodded. "It will be fun."

John slowly shook his head. "Thanks, but I can think of lots of things I'd rather do than be the third wheel on a fishing expedition."

Carlos's jowls sagged with disappointment.

"Besides," John continued, backing into his house. "I've got work to do."

Carlos leaned forward and grabbed him by the shirtsleeve. "Amigo," he rasped under his breath. "You don't understand. I've never taken a city woman fishing!"

"Oh, no you don't…" John chuckled and started closing the door. "You got yourself into this; you get yourself out."

Carlos stared at him with pleading eyes. "I'll give you half my catch."

"Half of nothing is zero. We don't need our accountant friends to tell us that."

Carlos stuck his foot in the door before John could close it. "When have I ever not been there for you?"

"Lots!"

"Okay, maybe that's true. But here's the chance for you to be the bigger man."

"Good-bye Carlos," John said, kicking his foot out of the doorjamb.

John shook his head at Mason as they walked back to the table. "And people say *women* are complicated."

Back at Winterhaven, Christine carted the last of their suitcases downstairs.

"I can't believe we're really leaving," she said, glancing around the comfortable space that, in such a little while, already felt like home.

"We'll miss it here," Tyler said, holding Jasper close.

Christine smiled tenderly at her son. "At least Santa brought you some Lincoln Logs to take home."

"Yeah. That's cool," he said his face brightening.

Christine gave the house one last perusal. Everything was pretty much in order, other than a few odds and ends. She didn't really want to put all the things away in the event Ellen might need them. She'd even bought some extra wine when she'd purchased her replacements, thinking Ellen and Carlos might open a few bottles later.

Ellen had called her cousin in London to gently break the news about her blooming affair with Carlos. To her happy surprise, her cousin, by now involved with a handsome Frenchman, was delighted. Carlos was nice enough, she'd stated, just a little too used to *taking a walk on the wild side* for her taste. Christine sighed, glad that life had a way of working out much of the time.

"I guess we'll let Auntie Ellen do the rest of the picking up."

"Why isn't she flying back with us?" Tyler wanted to know.

"Your Auntie Ellen had a few things to take care of," she said, thinking of Carlos.

About ten miles away, Ellen stood in designer boots perched over a fishing hole cut in the ice. She couldn't believe she was doing this! Fishing in the wilds of Vermont! It was positively to-die-for adventuresome, particularly with one hot Latino along. His tender ministrations to her scorched skin had worked wonders. While she wasn't exactly as good as new, she had improved enough to enjoy his attentions—and layer into this bulky coat.

She felt a tug on her line and squealed with delight. "I've got one! Carlos, I think I've got one!"

"Looks like a big one, too," he said, stepping up behind her.

The beast tugged harder, threatening to pull her in. "Whoa… oh! Carlos!" she yelped, starting to freak just a little. Maybe it was enormous and had teeth! Ellen wasn't sure whether they had piranhas up here, but decided now was not the time to find out.

"Hold it steady," Carlos offered. "Let me help

you."

He sidled up behind her, positioning his legs on either side of hers and wrapping his firm grip around the pole before them. She almost swore she felt his pole pressing up against her backside. She squirmed with excitement, suddenly too hot in her heavy clothing.

"This isn't working out so badly," he said in a sexy whisper that nearly melted the ice beneath them. If she weren't so dearly afraid for her life, she might have found herself turned on. For now, Ellen just hoped to live until lunchtime.

The line yanked forward as they wrestled with their footing. "Do they have sharks up here? Great whites?" Ellen asked. She dug her heels into the slick surface below her, thinking maybe practicality should have trumped fashion just this once.

Carlos settled her hips and bottom against him with one arm, to keep her from sliding, then said in a commanding voice, "We're going to take that sucker for what he's worth. You ready?"

As long as he was in charge and they weren't going under, Ellen was prepared to do anything Carlos said. She nodded, grimacing at the strain of holding the pole that arched over in their grip.

"When I say go…"

"What happens on *go*?" she asked, glancing quickly over her shoulder.

His eyes danced with mirth as he gave her a peck on the cheek. Her skin tingled at the brush of his beard and she saw a flash of bright light. Either she was dizzy from the contact or going snow-blind. "We pull that baby out of the water." He leaned back a bit and added with a chuckle. "Though something tells me it's an awfully big baby.

"Ready…" he started, strengthening his hold on both her and the pole. "Set…"

Ellen's heart thundered at the thought she was about to do it. Something so recklessly primitive as catching a fish!

"Go!" Carlos shouted, wrenching back with all his might. Ellen gave it everything she had, yanking hard. The monster strained against them. They pulled, it tugged… they pulled, it tugged. Then finally they pulled harder, and—*wham*! Ellen and Carlos fell back in a heap, with her landing squarely on top of him.

"Are you all right?" he asked, gripping her breasts through her coat as she stared up into a clear, blue sky.

"I think so," she said, spinning over on top of him. Six feet away, the most enormous fish she'd seen in her life flip-flopped on its side beyond their tackle box.

Ellen grinned. "We got him!" she shouted, happily pounding Carlo's chest with her gloves. "By God, we got him!"

Carlos laughed with delight and pulled her toward him for a kiss. "Damn good fishing for a city woman."

Christine and Tyler made their way through the busy crowd at the airport, dragging their rolling carry-on bags behind them. They were almost to security when Christine heard a distant cry. "Christine! Wait!"

Tyler turned first. "Mommy! Look!"

She spun on her heels to find John sprinting toward them in his Carolina sweatshirt, a large manila envelope in hand.

"Thank God I caught you." He leaned forward panting, hands resting on his thighs. "I thought I was too late."

Christine stared at him is disbelief. "What are you doing here?"

He huffed and puffed, still catching his breath. "I couldn't let you leave without this," he said, extending the manila envelop toward her.

"I'm not sure I understand. What is it?"

John caught his wind, straightening. "A business plan, Christine. This is it! A solution. A way to get from point A to point Z!"

She stared at him flatly unable to mask her disappointment. "Oh."

He appeared confused, thrown off guard. John ran his fingers through his short dark hair, settling his gaze on hers. "But this is what you've wanted. Your own line. Your own company, even. I…" He surveyed her once more, his cheeks sagging. "I thought that you'd be pleased."

"Pleased, John? When you didn't even bother to tell us good-bye? Just sort of dropped out of the picture? And now you suddenly appear with *this*." She eyed the envelope with disdain, causing him to flinch and step back.

He wrinkled his brow, pleading. "Won't you at least take a look? Glance over it on your flight?"

She'd spent these last three days trying to forget him. The last thing she needed to do was carry reminders home. "Thanks, but I've got to make plans for my life in Chicago."

"But this *is* for your life," he said, attempting once more to hand it over. "Christine, please…" He released the envelope, but she failed to grasp it, letting it fall to the floor. Tyler eyed them both uncertainly, then scooped it up.

Christine set her chin and willed it not to tremble. Here was this gorgeous man with whom she thought she'd made a personal connection, and all he cared about was cold, hard business. Perhaps he'd never felt anything for her at all, or for Tyler, either.

"Thanks for a swell New England vacation," she said, turning away and taking Tyler's hand. "It was nice knowing you." She walked her child toward security, the pain in her chest searing. After Christmas night, she didn't believe her heart could break again, but she'd been wrong.

Tyler looked sadly over his shoulder as they slipped away, milling in with the line passing through the security scanner. John couldn't stop the burn in his throat any more than he could the heat in his eyes. He'd thought she'd be happy to see him. Instead, she'd greeted him with chilling disdain. He'd spent untold hours on that plan, believing it was the best thing he could do for her. Wasn't helping her build the life she wanted the right thing? Her world was in Chicago; his life was here. There were no two ways about it.

John pursed his lips, recalling toboggan rides and warm nights by the fire… Little Tyler's *Whoohoo!* when he was thrilled about something. Then, there was the memory of Christine in his arms as they danced through the night, and his inward desire to never let her go. But the hard fact was that he couldn't hold on forever.

"You did *what*?" Carlos asked with disbelief

when they met for coffee a few hours later. "Followed her all the way to the airport to deliver a *business plan*?"

"Come on, man," John said, feeling gloomy. "I thought that you, of all people, would understand what a gesture that was."

"No. What kind of gesture was it?"

"A very generous one! I put my heart and soul into that proposal!"

"Harrumph."

"What's that supposed to mean?"

"Let me guess. She wasn't exactly thrilled to see you."

"No, in fact she wasn't," John said, still reeling from the shock. "Frankly, she was pretty ticked off."

Carlos slowly shook his head then met John's eyes. "You know, for a very smart man, you can be a really big dummy sometimes."

"What are you driving at, Carlos. Just spill it."

"John, John... You meet this pretty single mom up here on vacation. You wine her and dine her and make her think something is possible..."

"Hang on just one second! She did every bit as much wining and dining as I did!"

"You're only proving my point."

"Which is?"

"You may not have wanted it to happen. By some Christmas miracle, maybe even the two of you didn't see it coming. But, one way or another, you and Christine were drawn to each other, found yourselves falling—"

"Precisely why I had to stop it!" John shot back. "Can't you see? That was the best thing—the right thing—for us both!"

Carlos slowly stroked his beard. "Was it?"

Mason, who'd been sitting at John's feet, shot him a dirty look.

"You," John admonished the dog, "stay out of it."

Chapter Fourteen

It was New Year's Eve in the elegant bistro. Carlos poured Ellen a glass of champagne as they sat at a romantic table for two.

"I'm having a hard time feeling festive with things ending so badly between John and Christine," she said.

Carlos took her hand. "I know, *querida*. But it's their business, and their problem to work out."

"What are the odds?"

"In love, everything's uncertain, yes?" He lifted her hand giving the back of it a kiss. "Sometimes you win, sometimes you lose. Then you head back to *go* and start all over again."

"That's just it," Ellen said with a worried frown. "I don't know if Christine will ever head back to *go* after this." She sipped from her champagne. "Where's John tonight?"

"Likely moping about his place with that old mutt of his," Carlos answered. "What do you think Christine's doing?"

Ellen sighed. "Probably sitting around in her apartment with Tyler, watching the ball drop on TV."

The two of them sat for a moment in silence.

"Do you think Christine will be okay?" Carlos asked with concern.

"Oh yeah, she'll bounce back. She's tough. I don't know about in the love department… but, otherwise, she'll get her life together. Christine always gets her life together. She's got to, right? She does it for Tyler." She pursed her lips and looked at him. "What about John?"

Carlos shrugged. "Tough as nails, too. He'll be fine."

But, by the way the two of them stared at each other, it was as if neither one believed it.

Carlos perused Ellen thoughtfully. "What time do you leave in the morning?"

"Ten o'clock."

"Then let's not let tonight go to waste," he said, clinking her glass.

Ellen smiled warmly, thinking what a rare and unexpected treat it was that the two of them had met. "To us," she said, toasting back.

"And to living in the moment, when the moment's right."

Tyler dozed in a large leather chair, a New Year's hat askew on his head, as Christine watch the ball drop in New York's Times Square on television. *Happy New Year, indeed.* She shared a silent toast with the air, then frowned. Everything felt wrong about how things had ended with John, but she hadn't really seen another way around it. What was she supposed to do? Fall at his feet with gratitude when he'd surprised her at the airport with that ridiculous plan?

She tapped her glass with her fingers, eying the manila envelop on the end table. What could be so hellfire important that he'd raced to catch them before they boarded their plane? *A way to get from point A to Z?* Well fine. John could keep his unsolicited advice, and Christine wished he had. Seeing him at the airport had just made things worse. She'd known he'd really hurt her, but hadn't understood how badly until he'd appeared at the last minute and caused her battered heart to hope. For an instant, she believed him to regret letting them go without so much as a word. But he'd shown no hint of remorse at all, only confusion in light of his damnable insistence that she read what he'd brought.

Christine drew a deep breath, steeling her emotions. She didn't need a sexy professor from New England anyway. She and Ty had done just fine before he'd come along, and would do great going forward without him. He could keep all that snow, and those tobogganing hills, the warm nights by the fire, and his dog. Christine sighed, recalling Tyler's joyful bonding with Mason. Maybe she'd have to get him a puppy. But not any time soon. There was enough going on in the balancing act between being a single mom and working.

She took another sip of champagne, weighing the demands of her job and all it entailed. The truth was that she'd been asking for more responsibility at work, but Ellen had been resistant. Perhaps it was true that Christine had seemed out of focus before, but the trip to Vermont had done her good. She sensed greater clarity now. While John had been wrong in many ways, most especially in the way he'd treated her, he actually was correct in assuming Christine wanted more for herself than what she currently had. She was capable of it too. She knew she could develop her own line, and had several ideas for interactive products with Internet potential as well. It would likely take time, but she was still relatively young, so time was on her side. John's prescient words came back to her like a haunting refrain. *The future is long...*

She set down her champagne and lifted the manila envelope, almost afraid of its contents. What if John's plan was more helpful than she'd imagined? She had enough of a level head to separate a business opportunity from a personal disappointment, didn't she? If she ultimately had a different path for herself in mind, wouldn't it make sense to think out the logical steps to achieving her goal now? She tentatively broke its seal, her heart pounding. It was just a stack of papers. So why did Christine have a premonition her whole life was about to change?

John flipped off the TV and set down the remote. On the coffee table before him, a bottle of champagne in bucket of ice sat untouched. He'd considered inviting one of his lady friends to join him for the evening, but somehow the thought of entertaining was distasteful. He didn't really want to have anyone else over when the only person he could think of was Christine. While it had never been a big deal before, being physical with a casual acquaintance suddenly didn't appeal to him. He'd only kissed Christine once, but their kissing session had felt as intimate as they come. She'd been so warm and willing in his arms, her flesh molding against his as their mouths melded. He'd never longed to make love to a woman more, slowly and tenderly, employing all of his manly talents. He knew he could treat her right, and would take every care to ensure her happiness in bed. Sadly, he hadn't done such a hot job of filling her with joy outside of it.

He glanced at Mason, still mad at him, on the other side of the room. The dog turned his back on John, sitting beside the Christmas tree.

"Come on, boy. You're not going to hold a grudge forever?"

Mason walked his paws forward, slinking into a lying position. After a few moments, John heard him gnawing and knew he'd locked onto his giant rawhide bone. John sagged forward, his elbows resting on his knees, head in hands. If he'd really done the right thing with Christine, then why was everybody here trying to make him feel like he'd done something terrible?

John thought back to Christine's admission in the kitchen. He *had* made her happy out of bed, but then he'd gone and blown it big-time. But she'd caught him so off guard, he hadn't known how to respond. What could he have said? That she made him happy too? John stared at the Christmas tree, mentally reliving every moment. Of course, she'd made him happy. She and Tyler both had, each in their own way. When he'd been with the two of them together, they'd been almost like a family. Although it had been pretend, he'd felt contented in that role. He'd just been so unfamiliar with the feeling, he hadn't known what it was.

John swallowed hard, thinking there'd been another emotion present, something deeply personal and just between him and Christine, but he'd been in denial of that as well. He had his hands full these days and building his career to consider besides. Despite the common myth of the easygoing life of the college professor, the hard truth was that competition in academia was exceedingly tough. You had to publish or perish, and keep forging ahead. John was an ambitious man who'd carved out a path for himself. His own dad had been an unsteady worker who was often unemployed and barely able to keep food on the table for John and his younger sister.

John had vowed at thirteen to work his way past that. And, from that first job tending the golf course at that upper-crust country club to his full graduate school scholarship, he had. Still, John believed he shouldn't become serious with any woman, or consider having a family, until he found himself in a financially stable position. He'd be damned if he was going to repeat the past, when he was capable of charting his own future. Of course, he was contemporary enough to understand his wife would have her own career, but that didn't negate the sense of responsibility that had been pounded into him each time he'd seen tears of desperation welling in his mother's eyes. Because his late dad had been unable to prepare for it, John was now making arrangements for his mom's welfare too. He also helped out his kid sister, as he was able. She was a single mom and putting herself through school besides. There was a lot on his plate, a hell of a lot more than Christine, or anyone else—including Carlos—knew.

John decided to open the champagne, thinking he might as well have a glass. There were so many emotions churning inside him, it was almost like he didn't know where to turn. *Man's best friend* had denied him, and it appeared his own heart had betrayed him too. He'd not even understood what he'd been feeling until now. And now, it was too late. The truth was that his promotion put him in a different place. Yes, he'd be working harder, but he'd also be making more money. *A lot more money,* he thought, popping the cork. It sprang forth in an arc as bubbles gurgled from the bottle. John picked up a cloth to wipe it, reaching forward for the cork on the floor. His fingers made contact with something else set back a little farther under the coffee table. What in Hades was that? John pinched the wooly fabric between his fingers, then slowly withdrew a bright red object from its stowaway perch.

Mason stood, turning toward him.

"Well, what do you know...?" John said aloud.

Ellen melted in Carlos's rapturous embrace at the airport. It was January first and her vacation had ended. "I'm not going to ask when I'm going to see you again," she said sadly.

Carlos pressed his forehead to hers. "Now you're hurting my feelings."

Ellen stared into warm brown eyes knowing she couldn't stand to say good-bye forever. "When's the last time you came to Chicago?"

"Nineteen seventy-nine."

"Then you're overdue!"

"I have a problem with that," Carlos said, pulling back.

"Oh?"

"My old college chum, the one I used to stay with . . ." he began seriously, "has moved away."

She knew what he was getting at, but couldn't resist teasing him. "I know some good hotels in the area."

Carlos feigned shock. "You wouldn't toss an old man out in the snow?"

Ellen kissed him soundly his bristly beard tickling.

"Call me," she said, breaking away.

Carlos beamed as she picked up her luggage and

set it on the conveyor belt. He withdrew his cell from his pocket and waved it in her direction. "I've got your number!"

Chapter Fifteen

Christine sat at her drafting table intent on her sketch while classical music played in the background. All the Christmas decorations were tucked away, leaving her apartment with a neat array of modern furniture and clean open spaces. This drawing was whimsical and fun, with a family of snowmen tobogganing down a pine-studded hill. While there was computer software for graphic design, Christine preferred importing her hand-drawn illustrations into her layout program by using a scanner. This gave her the ability to create high-tech products with down-home appeal. It would take at least five years on her current income to save up enough to start her own company. In the meantime, she was determined to build a preliminary catalogue.

She took a sip of coffee as sunlight streamed through the windows. It was still windy outdoors, but the mid-January snow had abated despite the freezing temperatures. A vague sound buzzed upstairs and she heard something thumping down the steps. Christine looked up to see Tyler headed downstairs, his tiny cell in one hand, dog-eared Jasper in the other. "Good morning, Sunshine!" she called happily from her stool.

"Do I have school today?" he asked sleepily.

"Yes baby, you do. But first," she said, standing, "you're in for a treat."

"Huh?" he asked warily.

"I made homemade blueberry muffins."

He squinted his eyes. "You're cooking before

dinner?"

Christine spurted a laugh and set a hand on her hip. "Your mom's a pretty capable woman."

He studied her for a prolonged beat. "I thought so, but wasn't sure."

He had such a way to fill her with confidence, Christine thought jovially. She was happy inside, happier than she'd been in a long time. Maybe she didn't need a college professor to make her feel it, but it likely had helped that he'd pointed the way. Until Christine went to Vermont, it was like a part of her lay dormant, just waiting to be reawakened. Though her initial parting from John had left a bitter taste in her mouth, Christine realized after a while that she was the type who used lemons to make lemonade. Perhaps knowing John had been bittersweet, but being with him while reconnecting with Tyler would pay dividends for months to come. She not only got along better with her son, she'd gained additional confidence in herself. Confidence that she could do anything she put her mind to, given enough time. *The future is long indeed,* she thought with a melancholy smile.

John waited in Ellen's office with Mason, hoping he wasn't being an egregious fool. But, the more he'd thought about it, the more right this step seemed. John wasn't a reckless man. He weighed everything carefully, considered all the angles. And every way he posed the question, the answer came up the same. His semester started on Tuesday and he'd put off coming here until the last minute, needing to ensure everything was in place.

John twisted Christine's red Christmas scarf in

his hands, wishing with all his might that she'd be glad to see him. Both Ellen and Carlos had assured him she would. Then again, those two were turning out to be incurable romantics. He'd been pleasantly surprised by Carlos's sudden attachment to vivacious Ellen. He'd never seen the old boy fall quite so fast, or so hard. Of course, she seemed fairly well smitten with Carlos too. What serendipity that Ellen had joined Christine in Vermont at the last minute. Sometimes the fates really knew what they were doing.

John felt a rash of heat at his neck, realizing that this was the big time. He was more nervous now than when he'd defended his dissertation. He hoped he could turn that fear into a focused delivery. Yeah, he'd been a total jerk, and he knew it. He was fully prepared to apologize for it. Hell, even grovel. If that's what it took for Christine to give him half a chance.

Christine dropped Tyler at preschool and headed for the office. It was a little unusual for Ellen to call a personal meeting at nine o'clock. Generally her friend reserved individual conferences for after lunch. Mornings were good for settling in, answering phone calls and e-mails, and meeting with the general staff. Ellen also liked to give her people a few extra hours to polish any mock-ups they were working on before discussing them one-on-one. The funny thing was, as far as she knew, Christine didn't have anything specific to talk to Ellen about. Her projects were humming along fine and she'd kept her personal ambitions separate. Ellen didn't know she was planning to go out on her own, and keeping things to herself seemed the best policy right now. Given that Christine wouldn't be leaving the company tomorrow, there was no point in upsetting any applecarts with distant future plans.

Christine breezed into the lobby of her skyscraper building, her coat collar turned up against the cold. For the life of her, she wished she could recall where she'd left her favorite scarf, but she'd given up looking, thinking she must have forgotten it on the plane. She pressed the elevator button with a gloved hand, mentally going through a checklist of all she had to do today. The schedule was so tight, she wasn't sure she'd be able to make time for lunch. It was a good thing she and Tyler had shared a healthy breakfast. It had been great sitting in the kitchen with her little man and making cordial early morning conversation. Christine didn't know where that grumpy other person she'd been had gone, but she didn't want her returning any time soon.

When Christine reached the tenth floor, she was surprised to see Ellen standing outside her office door chatting with the secretary. Normally Ellen was nose-to-the-grindstone hard at work by eight o'clock and didn't take a breather until noon.

"Hi, Ellen. Good morning, Sarah," Christine said to the secretary, who gave her a dopey smile. Though she was acting a bit loopy, Christine cut her slack. She was only nineteen and had probably picked up a new boyfriend. This girl traded boyfriends like some people exchanged hasty purchases. Christine used to find it fitting that Sarah was Ellen's secretary, given Ellen's similar penchant for variety. Now, however, it appeared Ellen's shopping days were done.

"Let me just drop my things in my office and I'll

be right there," Christine told Ellen as she passed her by.

"Take your time," Ellen said, shooting Sarah a sly smile. "Just don't take too long."

Christine wrinkled her nose, thinking Ellen was acting strange. Did she smell something going on, or was she just imagining it? She dumped her purse, coat, and gloves on the loveseat in her office, and headed back the other way. Sometimes you just didn't know with Ellen. She could be the most wonderful person in the world. But she had a sneaky side, too. Like when she'd broadsided Christine with that vacation in Vermont.

She approached Ellen's office, then suddenly stopped. Both Ellen and Sarah studied her weirdly. Christine turned a suspicious eye on Ellen, and then on Sarah.

"Is something going on?"

"No," Ellen said, a bit too emphatically.

"Not at all!" Sarah chimed in, focusing on her computer.

Just then Christine heard a strange yelp. For the life of her, it sounded like a barking dog. She stared at Ellen, but Ellen just shrugged.

"I don't know," she said mysteriously. "Maybe you should look and see?"

Christine felt her face flash hot. She couldn't possibly mean…?

"Well, go on," Ellen prodded. "Daylight's burning."

Christine laid her hand on the doorknob, every ounce of her tingling from her head to her toes. She shot a quick glance at Ellen, then pressed forward, her heart pounding. It was a vision so surreal she had to blink hard to ensure it wouldn't fade away.

"I must be some kind of absentminded professor," John said, sitting in Ellen's desk chair, Mason perched in his lap. "Because sometimes I forget things. You know, fail to get the details right."

Mason bounded to the floor and happily swaggered over to where Christine stood, dumbstruck. The dog sat expectantly by her side and looked up, wagging his tail. Christine patted his head and stared agape as John rose and walked forward.

"Details?" she asked, her head reeling.

"Like when I put together that business plan."

Christine felt as if she might faint, but was determined that she wouldn't. She had to learn what John was doing here, and why he'd come all this way. It couldn't really be about the paperwork, could it?

"This is about the business plan?" she asked, confused.

John stepped toward her. "I left something pretty important out."

"No, wait," she said, collecting her presence of mind. "John, it was good. I actually read it. And you were right. It's a way to get from A to Z…" She'd nearly forgotten how brilliant his eyes were, their gorgeous blue color offsetting his striking dark hair and handsome face. "Maybe not this year," she continued, "or even the next. In fact, I've figured out that it will take at least five—"

"And naturally, you'll need a nanny."

"A nanny?" she asked as if she hadn't considered it.

"Starting a new business can be very intense. There's no guarantee childcare hours could cover it."

"Well no, maybe not. I haven't thought that far a—"

"Perhaps you'd consider a tag-team approach?"

"Tag team?"

"Sure, you know. People do it all the time."

Christine thought quickly, but there was no one around here she could trust to watch Tyler after hours. There was only Ellen and she had her own life, after all. "I don't think Ellen would be willing… What I mean is, that's a lot to ask."

John's lips turned up at the corners as he gave her a longing look. "I wasn't talking about Ellen." He amazed her by pulling her bright red Christmas scarf from behind his back. He now stood just inches away. Christine swallowed hard, her pulse racing. She felt hot, then cold, then warm all over.

"You left this back in Vermont," he said, his voice husky.

"You came all the way to Chicago to return it?"

"For that and something else."

She stared at him, her tender heart daring to hope.

"Christine," he said. "It wasn't until after you'd gone that I realized what an idiot I'd been… what a terrible mess I'd made of everything."

"But I thought you said—"

"Just one more minute. Please hear me out." He shot her a pleading look that sent wild butterflies fluttering inside her. She felt like a child on Christmas morning about to get everything she'd wished for. "I never in a million years expected to meet a woman like you. I mean, I had women friends, sure. But somehow we never… clicked. Then one day this beautiful woman from Chicago nearly ran me off the road. Practically killed me, really."

"Hey!" she protested, but John pressed on.

"But that was nothing next to the near-death I've experienced these past few weeks. I know we have distances to conquer and careers to plan for. But somehow when we're together, everything fits. We're good together, you and I. You, me—and Tyler." Mason barked and John shot him a glance. "And uh, yeah, Mason, too."

Her spirit leapt with joy. She'd tried so hard to push all thoughts of a life with John out of her mind that she hadn't realized how deeply she'd dreamt of one until now.

He draped the scarf around her neck. "Christine, you made me happy too, more happy than I've ever been with anyone. I know I was a jerk in not telling you earlier, and I'm sorry. It just took me time to realize it myself. I had other things that I thought stood in the way, but I was wrong about that too. Please tell me there's still a way to make things right?"

Christine battled the heat in her eyes and forced out the words. "Just what are you saying?"

"That I can't imagine a life without you. I don't *want to* envision my life without you. I believe there's something good here. Something worth fighting for. I think that we stand a chance, Christine, of being together forever. I'm willing to give it my all, if you are. But here's the thing…" He withdrew a small box from his pocket. "I need you with me, you and Tyler both, twenty-four-seven. Day in and day out. Long-distance won't do." John opened the box, exposing a glorious two-carat solitaire. Christine gasped with surprise and met his gaze, her eyes moist.

"I know I haven't done this exactly right," he said, "but I hope you understand my intentions are sincere."

Christine spoke past the lump in her throat. "Yes, yes, I believe you."

He plucked the ring from the box and dropped to one knee as he took her hand.

"I love you desperately, Christine, more desperately than I thought a man could love a woman. Come away with me to Vermont where we can be a family. Where we can build our dreams... But first, tell me you'll be my bride." He slid the ring on her finger and met her eyes with a hopeful gaze. "Say we have a future?"

Christine fought for the words as tears streamed down her face. John was intelligent, loving, and kind. He was just the sort of man she'd always hoped would come and carry her away. Her, and her precious boy too. "The future is long," she said with a shaky smile.

John stood and asked tentatively. "Does that mean yes?"

She nodded and he scooped her into his arms.

"Oh John, I love you too."

"Whoohoo!" he said with a kiss.

Epilogue

Two years later, John set Tyler on his shoulders to crown their Christmas tree with a glistening star. A tiny toboggan ornament sat on a high branch nearby. Christine sighed contentedly, massaging her blooming belly. Last Christmas, they'd shared an intimate mistletoe wedding at Winterhaven. Next year, there'd be another stocking hanging from the mantel and Tyler would have a baby brother or sister. Christine couldn't have imagined a better existence for herself. John was the perfect husband and father, and—with his support—she'd been able to launch her business early. With the New England countryside providing ample inspiration, she'd come up with a number of award-winning designs and her Internet company had taken off, profits skyrocketing. And to think, she owed it all to her pushy best friend who'd insisted she get away to pull her life together.

Christine smiled at Ellen and Carlos, sipping their eggnogs by the fire.

"I'm happy to see you finally broke down and got a Christmas tree," Ellen quipped.

"I had a little help," Christine said, gazing lovingly at John.

"Yeah, and Carlos has offered to help me take it down!"

"I what?" Carlos sputtered, as the rest of the group burst out laughing.

"You lazy old goat," John said, ribbing. "Nobody can get you to do anything at Christmas but eat."

"Oh, I wouldn't say that's exactly true," Ellen

said with a mysterious grin.

Christine turned to her, her cheeks flushed with delight. "Ellen?"

Ellen stretched out her left hand and a gemstone glistened on her ring finger.

"Does this mean what I think?" Christine asked with pleased surprise.

Ellen nodded triumphantly.

John put Tyler down and patted Carlos's shoulder. "Way to go, old man!"

"He's not so old," Ellen said, her voice low and sexy.

Carlos turned the color of Santa's suit as Tyler looked cheerily around the room. This was just the Christmas card Christine wanted, she thought as John took her hand. The best part was she got to live it all year through. Tyler hugged Mason and the dog licked his face.

"Merry Christmas, everybody!" the boy said, his cheeks aglow.

Mason barked twice.

THE END

Holiday Brides Book 2

THE HOLIDAY BRIDE

Chapter One

Lucy hoisted her waitressing tray high and snaked through the crowd at the packed diner. Paper Christmas decorations plastered the walls and plastic holly was draped from the counter to the floor. Customers hunkered forward over steaming cups of coffee and generous wedges of pie, as their heavy coats overburdened hooks by the door. Lucy spied a couple across the way snuggled giddily together on one side of a booth. Suddenly, the man involved slid from his seat and dropped to one knee. Lucy paused in her tracks, her heart thumping below the loud chatter. Though she couldn't hear his words, his intent was clear as he pulled a ring box from his pocket and took his companion's hand.

"Hey! Watch it, will ya?" Belle shouted, nearly crashing into her. Belle had worked here forever, and her years of experience were etched in her face.

Lucy lowered her tray, steadying it in her grip. "I'm sorry, Belle. I didn't see you coming."

Belle's eyes fell on the happy couple across the room, both now standing and engaged in a joyful embrace. "Maybe if you kept your eyes on *your* customers, instead of mine, you'd be more aware."

Lucy sighed, her gaze skimming the tiny solitaire on her left hand. It was hard not to think of Mitch and make a comparison. He hadn't even bothered to ask her officially. Instead, he'd just shrugged and said, *Well, you know what this means,* handing over the ring. "I'll try to be more careful."

"You just do that," Belle said, raising her own tray and stepping past her.

Lucy swallowed hard, collecting herself. Though Belle came off as gruff, she wasn't all bad. Everyone here was cranky by now. They'd been working like crazy all season long. Here it was Christmas Eve, and business hadn't let up one bit.

Lucy adjusted the silly Santa hat that Gus had forced her to wear and pasted a smile on her face. She'd been on her feet for ten hours and every one of her muscles ached. One of these days, she was going to get a better job, one that allowed her to sit once in a while. From the looks of this crowd, she thought, trudging through the sea of elbows and clattering dishes getting tossed in bus buckets, that day wouldn't be anytime soon.

On the other side of town, William Kinkaid stood by the snowy window as his five-year-old daughter said her prayers. Springy chestnut curls spilled forth as she bent her head, fingers interlaced. "God bless Daddy and Justin, and Mommy in heaven..."

William felt the familiar ache in his chest, just as he did every time the kids mentioned Karen. It wasn't that he didn't want them to remember her. Maybe it was more that it was hard for him to remember her himself.

"Okay, pumpkin," he said fondly as she finished up. "It's into bed with you."

Carmella hopped into bed and scooted down under the covers. "Will Santa really bring me what I asked for?" she asked, looking at him trustfully with big dark eyes.

"What did you ask for, sweetheart?"

"Uh-uh," she said, shaking her little head. "It's a secret."

"Santa's not going to bring you *that,* fuzz brain," Justin called from the doorway. William turned to find his twelve-year-old son standing in the threshold.

"Be nice, Justin. And you go to bed, too. Or else, Santa won't bring you what you asked for either."

Justin shrugged and strode away, his shirttails hanging around the slouchy jeans that draped loosely on his lanky frame.

William returned his attention to Carmella, still waiting on his answer. "Of course, sweetheart. You bet. Santa will do everything in his power to bring you what you want."

Carmella grinned, settling her head on her pillow. Something crackled underneath.

"Carmella?" William asked, leaning forward to check and see where the sound had come from.

Carmella flipped over and hugged her pillow. "It's all right, Daddy. You don't need to see."

He studied her, stroking his chin. "Why don't I?"

"Because it will only make you sad."

William steadied his emotions, thinking his precocious little girl always had a way to read him. At times, it seemed she was five going on thirty-five. Maybe that was because she spent most of her time around much older folks.

"Your old man's pretty tough, you know." He extended a hand, expecting her to turn over her hidden stash. How bad could it be? A handful of pilfered candy canes? William resisted a chuckle, maintaining his stern daddy pose.

Reluctantly, Carmella pulled a stack of papers from under her pillow. William was stunned to see they were advertisements, torn from catalogues and magazines. "What's this, pumpkin?" he asked, fanning through them. There were pictures of families, and mothers with daughters, all dressed in the finest fare.

Carmella blinked, then said urgently. "I was looking at clothes, Daddy! Girls like fashion!"

William stroked his chin, and eyed her suspiciously. "So I've heard..." Something about this didn't add up. He didn't think pressure was that keen to keep up with labels in kindergarten. Although his mom had repeatedly warned him: *You can't have those children walking around like ruffians, William. For heaven's sakes, buy them some decent clothes.* That's where all the catalogues had come from. They were entirely his mom's idea. Though William didn't believe his kids looked *that* bad. He basically let them wear what they wanted, and always shopped at the upscale malls. "Well, if it's fashion you're after, we can hit the stores the moment they reopen after Christmas."

"All right," she said with a big, bright smile.

William kissed her on the head and said nighty-night, still feeling as if something were amiss. He'd really thought she'd wanted that enormous white teddy bear she'd already named Cubby. Hadn't she ogled it each time they'd passed the window of that store?

He switched off the light, as she snuggled contentedly under the covers. "I know I'm going to get it. I just *know*."

"And I'm sure you will, pumpkin," he said, smiling softly.

William turned and ambled toward the door with

a heavy heart. He couldn't stand to disappoint his daughter. He hoped to goodness he'd gotten this Christmas right.

Lucy turned in a hurry, nearly crashing into Belle again. "Watch it!" the older woman shouted, clearly agitated. Even her patience was wearing thin, and Belle was long on patience. Lucy quickly backed up, but not in time to avoid splashing two new coffees down the front of her uniform. *This is great, just super,* she thought, on the verge of tears. Her last customer had stiffed her a tip, all on account of some burnt toast that she'd had nothing to do with. And now, *this.*

"Say, Luce!" the kindly older cook called from the griddle. "Why don't you call it a night? You've worked two hours over already!"

Belle offered to hold her tray as she dabbed her apron with a rag. "But this place is packed!" she told Gus, her voice cracking. Lucy hated that her tone betrayed her. She was only thirty-one and was supposed to be tough. At least as tough as old Belle here. She thanked the other waitress and took back her tray.

"Packed or no, it will go on without ya. Now, scat! Consider it an order." He motioned to Belle to take Lucy's tray back and Belle sighed with resignation.

"Sure, yeah. You go ahead," she said, accepting the mess. "Least you've got a life waiting on ya."

Lucy swallowed hard, wishing that were true.

"But first," Gus commanded, patting the counter, "come, sit. Woman can't live by stress alone."

Lucy gratefully took an empty stool near the

register, feeling her tension ease. She hadn't even realized how hungry she was until Gus set the big stack of pancakes before her. "Fresh blueberry. Your favorite."

"What would I do without you?"

"Starve, more than likely."

He poured her a glass of milk as she lifted her fork and waited.

"Oh no you don't..." he joked, "you're not dragging me into that disgusting habit of yours."

"Please, Gus? It's Christmas."

He pulled a bottle of chocolate syrup from the fridge and set it on the counter with a thunk.

"There really *is* a Santa Claus," Lucy said, greedily uncapping the bottle and pouring. Before she could ask, Gus had produced a can of whipped cream and spritzed a sweeping circle onto her chocolate-covered flapjacks.

"Yeah, and if he's watching, the old guy is sick to his stomach."

"It's good," Lucy said, digging in. "You ought to try it." The blueberry confection coated in chocolaty whipped cream melted in her mouth like a warm bite of heaven. "Mmm. Delicious."

"Thanks, but I give Pepto-Bismol enough of a workout."

"You act like I'm the only person on the planet who eats this."

He studied her with a mixture of affection and amusement. "That, sweetheart, is because you are."

Her gaze trailed to the ancient tube television mounted in the corner. An old black-and-white rerun from one of her favorite nineteen-fifties shows was playing, the sort with the ideal intact family and happy mom and dad. "If only real life were like that."

"Yeah, but life ain't no TV show. Perfection like that only exists in—"

"I know, I know. Fairy tales."

"The Classics Channel is full of them. Maybe you should watch it less, and live a little more."

"God knows I'm trying."

"So, where's the lucky fellow tonight?"

"Working, as usual."

"Socking away the dough for that love nest of yours?"

"I guess," she said, knowing she sounded less than convincing.

"Somehow you don't sound so excited."

Her gaze panned back to the television. "Like you said, perfection only exists in fairy tales—and on the Classics Channel."

Gus cleared her empty plate. "Sometimes you've just got to take what life serves you up. Even if it gives you indigestion."

"Thanks, Gus," she said with a weary smile. She stood and grabbed her coat off a nearby rack.

"Any time, kid. You have a merry Christmas now."

"Yeah, you too."

The moment Lucy stepped onto the street, a frigid blast of air hit her smack in the face. She bundled her scarf around her head and neck and trudged down the street through the blinding snow. What had started as light drifts had turned into a heavy sludge that dropped from the sky in icy strips. At least she and Mitch had plans for tonight and she could look forward to a cozy evening indoors. While

Mitch wasn't much on romance, he'd promised for weeks that tonight would be special. As soon as her shift ended, he'd be taking off from work as well, so just the two of them could spend the time together they so badly deserved.

Lucy was glad to see the lights from Mitch's real estate office burning brightly up ahead. He was always the last one working, though he maintained it was for a cause.

Lucy pressed through the heavy glass door, enveloped in a swirl of snow and sending its door chime tinkling. Whistling winds howled as she pushed the door shut.

Mitch didn't even look up.

Lucy strode to where he sat and set her gloved hands on his desk, palms down on either side of his laptop. "Um-hum," she said, leaning forward and hoping to get his attention.

Mitch looked up with a start, and removed the pen clenched in his teeth. "Sweet Merry Christmas, Luce," he said, studying the flakes stuck to her honey-blond hair. "You look like a blasted snow bunny!"

"That's because I *am* a blasted snow bunny. Haven't you even looked outdoors? It's really coming down out there."

Mitch craned his neck to peer over Lucy's shoulder. "So it is," he said with apparent surprise. "Sure wasn't doing that this morning."

"You didn't even break for lunch?"

Mitch angled toward her, trapping her hands in his. "Babe," he said, with serious brown eyes. "This is the big one." His cell rang and he motioned for her to wait.

"Magic Maker Mitch, at your service!" he said

into the mouthpiece before flashing Lucy a grin. She knew his spiel so well by now, she could practically spout it herself. "Closing on the thirty-first?" he continued. "No problem."

Lucy's heart skipped a beat. "But Mitch, that's our—"

He quickly covered the mouthpiece to assure her, "I'll have this all wrapped up by six, no problem."

Lucy pursed her lips, wishing she could be sure. With Mitch she never knew. New Year's Eve wasn't some casual date. It was their—

"Can do, that's my motto! Four o'clock on the thirty-first it is!"

He ended the call and ran a hand through the stubby brown hair he always wore in a Marine's cut, though he'd never actually been in the service. *Makes the clientele totally trust me,* he liked to say, *real apple-pie-like.*

"Mitch," Lucy said, speaking past the lump in her throat. "December thirty-first is our wedding."

"Of course, I know that." He stood and pulled her into his arms, soggy coat and all. "That's precisely why I'm doing this. For you!"

"Me?"

"Baby," he said, tilting up her chin and meeting her eyes. "You've got to trust me when I say this is the big tamale. We're talking swimming pools, movie stars, the whole nine yards. Once this deal's cut, we'll get twice the house for our money."

"But I already told you, I don't need a big house."

He jostled her in his arms. "You just say that because you've never allowed yourself to believe you deserve it. But I know better, you hear? And I intend to see that you, little lady, get all the happiness you deserve."

Lucy's cheeks warmed with a hopeful flush. "You mean you've changed your mind about having kids?"

Mitch studied her with alarm. "Kids? Hoo boy, Luce. I was talking about you and me! I don't recall that discussion being on the table."

"That's because you keep taking it off," she told him. "It's important. A big thing we need to talk through."

"You bet, and we will," he said, releasing her. "Tomorrow, at my place. Turkey with all the trimmings!" He smiled sheepishly and lifted a stack of papers from his desk. "But first, I've got some files to go through."

"But I thought you promised tonight—?"

"I know, baby, and I'm sorry. Really I am. But this deal will be worth it. Just you wait and see."

"Yeah, sure," Lucy said, resigned. Every new deal was the big tamale… or taco… or enchilada, and Lucy was growing weary of Mexican food. She shoved her hands in her pockets, feeling let down. It was their last Christmas Eve as single people and she'd really hoped that they'd spend it together. "Won't I be seeing you later?" she asked with a tentative glance.

"Of course. You bet. I'm still planning on stopping over. Just as soon as I wrap up things here, and deliver those packages."

Lucy followed his gaze to a stack of neatly wrapped gifts by the copier. "What are those?"

"Just some things I said I'd take care of for a client."

Lucy checked the clock on the wall, thinking that he'd never make it to her apartment at this pace. Maybe if she helped out, she'd speed things up a bit, so they could at least enjoy one glass of eggnog in tandem before midnight. "What's the address? I'll take them."

"You'll what?" he asked with surprise.

"I said I'd take them, Mitch. Just let me know where they're going and I'll drop them off."

"Gosh, Luce! Are you serious?"

She nodded, then spoke under her breath. "Got nothing else to do."

"You're the best!" He took her by the shoulders and planted a big kiss on her lips. Then he scribbled an address on a post-it note and stuck it to the top package. "It's not too far from here. Actually, it's kind of on your way."

Lucy had barely gone fifty feet when she started regretting her decision. It was as cold as Siberia out here, and the sidewalk was slippery besides. She adjusted the bulky sack holding the packages in her arms, wondering what sort of client couldn't do their own Christmas shopping and delivery. Mitch really went overboard sometimes, forever banking on his zealous devotion paying off. If only he were a little less devoted to his work and a tad more attached to her, she would be happy. But what was happiness, anyway? Like Gus had just said, life wasn't some fairy tale.

Lucy blinked at the glare of headlights meeting her head-on. She was approaching a crossing, and the driver apparently didn't see her coming. He barreled straight ahead, obviously not spotting the stop sign, either. Lucy had been scurrying along, trying to make haste in completing her task, so she could get home. Now, she had to call herself up short and stop on a dime to avoid walking into the path of the oncoming car. She gripped the sack with a start as her sneakers skidded against slick pavement beneath her. Their soles were coated in a film of ice, lending her no traction at all. "Ohh, whoa!" she shouted, hydroplaning toward the intersection. She was sliding faster now, with no way to stop herself. Then, *bump,* she went over the curb and felt herself falling backward toward the sidewalk. Taillights streaked away as the back of her head came down hard.

The last thing Lucy saw was a tiny post-it note fluttering high into falling flakes and twirling away, as sleigh bells chimed.

Chapter Two

William cinched the tie on his robe and paused at the bend in the stairs. Carmella raced down the steps ahead of him, dashing to the large beige sofa facing the fireplace. Two stockings brimming with goodies hung from the mantel.

"Oh boy, oh boy!" she cried, springing on her heels in a happy dance. Justin appeared on the landing beside his dad.

"What is it, fuzz brain?" he asked with a yawn.

Carmella looked up at them, her cheeks aglow. William had never seen her so excited. "He did it! Santa really did it!"

William descended the stairs feeling pleased with himself. He did know a thing or two about fathering, after all. "Well? Is it what you wanted?"

"Boy, is it ever," Carmella said with a happy gasp.

William strode around the sofa, feeling smug. Then, suddenly, he halted, nearly tumbling over the coffee table.

"Wow," Justin said, gazing straight ahead of him.

William stared in shock at the lovely blonde on the sofa who was clutching Carmella's teddy bear! She didn't look much over thirty, and was very reasonably put together.

The woman opened her eyes with a start and tried to sit, before quickly lying back down. "Where am I?" she asked with a pitiful moan.

"Don't you know?" Carmella asked, taking her hand. "Santa brought you home!"

She pushed herself upright, grasping the back of the sofa. "Home?"

"You're our new mommy!"

William stared at the woman, who stared back in shock.

"Our new...? Oh no, no, no, no, *no.*" William suspiciously studied his son. "Justin William Kinkaid, did you have something to do with this?"

"No, Dad! I swear!"

"I bet it was Eddie," William said, stroking his chin. "Eddie, from the bank. I gave that scoundrel our key to water the houseplants at Thanksgiving, and he never gave it back."

Blue eyes flashed beneath long dark lashes, as the woman took all of them in. "Do I... know you people?"

William strode toward the sofa and spoke in a coarse whisper. "Listen, missy, I don't know who you are, or what—"

"I don't either," she said, sounding alarmed. "How did I get here? Was I abducted?"

"Ab—*what*?"

"Why are you two whispering?" Carmella piped up. "I want to hear what she's saying."

"Ditto that," Justin added. "Ought to be a doozy."

William scowled at the woman, thinking this little practical joke had gone too far. "Would you mind having a word with me in the kitchen?"

She gripped the bear and scooted back on the sofa. "I don't know. Maybe I *would* mind. You seem a little unstable to me."

"Don't be afraid," Carmella said kindly. "Santa wouldn't send you to a bad place."

"Santa? But there's no—" the woman began

before William cut her off with a silencing look. "...way he could have told me what a pretty little girl you are," she finished, picking up on the cue not to let the *there's no Santa* cat out of the bag.

"If you don't mind?" William said, motioning toward the kitchen door.

Lucy stood in the kitchen, her head still woozy. Her legs felt like spaghetti that had been way overcooked. She held on to the center island to steady herself as the man ranted on. He was impossibly irritated with her, and she hadn't a clue why. In fact, she was having a hard time remembering much of anything.

"Okay, we're away from the kids now," he continued, "you can drop the act." For someone so obviously agitated, he was terribly handsome. With that solid six-foot frame and those chiseled features offset by morning stubble, he almost looked like a star meant for television. But then, why was he wearing a robe? "I don't know what you mean."

"Listen, I don't know what Eddie paid you—"

"Isn't Eddie the one who hired the stripper for your birthday?" the boy asked from the threshold. He held a big bag full of packages and looked to be twelve or thirteen. From the smirk on his lips, he liked to think he was older.

The man's naturally ruddy complexion took on a deeper flush. "A *dancer,* son. She was a dancer. I thought I explained all that. Just what have you got in your hands?"

The tween cast Lucy an appreciative eye. "Looks like your mystery date brought gifts. Loads of them." He checked a tag and grinned. "By the way, her name is Bridget."

Lucy and the man exchanged glances, but all she drew was a blank. Bridget didn't sound quite right. Then again, it wasn't completely unfamiliar.

"Fine, fine," the man told the boy, "thanks for the update. Now could you please..." He motioned for his son to leave and the tween skedaddled. He turned his gaze back on Lucy and she noticed his honey brown eyes were dabbled with flecks of gold right around the irises. "All right, Bridget. Let's get one thing straight. There will be no disrobing in this house. Do I make myself clear?"

She set her hand on her hip, affronted. She might not recall much at the moment, but she was certain she wasn't a stripper! "Give a break," she said. "Do I look like a stripper to you?"

He scrutinized her, apparently deciding.

"Look," she said, "there's obviously been a big misunderstanding. I don't know someone called Eddie, and I certainly don't know any of you."

"Well then, there's no other explanation. You broke in here."

"Come on! I don't know a lot, but I know that I'm no thief. Listen, I'm just as upset about this as you are. Maybe more. I wake up on some stranger's sofa, whose kids think Santa brought me—"

"And we both know that's not true," he said, tilting his decidedly masculine chin.

"Oh!" Suddenly, all the commotion hit her and she felt incredibly light-headed.

"What is it? What's wrong?" he asked, his face softening with concern. Maybe, just maybe, he believed her and trusted she wasn't putting this whole thing on.

"My head. It's..." She reached for the back of her head and instantly winced at the pain.

He gingerly lifted his hand toward her scalp. "May I?"

She nodded, increasingly dizzy.

"No wonder you feel faint," he said. "You've got quite a bump back there."

Lucy stumbled forward and he caught her in his sturdy arms. "Bridget?" he said, searching her eyes. *He really is incredibly gorgeous,* she thought in the split second before the lights went out. And then, Lucy felt herself falling into someplace totally dark and warm.

William stared down at the woman who'd collapsed against him, at a total loss. What on earth could he do? He clearly couldn't leave her slumped over like this. As carefully as he could, he slipped one arm beneath the back of her legs and lifted her into his arms. Cradled against his chest, she looked almost like a princess from a fairy tale. Her hair was blond and fine, tucked back at the top with some pins, and falling in some sort of uneven arrangement around her chin. Her complexion was fair, although she looked even paler now that she'd fainted away completely. Ordinarily, he'd take her to the hospital, but he wasn't sure of his odds of getting into town with the snowstorm upon them and the one-lane bridge closed. He'd call the doctor first, that's what he'd do. And then start phoning around. The police, the missing persons bureau... She had to be on the level, and was clearly injured besides.

A moment later, William carted Bridget through the living room as Carmella sprang from her chair.

"Where are you taking her?"

"Probably back to the loony bin where she belongs," Justin said from nearby.

"Justin!" William corrected sternly.

Carmella raced to the front door and flung herself against it, arms outstretched. "Oh no you don't!" she told her puzzled father. "Bridget was *my* Christmas gift, remember? No exchanges, no returns!"

"I'm not taking Bridget anywhere," he kindly told his daughter. "Except for up to bed."

Justin lifted an eyebrow, but William just cleared his throat and headed for the stairs. "You know what I mean, son."

"She's good, I'll give her that," Justin said.

"She's not playacting," Carmella retorted soundly. "She's just tired. Bet it was exhausting riding all the way around the world in that sleigh."

"Yes, well," William said, taking his leave. "I think I'll just take her upstairs and let her get some rest."

William carried Bridget to the master bedroom and tenderly set her down on the bed. As cautiously as he could, he removed one sneaker and then the next. Her instep dropped into his hand and he halted, looking up at her legs with a flush. She wore nylons and a short white dress marked with dark stains that appeared to be some kind of uniform. William hadn't thought about women's legs in a long time, and certainly hadn't been this close to any. Definitely none this lovely. He quickly lifted a throw blanket to cover them, and the rest of Bridget's womanly figure as well.

He caught a glimpse of Karen's picture on the

nightstand and felt his face redden, suddenly overtaken with guilt. He hadn't looked at another woman since Karen died, and had honestly had no desire to. What with being a single dad and managing the bank, he scarcely had time for a female friend. He was nearly forty besides, and well out of practice with the ladies. With Karen, things had been easy. They'd been companionable college friends who'd become lovers, then later had married. He'd felt lucky to have been spared the trials and tribulations of playing the field that so many of his buddies purported to delight in, but secretly disdained. It really was a jungle out there, and William Kinkaid's swinging days were done.

Something sparkled on Bridget's left hand, and he realized with an odd sense of sadness that she wore an engagement ring. Well, of course she would, wouldn't she? Pretty young woman like that was bound to be taken. Was sure to have a wonderful life—and fiancé—waiting for her somewhere out there. And wherever they were, William was going to help find them. It was the least he could do for a stranger, especially at Christmastime.

"She's so beautiful," Carmella's soft voice rang out behind him. William turned in surprise to see his daughter had entered the room.

"Bet she escaped from prison," Justin said, trailing behind her.

Carmella puffed out her cheeks. "Did not!"

William shooed them out of the way and quietly shut the door. "Now, come on, you two. I'm sure she didn't escape from prison."

"Yeah. The elves made her," Carmella informed

them.

"Elves don't make people, fuzz brain."

William shot Justin a look, and then stooped low to speak to Carmella. "Is that what you asked for, Carmella? A new mommy?"

"Oh, yes. And isn't she perfect? A little younger than I asked for, but I guess that's okay."

A lump welled in William's throat. "Sweetheart," he said softly. "I know how much you miss your mother. We all do." He pursed his lips a beat. "But I think that you should know—"

"There's no such thing as Santa!" Justin proclaimed with mirth.

The child gasped, pain streaking her eyes. "Daddy, say he's wrong!"

William huffed and glanced at Justin, agitated. "Downstairs. *Now.*"

Justin skulked away, saggy pants drooping, as Carmella clutched her teddy. "But he brought me Cubby! And a mommy! You said he was real. You wouldn't lie, would you, Daddy?"

William set his jaw, feeling like a big fat fake. He couldn't tell Carmella that Santa wasn't real and break her little heart. She still had so much of childhood left, and her childhood had been hard on her already. Growing up without a mother had left her longing for things he couldn't provide. William saw that now and felt awful about it.

"Of course there's a Santa," he said, drawing his daughter and her bear into a hug. "You bet there is." He pulled back and thumbed her nose with a smile. "You got your Cubby, didn't you?"

Chapter Three

One hour later, William lowered his voice and spouted into the mouthpiece, "What do you mean I have to wait forty-eight hours to report a missing person. I just told you, she's already here!"

He set down the phone and massaged his temples just as the doorbell rang. Cheery voices and laughter rang out from the foyer as Carmella raced into room.

"Grammy and Poppy are here!"

William sighed, wondering how he was going to explain Bridget to his parents. They were overbearing enough when he led the life of the unencumbered single dad. Who knew how they'd take the news of a stranger landing on his sofa?

He walked toward the front door and helped his mother with her coat. She was neatly prim as always, in a crisply ironed skirt and buttoned-up blouse. His father was a mess, as usual, with none of his patterned items matching. "Mom! Dad!" William said, greeting them both with hugs. "How was the trip? Any trouble getting here?"

"Well, the walk was a little slippery," his mom said.

"Other than that, it went just fine," his dad finished for her.

William supposed it helped that they lived next door. Otherwise, with the storm pelting, they might not have made it.

Emma leaned forward and whispered in his ear. "Carmella says Santa left something on your sofa..."

"Something life-size," Grant chortled with a grin.

"Actually, it's not like that at—"

"Sure it is, Daddy!" Carmella butted in. "You said so upstairs. Just after you took her to bed, remember?"

Emma fanned her face with her purse as William reddened. "I don't really think this is appropriate," she hissed under her breath. "Not with the children—"

"He's a grown man, Emma," Grant cut in. He leaned in toward William. "But your mother's right, son. You should have asked her to leave before the kids got up."

"No, he should have asked her to *wait* until after the wedding," Emma said a little too loudly.

William croaked, *"Wedding?"*

"Oh boy!" Carmella crowed. "She'll look just like my Bride Barbie! Wait until you see her!" she said, shooting her grandparents a sunny smile.

Justin guffawed and William cupped his mouth with a hand. His parents were nearly to the stairs, his mom led by Carmella.

"Mom! Dad! Before you go up there—"

"She *is* decent, son?" his dad asked.

"She's just like Goldilocks," Carmella said.

Grant studied his son with admiration. "A blonde, eh? Well, why not."

Carmella tugged at her grandma. "Come on, but shhh... She's sleeping."

"Mom, wait!" But it was too late. They were already to the landing. William sighed and chased after them.

Justin gallantly rushed ahead, holding open the door for his grandparents.

"Very nice, Justin," William said under his breath. "Ultra helpful."

"Oh my yes," Emma said. "Lovely, really lovely."

"Of course, you can't see much with that blanket in the way," Grant quipped.

Emma turned to William. "Does she always sleep this late?"

"Not a drinker, is she?" Grant wanted to know.

"Please," William said in hushed tones. "Let's all go back downstairs. Mom and Dad, I've got some cocoa for you in the kitchen."

Justin triumphantly shut the bedroom door. "Sounds good. I'll come, too."

"Adult cocoa, Justin. Not for you."

Carmella looked hopeful.

"Or for you either, pumpkin."

"Can we open some of our presents?" Justin asked slyly.

"You bet," William said. "Just don't touch any of the ones brought by you-know-who."

Emma snatched the bourbon bottle from her husband and poured another liberal dose into her cocoa mug. "Oh, dear. This won't do at all."

Grant drained his mug, then set it aside. "Aren't you a little old to be picking up strays?"

"Look," William said, "I don't know what else to do! The police say no one has filed a missing persons report. I tried the hospital, too. But nobody's called there looking for her, either."

"Maybe you should take her to the hospital," Emma said seriously. "Maybe she's not *right*."

"The fact that she can't remember anything

doesn't make her a psycho, Mother. Besides, you saw what it's like out there. Nobody's going anywhere until the plows get through."

"What about Dr. Mass?" Grant asked.

"I phoned him, too." William checked some notes on the table. "He gave me some instructions about waking her up every hour. Checking her pupils with a flashlight."

"So you're just going to let her stay here?" Emma asked.

"Dr. Mass says that–unless she takes a turn for the worse–he'll see us in his office in the morning, assuming the streets get cleared."

His mom tapped the side of her mug with neatly trimmed fingernails. "I still don't know if this is such a good idea. A damsel in distress... a lonely widower..."

"It's almost two o'clock on Christmas Day," William said. "I can't just toss her out in the snow!"

"No, I probably wouldn't toss her out of my bed, either," Grant said thoughtfully.

Emma swatted his arm.

Grant leaned forward with a conspiratorial whisper. "Say, what if she's escaped from prison? That would give her plenty of reason to forget who she is!"

William huffed with exasperation. *"She is not on the lam, okay?"*

Both of his parents pushed back in their chairs and stared at each other.

"Don't you think the cops would have mentioned it?" William asked, a slight edge to his voice.

William couldn't believe it. His dad almost looked disappointed. "Yeah, I guess you're right."

"Besides," William added, "she doesn't exactly look like the hardened criminal type."

Emma shook her head. "What about the children? How are they taking it?"

William frowned. "Carmella thinks Santa brought her."

Grant chuckled and William cast him a cursory glance.

"And Justin?" Emma asked.

In the next room, Justin eagerly pawed through Bridget's gifts. "I say we open all of them."

"You heard what Daddy said."

"Yeah... don't touch! So, I won't. I'll just open and peek inside." He yanked off the gift tag, hooting. *"For Koochie, for us to be naughty and nice..."*

"Koochie?" Carmella puzzled. "Do you think that's for Daddy?"

"One way to find out!"

He tore back the wrapping of a long box and Carmella lunged forward. "Justin!"

Before she could stop him, he'd dispensed with the rest of the paper and flipped open the lid. "Well, well, well..." Justin fell back whooping holding up a skimpy black-and-red lace teddy.

Just then, the adults entered the room.

"Why son," Grant said discreetly to William. "You buy that getup for Goldie?"

"Goldie? Hey, no! Wait!

Carmela stuck out her bottom lip. "No, Poppy. These are *from* Bridget." She purposefully collected the lingerie and deposited it with William. "Here, Daddy. I think this is for you."

William held the lace teddy, which dangled

down in front of him. "No, honey, I don't think it's my size." If someone had stuck hot coals to his face, it couldn't have felt any warmer. Then he looked up to spy Bridget on the stairs, and felt himself combust from heat all over.

Lucy stopped walking and gaped at William holding a racy teddy and standing beside the Christmas tree. His face was the color of cinnamon, while Carmella pouted and the tween rollicked with laughter on the floor.

"Hello, dear!" a neatly dressed older woman called.

A man with abysmal fashion sense stood beside her and grinned. "You must be Bridget!"

"You're awake," William said, his voice cracking.

Frankly, this moment seemed a fine time to turn around. "No, actually I'm—"

"Sleepwalking?" Justin asked.

Carmella shook her head at her brother. "She's not sleepwalking, you Dumbo. Can't you see?"

"Why don't you come on down here and join us?" the older man said.

"Yes, dear," his wife agreed. "We'd like the chance to get to know you better."

That would be ideal, if only she had a way to understand herself. Who was this family, and how had she gotten mixed up with all of them? She recalled the sofa, remembered waking up here this morning quite well. It was all that came before that was a blur.

William shoved the lace teddy in his pocket with an embarrassed look. "Do come downstairs, if you're able. Do you need help?"

"No," she said uncertainly. "Thanks. I think I've got it."

A little while later, they sat around the family dining table where William carved a large turkey. Lucy had learned his parents were named Emma and Grant, and that the tween's name was Justin. Justin was slightly snarky, but Lucy supposed that came with the territory. Little Carmella, on the other hand, was simply adorable. She was so intent on Lucy being her *Mommy,* Lucy hadn't known what to think, or say, about any of it. While she'd gathered from the conversation that William had lost his wife some time ago, she wasn't sure how long it had been or under what circumstances. How hard that must be on William, handling this all on his own.

"White meat or dark?" he asked, meeting Lucy's eyes. But she truthfully didn't know. Lucy shrugged and Emma laughed, warmly patting her hand. A light mix of 1940s jazz played in the background. The music was comforting, and familiar, to Lucy at once, and yet—she couldn't place it.

"Don't worry, dear. It will all come back, eventually."

"The trip to the doctor's sure to help," Grant said.

"Doctor?" Lucy wondered.

William laid another slice of turkey on a platter. "I forgot to mention. I'm taking you to see Dr. Mass tomorrow."

Emma smiled reassuringly. "He's been our family physician for years."

Lucy felt her face warm. They were all being so kind to her. Had to be the Christmas spirit. "You

don't know what it means to me, how nice you've
been. I mean, I could have wound up anywhere,
really. There are bound to be terrible places out
there."

"Yes, right," Grant said.

"Bound to be," Emma added.

Dinner passed with Emma and Grant asking the
grandkids what they'd been up to, and how their
friends were in school. Everyone seemed to get on
reasonably well, even William with his parents,
despite their eccentricities. Serving plates circled
round and round until Lucy was sure she'd eaten
enough to hibernate for winter.

"More stuffing, dear?" Emma asked, hovering a
brimming ladle over her dinner plate.

"Oh no, I couldn't," Lucy said. "I'm stuffed!"

"Tell us about the elves," Carmella said sweetly.

Justin grinned in her direction. "Yes, do tell us
about those elves. Are they ordering from Victoria's
Secret now?"

William and Grant turned on him at once,
parroting together, "What would you know about
Victoria's Secret?"

Carmella looked around the table. "Who's
Victoria and what's her secret?"

Emma gave Grant a hard elbow and spoke in low
tones. "What would *you* know about Victoria's
Secret?"

Grant coughed loudly, as William cleared his
throat.

"I'm sure Bridget has better things to talk about.
Don't you, Bridget?"

He met her gaze, and Lucy's heart stilled. With
him sitting there, and her sitting here, at opposite ends

of the table, she could almost imagine them as husband and wife. And what a marvelous husband he'd make, too. He was accomplished, and settled, she thought, glancing around at the comfortable place. Not rich, but well off enough, and boy did he ever seem to love his family. From the happy feel in the room, the emotion was mutual. Not only that, he was easy on the eyes. Way too easy. Lucy tucked the hand wearing the engagement ring in her lap, wondering if the guy she planned to marry was half as grand. A sultry rendition of Billy Holiday singing "All of Me" played in the background. *Take my lips, I want to lose them... take my arms, I'll never use them... How can I go on without you...?*

William stared at her expectantly, and Lucy realized he was waiting for her to say something.

"This stuffing *is* delicious," she said, suddenly lifting the serving bowl. "I think I *will* have some more."

"Do you cook much, dear?" Emma asked.

Lucy realized she was making a glutton of herself, nervously heaping mound upon mound on her plate. She stopped and looked up. "Um... cook?" Now, that was something she was used to being around. But, doing? Hmm. "Honestly, I can't exactly tell you. But I do know this, I'm totally used to being around food."

William grinned at her, oddly charmed by this. "Anything in particular, or everything in general?"

Lucy thought hard, willing even the tiniest tidbit to come to mind. Her eyes fell on a candy dish of green-and-red-wrapped holiday chocolates sitting on the sideboard. "Chocolate," she said brightly, knowing that was right. "Anything—and everything—chocolate."

Carmella appeared inordinately pleased. "No fooling? Daddy loves chocolate, too."

Justin lowered his eyebrows. "Yeah. He does the most disgusting thing with—"

"Justin, knock it off," William said, plainly embarrassed.

"Yes well, enough of that," Emma said. "Just let me clear the plates and I'll serve dessert."

"Bodacious bourbon pecan?" William asked.

Emma nodded.

"Make mine a double!" Justin said.

Lucy felt awkward not offering to help. "Here, let me take some of these," she said standing. At once, her knees buckled, sending her back into her chair.

"I think you'd best stay off your feet a bit longer," William said with a kind look. "At least until your legs feel steady."

Lucy met his eyes and her cheeks caught fire. He was so kind and caring. With that sensible banker haircut, she might never have known it just passing him on the street. But in here, all cozied up with his family, she saw William for who he really was. He was the sort of man who looked after people. It was a feeling that Lucy hadn't known in a long while. That much, she believed was true. Even if she couldn't trust in anything else.

By the time coffee and dessert were over, Lucy had gathered her reserves and was feeling much better. She'd insisted William let her dry the dishes, and after a bit of lighthearted banter, he'd given in.

"You don't stay put very well, do you?" he asked, as she finished up.

"Please, William. I want to... need to do something to help." She set a clean pot on the counter and capped it with its lid. "The dinner was delicious, thank you."

He studied her with earnest brown eyes. "And I want to thank you, too. Thank you for playing along with Carmella. It would break her heart if she knew the truth."

"I'd sure like to know it. I'm hoping the doctor can help tomorrow."

He leaned back against the counter, studying her. "You know, I don't believe in that Santa bit, of course, but I'd sure like to know how you got in my house."

"Yeah, me too. You say everything was locked up tight?"

"As a drum."

"Maybe there's a rusty basement lock, or unsecured window?"

"What kind of father do you think I am? I double-check this place every night. It's just like Fort Knox."

Lucy drew a breath. "Well, I certainly didn't drop down the chimney."

He met her eyes and his gaze lingered. "At least we've agreed on that."

The seconds ticked by as Lucy watched him watch her, her heart pounding. She didn't know this man from Adam, but still, when she was with him, she had an uncanny sensation of being home.

"Still nothing doing on the memory?" he asked.

"Except for some weird little details, like knowing I love chocolate, I just draw a blank." She hung her head. "I feel really terrible. I've ruined everyone's Christmas."

William reached over and gently raised her chin in his hand. "Don't you go worrying about that. You haven't ruined our Christmas at all. But someone out there is sure to be having a rotten night." He glanced down at her engagement ring, then once more met her eyes. "Someone's bound to be looking for you."

A few miles away, Mitch checked the wall clock in his real estate office, cursing out loud. It was snowing even harder than yesterday. He hadn't even made it home last night, despite his four-wheel drive. He'd had to sleep at the office. Mitch stared through the plate-glass window at the pounding snow, knowing his chances of getting out of here now were slim to none. But heck, he had lots to take care of anyway. He could get a jump on those closing papers, and snooze in the break room when he needed to. Yeah, there was a plan, he thought, taking another swing of eggnog from the quart carton on his desk.

He scooped up his cell and dialed Lucy's number.

Hi, it's me. Leave a message at the beep.

"Hey, sweetheart. Merry Christmas. It's me, Mitch. Say, I really hate to do this to you again. But Luce, if only you knew the size of this deal. I'm serious. This one is the grand tostado. I mean, *loaded.* We'll have everything we always wanted, just you wait and see. The two-car garage, a whole closet full of clothes just your size. Luce, you'll even be able to cut back on your hours at the diner. Maybe quit your job completely.

"The only thing is, hon, I've got to get this contract faxed by midnight. Now, I know this is a holiday and all, and I feel so totally terrible about you spending it alone. But, I swear, I'll make the whole thing up to you. Next year will be completely different."

Out on the porch, William said good night to his parents. He'd tossed on his coat so he could speak to them in confidence, but the down parka was a poor barrier against the biting wind. "Mom, Dad," he said, as Grant wrapped himself in his big, brown scarf, "I want to thank you both for everything. The gifts were really terrific."

"Yeah, especially the pretty blond one," Grant said.

Emma tugged at her gloves, adjusting their fit. "What are you going to do with her?"

"Like I said, I'm planning on taking her to the doctor tomorrow. Maybe he can help us figure out why she can't remember."

"Or *what* she can't remember," Emma said. "I want you to be careful, William. Now, I know she seems nice... But sometimes the quiet ones turn out to be the most dangerous."

"Your mother's right, son," Grant said. "You really don't know anything about this girl. Are you sure you want her spending the night? This isn't college, you know."

"I appreciate your concern, both of yours. Really I do. But I can take care of myself."

His mother met his eyes. "It's the children we're worried about. Little Carmella really has her hopes up. We had no idea."

"I know, Mom," William said sincerely. "I had no clue, either."

A fire blazed in the hearth as Carmella snuggled up against Lucy, who read to her on the sofa. *"And laying his finger aside of his nose and giving a nod, up the chimney he rose…"* Carmella's eyes drooped and she cooed happily, gently fading into slumber as Lucy uttered the final lines, *"Happy Christmas to all, and to all a good night."* Lucy quietly closed the book, yawning herself. It had been such an eventful day, and who knew what tomorrow would bring? At the moment, she was cozy and warm, and way overstuffed with stuffing.

Justin looked up from a wing chair beside the Christmas tree, where he'd been engrossed in a handheld game. "You act like you actually know something about it," he said bitterly.

Lucy glanced down at the book, then met his eyes. "Well, I do. I mean, this story, of course. It was always one of my favorites to read." She wasn't sure how she knew that, but she did. *What is it about this place? This room?* "Right here, by this fire."

"Yeah, right."

"Justin," she asked, her eyelids growing heavy. "Just what is it that you don't like about me?"

"The same thing I don't like about all girls. You're weird. In fact, you're the weirdest. If you think I buy that *Santa dropped me down the chimney* business…"

She wanted to stay awake, really she did. She needed to talk to William about tomorrow, and sleeping arrangements for tonight. But the firelight was so soothing. She and Carmella together felt so right. It took her back to an earlier time, a time when the world was safe and family meant home. Even

Justin's snarking couldn't combat the lull of the Sandman, beckoning her to drift away. A song came back, a lullaby, she thought... her mother's voice, rich and warm. And then, she felt her body sag into the sofa, all tension letting go.

When William reentered the house, he encountered an idyllic scene. Bridget and Carmella dozed together on the sofa, *The Night Before Christmas,* by Clement C. Moore, clutched in Bridget's hand. It was an old edition, one his parents had read to him as a child many years before.

He quietly hung his coat on the rack, not wishing to disturb them. William swallowed hard, resisting the warmth in his eyes. He couldn't recall having seen Carmella so contented in a long, long time. At least that made one of them, William thought, noting Justin's glum appearance in the wing chair nearby. He played his new video game with intensity, yet his expression was sullen.

"Time for bed, Justin," William said softly.

"But, Dad..." he protested

"Up!" William commanded, thinking it had been a full day for all of them.

Justin rose begrudgingly, casting a wary eye on Bridget. "Who is she really?"

"I don't know, son. But I'm sure as heck going to try to find out."

"Yeah, well, you'd better. Before she does any more damage around here."

"Damage?"

"Just look at them, Dad. How do you think Carmella's going to get over this? She's already lost one mom."

"Yes, son. And so have you."

"Here's the different between me and the fuzz brain. I don't want another mom any time soon. The one we had before was good enough to last me."

He stormily trudged upstairs, leaving William confounded. Justin was at such a hard age, William didn't know how to handle him half the time. And lately, he'd been more and more out of sorts. Having Bridget intrude on his holiday apparently hadn't sat well with him, either. But William needed to work on the boy. It was good for him to understand that charity came first, at the holidays especially. It wasn't like Bridget had chosen to come here. She was just as confused about her circumstances as the rest of them were.

Well, best to get everyone settled for the night so they could move on with solving things tomorrow. William leaned forward to scoop the sleeping Carmella into his arms, then suddenly he pulled back. He studied the portrait before him, a deep melancholy taking hold. They truly were a picture together, Carmella in her springy curls and Bridget with her arm wrapped protectively around the little girl. William stood there for a long while, firelight lapping at his face. He crossed his arms over his chest, trying to stem the tide of his emotions. But they welled within him, anyway. And, in that moment, William understood that Carmella hadn't been the only one hoping for someone else in this house. In his heart, he'd wanted someone, too.

Chapter Four

Lucy was called out of deep slumber by a piercing white light. She sat up with a start to find William hovering above her with a flashlight. "What are you doing?" she asked, pulling the covers to her chest.

"Checking your pupils." He grimaced apologetically. "Doctor's orders."

Of course, she remembered now. That part, anyway. "Sorry," she said, settling back on the pillow and opening her eyes wide. "I forgot."

He angled the beam toward her, causing her to squint.

"Still nothing doing on the memory?" he asked.

She blinked as he turned off the flashlight. "Not a thing. I mean, other than everything that's happened here."

"Hmm."

She watched him study her as fine light filtered in through the window. "Is that the moon out there?"

"Lucky for you, we've had a break in the storm," he said with a smile. "I'm sure I'll be able to get the SUV out tomorrow."

"Oh," she said, wondering why that notion depressed her. Of course she wanted to go the doctor and learn what was wrong with her. This wasn't her house; it was theirs. And they likely wanted her out of it as soon as possible. She brought her hand to her cheek, mildly pained at the thought. Why did the idea of feeling unwanted ring so familiar?

"Bridget," he said, as her solitaire glinted in the

moonlight. "There *is* a man in your life, isn't there? Somebody waiting for you?"

"I'd like to think so, yes," she said, unable to resist the ache in her heart.

His gaze lingered on hers and for a moment she suspected his heart ached, too.

"That's what I figured," he said.

"William?"

"Yes?"

"What's that disgusting thing you do with chocolate?"

He bellowed a laugh. "Your memory's not all bad, now is it? I'll never tell." He stood from where he'd sat on the edge of the bed. "Now, lie back down and get some rest. I'll be back to check on you in an hour."

"Is that a promise?"

"Yes," he said in a way that made her believe it. His eyes trailed to a photo of a pretty brunette on the nightstand. He picked up the frame a bit awkwardly, and took it with him. "I'll just... move this downstairs," he said.

Lucy snuggled under the covers, thinking what a happy woman she must have been to have someone like William for a husband. "William?" she said, as he slowly shut the door.

He paused and looked at her, picture frame in hand.

"Thanks."

William sat on the living room sofa with a guilty heart. He'd brought a pillow and a blanket downstairs and had taken care to wear a robe, as he knew he'd be checking on Bridget later. He lifted Karen's photo from the coffee table and addressed it as if she were there. "You don't know how much I miss you. How badly all of us do..."

His gaze slowly panned toward the stairs. Here he was with another woman in the bed that he and Karen had shared. Although it wasn't like he was up there *with* her. William swallowed hard, trying not to imagine what that might be like, he and Bridget together. She was so soft and womanly, with that curvaceous body and those sensuous lips. And her eyes were as blue as the heavens. They were an angel's eyes, really.

William fretfully stared down at the photo in his hands. "Forgive me, honey. I didn't mean it. There could never be anybody for me but you. I could never go there. Not in a million years... Not unless the gods sent me an earth-shattering sign." He settled down on the sofa, laying the frame facedown on the floor beside him. "Like that's going to happen."

William awoke the next morning to the smell of bacon frying and coffee brewing. He quickly sat up and swung his feet to the floor, trying to place where he was. The living room, that's right. That's where he'd slept, or gotten some semblance of sleep anyhow. Not that he regretted going up to check on Bridget. In fact, he'd sort of looked forward to it. Didn't matter that he'd had to set his cell to wake him hour after hour. The truth was, even when he'd been sleeping, she'd occupied his dreams. Once or twice, he'd awakened with a start because he'd thought he'd felt his arms around her. In reality, it had just been a throw pillow. William felt himself flush at having these thoughts, especially in light of his late-night promise to Karen.

He stood and something crunched under his slippered feet. William looked down in horror to see he'd smashed the glass on Karen's picture frame. He sat back down and lifted the broken frame in his hands. Karen's smiling face gazed back at him. *"An earth-shattering sign?"* he mused. No way. No earthly way. Clearly it was coincidental, him breaking the glass.

Noises sounded from the kitchen. Someone was cooking in there. William carefully picked the errant shards off of the carpet and set them on the broken frame, which he laid on the coffee table. Then, he slipped on his robe and headed to the kitchen to investigate.

Lucy whisked about the open space, attempting to put together a very fine breakfast. She had bacon on the stove and bread in the toaster. Next, to find the eggs. She whirled toward the refrigerator, nearly colliding with William as he entered the room.

"Good morning!" he said with surprise. His gaze traveled to her bare legs and quickly back up to her eyes. He'd left her one of his shirts to sleep in, but plainly had forgotten about it until he saw her wearing it skimming her thighs, its cuffs rolled up. Lucy had washed out her short dress and it was hanging to dry in the bathroom. That, along with her undies. She'd planned to dash back upstairs and get dressed before the family had awakened. A rash of heat enveloped her as she feared for a second that William might know she'd gone Commando. But no, that was silly! He couldn't possibly guess. He didn't have X-ray vision.

"Hello," she said smiling tightly. His eyes really were flecked with gold, she could see that quite clearly now, and my, were they gorgeous. A man built like that was particularly dangerous in a robe, not to mention that sexy morning stubble. Lucy's knees buckled slightly, and he reached out a hand to steady her.

"Bridget?"

What was it about that name that still felt wrong. "Huh?" she said, noting his waist tie had come loose and his robe gaped slightly. Beneath it he wore plaid pajama pants and no shirt, just a broad and muscled chest sporting a perfect smattering of light brown hair.

"Are you sure you should be up doing all this?" he asked, glancing around.

"Oh yes, I really am!" she said, turning toward the coffeepot, needing to redirect. "I'm feeling so much better. Honestly." *What* had she been doing ogling William's pecs? Is that the sort of woman she was? One that took advantage of every opportunity to pounce on a man? She had pounced before, hadn't she? She lifted a mug to pour, spotting the ring on her hand. Of course she had, rightly so. "Coffee?" she asked weakly.

"Coffee would be super, thanks." He glanced down and saw that his robe had slipped. "Sorry," he said a bit uncomfortably, before retying it and covering that marvelous chest.

She handed him the mug and he took a sip. "Delicious, thank you."

"As long as I was the first one up, I thought I'd make breakfast."

"I still don't know if it's a good idea for you to

be so active."

"Why don't we let the doctor be the one to decide about that?"

"All right." He studied her thoughtfully over the rim of his mug. "This is really nice. I haven't had anyone make coffee for me since... in a very long time."

Fine lines creased his brow, and Lucy suspected he was remembering his late wife. "I'm really sorry about your wife, William. Has it been long?"

He pursed his lips a beat, then met her eyes. "Karen died of ovarian cancer three years ago. It came on very quickly. There was nothing the doctors could do."

The pain in his eyes was unmistakable. He clearly wasn't over it. But then, how could he be? What an awful thing that must be, to lose someone... Lucy felt a sharp tightness in her chest, stirring some recognition. "You loved her very much, didn't you?" she asked softly.

"More than she knew."

Lucy hated to think of someone as wonderful as William being alone. Certainly there were boatloads of women who would eagerly snap him up. "You'll find somebody else. One day. Don't you think? I mean, some day when you're ready."

"To tell you the truth, I've never really thought about it."

"Well, Carmella apparently has. And I'm betting Justin has, too."

"Justin?"

"Boys his age need a woman to talk to just as much as a father."

He set down his mug and leaned into the counter.

"How do you know so much about kids and family?"

"Probably from watching too much late-night television," she said, laughing.

"The Classics Channel?" he asked with pleased surprise.

"Why, yes! That's right! I know it is!" She stared at him and grinned. "You mean, you watch those shows, too?"

"Well, sure." He cleared his throat. "I mean, when the kids are with me and they insist."

Lucy struggled with a murky memory, the odd refrain coming back to her. "But real life isn't like fairy tales."

William blinked, then asked with mock offense, "Who told you that?"

This part, Lucy knew absolutely. "Gus!"

"Gus? Who's Gus?"

"I don't know. Someone from my past. Yes, that name. It's important, for certain."

William drew nearer. "Your father? Brother? Fiancé...?"

Lucy felt mildly sick to her stomach. "Fiancé? No!"

"Well then?"

"Argh! This is driving me nuts! It's like something's right around the corner, but I can't quite grasp it. None of this makes sense. How can I remember the Classics Channel and not even recall my own name?"

"It's Bridget, isn't it?"

"Is it?"

"I have no idea, sweetheart. But I can tell you one thing. Whatever that old cynic Gus had to say was way off base."

She watched him wide-eyed, still stuck on the fact that he'd called her sweetheart. *Sweetheart*. Ooh, she liked the sound of that, especially coming from his warm, expressive mouth. Was she swooning? Was that even a word?

"Because let me tell you something, " he continued, stepping closer, "when a guy finally meets the right girl, the whole world becomes a fairy tale."

Their eyes locked and Lucy's heart skipped a beat. Yep. She could buy that, every word of it, and she was staring straight at a prince.

"Bridget?" he asked, his gaze diving into her. He smelled so good and manly, like sandalwood and spice. Oh God, she didn't remember this. Couldn't recall ever feeling this way. Surely, she would recall emotions like this.

"Huh?"

"Do you smell something burning?"

A smoke alarm blared and Lucy brought her hands to her head and yelped. Black smoke curled from the toaster, which immediately burst into flames. "Oh no!" A split second later, the frying pan caught fire.

William looked around in shock. "Jesus." He raced beside the refrigerator and yanked a fire extinguisher from its holder on the wall. In a flash, he'd pulled its pin and doused the toaster and the whole stove in white foam.

An hour later, Lucy sat in a family-style breakfast place with William, Carmella, and Justin. The snow had let up long enough for the plows to get through, and the one-lane bridge leading to the Kinkaids' suburban neighborhood had been cleared.

The day's forecast called for nothing more than light flurries.

"I still don't understand why we couldn't have breakfast at home," Justin complained.

Carmella looked up from the kiddie placemat she'd been coloring with crayons. "Because the elves didn't build in cooking skills, silly."

Lucy turned toward the little girl. "Build in?"

"Sure, you know, like how some dolls have built-in talking machines. Things like that."

Justin eyed Lucy suspiciously over his glass of orange juice. "Yeah, and others are made plain lucky."

William shot Justin a stern look. "I'll ask you to remember your manners."

A waitress appeared with a notepad and Lucy felt a twinge of familiarity. "Do I know you?" she asked, puzzling at the woman.

The gal, who looked to be in her fifties, turned her eyes on Lucy. "Don't think so, love." She returned her attention to the table. "You folks ready to order?"

"Bridget?" William prodded.

"I'm not really sure what I'd like. Why don't you all go first?"

Justin set aside his menu. "I'll have the Western Omelet with extra sausage and hash browns."

"I'd like the chocolate chip kids stack," Carmella said. "With bacon."

William twisted his lips, scrutinizing the menu. "Could you make mine the tall stack of blueberry pancakes?" He glanced sheepishly at the waitress. "And bring some chocolate syrup, please?"

Lucy abruptly set down her water, sloshing it

sideways. "Make that two of those!" Her eyes met William's. "With whipped cream."

His jaw dropped, before his lips tugged into a grin. "Can't forget the whipped cream," he told the astounded waitress.

"Are you folks serious?" she asked with a disgusted look.

Lucy and William locked eyes.

"Yes," she said.

"Most definitely," William followed.

"Suit yourselves," their waitress said, "just don't expect me to bring the Tums."

She departed as William stared at Lucy, dumbfounded. "I can't believe you like your pancakes that way."

"But only on blueberry," she said, feeling herself smile.

"Only on blueberry," he said. "There's something about that fruit and chocolate mix."

"Yes!"

"How did it happen for you?" he asked.

"I'm not sure." She studied the table a beat. "It may have had something to do with my mixing up the pancake syrup and—"

"The chocolate meant for your milk?"

Her eyes flashed in recognition. "I think that's right."

"No way," he said, sipping from his coffee. "That's what happened to me, too."

Carmella turned smugly to Justin. "You see, Bridget's made just the way she's supposed to be. Just right for Daddy."

"Find me a bucket. I think I'm going to hurl."

Lucy tried not to be stung by Justin's constant barbs, searching her heart for understanding. The boy was hurting more than he let on and covered those wounds in a patina of sarcasm. It must be terribly hard to lose a parent at such a young age. In some ways the absence of his mom troubled him even more than Carmella, because he'd had more time to spend with her before she'd gone. Lucy felt a lump in her throat as an old familiar ache arose. She couldn't quite place it, but it was there deep inside, telling her not to judge Justin too harshly. His father, however, filled another role.

William sighed and frowned at his son. "I'd appreciate it if you revised your attitude. Especially since I need your help later this morning."

"Help?"

"I want you to watch Carmella—"

"But, Dad—"

"So I can take Bridget to the doctor."

"Why's Bridget going to the doctor?" Carmella's face clouded over. "Is she sick?"

"Who knows?" Justin said with a smirk. "Maybe she's pregnant."

"Pregnant?" both William and Lucy said together in shock. He stared at her.

"No, no, I don't think so," she said, laying a hand on her belly.

William shook a scolding finger at Justin. "You, young man, have been spending *way too much* time online."

A little while later, William sat with Bridget in the physician's office. She'd already had a complete check-up in private. Now they were awaiting the results of the examination. "Dr. Mass? Please tell me," Bridget asked with concern, "is it bad news?"

The big-bellied, white-haired physician removed the stethoscope from around his neck. William noted it still had the same small stuffed reindeer attached that it had sported for years. "Please, call me Chris, dear," he told Bridget with a warm smile. "All my patients do. Except for ones like him" he said, tilting his head toward William, "who I've been treating since they were in diapers."

"Well, don't keep us in suspense," William urged.

Dr. Mass steadied his small circular glasses above his plump round nose. "I'm afraid it's a clear-cut case of amnesia. The bump on the back of her head, combined with the memory loss, can point to nothing else."

Bridget lifted her brow with concern. "How long will it last?"

Dr. Mass stroked his snowy beard. "That all depends. Sometimes these things resolve themselves in a matter of days. Then again, they can drag on for months."

"Months?" William blurted involuntarily. He'd been prepared to help Bridget out temporarily. But for the long term? He just didn't know. He met her blue-eyed gaze and thought he heard angels sing. William shook his head, thinking he'd had one too many hit of bourbon pecan pie. But wait a minute... That was *yesterday*.

"Have you tried the police?" Dr. Mass asked him. "The missing persons bureau?"

"Everything I could think of," William assured him. "I plan to follow up more when we get home today."

"That's good, son," Dr. Mass said. "Might even want to try one of those Internet postings. I hear they can be very helpful. Someone's bound to be looking for her."

William glanced at Bridget, regret brimming inside him. "I'm sure of it," he said, wondering where that sentiment had come from. It's not like she could stick around forever. She had a life—and a fiancé—to return to, after all.

"Chris," Bridget said. "It's very strange. There are some things I remember, little things really, that don't make any sense. But the bigger picture is all a blur."

He eyed her with understanding. "Par for the course, dear. The memories should all come back, but won't necessarily surface in the expected order.

"The good news is that you're perfectly healthy, other than the amnesia. The scans were clear and all your tests came back negative. The best I can suggest for the short term is that you engage in things that might spur your memory."

"Such as?" William asked.

Dr. Mass turned toward Bridget. "When you arrived at the Kinkaid house, did you have anything with you? Anything at all?"

Chapter Five

Lucy perched on the edge of the bed in the master bedroom. William shut the door and came and sat beside her, a stack of presents in hand.

"You're right about doing this away from the kids," he said.

Lucy had insisted on utmost privacy for the rest of the gifts' unveiling. Judging by the item in the package that Justin had opened, she couldn't imagine what might be in these other boxes. Hopefully, nothing too scandalous for her *Koochie*. Boy, that just seemed wrong. Who on earth calls somebody that?

"Ready?" William asked, passing her box number one. She felt her face warm and he reddened in return.

"Maybe I should... um... Open them alone?"

"I was a married man once, you know."

"Sure," she said, smiling tightly and feeling as if her cheeks might burst from the pressure.

"This one looks interesting," he said, peering at the tag. "*My love will set you free.* I wonder what that means?"

Lucy shrugged and peeled back the wrapping with trepidation. It was as if, with each layer of red and green foil, she was stripping away herself. Oh my God, she thought, staring into the box. Perhaps she was a stripper, after all!

William chuckled and raised a pair of fur-lined handcuffs from the unfolded tissue paper. "Well, well." He studied her in a new way that told her maybe he was reconsidering her profession, too. "Any flashbacks?" he asked with a wry twist to his lips.

"Not a one!" she declared a little too loudly. All at once it felt terribly hot in here. Was that because she was used to going without clothes? Lucy cringed, thinking that forgetting might have its merits.

He handed her another box. "Try again?" he said, both looking and sounding mildly amused.

She peeked at the tag and then stood abruptly. "Oh no, I don't..." There was no way on earth! "I think I'd better open this one in the bathroom!" She grabbed the box and scurried out of William's sight, barricading herself behind the door. Seconds later she flung open the package and wailed, *What kind of woman am I?"*

William sat up with a start on the bed. Perhaps there was more to Bridget than he'd imagined. She certainly seemed to have a secret side. Not that he minded, or that it was really any of his business. He was only interested in helping learn who she was, sparking her memory, that's all.

Bridget burst back through the bathroom door, hastily gathering the rest of the packages in her arms.

"What are you doing?"

"Hiding these away somewhere where the children won't find them!"

"That bad?" he asked, wide-eyed.

"Oh, much worse," she assured him, without surrendering any details. "Do you have something like duct tape?"

William appeared taken aback. "Duct tape? Is that something else you like to—?"

She turned bright red. "Oh God, no. It's nothing like that! I just want to close these securely. We can't take any chances."

He handed her the fur-lined handcuffs, which she flung back in the box like they carried something communicable. "Hmm, yes. I see what you mean."

She stared at him, mortified. "Wait a minute. You don't actually believe those are *mine*?"

"No," he said, ribbing. "I know they're for Koochie."

She heaved a sigh, big blue eyes brimming with tears. "This is so very awful. I don't see how this has helped one bit."

"Listen," he said standing and taking the packages from her. "There could be dozens of reasons why you had those presents with you."

"Really?" she asked, looking hopeful.

"Why, sure," he said, unable to think of any.

"So you're not judging me?"

"Judging? Sweetheart, I don't know you well enough to judge you."

"But if you did, would you?"

She tilted up her chin and William realized in a flash that she was within kissing distance. It wasn't like he'd done it in a long time, but he clearly recalled the instinct. He guessed it was like riding a bicycle, only softer... more curvy... and feminine. Heat warmed the back of his neck. "Would I?" he asked, lost in the moment.

"Judge me," she repeated, dark eyelashes fanning wide.

William drew a breath and counted to ten, telling himself not to lose his head. Here he was with a beautiful woman beside a large comfy bed on a wintery afternoon. *And my children are right downstairs,* he reminded himself, swallowing hard.

With my mother and father! "No, absolutely not. Never." He took a giant step back, drawing the gifts in toward his chest. "I mean, never in a bad way. Listen, Bridget, I'm a very fair-minded individual. Whatever other people choose to do in their personal lives is their business, not mine. I mean, as long as everyone's a grown-up and agrees."

"Yes, that's what I think too," she said, taking a step back of her own.

"I think you're right, and we'd better find a place to stash these."

"Good," she said with a nod.

Downstairs on the living room sofa, Carmella snuggled between her grandparents as her Grammy read her a storybook. Her Poppy sat on her other side, reading the sports section of the newspaper.

Emma turned the page and Carmella looked up with a pout. "Why did they go upstairs?"

"They needed some privacy, dear," Emma said.

"For what?"

Grant chuckled. "Likely discussing North Pole secrets."

"But I want to hear how Santa got her down the chimney!"

Grant glanced at Emma. "I'd be interested in hearing that myself."

"Shush," she told him.

Carmella stared at Emma with big, brown eyes. "Bridget's not sick, is she Grammy?"

"Oh no, dear."

"Dr. Mass says she's healthy as a horse," Grant said. Then he added under his breath, "Not even pregnant."

Emma glared at him, but Carmella just said, "Darn!"

Her grandparents exchanged glances, then looked at her.

"I was hoping for twins," the child explained.

William entered Justin's room to find him working at his computer. Justin glanced in his dad's direction, then closed a series of pop-up boxes.

"Justin, I'm going to need your help with something."

"Sure thing, Dad," Justin said, still furiously clicking the mouse. "Name it."

William scrutinized his son a beat, and then met the boy's gaze. "Do you know how to build a Web page?"

"Piece of cake."

"Good, because I was thinking we could put up one of those Internet postings."

"An advertisement?"

"Well, no. Yes. Something like that. What's the name of that local site where you can get anything and everything?"

"Dave's List?"

William nodded soundly. "That's the one. Do you think they've got a section for Lost and Found?"

Justin smiled securely. "No worries, Dad. You can leave *everything* to me."

William sighed with relief. "That's my boy. Now," he asked, "What do you need?"

"We probably need a picture. We can use your digital camera."

"Great thought. I'll go and get it," he said, turning away. "Bridget, too."

"Uh, Dad?" Justin called after him. "I was just thinking... Maybe it would help if Bridget modeled some of that stuff she brought with her? You know, make her more recognizable?"

William shot him a stern look and shook his head. "Don't think so, Justin."

A big-busted woman strode into Mitch's real estate office with a combative air. She slapped her purse on his desk and Mitch looked up at the bleached blonde in a leopard print coat smacking her gum. She removed her dark glasses to glare at him. "What's the big idea?"

"Bridget!" he said with surprise. "Ain't you a sight for sore eyes. So, you decide on that six mil mansion?"

"No, you slimy cheat. What's your excuse this time? Still haven't gotten over the fact that I dumped you for Roger?"

He blinked at her. "I don't know what you're talking about."

"My packages!" she cried with dismay. "You promised you'd bring them by."

"I did! I mean, I sent... Wait a minute. Are you saying you never got them?"

She pulled herself upright on her petite frame and studied her manicured nails. "I knew you didn't have it in you to be a gentleman, despite all that stuff you said." She lifted cat-green eyes to his. "You're still getting back at me, ain't ya?"

"No, Bridget! I swear! I'd never—"

She licked her lips and he squirmed in his chair. "Though you're still pretty good to look at, Mitch-o. Despite your conniving."

She leaned forward, her coat gaping to reveal the low-cut blouse beneath it.

Mitch gulped. "And you're still looking good, too. How's Roger?" he asked with a squeak.

"Getting bored with marriage, I think." She inserted herself between Mitch and his desk, then purred in a sexy whisper, "I always thought you worked too hard."

"Ditto, sweetheart," he said with a hard stare.

She flinched. "Ooh, was that a cut?"

Mitch rolled his chair back a foot and spoke matter-of-factly. "Listen, Bridget, I've got stuff to do. I'll find out about those packages ASAP. Okay?"

"Yeah, well, you'd better. I spent over three hundred smackers at The Naughty Shop!"

His cell rang and he reached around her to snag it off the desk. "Magic Maker Mitch at your service!"

Bridget rolled her eyes and sauntered toward the door. "Magic Maker, hoo. You'd think that new gal of yours could find someone better."

Chapter Six

As William bent down to lift his morning paper off the stoop, he heard a mounting commotion. His raised his eyes in disbelief to the pandemonium around him. Their quiet residential street was flooded with vehicles and hordes of men were pouring into his yard. There were jocks dressed in sports uniforms, Wall Street types in suits, military men, construction workers, guys in tuxedos carting flowers. Holy cow! William's jaw dropped as he stared up at the noisy helicopter hovering above and some lunatic parachuted in for a landing. A knight on a white horse galloped in through the front gate, trailed by a rowdy group, a few of them on motorcycles. The mass stormed toward the house, calling out to him in competing voices, "She's mine! She's mine!"

William raced inside, sweat beading his brow. He quickly bolted the door, seconds before its chime sounded. *Ding-dong... ding-dong... ding-dong!* The landline rang next, trilling loudly on the hall table. William lunged for it, picking it up. "Bridget? No, she's still sleep—What? *What?*" He held out the receiver in shock, then pressed it back to his ear. "Well, I don't know whether she'll give an interview."

A pounding sounded outside the door. "Mr. Kinkaid! This is WKVX News! Can we get a statement?"

William hung up the phone and strode toward the stairs, taking them two at a time. An instant later, he burst into Justin's room, popping the boy on the head with his up newspaper. "Justin William Kinkaid," he said. "I want to see that Web page you built, and I mean *now*."

William gaped at the computer screen. It was Bridget all right, only better. She was very scantily dressed in some sort of sexy elf outfit, jingle bells dangling from strategic places. William frowned and stared down his son as the boy flushed red.

"*Sexy Cyber Mom Seeks Home? Justin! Just what kind of junk have you been reading?"

"The personals?"

"But, son! You gave our home address! A MapFinders link, even!"

"You told me to list contact information."

"I meant an e-mail address, telephone number, maybe. Not this!" He shook his head and stared again at the computer screen. "We don't even *know* if she's got kids, for heaven sakes."

"She's the right age, isn't she?"

William blew a hard breath, his eyes glued on Bridget's photo. "How did you do that? You know she wasn't wearing that when I took the picture."

"Computer program. Really simple." Justin gulped. "Even allows enhancements."

"So I see." William ran a hand through his hair, wondering how he was going to get out of this mess.

"I thought the jingle bell tassels were a nice touch," Justin said with an impish grin.

Carmella pressed into Lucy's room with a worried frown. "What's all that noise?"

Lucy quickly released the curtain she'd pulled back to peer outside. "I'm not sure."

"Then what were you looking at?"

"Just some birds out on the lawn!" she said above the hum of copter blades lifting away.

"Birds? But all of those have flown south for the winter."

Carmella strode to the window with determination and threw back the curtain. "Oh my! Who are all those people?"

"I don't know," Lucy said, standing behind her. There was an incredible crowd out there, and it appeared testosterone heavy. In fact, the only woman Lucy saw seemed to be a television reporter. She held a huge microphone and spoke through a broad smile to a couple of cameramen by a truck.

Carmella spun toward Lucy, gripping her legs. "You don't think they heard about Santa, do you? And they're coming to take you away? Sort of like they do with aliens?"

Lucy bent low to hug her. "Oh no, sweetie. Don't you worry one bit. Nobody's taking me anywhere. I'm sure those fellows are all just here for a visit."

Carmella looked her in the eye. "It's awful early for visiting. We haven't even had breakfast yet."

Lucy studied the little girl, the truth paining her. Sooner or later, Carmella was going to have to know. From the looks of the horde outside, *sooner* was going to come first. "Carmella," she said, "About Santa... There's something I think you should know. I don't really believe—"

"Of course Santa brought you!" the child said, throwing her arms around Lucy's neck. "Even Daddy said so!"

Carmella hung her head, then looked up with misting eyes. "You know, when Mommy died, I was very little. Just two. So I barely remember her at all. But, I do remember one thing. She used to sing to me."

"I'm sure it sounded beautiful," Lucy said kindly.

Carmella gulped, wiping away her tears. "So when... you know... I asked Santa for a new mommy, I was kind of hoping that..." She stopped and met Lucy's gaze. "That you would..." Her voice trailed off, her little chin trembling.

Lucy sat on the bed and pulled Carmella into her lap. "Shh... Shh, now. Everything will be all right. I'm sure soon enough Santa will send just the right mommy for you."

"He already has." Carmella looked up with pleading eyes. "Sing to me? Please?"

"But I'm not sure I know any songs."

"They must be in there somewhere. The elves wouldn't have messed that part up."

At the senior Kinkaid house next door, Grant perused the paper while Emma poured him coffee. "What's all that commotion, dear?" she asked.

"I don't hear anything," he said. Then again, Emma suspected he was going deaf. She glanced at the television on the built-in desk in the kitchen. There was some sort of reality show on. *That's odd,* Emma thought, *generally at this time we see the morning news.*

Grant lowered his paper to take a sip of coffee. An instant later, he spat it back in his mug. "That's William's house!" he spouted, staring at the television.

"Well, so it is!" Emma said in shock.

On the old black-and-white tube set, a farmer on

a tractor bulldozed through the crowd in the street. He wore a straw hat and a big chest plaque stating *Bridget or Bust!* "Let me through! That's mama's mine!" he bellowed, barreling past the reporter extending her microphone.

Emma drew a hand to her mouth. "Oh my!"

Grant set down his mug and stood. "We'd better get over there and see what's going on."

They pulled on their coats and rushed outdoors, where the situation looked even more overwhelming than it had appeared on the small screen.

"It's like the whole world's gone crazy," Emma said with a gasp.

"Crazy for a certain blonde, I'd say."

"Gracious," Emma cried, "Is that a real set of armor?"

They elbowed through the crowd, as Grant spoke in agitated tones. "This is worse than Mardi Gras in New Orleans!"

"How do you think these fellows got wind of Bridget?"

Grant shook his head and pressed ahead. "Don't know, Emma, but I'm hoping William does." He parted the crowd with his hands, shouting gruffly. "Let us through! We're the parents!" A hush fell as heads swung in their direction. Emma's heartbeat picked up a notch. "We've got to get out of here," she told Grant, as someone in a paratrooper outfit raced toward them.

"Please, sir!" he petitioned Grant. "Can I have your daughter's hand? Sir!"

"Not *her* parents," Grant grumbled, trudging ahead. *"His!"*

Emma scurried after him. "Best to try the back

door," she said.

"Probably safer," Grant agreed.

William struggled to collect his thoughts on how to deal with this. He'd have to address the thronging masses somehow, and *who knew*? It was possible Bridget's betrothed was among them. William hoped he wasn't one of the loony ones. Several of the contenders seemed slightly off kilter. But perhaps that was just at first glance.

William peeked back out of Justin's window, deciding his first impression wasn't all bad. Hang on. Were those his parents cutting through the crowd? Good. It appeared they were headed for the back door. He'd need to go down and let them in. But first, he'd have to check on Carmella. He hadn't seen her or Bridget all morning. They couldn't have possibly slept through this?

"Wow," Justin said, eying the lawn. "Dave's List is pretty effective, huh?"

"You and I will square up later," William said sternly before leaving.

He passed Carmella's room, noting that her bed was empty. He strode toward the master bedroom, but slowed his steps at the sound of singing. Bridget's melodious voice rose in a sweet tune, *And if that mockingbird won't sing, papa's gonna buy you a diamond ring*... William halted and peered around the doorframe to spy Carmella cradled on Bridget's lap. The little girl sighed happily, her tiny frame molded against Bridget's. Neither one had seen him, so he quietly slipped away, fighting the fire in his eyes. They were a pair, the two of them. If only Carmella was right and there really *was* a Santa Claus, he could convince himself this portrait was more than make-believe.

The doorbell chimed once more downstairs and William realized he'd better get moving. He had to meet his parents around back and get them indoors before one of the new reporters who'd just arrived discovered them.

Emma blustered in the door, trailed by Grant. "What on earth is going on?" she asked, removing her hat and shaking it out.

Grant quickly turned to bolt and chain the door. "Yeah, what?" he asked, his cheeks ruddy from the cold. There'd been a brief lull in the snow, though apparently it was long enough to allow all the marauders through. The light sprinkling that had started back up was obviously doing nothing to dissuade them.

"It's Justin," William said, out of breath from racing down the stairs. "It seems that the Internet missing-person posting he designed revealed a bit more than we hoped for."

Justin, who'd been standing nearby, quietly slunk away.

Emma's sympathetic gaze followed him. "Oh now, I'm sure he didn't mean it."

"I'm sure that he did," Grant said removing his coat. "The boy's older than you think, Emma."

"Yes, well, I plan to talk to him more about that later." William glanced through the door window to see more suitors storming the house. "But for now," he said, quickly shutting the blinds, "what are we going to do?"

Grant parted two blind slats to peer between

them. "We could make a run for it."

"Very funny."

"I'm serious!" Grant told his son. "Out the back way and around to our place."

"Don't kid yourself, Dad. The backyard's filling up, too."

"Have you called the police?" Emma asked.

"Yes," William answered, "but they said they already had a few officers on the scene. Didn't mention they were carrying corsages!"

Emma studied her son with kind brown eyes. "Do you think any of those men might actually know her?"

William sighed. "I'm afraid there's only one way to find out."

The trio looked toward the hall as Bridget and Carmella entered the kitchen.

"Who are all those people out there?" Carmella wanted to know.

William glanced at his parents. "Just some nice folks who've come to see Bridget."

"I knew it!" the child cried, wrapping herself around Bridget's legs. "It's just like *E.T.*" She looked up. "They're coming to take you away!"

Lucy's heart pounded at the implausibility of it all. Could Justin's Web notice really have sparked this pandemonium? She'd made a wreck of the Kinkaids' holiday ever since coming here. And now, things had actually gone from bad to worse.

"No honey," William said. "They only want to talk to her, that's all. Bridget won't be going anywhere..." He paused, shooting Lucy a telling look. "Until she wants to."

Carmella studied him with moistened eyes. "By why would she want to? She's *ours,* Daddy! You said so! Santa brought her to *us.*"

William heaved a breath and Lucy dropped to her knees to address Carmella at eye level. "Don't you worry, sweetheart. I have a feeling everything will work out just fine." Despite the ruckus outdoors, perhaps some good would come of it. Maybe her intended was one of the men who'd come to whisk her away. Somebody good and kind like William, she thought, warming under the heat of his stare.

William pulled his gaze from hers to address his daughter. "Why don't you stay in here with your Grammy and Poppy and have some breakfast?"

"If I have to," Carmella said, regretfully letting Lucy go.

"Mom? Dad?" William asked them. "If you don't mind? Pancake mix is in the cupboard."

"Of course," Emma said, helpfully heading for the stove.

Lucy walked to the living room window and peeled back the sheers. "There are even more of them than before! Bless Justin. He must have built quite a Web page."

"Oh, I wouldn't go blessing him just yet," William said flatly. "I think you should know the boy built a... very explicit ad, urging the man who knows you to come and take you home."

"Explicit how?"

William swallowed hard. "You were scantily clad in items that looked like they came from some of those boxes. He used some sort of photograpy program."

"Oh!" she cried, her cheeks coloring.

He leveled her an apologetic look. "Justin will be punished for it."

"Oh, no. I don't think you should... I mean, just look at the results!"

"Yes well," he agreed, following her gaze out the window. "One could certainly claim the ad was successful."

She dropped the curtain and turned to face him, an unexpected melancholy taking hold. "I suppose this means I'll soon be out of your way." If it was possible, he appeared even more handsome than he had the day before, small flecks of gold warming his light brown eyes. "You must be relieved."

"No," he said stepping forward. He paused and seemed to collect himself. "What I mean is, Carmella will really miss you."

Lucy's heart warmed at the mention of the little girl. She was so sweet and trusting, and had cared for Lucy immediately in that hopeful childlike way. Lucy would have to be made out of stone not to start feeling some emotion for the child as well.

"She's a very special little girl," she said.

"Yes." He studied her a prolonged beat. "Bridget, I have something to tell you. I heard you earlier, singing to Carmella upstairs."

Lucy felt her cheeks flame and dropped her chin. "Oh. I'm afraid my voice is—"

"I thought it sounded heavenly," he said.

Slowly, she raised her eyes to his. What was it about him that sent her heart all out of kilter? "Well, I don't know when... Can't exactly recall singing before."

"And still you felt at home?"

"Yes."

William stared down into Bridget's big blue eyes. If he weren't careful, he feared he'd tumble right inside them and get lost swimming there forever.

"Can I ask you something?" she asked.

"Anything," he said, his voice gone husky.

She tilted up her chin and he had that overwhelming sensation again that he needed to kiss her. Kiss her like he was damn sure he could do, and do right.

"Did you always know you wanted to have kids?"

"For as long as I remember," he answered.

"Yeah, me too," she said. "Just somehow I never thought I'd really have them."

"You? Why not? Dr. Mass says you're as healthy as they come. Apart from that little, you know." He playfully tapped his forehead and smiled.

"It's just something I can't remember," she said, shaking her head. "Silly, probably."

"Well, somebody's going to be awfully lucky to have you as a mother... someday. When the timing is right."

She looked at him and grinned. "And Justin and Carmella are very lucky to have you."

Something pounded on the front door as a man's voice shouted. "Say! Can we get this show on the road!"

"Yeah, and look how lucky I am to have Justin," William said with a wry twist to his lips.

"Do I really have to meet with *all* of them?" she asked, clearly overwhelmed. How he wished he could rescue her from this, but he didn't really see a way. If Bridget were his fiancé and missing, he'd be crazy with worry, no doubt. He didn't think he'd don a suit of armor, but that wouldn't dampen his urge to up and carry her away. William swallowed hard, realizing he was the one getting carried away. Totally swept up in some alternate reality where Bridget could actually be his. But she wasn't, and as the man in charge, it was his duty to look after her. Even if that meant helping her find the man she was destined to be with forever.

"I suppose you ought to look at them, at least. I mean, how else are you going to know?" he said.

She frowned and glanced at the door. "Oh William. It's just so much. There must be two hundred men out there!"

Maybe more, he thought, thinking he spied a small figure through the sheer curtain covering the window. That couldn't be Justin outdoors? Positioned at a table by the gate? "Well, we don't have to do it all in one day," he said, his attention back on Bridget, who was now standing in the threshold. "We can have some of them come back again tomorrow, if you'd like."

"Do you mean it?" she asked with a hopeful gaze.

"Why sure, or the day after that." *That's right, just keep talking, William. Why not go on and admit you'd prefer that none of them return until well into the New Year?*

She blushed sweetly, fine wisps of honey-colored hair framing her face. "But I've already taken up so much of your time. Been so much of an imposition."

He moved forward without thinking and took her by the elbows. "Oh no, you haven't."

His eyes locked on hers, then simultaneously they both looked up to see they were standing below the mistletoe. Bridget stared down at her hand, her diamond glinting in the early light. William released her and abruptly stepped back.

Bridget anxiously twisted her engagement ring. "You're right. I'll need to look at all of them."

"Yes. I suppose you should."

William tugged on his parka as he walked through the kitchen. "Has anybody seen Justin?"

Emma turned from the stove as Grant buried his face in the paper. "I think he went outside, dear."

"Out in *that*?" William asked peering through the back door window. Just as he'd predicted, the backyard was also flooded with interested suitors. But the figure he'd spotted and thought was his son was around front. "What on earth is he doing?"

"I'm not sure," Emma said, absentmindedly flipping a flapjack.

"He said he was selling lemonade!" Carmella proclaimed between mouthfuls.

"Lemonade?" William queried. "But it's December!"

From behind his splayed paper, Grant just shrugged.

William pressed his hand atop the sports page, lowering it to face his father. "Dad? Do you know something about this?"

Grant coughed lightly. "I don't see what's so wrong with a little ingenuity."

William twisted his lips in thought, deciding something didn't add up. And wherever the math had gone faulty, his dad was sure to be involved. He generally was. "I think you should come with me," he told his father.

"But it's snowing out there!"

"Don't be such a big baby," Emma scolded from the stove. "Pull on your parka!"

William cut his way through the crowd, Grant reluctantly trailing along. "Excuse us! Coming through!" William called as two reporters and several men sprang at him. *"I said, no comment,"* he told the persistent news angler.

When they got to the gate, William could scarcely believe his eyes. There sat Justin, all decked out in his leather jacket and shades, holding court at a folding table he must have dragged out of the garage. A poster stuck to the fence behind him boldly stated, "Pay to Play: 10 Bucks!" There was a coffee can at his elbow stuffed with cash, and William watched as a beleaguered groom inched up to the table and dug a hand in his pocket.

"Got change?" he asked, holding out a twenty.

Justin lowered his shades and solemnly shook his head.

"Didn't think so," the man grumbled shoving his bill in the can.

"Hey! Wait!" William called, snatching the cash out of the can and handing it back to him. "There's no charge here."

He turned his gaze on Justin, who slunk down in his chair and cast a panicked look at Grant over the rim of his glasses.

"You, young man," William said with a shake of his finger, "are in *deep*."

"Really, son," Grant added. "What were you

thinking?"

"But Grandpa!" Justin gasped. "Charging an admission fee was your idea!"

William huffed and turned toward his father. "Both of you, in the house, please. Now."

Chapter Seven

A few hours later, Lucy yawned on the sofa. They'd been at it all day, only breaking briefly for lunch, which Emma was kind enough to make. One by one, William had escorted each man in the house and asked for his credentials. After he'd supplied reasonable identification, the guy was asked to remove his hat, helmet—or whatever—and take a seat. All of the Kinkaids partook in the questioning, even little Carmella seated beside Lucy. William was on her other side, protectively close.

By now, Lucy had lost track of the assorted construction workers, farmers, and sportsmen with implements in tow, which William had very wisely insisted they leave on the porch. But it was the undertaker who gave her pause, pasty pale in his approach, assuring her that their place was nice and quiet, dark and cool, too. Chill bumps raced down her spine saying, for sure, he wasn't the one. Neither was the pilot asking her to *come fly with me,* the sheik in a turban, or the knight with a proclaimed penchant for the chastity belt!

Finally, here before her sat a reasonable looking person, a mid-thirties naval officer who was really quite handsome, his blue eyes complemented by his uniform.

"I've spent six long months at sea," he said sincerely, "thinking of nothing but you."

Lucy sighed, almost daring to believe it. He seemed decent enough, fine and upstanding. Broadly built across the shoulders, too. She caught William watching her careful perusal of his chest and coughed.

"Where did you say we lived again?" she asked, taking a sip of water Emma had placed on the coffee table for her earlier. All this talking had left her parched. Maybe, here at last, she'd come to her oasis. She looked the officer in the eye and he shared a winning smile.

"In the prettiest little house, with a white picket fence."

"Oh," she said, charmed. "That sounds lovely."

William stroked his chin and glanced at the guy. "White picket fences are a pain, you know," he told Lucy.

Grant leaned forward in his wing chair. "It's true. Have to paint them every year."

"No worries about the little lady lifting a finger," the officer said. "She can leave all the manly work to me."

William shifted uncomfortably as Grant watched his son. Emma surveyed them both before jumping in. "So what about ID?"

The officer turned toward her, confused. "My military credentials? I already showed those."

Grant nodded approvingly at his wife. "Not those. We're talking something more personal."

"Personal?" the man asked.

"You bet," William said.

"Something to prove you're the real McCoy."

"Proof! Yeah, we want proof!" Carmella butted in.

Justin sat nearby watching the show with interest, but didn't say a word. Lucy glanced at him and then at the others.

"Proof's not a bad idea," she said, guessing what

the Kinkaids had in mind. She studied her engagement ring a moment and looked the officer in the eye.

"Well now, I was out at sea," he faltered, "I'm not sure how much you think I—"

"You would certainly know your nickname?"

"Nickname?"

"Sure, you know," Lucy said brightly. "Something I might have called you. Something…" She flushed a little in spite of herself. "…intimate between the two of us. A pet name?"

He stared at her, dumbfounded, then searched all of their faces. "Fido?"

William closed the door a few seconds later as Emma spoke. "And to think, it looked like we were getting close there for a minute."

"Harrumph," Grant said, shaking his head. "All a bunch of nut jobs."

"I'm afraid you're right, Dad," William agreed.

Lucy sighed, exhausted. At this rate, they'd never find her true home.

William regarded her sympathetically. "How about we take a break? You look as if you're done for the day, and you still should rest after that whack on the head."

"That would be terrific," she said, feeling her tension ease. Who knew it could be so hard trying to find the man you were in love with? "But what do we tell the others outside?"

"Don't worry," William said, "I'll take care of it."

William stepped out on the porch as Emma and William took Carmella into the kitchen for a snack.

Justin lingered behind, eyeing Lucy.

"You've really got them lined up around the block," he said.

"Thanks to your Web page," she said, attempting to be pleasant.

"Naw. I'd said it's thanks to whatever it is Dad's been staring at."

"What do you mean?"

"I think you know what I mean. He's been looking at you all goo-goo-eyed ever since you got here."

"Your dad's just trying to help."

"Yeah, and so are you. Help yourself to this family," he said with a bitter edge.

"Justin, that's not really fair. Nobody wants to know who I am any more than I do, believe me."

"Meanwhile, you've got it awfully cushy not knowing, don't ya? Cushy enough to worm your way into my dad's heart."

Lucy's face warmed. "I... You don't know that's true. Besides, my stay here is only temporary. Very soon I'll have my old life back and be out of your way. But Justin, in the meantime..." She studied him sincerely. "I'd sure like it if you and I could make some sort of peace."

"You mean like, if I'm not nice to you, you'll tell?"

Her shoulders sagged as she hurt for him. She knew the boy was having a rough time, but she honestly wasn't here to make things any tougher. "I'm not saying that it's mandatory."

"Man-da-who?"

"Nothing's mandatory, Justin. I'm not forcing you to do anything, because I know that I can't.

You're practically a man now. Old enough to make your own decisions."

He eyed her suspiciously. "Well, if you're not forcing me, just what are you doing?"

"Asking you." She raised her brow. "Pretty please? Your choice."

Just then, William came inside carrying a stack of mail. He looked from Lucy to his son, and then back again. "Is something going on in here?"

Lucy stared at him innocently. "Nothing at all."

William turned toward his son. "Justin?"

"Nothing, Dad. It's nothing, okay?" He turned and ducked into the kitchen, as something in William's stack of mail caught Lucy's eye.

There was a picture of some guy on the back of a real estate brochure. A face with short dark hair and big black eyes floated over a fairy-tale scene, a castle with hot pink turrets. What was it about the banner fluttering from one of the turrets—*Let Magic Maker Mitch Find the Castle of Your Dreams*—that called her up short?

William's voice hummed from far away as her whole world went woozy.

"Bridget? Are you all right?"

She felt a sharp stab of pain above her left temple. "Oh! Oh, my head." Lucy blinked hard, stumbling toward him.

William caught her in his strong arms and shored her up against him. "Bridget? What's wrong?"

Bridget? Why was he calling her that? Lucy felt herself spiraling into a dark tunnel, visions swirling around her: Gus serving up pancakes... Mitch handing her packages... Waking up on the sofa here... And, huh? Her parents dancing to Billie Holiday...?

"I'm... not really me," she breathed as William embraced her.

Sleigh bells sounded as her world went black and something strong lifted her up and carried her away.

William addressed Dr. Mass, his voice tinged with concern. "She's going to be all right, isn't she, Doc?" Beside them, Bridget was stretched out on the sofa, covered by a throw blanket.

"Oh yes, fine," Dr. Mass said. "It's not as bad as it looks. She's just getting over the shock."

"You mean, about who she really is?"

"Could very well be."

"But why would that make her faint?"

Dr. Mass stroked his snowy beard. "At times, these amnesia cases involve some sort of internal conflict. When the memories start to resurface, they're not always a welcome relief."

"You're saying she's scared to face the truth about who she really is?"

"That all depends on what she has to gain—and lose—by becoming herself again."

William cast his gaze on Bridget, slumbering like a beautiful princess. Perhaps he'd been reading too many fairy tales to Carmella, but he couldn't help but think she looked like she'd stepped right out of one of those storybooks' pages. But in the tales he'd read his little girl, it was always a handsome prince that came along. Not some wayward banker with a middle-class mortgage and a couple of kids.

"Dr. Mass," he said, meeting the older man's eyes. "Can I ask you something?"

"Go right ahead."

"Well, I know this sounds crazy. Loony, for sure.

Asking you of all people... But something has happened in this house, something that defies all... What I mean to say is—" He drew a breath. "Do you believe in Santa Claus?"

"Believe in Santa Claus? Who me?" Dr. Mass chuckled and thumbed his chest. "Why, of course I do!"

"You what?" William sputtered.

"William, my boy," Dr. Mass said, packing his medical bag, "I've known you your whole life. I've seen you grow from diapers until now, and you've become a very fine man indeed. But somewhere along the line, you changed. I'm not sure when. Maybe it was when you lost Karen. You seemed to lose your faith."

"But, Santa! I'm talking the guy in the red suit!"

"Yes, yes. The one who comes on Christmas Eve. Is that the one you mean?" He snapped his bag shut and looked up. "But see, that's where you've gotten things mixed up."

"Mixed up how?" William asked, perplexed.

"I don't know who on earth started that myth, because that's what it is, a flat-out untruth."

"Aha! So there *is no Santa.*"

Dr. Mass, who'd started toward the door, stopped walking. "There is a Santa Claus, indeed," he said, meeting William's gaze. "But can't you see? He doesn't just exist on Christmas Eve. He's here the whole year through!

"June, September, yes, even in January. It's not so much about the man in the red suit as it is about what's in your heart. All you have to do is open yourself up to the magic and believe."

Emma entered the living room to find William sitting in a wing chair by the sofa.

"Is the doctor gone?"

"Yes."

She quietly shut the kitchen door behind her. "You're really worried about this girl, aren't you, son?"

"I'm worried about her and Carmella, too. About what the truth is going to do to all of us."

"Maybe you shouldn't have lied to Carmella."

"Mother! I never lied!"

"You evaded the truth."

"No, I didn't know it," he said firmly. "In fact, I'm still not sure I do."

She sat in the chair opposite his and spoke with a kind smile.

"Come now, William. You're a little old to believe in Santa."

He longingly studied Bridget, sleeping on the sofa, then met his mother's eyes.

"Am I?"

"What are you saying? That you've fallen in love with a total stranger?"

"I never said that, precisely. Only..."

"What?"

"You know how it's been since Karen died.

Emma studied her son. "Lonely."

"Yes."

"But surely you can't believe—?"

"In miracles, Mother? Why not?"

Just then, Carmella entered and rushed to Bridget's side. "Is she going to be okay, Daddy? Please tell me that she is."

"Yes, sweetie," he assured her, "she's going to be

just fine."

The child's face brightened as she turned toward her Grammy. "Did you know she sings really pretty? She sang to me, and it was just like Mommy."

A tear glistened in Emma's eye as she looked from Carmella to her son. "Why not, indeed," she said softly.

Chapter Eight

Mitch hustled toward his desk, where an assistant sat goggling at his computer.

"If you don't mind?" he said, shooing the underling away.

The girl stood and scurried off, casting him an odd look.

Good help really was hard to find. Probably shopping on Q-Bay.

Mitch dropped into his chair with a sigh. Seconds later, his gaze locked on the computer screen. "Sweet Merry Christmas!" he cried aloud. "That's my Luce!" And it was, too, only more bodacious. He'd never known Lucy to go for getups like that. Hey, wait a minute. What did it say? She weren't no mom, for God's sakes. And how could she think her name was Bridget? Was it possible she didn't really know?

Mitch panicked briefly, wondering if this was some sort of trick she was playing. Maybe an attempt to make him reconsider the whole kid thing. Or maybe, just maybe, she was getting back at him. Yeah. That could be it. They were supposed to be together for the holidays, and Mitch suddenly realized he hadn't seen her for five days! *Nope,* he thought shaking his head. *Doesn't seem like my Luce. She don't play no mean tricks. She's a good girl. Really simple.*

He ogled the jingle bell tassels, eyes popping. And now her *simples* was protruding out all over the place. Jesus. Was this any sort of way to behave at the holidays? Mitch quickly crossed himself, hoping his parents hadn't seen. Then he gave the office a slow, studied perusal. Other agents sat at their desks, smirking at their computer screens. They couldn't all be tuned in to this?

"Hey, Magic Maker Mitch!" Amanda called from the front. He'd never liked Amanda. She was always into everybody's business. "You going to go over there?"

Mitch stared at the copy under Lucy's picture seeing   an address was listed. Then, ignoring Amanda and the other gawkers, he grabbed his coat and headed for the door.

Grant, Emma, and the kids stood in the foyer, wearing their coats.

"Mom, Dad," William said. "Thanks so much. It's really nice of you to do this."

"Bosh!" Emma said. "The kids love ice-skating. Besides, they need a break from the madness."

"We all do!" Grant proclaimed.

"I don't see why I have to go, too," Justin said with a scowl. "The fuzz brain's the one who likes to skate, not me."

"Just cooperate, Justin," his dad said. "The fresh air will do you good."

"I already got some fresh air."

"You probably shouldn't remind him," Grant whispered gruffly in Justin's ear.

William saw them off from the porch, grateful that the snow had stopped and his lawn had cleared. Even the television trucks had moved on. Thank God. What a circus!

He came back in the house and was surprised to see Bridget sitting unsteadily on the sofa.

"You're up."

She rubbed her eyes and glanced around the room. "Oh, yes. I know this place."

He strode over and sat beside her, gently taking her hand. "Sure, we're in the living room."

"Our living room?" she asked, squinting her eyes.

"No, I'm afraid it's mine."

"No, it's not," She squeezed his hand firmly and met his eyes. "William, it's mine."

He kindly patted the back of her hand with his free one. "I'm afraid you've gotten things confused."

She pulled free of his grip and studied the decor. "Of course, the wallpaper is different."

William ran a hand through his hair. Dr. Mass had been wrong about Bridget. She wasn't getting better. In fact, she seemed even worse! "Bridget, listen to me—"

Blue eyes flashed as she centered her gaze on his. "Why are you calling me Bridget?"

"That's your name, isn't it?"

"No, I don't think so. I mean, it's familiar."

"Do you remember how you got here?"

She gripped the arm of the sofa and stood, staring around her. "That much is a blur. But this place, yes. I remember it. Recall it quite well." Her eyes traveled to the mantel brimming with Christmas decorations, then settled on a spot to the right of the hearth. "Especially the hidden passageway behind the bookcase."

William felt his anxiety spike. She wasn't just confused; now she was growing delusional. "Wait right there. Don't move for a second," he said, snatching his cell off the coffee table. "I think I'd better call Dr. Mass."

"But Chris Mass has already come and gone!"

"You remember that?"

"I thought I heard talking."

William felt himself flush, wondering how much of the conversations she'd overheard. First the one with Dr. Mass and then the one with his mother. "We thought you were sleeping."

She lightly shook her head. "Maybe it was a dream I had. Some talk about Santa Claus?"

William's neck flashed hot. "This will just take a sec," he said, starting to dial. "Why don't you sit until I get back? Just to be sure?"

Lucy took a seat in a wing chair as William slipped from the room. He was trying to whisper, but his voice rose in apparent panic. "What do you mean you can't come? I just told you she's acting delusional! A baby? Well, tell the woman to wait! I don't know. Cross her legs!"

Lucy didn't know much about what was happening, but she didn't believe herself to be delusional. The truth was, everything was getting clearer. So clear, in fact, that now she was certain she'd been right about the bookcase. She stood with determination and steadied herself. While the wood at the back of the built-in shelf had been painted white, she was betting she could still find that loose panel. Lucy carefully moved a few books out of the way, setting them on a lower shelf. *Tap-tap, tap-tap... It was right around... here...* She laid a fingernail under the edge of the panel and tugged lightly. To her amazement, it moved. Gingerly, she slid it sideways. A small dark hollow gaped open. Inside it sat a single switch. She lifted it and loud humming noise sounded. Slowly the bookcase before her began to move.

Lucy stepped back with delight. *I knew it. I just knew it!* Suddenly, everything came back in a flash, as blinding and bright as the whitest snow blizzard. This *was* her house. She had lived here!

William appeared beside her, slack-jawed. "You weren't kidding about that passageway," he said, staring ahead into the cavernous space.

She turned toward him, cheeks aglow. "William," she said. "I know how I got in your house."

He looked at her in disbelief. "Don't tell me you came from in there?"

"I used to play in there all of the time. Just like Nancy Drew."

"Wait a minute. What are you saying? That you used to live in this house?"

"When I was just a kid."

He stared back into the deep, dark tunnel. "Where does this go?"

"Come on," she said, "I'll show you."

She stepped forward and he laid a hand on her shoulder. "Maybe I should go first."

"All right," she said, smiling. Of course this was her house! Something about the shock of hitting her head, and not knowing who she was, must have sent her back to it. Back to the one safe haven she remembered, even if she couldn't recall anything else.

William attempted to scoot past her in the narrow space, bringing them almost chest-to-chest. He paused, looking down into her eyes. "Who designed this place?"

"Someone who used to work for the government. Paranoid schizophrenic, some say."

"Nice."

They were so close, nearly touching, that for a second Lucy couldn't breathe. He was the best-looking man ever, in many respects way more attractive than Mitch. He had all of the qualities Lucy wanted, everything she'd hoped for in a man. She'd convinced herself he didn't exist. But he did, and here he stood, in the flesh. Funny thing was, they'd never been properly introduced.

"My name's Lucy," she said, her voice coming out as a squeak.

A slow smile worked its way across his handsome face. "That so?"

"Lucy West. I'm a waitress at the diner downtown and live on Ninth Street."

Brown eyes sparkled with delight. "I never thought you were much of a Bridget."

"No."

He studied her for a prolonged beat and for an insane moment Lucy hoped that he might kiss her. She'd harbored the same wish under the mistletoe. Although then, she hadn't fully recalled that she had a fiancé. There was no more denying that now.

"Shouldn't we... You know?" he said, tilting his chin in the direction of the tunnel.

"Yeah, right," she said, stepping back so he could move forward.

At the outdoor skating rink, Justin reluctantly dragged himself onto the ice beside his sister. In a gaggle of girls nearby, one young lady in particular had her eye on the boy. Emma nudged Grant. "Look over there."

"Where?" He craned his neck to spy the pretty brunette giggling into her hand. "Well, I'll be..."

"Do you think Justin has any idea?" Emma asked.

Grant chortled. "Seems like he's going to now."

Emma watched with amusement as the girl skated toward Justin, puffy earmuffs framing the long brown hair flowing behind her as she went. She tapped Justin on the shoulder just as he was about to break into a stride. He turned to stare at the girl in surprise, his neck and the tips of his ears reddening.

"Just like his father," Emma said with a warm smile.

"Hmm," Grant replied. "Looks like she's asking him to skate."

Carmella stood between her brother and the girl, glancing happily from one to the other. "Go on!" Emma heard her shout. "I'm going to have cocoa with Grammy and Poppy."

"I'll come, too," Justin said, racing after her.

The girl's face fell. But then little Carmella took charge. "Oh no you don't," she said, shoving Justin back on the ice. "Not enough cocoa for you."

Justin whirled to face the girl, his whole face beet red.

Grant laughed and then whispered to Emma, as Carmella approached, "Good to see his sister didn't let him chicken out."

Seconds later, the girl held out her hand and Justin took it, letting her drag him onto the ice.

"Looks like Justin's got a girlfriend," Carmella chirped, trudging forward.

Emma and Grant looked at each other and

grinned.

Mitch exited his SUV and stormed up the walk to the front door of the Kinkaid house. Something funny was going on here, and whatever it was, he was going to get to the bottom of it. He rang the bell and waited. Then tried again. Nothing doing. Hmm. There was still a car in the drive. Maybe they hadn't heard him, he thought, deciding to use the knocker. Mitch checked his cell for the time, guessing he'd already been standing here ten minutes.

Well, he sure didn't come clear across town for nothing. He laid his hand on the doorknob, turning it easily. Folks should really take more precautions. Leaving your door unlocked these days could only invite trouble.

He tentatively pushed the door open and called inside, but got no response. Maybe they were in the back or were watching television. He walked a few feet indoors and yelled louder. It was then that he saw it, the big gaping hole in the wall. "Sweet Merry Christmas! What's *that?* Looks like somebody bombed this place." Or maybe that's what this was, some sort of bomb shelter. *Yeah, I'm betting that's right. This whole setup just gets weirder and weirder.*

He took a breath and stepped into the darkness.

William laid his hands on the back of the old pegboard, once meant to hold garden tools, and gently pushed. To his amazement, the pegboard popped off in his hands. He grappled to catch it before it spilled forward, then set it aside, leaning it against a nearby wall. "This is incredible," he said, looking around the crowded space. Cobwebs were everywhere inside the

old garden shed, several coating the lawn mower.

"Don't do much yard work, do you?" Lucy asked.

He shrugged apologetically. "I hire a lawn service."

"I must have remembered this place," she told him with growing confidence. "Even when nothing else made sense to me. William, this is how I got in your house."

"How long did you live here?" he asked in awe.

"Only until my parents died. I was twelve and a half."

"Oh Lucy," he said, his heart aching for her. "I'm so sorry."

Her eyes misted slightly. "After that, I went to live in a group home. Everyone there was very nice, but it wasn't the same."

Of course, it couldn't have been. How horrible for her to have suffered that tragedy, and at such young age. "Didn't you have any brothers or sisters?" he asked.

"No, it was just me."

No wonder she'd asked about having kids. Perhaps she wanted the sort of family for herself that the fates hadn't allowed her to have as a child. William spoke past the lump in his throat, wishing he could find a way to make things all better. He'd give anything to take away the pain in her eyes at the memory of her loss. "So, it's just you then? You're all alone?"

She drew a breath and forced a brighter look. "No, I've got Mitch."

"Who's Mitch?"

"That would be me," a contentious voice said.

"I'm the intended."

William spun in surprise as a stout, dark-haired man stepped out of the passageway and into the crowded space with them.

"Mitch!" Lucy cried with alarm.

"Luce!" he answered, throwing his arms wide. "I thought I'd lost you!" He pulled her into a hug, snug up against him. She shot William a helpless look and his neck flushed hot. What could he do? He couldn't possibly break up the happy reunion.

"Did this fellow hurt you?" Mitch asked, when Lucy pulled back. "Because if he did, I swear—"

"No, Mitch. Seriously. It's not like that at all."

"How is it, then?" he asked, suspiciously eyeing William. In all of his thirty-eight years, William had never felt so entirely sized up.

William stuck out his hand, unsure of what else to do. "I'm William Kinkaid."

Mitch raised an eyebrow at him, then turned back toward Lucy. "Is this on the level? This guy's all right?"

"Yes, Mitch." Lucy sighed heavily. "It's a really long story, but William had nothing to do with me coming here. He's been nothing but the perfect gentleman, I swear."

"Let's hope so," Mitch said, turning to take William's hand. Before he could do it, he stopped. "Wait a minute... What about those, you know..." He cupped his hands in front of his chest. "Jingle bell things."

"That wasn't William," Lucy rushed to explain. "That was Justin."

"Justin? Was this some sort of threesome going on?"

"Mitch!" Lucy shouted in shock.

"Hold on one second," William said, offended. "Justin is my son."

"All the worse!" Mitch's temples bulged and Lucy reached up to sooth them.

"Baby, a lot has happened in this house, but nothing like that. The Kinkaids are a very nice family. They were nothing but good to me."

Mitch scowled, then shook his head. "Well, all right. If you say so." He started to take William's hand again, but stopped. "No monkey business, huh?" he asked Lucy. "Not even with this good-looking ape, here?"

She blushed bright crimson. "No, Mitch."

"Well, good!" He gave her a quick peck on the lips that made William feel slightly sick to his stomach. He'd naturally known all along that Brid—uh, Lucy had a fiancé and another life waiting for her somewhere. He just hadn't realized how unsettling it would be to see it.

Finally, Mitch extended his grip. "Nice to meet you, fellow," Mitch said. "I can't wait to hear this story."

Emma and Grant entered the house holding fast-food bags and sent the kids upstairs to change. As they approached the kitchen, Emma halted, holding up a warning hand to her husband. Grant looked past her to William, sitting glumly at the kitchen table. Emma glanced at Grant with a worried frown. Something didn't feel right in here. Plus, it was awfully quiet.

She put on her sunniest face and carted the burger bags to the kitchen's center island. "We stopped and picked up dinner on the way home."

"Kids already ate in the car," Grant added. "Justin ate like a horse."

William met his parents' eyes with a sad gaze. "Thanks, guys."

"Where's Bridget?" Emma asked.

William sighed and set his palms on the table. "Mom. Dad. I have something to tell you."

Grant walked over and took a seat as Emma slid into another chair.

"What is it, son?" Grant asked.

"Her name's not Bridget," William answered, with red-rimmed eyes. "It's Lucy."

"Well, Lucy's a very nice—" Emma began.

"She's gone."

"Gone?" Grant was visibly surprised.

"Who's gone?" Carmella asked, entering the kitchen.

William stared at his little daughter, hating to break the news. "Bridget, honey. I found out where she lives and—"

"No!" Carmella cried, lunging toward him.

"Hang on, fuzz brain." Justin had appeared and wrapped his arms around her.

She glared at her father, tears streaking down her face. "But it can't be true!"

"Is it, Dad?" Justin asked, his brow creased in concern.

William pursed his lips for a remorseful beat before speaking. "I'm sorry, kids. I wish—"

"But you promised!" Carmella shouted. "*Promised,* Daddy!"

He stood, stepping toward her, but she backed against Justin, who held her tight. Emma's heart broke at the scene. Everyone here was falling apart, not the least of whom appeared to be her son.

"Pumpkin," William said, his voice cracking.

"Don't you 'pumpkin' me!" she said, breaking out of Justin's embrace.

Before they knew it she was through the door, her small footfalls racing upstairs.

"I'll go after her," William told the others.

"Carmella, please honey, talk to me," William said as she hunched forward, burying her face in a pillow. He swallowed past the burn in his throat. "I'm sorry, Carmella. Really, I am."

"But you said she was my mommy!" her muffled voice returned.

William patiently removed the pillow and stroked her damp cheek with his thumb.

"I never said that, sweetheart. You did. I only said I believed in Santa."

"But I don't get it." Pain streaked her eyes, threatening to cleave William in two. "If Bridget's not her real name and Santa didn't bring her... Then..." Her voice faltered again. "There's no Santa at all."

"Now, hang on one second," William said. "We don't know that's so."

"But you can't believe. You just can't. Especially not now."

"Why not?"

"Because he didn't bring you what you wanted, either."

"How do you know what Daddy wanted?"

She stared at him with moistened eyes. "Because I've heard you . . . crying at night." William blinked, turning away. "You wanted somebody, too. Didn't you?"

"Yes," he said in a whisper.

She reached out and touched his arm. "Then, there is no Santa Claus," she said softly. "And if there is, he let us both down."

If that was the truth, then why did Carmella's statement ring so false in his heart? Maybe things hadn't worked out as they might have, but he would never call having had Lucy here a mistake. In fact, having her presence in this house—even if for just a little while—had been the greatest of gifts.

"Oh, I wouldn't say that," William said, pulling his daughter into a hug.

Chapter Nine

Time passed painfully slowly for Lucy. Nothing about it seemed to go right. When she got back to her tiny apartment, it appeared dark and cramped, and absent of holiday cheer. All of the Christmas decorations, including her miniature Christmas tree, were artificial. And each of her potted plants had wilted. She'd never been much of a gardener, anyway. Something like William, she supposed, noting the comparison only further dampened her spirits.

She hadn't realized how attached she'd grown to him until the time had come for her to go. He was just the sort of guy she'd always dreamt of, almost like someone from one of those late-night TV shows. He was an excellent father, too. He was good with his kids, loving yet firm. He was there for them and they knew it, just as his parents remained there for him— and vice versa. Lucy sighed, reliving her moments in that happy home. What the Kinkaids had was a real family, and *family* was a feeling Lucy had nearly forgotten.

She sorted through the mail on the kitchen counter, hoping to find something of interest among the solicitations and bills. She paused, gripping a bright red envelope with no return address in her hands. It could be a Christmas card. Or maybe... just maybe... something from the Kinkaids? Her heart pounded as she recalled the gold flecks in William's eyes. Him holding her under the mistletoe... Their *almost* kiss. She slipped a fingernail under the seal and popped it, then pulled the shiny red foil-covered card from its sleeve. *Hoping Santa's good to you this Christmas* it said on the front. She flipped it open to read the message inside. *And brings you a bag full of joy.* Then, in his charming scrawl, *Gus.*

Lucy's heart warmed despite her frown. Of course it was from Gus. He always ran a week behind and a dollar short. But he was the best darn boss a girl could hope for. Lucy stared out the window at the drifting snow, realizing how foolish she'd been. Thinking she might actually hear from the Kinkaids in general. William, in particular. Naturally, now that she'd gone, they'd all returned to their lives as normal.

That thought didn't stop her from racing to the door a few hours later when the doorbell rang. She opened it to find a florist standing with a huge white box. "Two dozen of our best," he said merrily. She thanked him with a blush and hurriedly took the box inside, ripping into its card. *This time, I promise, I won't let you down. Love, Mitch.*

Lucy gave a melancholy smile, thinking Mitch wasn't such a bad guy. In fact, he was a great guy, and the right guy for her. While it was true he got distracted at times, he was basically a decent man with a good heart. Someone who cared for her, and probably only overworked himself in order to do right by her. Besides, they'd been going out forever and sort of *fit*. He wasn't a bad man and would treat Lucy right, wouldn't run around on her, or purposely be unkind. Over time, they'd work out the baby thing. Once his business had settled down and he wasn't so stressed, he'd be more willing to talk about it.

Lucy eyes misted at the memory of reading to

Carmella by the fire and singing her early morning lullabies. Even Justin had seemed to be coming around. Perhaps slowly, but she had a gut instinct she could break through to him if she just kept trying. But these were silly things to dwell on when she had a wedding to plan. She and Mitch were getting married—*married*—in just a few days. There were so many things to check on, and loose ends to tie up.

Lucy felt a tad guilty for not being overwhelmed with joy at the thought of her upcoming nuptials, but knew that she'd get into it eventually. She was sure that when the big moment came, she could look Mitch in the eye and say *I do* with the hopeful expectation of any bride. The sooner she put the illusion of William meeting her at the top of the aisle instead of Mitch, the better. William was this banker prince, and here she she was, this diner Cinderella. It would do her good to keep her life in perspective and stick with the world she knew. At bottom, it was the only world she had.

William sat by the fire with his parents, sipping eggnog. "I want to thank you both for everything you did to help with Brid—I mean, Lucy."

"Takes some getting used to, doesn't it?" Grant asked.

Emma smiled. "Lucy's a nice name. Comes from Lucille, bearer of light."

"And that's how she was, too," William said thoughtfully. "Just like a candle in a window that had been darkened too long."

"Why son, that's very poetic," Grant said with surprise.

William shot his parents a sad smile. "And the

funny thing is, I haven't thought much about poetry, or anything else romantic, in a very long time."

"We know, son," Emma said kindly. "And we've kind of been hoping there'd come a day when those things would change."

"What your mother means is, we've been wondering when the day would come when somebody special would turn your head."

"We just never dreamed she'd get dropped down the chimney!" Emma said.

William set down his drink and stared at her in surprise. "Why Mom, aren't you a little old to believe in Santa Claus?"

"Oh no, honey. It's never too late to…" She swigged from her glass. "…renew one's faith. Is it, Grant?" she asked, glancing at her husband.

Grant drained his glass and winked at William. "Never too late, indeed."

A ways beyond their view and at a high bend in the steps, Justin had been sitting and eavesdropping on their adult conversation. He'd never seen his dad this way, all moping about like he'd lost his best friend. When his mom died, his dad had been tough. Super strong for all of them. Justin saw now that maybe that was because he felt he had to be. On the inside, he must have been hurting. Just as much as Justin and Carmella, in some ways. Maybe more.

Justin pulled the small wallet-size photo of Mary, the pretty girl from the skating rink, from his pocket and studied it. She had the sweetest looking face in all of the seventh grade, and he was betting she'd be the best-looking girl in the eighth, too. If he didn't get her to go with him now, it would be over and done with by high school. All the more athletic and smarter boys would have moved in, leaving Justin out in the cold.

He stared down the flight of steps, imagining his dad's long face. While he couldn't precisely view his profile from his hidden spot on the stairs, he could envision how it might look, his brow all creased with worry, his lips taking a downward turn. Justin returned his gaze to Mary's photo and her beautiful, cheerful smile. When that smile was meant for him it made his guts turn inside out, but in a good way. He guessed when Lucy had smiled at Dad, it had made him feel something similar. Maybe something he hadn't felt in a while. For all of Justin's life, his dad had done stuff for him and the fuzz brain. He was a good dad who loved them a lot. Maybe it was time that they let him know they loved him back.

Justin stealthily rose to his feet and crept back up the stairs, an idea taking hold. He tiptoed to his sister's room and snuck in the door.

"What are you doing?" she asked looking up from her Barbie dolls.

He quietly shut the door and rasped under his breath. "Carmella, I have an idea."

"Oh no you don't," she said, firmly shaking her head. "Your ideas get you in trouble, and I don't want any of that."

"Not even . . ." he asked, with a tempting smile. "If they get Lucy back?"

Forty-five minutes later, Carmella goggled at Justin's computer screen. "Looks really good. Do you think it will work?"

"In getting her attention? You bet." He'd done his best with it, computer program modifications and all. It certainly got the message across.

"I still don't know about that word." She frowned. "*Man-a-tory?* Are you sure she'll know what that means?"

Justin shot her an informed look. "Do reindeers fly?"

Carmella studied her brother. "You're some kind of softie, aren't you?"

"Let's just say I had some growing up to do."

"Does this have something to do with Mary?" she asked astutely.

"I don't know. Maybe."

"Wouldn't hurt to have another girl around. I mean, a grown-up one like Lucy, to ask all those mushy love questions to."

"Love...?" Justin surveyed his sister, wondering how she knew so much. "Go back to bed," he said, playfully swatting the side of her head.

William nearly bumped into Carmella exiting Justin's room. "Well hello, pumpkin." He did a double take. "Wait a minute. Didn't I tuck you in over an hour ago?"

"Uh-huh," she said, staging a yawn. "And I'm really tired."

"Then what...?"

"Oh! I had a little bit of a bad dream, so I went to see Justin."

"And Justin helped you out?" he asked uncertainly. The boy did appear to be turning over a new leaf. "Oh yes!" she said brightly. "All better now!"

"Hmm."

"Well, good night, Daddy," she said, giving him

a quick hug around the legs and darting to bed. "Sleep tight!"

"You too, pumpkin," he said, thinking something didn't add up. William rapped lightly at Justin's door, then went in.

Justin sat nonchalantly on the bed, scribbling something on a notepad. William couldn't believe his eyes. Was that Justin—writing poetry?

"Hey Dad. What's up?"

"Uh, I just wanted to... About Carmella...?"

"Oh yeah, the fuzz brain had a bad dream. It's okay, though. I told her the monsters weren't real and that she could leave on the lights."

"Very good of you, Justin, thanks," William said, impressed. Who had taken his snarly preteen and replaced him with somebody older and wiser? Not to mention, a bit kinder to his kid sister?

"Was there something else?" Justin asked, apparently ready to get back to his writing.

William had the sneaking suspicion Justin was up to something. For some odd reason, he suspected it had something to do with girls. "Everything all right?"

"Oh yeah, Dad. Just dandy."

Dandy? "There's nothing you want to tell me about? Nothing you want to discuss?" *Like your raging hormones or possible new interest in girls,* William wanted to ask.

Justin smiled at him, tightlipped. "Nope."

Chapter Ten

William had been pondering a way to see Lucy again, but knew that it wouldn't be right just to pop on over there and say *hi* the day before her wedding. Still, he had her gifts to return. Bridget's gifts, anyway. William peered in the top box, his face firing red. Well, no wonder Lucy hadn't wanted him to look! He paused, wondering what had become of his sense of adventure. He wasn't even forty and yet it seemed he'd morphed into an old man. Something about the light in Lucy's bright blue eyes told him she could find a way to reawaken his youth. Hadn't he nearly been driven to pull her into his arms and carry her up to his bed half a dozen times? Okay, he had carried her upstairs that once. But given that they scarcely knew each other at the time, and she was effectively passed out, that didn't seem to count.

William sat on the side of the bed, feeling foolish. There really hadn't been anyone since Karen died. The fact was, when his wife had gone he'd been so devastated by the entire event, he didn't believe he'd ever love again. And then, this stranger waltzed into his house... More like sleepwalked... And suddenly, his heart was all over itself, unable to stop its pounding each time that she was near. There was something about her, he didn't know what, that just seemed so right. It was like she'd belonged in this house . . . and in his arms, he thought, as his neck flushed hot. Though he never truly got the chance to hold her like he'd yearned to do. He tried to imagine what that might be like, having a wife and mother in this house once more. He'd never before trusted there would be a way for that to work. The person would have to be very special. Extra special. To fit such a large bill.

But what was he doing entertaining such cockamamie notions? Tomorrow, Lucy was marrying Mitch. That was the life she was meant to lead, and had decided on, long before she'd wound up on William's sofa. It wasn't like a few days with his family were going to change her mind.

Lucy trudged through the snow up to William's house, her palms damp inside her warm wool gloves. For the past forty-eight hours, she'd been dreaming up any excuse she could think of to come on over. Then, she recalled Bridget's packages. Of course, she had to get them back and make that delivery. After all, she'd promised Mitch.

Maybe it was true that deep inside she longed to see William again. Ever since staying with the Kinkaids, she'd felt oddly conflicted about her upcoming wedding. Perhaps dropping by this morning would set everything right. She'd had a few days to gather her thoughts and distance herself from the disconcerting events that had occurred here, she thought, climbing the front porch steps. Lucy paused, taking in the pretty handmade Christmas wreath, tied up with a bright red bow and hanging from the front door. Everything in this house teemed with life.

Especially William! She looked up with a start when he opened the door, before she could ring the bell. He stood there in his parka, appearing more handsome than ever, light brown eyes sparkling with surprise. "Lucy!" he said, holding a stack of

Christmas gifts.

"Bridget's packages," she exclaimed, heaving a breath. "I was just coming to get them!"

He raised his brow. "You were?"

"Who's at the door, dear?" Emma called from inside. She appeared behind William a few seconds later, followed by Grant.

"Why, Lucy!" she said, rushing over to give her a hug. "What a pleasant surprise."

"Indeed," Grant said with a grin. "In fact, we were just talking about you."

William turned to his parents and parroted with Lucy, "You were?"

"Yes, yes, of course." Emma ushered Lucy inside and shut the door. "Come on in and out of the cold. I just put a pot of coffee on."

Hearing voices downstairs, Justin and Carmella decided to go investigate.

"Carmella, look," Justin whispered at the top of the steps as his Poppy helped Lucy off with her coat and his dad set down a stack of packages.

"Wow," Carmella whispered back. "That worked fast."

Justin nodded. "Guess that's what they mean by *instant upload.*"

"Hey kids!" William called upstairs. "Come on down! We've got company!"

Justin and Carmella smiled at each other, beginning their rapid descent.

"Justin! It's so good to see you," Lucy said with a happy grin. "And you know, I have something to tell you. I'm not mad at all about that Web page."

Justin glanced at Carmella, then spoke, his voice

lightly cracking. "That's great!"

"I know you kids were only trying to help," Lucy said sweetly.

Carmella beamed from ear to ear.

Lucy bent low and held out her arms to the little girl. "Come here, you."

Carmella rushed over and gave her a happy hug, as Justin's heart brimmed. He studied his father, who appeared equally pleased that Lucy was here. Sometimes it was nice to do a good thing.

"Let's all head into the kitchen, why don't we?" Emma said. "Gingerbread's in the making."

"Oh boy!" Carmella crowed.

Justin approached Lucy as she neared the threshold and spoke in a low, confident manner. "Good to see you, Luce."

She stared at him, her cheeks aglow. "Why Justin, that's very nice of you to say. It's awfully good to see you, too."

William sat in the kitchen with the others, thinking how good it was having Lucy back in this house. As they sat around the kitchen table, laughing companionably and sharing warm gingerbread, it was almost as if she belonged here.

"I thought the farmer was a hoot," Grant said, as they relived happy memories.

"I liked the knight on the horse," Emma said.

Justin sipped from his cocoa. "I liked the paratrooper."

"Yeah, well, I liked Daddy best!" Carmella chirped, looking around.

The adults chuckled as Lucy hung her head with a blush.

She looked up, meeting William's eyes, and his heart skipped a beat. "You really were the best out of all of them... I mean, as far as keeping everything organized. I don't know how I could have managed without you."

"William's very good at organizing things," Emma said.

"And he's an excellent provider," Grant piped in.

The tips of William's ears burned hot as Lucy's cheeks colored. "Yes, well..." William stumbled with the words. "The important thing is that we provided a place for Lucy when she was lost."

"Confused was more like it," she said. "I'm so very grateful to all of you. For taking me in and making me feel so much at home."

"It's amazing that this was your house once," Emma said.

"Yes," Lucy agreed. "It seems I have a happy history here."

"History has a way of repeating itself," Grant said with a knowing look.

What were his parents driving at? It was almost embarrassing the way they were throwing themselves at Lucy, dropping hints here and there concerning everyone's feelings for her. Including his own, he acknowledged, sentiment overtaking him. Here she was, this wonderful, beautiful woman, whom his parents and his kids obviously adored. And she was getting hitched to another man.

"You know, we've been thinking," Emma said as she stood to refill the adults' coffees, "Grant and I..." She cast her husband a look. "That, with the New Year upon us, it would be terribly good to get together and celebrate."

"At our house for a change," Grant added. "You know, card games, puzzles. Champagne at midnight. A good old-fashioned family New Year's Eve."

"Yes, dear," Emma said, her expectant gaze on Lucy's. "And we were hoping you could join us."

Lucy's eyes brimmed with gratitude. "That sounds lovely," she said. "Really special. You don't know how much I'd like to come. But I can't." She set down her mug resolutely, then looked around the room, taking them in one by one. "I'm afraid that I'm getting married tomorrow night at eight o'clock."

"Married?" everyone but William cried.

"Didn't William tell you?"

Grant studied his son. "No, I'm afraid he left that little detail out."

"Where is the ceremony, dear?" Emma asked kindly.

"Up at the Old North Church, out on River Road."

"Of course, we know it," Emma said. "Sweet little place."

"If I could, I'd invite you all," Lucy said. "But the chapel's small, and it's only family."

"Naturally, we understand." Emma took her seat with a heavy heart. William felt as if someone had ripped his heart from his chest and replaced it with a huge iron anchor.

William turned toward Lucy, sinking into the depths of her eyes. They were beautiful eyes, angel eyes. *But this Christmas angel belongs to someone else,* William reminded himself. "And we wish you and Mitch the very best," he said quietly.

Justin rubbed his forehead as Carmella watched her father with a frown.

Grant stood and warmly patted Lucy's shoulder. "Of course, we do. Congratulations. From all of us."

Chapter Eleven

Lucy stood glumly before her mirror applying the last of her makeup. Well, this was it. The big day had arrived. She studied her reflection, deciding she looked passable in the simple wedding dress she'd bought online. Mitch would never guess it was a second. The important thing was, she was wearing it for the first time with him. Lucy sighed and pulled on her heavy coat, expecting him at any minute.

She noted the light was blinking on her answering machine and hit *play*.

"Hey sugar, it's me, Gus," his voice said. "Don't get me wrong here. I'm still pleased as punch to be walking you down the aisle tonight, but all of us over at the diner found something on the Internet we think you should take a look at."

Moments later, Lucy sat at her PC typing in the URL Gus had provided. The page loaded and her eyes watered, threatening to overflow. Clearly this was something Justin had crafted, probably with Carmella's help.

There was a Kinkaid family picture and her figure had been cut and pasted in. The caption read: *Sexy Cyber Dad Seeks Mom. Only those answering to "Lucy" and perfectly matching this photo's description need apply. Personal experience with Santa and his reindeer team a plus. Extra room in her heart for two great kids mandatory.*

"Crazy, adorable kids," she said, as tears escaped her.

Mitch knocked at the door and she nabbed some

tissues off a nearby table to dab her weepy eyes. She had to pull herself together. The man who loved and wanted her was just outside and prepared to whisk her away and into a new and happy life. She would be happy, wouldn't she?

"Wow, you look gorgeous," Mitch said as she opened the door.

"You don't look so bad yourself," Lucy answered. And he didn't. Mitch had cleaned up very well, and looked really nice in his tuxedo and red rose boutonniere.

"So, ready to go and do this thing?" he asked with a grin.

Lucy forced a shaky smile. "You bet."

"Great. That makes two of us." He held out his arm to escort her. "Your carriage awaits!"

"Mitch?" she began tentatively.

"Yeah?"

"Have you ever tried blueberry pancakes with chocolate syrup on top?"

"Ew! That's disgusting! Why would you ask...? Wait a minute. You're not trying to prep me up for some of those pregnancy cravings, are ya?"

Lucy cast a sorrowful gaze toward her computer. "I can't really have the kids without the father, can I?"

"Now, you're talking crazy, Luce." He stopped walking and turned toward her. "Are you all right?"

"Yes, fine." She pulled herself upright and looked him in the eye. "I'm sorry, Mitch. I just had a weak moment, but it's passed. I know what I want to do."

The mood was grim at the senior Kinkaid house.

Grant and Emma couldn't get anybody to do
anything. Justin didn't want to play cards and
Carmella refused to work puzzles. Finally, the
grandparents gave up and turned on the television,
letting the kids watch a New Year's Eve show,
complete with stage performers and marching bands.

William was sure his mom had cooked a
delicious dinner, but the truth was that he hadn't been
able to taste a bite. It was like his whole world was in
a haze and he was detached from everything. He'd
meant what he'd said to Dr. Mass when he questioned
the older man about Santa Claus. Something unusual,
magical, had happened when Lucy arrived. And when
she'd gone, she'd taken all that brightness with her,
leaving him in this dark well of despair. How could it
be that the fates had brought home just the right
person for him... for all of them.. and then just as
suddenly snatched her away?

William looked up from where he sat on the sofa
and Grant motioned him into the kitchen—and out of
the earshot of the others.

"Want a drink, son?" his dad asked gruffly.

William glanced at the still untouched glass in his
hand. "Thanks, I've got one."

Grant met his gaze. "How about something
stronger? A kick in the ass?"

"Dad!" William said with surprise.

Grant massaged his chin and studied William.
"You know, son, we Kinkaids might be many things,
but I've never thought of any of us as quitters."

"Quitters?"

"Just look at yourself. All moping about and
giving up, while the woman of your dreams goes
waltzing down the aisle with someone else."

"That's just it! She's already marrying someone else."

His dad shot him a disappointed look. "Well, fine. Okay, then. Just throw in the towel if that's how you feel. If you really, in your heart, believe Lucy's making the right decision.

"But if you believe, even for a second, that she's making the wrong one, don't you think you owe it to yourself—and her—to go out there and tell her so?"

Gus and Lucy stood at the top of the short aisle. The small chapel was lovely, still decorated for Christmas with candles and holiday greenery. Mitch waited up front, beaming brightly beside the waiting priest.

"Remember," Gus said, taking her arm. "Just keep it nice and steady."

"Thanks for being here, Gus."

He leaned toward her, speaking under his breath. "I feel like I'm walking you to your execution."

"Sometimes you have to take what life serves you up," she whispered back, "even if it gives you indigestion."

"Right, but I won't tell Mitch that you said that."

William stared at his father, affronted. "Dad, are you calling me a wimp?"

"Why, yes. Yes, I suppose I am."

William set his jaw, knowing one thing firmly. He wasn't some coward who backed down from a challenge. Never had been. Who was he to step aside and assume Mitch was the right guy for Lucy? Shouldn't he let her decide that for herself?

"Now, I know things have been tough since—"

his dad went on.

"Hold that thought," William said, nabbing his keys off the counter. Damn straight Lucy should decide things for herself. But how on earth could she, when she hadn't even been presented with a choice?

"Atta boy!" Grant called, as William raced from the room. "Go get her!"

Emma and the kids stared at him, stunned, as he yanked on his parka and bolted for the door. "Be back soon," he said, as their faces all brightened in smiles.

William rushed through the snow to his SUV, noting it was coming down heavily again. He held up an arm to shield his eyes from the onslaught. When he was nearly to his driveway, a cascade of heavy wet flakes poured down on him "What on earth?" He squinted heavenward, almost swearing he'd heard sleigh bells. "No," he said, shaking his head. "No earthly way."

Ten minutes later, William burst through the door of the chapel covered in white flakes. "Hang on just one second!" he shouted. "I object!"

The priest eyed him curiously as he bustled his way to the front. "I'm afraid, young man, we haven't yet gotten to that part."

Lucy blushed mightily. "William!" she cried with unmasked delight.

"You!" Mitch declared, not nearly as happy to see him.

A man stood from the front pew. From his looks, he appeared to be Mitch's father. "What's the meaning of this?" he demanded.

"The meaning of this, sir," William said as he pressed his way to the front, "is that something's happening here that maybe shouldn't be."

Mitch's mother addressed him. "What's he talking about, son? Do you know this man?"

"I do!" Lucy shouted, nearly breathless. Boy, she was gorgeous in the pretty white dress. Just like a picture straight from heaven.

Mitch to turned her. "Hey! I thought there was no monkey business going on!"

"There wasn't," William stated calmly. "But that didn't prevent me from developing feelings for Lucy. Very deep feelings."

"You did? I mean, you have?" Lucy asked with a hopeful blush.

"I do," William said, his voice growing froggy.

"Oh my," the priest said.

"Hoo boy," Gus echoed.

Mitch spoke to Lucy, hurt etched in his voice. "Wait a minute. You can't possibly be saying that you love this guy?"

"Oh Mitch, I'm so terribly sorry. I never meant for it to happen."

"Was that a yes?" the priest asked.

"Was it, Lucy?" William asked, his eyes on hers.

"But Luce," Mitch inserted. "We... you said..."

She studied him kindly. "We said so many things. But can't you see? Neither of us really knew what we were talking about. You said you never wanted kids, and I agreed. Not because that's how I really felt but—"

Mitch blinked hard. "Are you saying you would have tricked me?"

"Tricked you? Never. But would I have tried to convince you to change your mind? Over time? Then yes, I'm sure. And when I realized I couldn't because that's how you really feel, then I would have made the two of us miserable."

"But you said I was the only baby you need."

"I know what I said, but I was wrong." She glanced lovingly at William. "Wrong about so many things. I didn't really know what having children was like until I had a chance to live that life for myself. It helped me understand how important that is to me."

"And she's going to make a wonderful mother, too," William interjected.

Mitch's cell buzzed and he reached a hand in his pocket to answer it. "Sorry folks," he said, checking the number. "Business." He pressed talk. "Magic Maker Mitch, at your service!"

Mitch's parents turned to each other and sighed while the priest drew a breath.

William smiled at Lucy and she grinned broadly in return.

"There's still a party invitation with your name on it," he said.

Lucy shot the small crowd an apologetic look, then took William's hand, as they raced down the aisle and into the dressing room to grab her things.

William and Lucy dashed out of the church and into the snow, where he pulled her into his arms. "I couldn't let you go through with it," he said as snow fell around them. "Not knowing what I know now, and how strongly I feel. The moment you walked into my world, Lucy, everything changed. And if that's not magic, then I don't know what is." He dove into her eyes, wanting to stay there forever. "Up until this year, I'd long ago given up believing in Santa Claus. I know it sounds crazy, but now I—"

She reached up and lightly stroked his cheek. "I know. I believe, too."

He settled his arms around her, holding her close. "I love everything about you, Lucy West. The way you eat your blueberry pancakes and burn the bacon... The way you are with Carmella and somehow broke through to Justin... The way you charmed my parents, and also me."

Tears glistened in her eyes. "And I've fallen for you, William. All of you. I never really knew what having a family of my own was like until I found you. And now that I do, I can't imagine a life without it."

"Then *don't*. Marry me, Lucy. Be my bride."

"Oh William," she said with a happy gasp, "if I had a whole yard full of grooms to choose from, I'd pick you."

"I'm glad," he said, closing the distance between them with a kiss. Her lips met his, warmly and willingly. He deepened his ardor and she returned it, every bit the taste of heaven he'd imagined.

Somewhere high above them, music chimed.

"Did you hear that?" she asked, pulling back. "It almost sounded like... bells?"

"Did it now?" he asked with a happy laugh. She was incredibly beautiful, so warm and feminine against him, and she was going to be his. *His bride* forever. Yearnings stirred within him he hadn't felt in a while. And boy, was he eager to make good on them. He bent low to scoop her into his arms, billowy white gown, winter coat, and all.

"I'm awfully glad you landed on my sofa," he said with a husky rasp. "You're welcome back there any time."

She wrapped her arms around his neck and

hugged him tightly as he carried her toward his SUV. "If that's an invitation, I accept."

"Shall we head back and tell my folks and the kids?"

She shot him a mysterious smile that made his heart soar. "Something tells me they already know."

Not far away, Grammy and Poppy stood with the kids, peering out their bay window.

"That's funny," Emma said. "I could have sworn I heard something. How about you, Grant?"

He shook his head and stared outdoors. "Just a slight ringing in my ears."

"Well, I heard it," Carmella said. "And I know who it was, too."

"Don't be silly, fuzz brain," Justin said, but this time with affection. Just then, he saw a flash of light up in the sky and something far away, trailing off into the night. "Oh no, no... no."

"What is it, Justin?" Grammy asked.

"Just been gaming too much, that's all."

"Sure," Carmella said. "But you know that there's a Santa because you got what you wanted, too."

"Yeah? What's that?"

"The same thing that I did," she said confidently.

"How do you know so much?" Justin asked.

"I asked Grammy and Poppy about *man-a-tory*."

Justin pursed his lips to steel his emotions. The truth was, he hadn't thought he was ready for a new mom, and didn't even believe he wanted one. When Lucy came along, though, everything had changed. "Do you think she said yes?" he asked his grandparents.

Emma and Grant exchanged glances and grinned. "Do reindeers fly?" they said together.

THE END

Holiday Brides Book 3

MISTLETOE IN MAINE

Chapter One

Carol Baker imagined herself in the snowy scene... An idyllic Victorian mansion sat high on a hill, overlooking a frozen lake. Holly draped from the railing of the wide wraparound porch, and a cheery Christmas wreath hung on its old oak door. She smiled beneath her warm woolen hat as fourteen-year-old Will and nine-year-old Ashley put the final touches on their snowman. Suddenly, Ashley turned on her big brother, hurling a snowball. "Oh no, you don't," he charged with a grin, scooping up some snow of his own and pelting back. Carol laughed heartily, joining in the fray. It was the first time she and her kids had enjoyed each other's company in months.

Carol sighed and closed the cover of the glitzy brochure she'd been perusing, setting it on the dining room table. How she wished she could really take her kids on that kind of family holiday.

"What's that?" Ashley asked. Her daughter had just come indoors from a rousing game of basketball, during which she'd no doubt whipped the tail of the ten-year-old boy next door. Her cheeks were pink from the nip in the air, her sweatshirt slightly speckled with moisture.

Carol glanced out the window, noting dark clouds rolling in. "Is it raining?"

Ashley pulled off her hoodie. "Just started. It's getting really windy too." It seemed they were in for another winter storm—all rain, with temperatures hovering right around forty. If only they had luscious snow like Carol had been dreaming about in New England.

Will emerged from the kitchen, snacking on a meatloaf sandwich. The boy always seemed to be eating these days. Perhaps that was because he was growing like a weed. "Is that where we're going on vacation?" he asked, motioning to the brochure on the table.

Ashley took it in her hands, fanning it open. "The Love Inn?" she said with a big, broad smile. "Sounds sweet!"

Will polished off his sandwich, peering over her shoulder. "Yeah, Mom, look. They've even got dog sledding."

Yes, Carol had looked in to that, and its incumbent price tag. She could nowhere afford that kind of fun on her public-schoolteacher's salary. "Dog sledding's expensive," she said with a sympathetic smile. "I'm afraid we can't swing that this year. In fact, we won't be making it to Maine at all."

Ashley shot her a worried look. "But you said we were going skiing."

"Yes, honey, and we will," Carol said brightly, producing a new pamphlet. "In Asheville!"

Her kids' faces fell as they studied the dismal brown condos hugging the side of a craggy mountain. Their placement looked Photoshopped as log-shaped lettering proclaimed: *Discount Family Vacations.* Lightning crackled outside, and the sky opened up in a downpour.

"Oh," Ashley said with a frown.

"For Maine, we'd have to buy airline tickets," Carol explained. "Asheville's within driving distance."

"Looks cool, Mom. Really." Will nudged his sister.

"Yeah," Ashley said, brightening. "I'm sure it will be great."

Just then, the doorbell rang. Carol glanced down at her sweatshirt and jeans. She'd been so busy grading papers, she hadn't even bothered to put on makeup today. "Are you two expecting anybody?"

Will and Ashley shrugged and shook their heads.

"Probably just a delivery person," Carol said, straightening her short brown ponytail.

Carol pulled open the front door to find a curly-headed man holding Christmas packages. Behind him, rain came down in droves.

"Hi, Carol, nice to see you."

"Jim." Her stomach clenched, making her feel ill all over. "You could have called."

"I thought I'd surprise the kids on my way to the airport."

Carol noted his dark sports car parked in the drive. A stunning, young blonde waited inside. Naturally, Jim was headed to the airport. He and Brenda hadn't stopped traveling since they'd hooked up. When he'd been married to Carol, he'd never taken her anywhere.

"Is that Daddy?" Ashley called from inside. She rushed out on the porch and wrapped her arms around him. "Daddy, it *is* you!" she said with a happy laugh. "Come in the house. You're getting wet!"

"Merry Christmas, angel," he said with a happy grin.

Carol burned to rail at him for every single Christmas, birthday, and special event he'd missed.

Instead, she pressed her lips together and cleared the way for him to walk indoors.

Will ambled in from the next room and cast his dad a wary eye.

"How you doing, son?" Jim asked in a jovial tone.

Will's gaze panned out the door seconds before Carol shut it. He'd obviously seen the sports car too. "We're headed out of town ourselves," he said, his gaze back on his father's.

Jim turned toward Carol. "That so?"

"Where are you going, Daddy?" Ashley wanted to know.

Jim chortled, apparently pleased with himself. "Brenda and I are headed down to St. John, little island in the Caribbean."

"That sounds nice," Ashley said, in all her innocence.

Carol squared her shoulders and spoke resolutely. "I'd prefer a white Christmas myself."

Jim stared at her, then glanced at the kids. "Just where is it you're off to?"

"Ash—" Will began, before Carol cut him off.

"Actually, we're going to Maine!" She didn't know why she'd blurted that out, but suddenly she'd been unable to stop herself. There stood Jim, with his expensive new car and high-maintenance wife, bragging...*bragging*... to them all about yet another extravagant vacation he would take. Well, she could be extravagant too, couldn't she? Her kids were worth it. Didn't matter how long it might take to pay down the credit card.

Will's jaw dropped, but Ashley didn't miss a beat. "Yeah," the little girl crowed. "We're staying in a *big* house that's sixteen stories tall! On the top floor even! We're going dog sledding and everything!"

"Dog sledding? In Maine? Imagine that." He slowly shook his head. "Your mom always was one for crazy ideas." He handed one of his two small gifts to Ashley. "This one's for you, sweetheart."

She accepted the flat, square box with a hopeful grin. "You want me to open it now?"

Jim nodded, crossing his arms over his chest. Carol could ask him to remove his coat and invite Brenda into the house. She could check herself into the insanity ward at the local hospital too, but she wasn't close to doing either.

Ashley eagerly unwrapped the small package and studied it with a wrinkled brow. *Oh no*, Carol thought, *not another one of Jim's homemade DVDs*.

"It's a picture story album," he told his daughter. "Complete compilation of all my trips."

Will glanced at Carol, and she knew what he was thinking. He'd likely gotten one too. Jim was nothing if not unoriginal in his gift giving. He handed a second package to Will that looked to be identical. The boy unwrapped it, seeing he'd received the same thing as his sister. "Thanks, Dad," he said with a tight smile.

"Wait!" Ashley spouted. "Don't go anywhere! We've got something for you."

She returned with a couple of boxes. Jim opened hers first, extracting a handmade tree ornament. "It's beautiful. Real special, sugarplum."

Ashley beamed while Will shifted uneasily on his feet. How Carol hated this for her children, the way Jim just popped in and out of their lives. If only she could figure a way to give them a better, more consistent one, she would.

Jim opened Will's gift and hooted, holding up the expensive, patterned tie. "Well, I'll be! I sure as heck won't be wearing *this* down in St. John!"

Carol shot him a look, and he self-corrected.

"Oh, right. Right," he said, softening his tone toward his son. "Very nice, Will. Ultra sharp. I'll be using it a bunch, I'm certain."

Carol followed Jim onto the porch as thunder boomed. "You can't keep doing this," she said as rain poured down all around them. "It's been two months—*two months*—since you've seen them."

He averted her gaze. "Brenda and I've been busy. We're building the new house and—"

"So busy you missed your own son's birthday? Again?" She felt fire welling in her throat but spoke past it. "He sat around all day, jumped up every time the telephone rang…" The memory of that day haunted her still. Though he was a young teen now, in his heart, Will was still that tender little boy his dad had walked out on. For Jim hadn't just left her; in many ways, in his midlife rush to find himself, he'd abandoned all of them.

Jim pursed his lips and turned toward her, rain splattering the back of his coat. There was a look in his eyes she hadn't seen there before, something akin to remorse. "I'm sorry, Carol," he said hoarsely. "Sorry about a lot of things."

Then he turned toward the car and walked away through the drowning rain.

In a faraway corner of northwestern Maine, Paul Love steadied the ladder in front of the Christmas tree and directed his son. "A little more that way. Yeah."

Daniel leaned back, appraising his handiwork. "I think the star's straight now."

Paul tried to deflect the deep sadness taking hold. Something about this time of year always left a raw ache in his heart. "Somehow this doesn't seem right without your mom here."

Daniel stepped down from the ladder and stood beside him. "I know it's still hard, Dad."

Paul thoughtfully studied his son. Though he was only seventeen, he looked just like Nancy in so many ways. He clearly had her bright blue eyes, but they were offset by Paul's dark hair. "When did you get to be so old?"

"I'm almost eighteen now. I know a thing or two."

"Let's just hope you don't know too much," Paul teased.

Daniel draped an affectionate arm around his father. It struck Paul that Daniel was nearly as tall as he was, six foot one. He'd likely surpass him in height by this time next year. "I'm going to college in the fall, you know."

Paul met his son's gaze with a mixture of pride and melancholy. Daniel had been accepted to Brown, Paul's alma mater, and would be leaving the nest soon. "I know, and I'm going to miss you."

Daniel tugged his dad toward him in a one-armed hug. "Maybe you should, you know?" He lifted his brow.

"What?" Paul asked, perplexed.

"Think about getting a life of your own."

"I have a life."

"No. You have a business."

"And business is good. So good that I'm thinking

of giving it up, in fact."

Daniel removed his arm with a start. "What are you saying?"

Paul walked to the window beside the huge stone fireplace crowned with an enormous moose head. Snow beat down furiously outdoors, coating the pines surrounding a frozen lake. Snowmobilers blazed trails across its glassy surface, while ice skaters pirouetted in the rink abutting Pruett's Barn. "I'm selling the inn."

"*Selling?* But, Dad, you can't!"

Paul faced his son, who ran a hand through his hair.

"Found a nice little place up in Montreal. Nice and peaceful, overlooking the water."

"Canada? You must be joking. Things are tough enough for Amy and me as it is with me going off to Rhode Island. How do you think it will work with me gone summers and breaks too?"

"I'll fly you—and Amy—up whenever you want. Besides, your grandma's still in Greenville. I'm sure she'll make a place for you if ever you get the hankering to visit."

Daniel set his hands on his hips, then hung his head. "I can't believe you'd sell this place, after all this time."

"Aren't you the one who was just telling me to get a life?"

Daniel looked up. "I meant, in *America*."

"Things will all work out, you'll see."

"Yeah, sure."

"In the meantime," Paul said, jerking a thumb toward the window, "the powder's looking awfully good out there."

Daniel cocked his chin in a challenge. "Don't make me embarrass you, now."

Paul chuckled aloud. "I wouldn't go counting any chickens before they hatch, if I were you."

One hour later, they were all suited up and on the ice, mounting matching snowmobiles. "Ready to ride?" Daniel asked as snow streaked down hard.

"More ready than you know!" Paul revved his engine, then took off, gunning it across the lake.

Daniel flipped down his goggles and raced after him. "Hey!"

"Whoo-hoo! Yes, sir!" Paul whooped, zipping along. He glanced over his shoulder to see Daniel in hot pursuit.

Daniel gritted his teeth and lowered his shoulders, leaning into the wind. "You asked for it, old man!" He unleashed his machine's full force, zooming past his dad and kicking up a blast of powder.

He skidded to a halt at the edge of the lake and waited, panting.

Paul pulled up beside him and cut his engine with a big, bold grin.

"What are you so happy about?" Daniel asked, surprised. "I just kicked your tail."

Paul wryly twisted his lips. "Just proves I'm a good teacher." He flipped his vehicle around. "Best two out of three?"

"All ri—"

Paul lowered his goggles and took off again before Daniel was ready.

"Argh!" Daniel cried, chasing after him through the blasting snow.

Chapter Two

The following week, Ashley used her sweater sleeve to wipe the fog off the airplane window. Icy snow slapped against it as the buildings of Boston below came into hazy focus.

"I hope we got a four-wheel drive," Will said, looking up from his smart phone.

Carol gripped the metal armrests framing her airline seat. She'd never liked flying, especially in bad weather. "We'll upgrade."

"You think we'll see any moose there?" Ashley asked her mom with a hopeful look.

Will shook his head and replaced his earbuds.

"What?" Ashley said. "There are moose in Maine. Right, Mom?"

"Of course there are, honey. Loads of them. Especially up in the North Woods, where we're going."

"Might even see a couple of reindeer," Will added with a twinkle in his eye. "Big, gigantic ones with flashing red noses."

Ashley huffed because she knew he was teasing her. Maybe if her daughter didn't invent such fantastic stories, folks would cut her more slack. But she had a knack for exaggeration that put the *tall* in tall tale.

"I thought you were listening to music?" Carol said sternly.

Will turned up the volume on his handheld device.

"If I saw one, I wouldn't tell *you*," Ashley told

her brother.

Carol drew a breath, hoping she'd made the right decision. Her kids didn't always get along swimmingly, and here she was about to confine them to the four walls of some rustic country inn for ten days. Suddenly, the notion of a good, old-fashioned family Christmas seemed farfetched. Could she really count on Will and Ashley to get along—and not drive her crazy—for that extended period of time? She glanced out the window at the driving snow, thinking it was good they were flying in today. This Nor'easter blowing through was predicted to get worse, so travel within the next day or so could get iffy.

At least she and the kids would be cozy inside their historic New England getaway by then. And, when the winds weren't too biting, they could bundle up and go play outdoors, just as she'd imagined them doing while mooning over that picturesque brochure. She'd budgeted carefully to allow for a least one day of skiing. Lessons and equipment rental were included in the Holiday Hills package she'd purchased for the three of them. Dog sledding, unfortunately, was not. That was part of the all-inclusive Winter Wonderland deal she figured only well-heeled individuals could afford. And boy, did it offer a cool slew of events, all the way down to a real horse-drawn sleigh ride through the scenic, snow-covered town.

Carol sighed, realizing she was letting her *wants* get the best of her. Here she was going to Maine! *Maine!* How exciting. It was the farthest she'd traveled north in her entire lifetime. It would be a terrific family vacation, and they'd savor the memories for months to come. Just because Jim had left her alone, that didn't mean he'd made her incapable. Carol was plenty prepared to deliver an awesome holiday experience for her kids. Even if she had to teach summer school next year to pay it off, it would be worth it. Every dime. She felt lucky the inn had received a cancellation shortly before she'd called. Normally they couldn't have accommodated her so last-minute. As it stood, an attorney couple that had reserved a few rooms for themselves and two of their children had been caught up in an ongoing court case and forced to postpone their trip.

She smiled softly at Will and then at Ashley, who gazed out the window, enchanted by the drifting snow. Yes, a white Christmas would be just the right thing for all of them.

A little while later, Carol stood with her kids outside an enormous SUV, second-guessing her decision to drive north in this weather. Will shifted the backpack on his shoulder, gaping at the bright red vehicle.

"Are you sure you can drive this thing?"

"Of course!" Carol said with more confidence than she felt.

Will and Ashley exchanged doubtful glances as their caps became dusted with flakes. Carol hit the Unlock button on her key and slapped a road atlas against Will's down parka. "You navigate."

Ashley rolled her eyes. "Good thing we got the built-in GPS."

Carol popped the hatchback, and they tossed their things inside.

"Can we strap her to the luggage rack?" Will asked, referencing his sister.

"Both of you in the car—now!" Carol commanded, wondering if this nice, family vacation was really such a hot idea.

A few hours later, she decided maybe it hadn't been. Trapping herself in this SUV with two bickering kids was driving her nuts. They'd made it through New Hampshire and into Maine, but once they'd hit the North Woods in the impending blizzard, the entire landscape had become one big blur. There was nothing along this desolate logging road but a tall stretch of pines and the creeping late-afternoon darkness. There wasn't another vehicle in sight. Fierce winds howled, and Carol gripped the steering wheel, wondering if they'd accidentally veered off course.

"Are you sure we're on the right road?" she asked Will.

"Yes, Mom, I see it right here! Route 16. It's a shortcut over to 15 North from 201."

The GPS chimed in with its annoying mechanical voice. "*Bleep, bleep.* When possible, make a legal U-turn. *Bleep, bleep.* When possible, make a legal U-turn."

Ashley gripped the back of her mom's seat. "We're lost! I knew it! We're lost!"

Carol felt her panic build as she glanced at Will.

"I said, keep going!"

Carol strained to see through the windshield that was piling up with snow. The furiously beating wiper blades could barely keep up.

Suddenly, Ashley shrieked. "Mom, stop!"

Carol instinctively hit the brakes, sending the SUV into a skid. She wrestled to correct it, maneuvering the vehicle onto the side of the road.

She turned to her child in the backseat, fearing she was sick. "Ashley, what is it?" she asked, breathless, her heart pounding. "Are you all right?"

Her face was ruddy with excitement, her eyes big and wide. "I saw it, Mom! I really saw it!"

Will turned toward her as well.

"Saw what?" Carol asked.

"A moose! A real live Christmas moose!"

Will turned back around. "O...M...G."

"Will, no cursing!" Carol said.

"I wasn't cursing, just abbreviating."

Ashley pouted in the backseat. "It's true! Why won't you believe me?"

Carol sighed and scanned the woods hedging the road. "Okay, Ashley," she said kindly. "Where's your moose?"

"It was right over..." Ashley stared out her window, pointing. "Well, it was there! Just a second ago!"

"Yeah right," Will spouted without looking at her. "Bet it was pulling Santa's sleigh too."

Ashley huffed, and Carol pursed her lips, thinking. She had to get them out of this wilderness and to their destination ASAP. From the look of the increasingly gloomy sky, the sooner the better. "Let me see that map," she said to Will.

Daniel cradled logs in his arms as his dad stoked the fire. Embers leapt into flames, filling the rustic room with a warm glow.

"I'm sorry we've got a smaller crowd this year," he told his dad. "I know you like a full house at Christmas."

"The weather and people's commitments can't be

helped," Paul said congenially. "At least we were able to fit that new family in."

"The mom and her two kids from Virginia?"

Paul nodded as a loud pounding came at the door. "Bet that's them now."

"Why don't I finish up so you can go answer?"

Paul stood, dusting off his jeans. "Thanks, son."

The knocking sounded again, this time accompanied by the ringing doorbell.

"Coming!" Paul called, headed that way.

He pulled back the heavy door, and the attached sleigh bells jangled.

Redheaded Velma threw her arms wide and beamed up at him from beneath her knitted cap sporting reindeer antlers. "Pauly!"

"Mom!" he cried in shock. Behind his compact sixty-something mother, a much younger man trudged up the walk in snowshoes and wearing a matching antlered hat. He carted several pieces of luggage as a long blond ponytail draped down his back.

"I hope you don't mind," Velma said with a little pout. "Our flight to Chicago was cancelled."

"Chicago?" Paul asked with surprise.

"That's where Zach's from." She leaned forward, then spoke in a whisper. "Isn't he the cat's pajamas?" Velma stepped past him and into the foyer as Zach lumbered in the door.

"Hey, man, nice to meet you," Zach said, rearranging his bags and extending a hand.

Paul shook it as another figure appeared through the driving snow. It was a stunning blonde dressed in a white coat and hat. As she drew closer, recognition alighted in her pale blue eyes. "Paul Love, is that really you?"

"Beth?" Paul asked, scarcely able to believe it. He hadn't seen his old high school sweetheart in years. The last he'd heard, she'd married and moved to Vermont.

"We ran into her at the airport," Velma explained. "Seems she was waylaid on the same flight." She batted her eyes at her son as she closed the door behind them. "Isn't it a small world?"

"Very." Paul swallowed hard, caught off guard by this turn of events. He hadn't thought of Beth in a long time. So long, he'd nearly forgotten how attractive she was, and her looks had withstood the test of time. Despite the fine lines that crinkled around her eyes when she smiled, hers was still a youthful face. If he didn't know better, he'd swear some magician had turned back the clock and deposited his first love—just as she'd been—before him.

"I hope it's not too much of an imposition?" Beth said, color lightly dusting her cheeks. "My parents already left on their cruise, but I suppose I could go back to the old homestead."

"And have you spend Christmas alone? We wouldn't hear of it, would we Pauly?"

For a second, Paul seemed to have lost his ability to speak. But he quickly called himself up short, realizing he was being impolite. "Not at all," he said, spewing out the words and then instantly hoping he hadn't sounded too desperate. But he was desperate. Desperate to know what his long-lost love was doing here after all this time. He cast a wary eye at his mother, wondering how much of the airport story was actually true. His mom was very dear but had a conniving side too. But surely he couldn't pin that kind of nature on Beth? "We have plenty of room here," he said, addressing Beth and then the group. "Room enough for all of you."

Beth removed her hat, revealing shoulder-length tresses. She glanced around the cheery room. "Oh, Paul, it's charming. I'd heard you ran your own place, but I had no idea that it was so quaint."

Paul stared at her, still broadsided. "Are you still in Vermont?"

She gingerly removed her gloves. Paul noted a wedding band was missing. "Chicago now. In advertising." Paul caught Velma beaming at him like a cat full of canary.

"So, how's old Jack holding up?" he asked. They'd all been friends in high school, but shortly into everyone's freshman college year, Beth had thrown Paul over for Jack. Paul later reasoned it had been for the best. She'd married Jack four years later, and after a while, Paul had met and fallen in love with Nancy.

Beth removed her coat, unveiling her trim, athletic figure, and hung it on the rack by the door. "Wouldn't know. We split."

"I'm sorry," Paul offered kindly.

"Don't be," she said. "It wasn't a bad breakup or anything. We just drifted."

This smelled more and more like a setup to Paul. Perhaps Beth really was innocent to it. Then again, maybe not. She had to know he'd been alone since Nancy died. And if she hadn't, Velma had surely filled her in on the details on the way in from the airport. Paul chided himself for being overly suspicious. Where was his holiday spirit, anyway?

Zach removed his snowshoes, looking around.

"Nice place, man. Thanks for taking us in.

"What is it you do, Zach?"

"Zach's a junk-metal artist!" Velma proclaimed with pride. She nuzzled up against his broad chest, then spoke in low tones. "One man's trash is another man's treasure. Right baby?"

Zach drew her into his arms. "That's right, Mama Bear."

Paul cringed, shooting Beth an embarrassed look.

Daniel entered the foyer and took in the busy scene.

"Grandma!"

"Oh now, honey," she said with a wave of her hand. "We're all a little grown-up here for that *granny* business." She wrapped her arms around her grandson and pulled him close, whispering in his ear. "Don't you worry one bit, baby. Your daddy's not moving anywhere."

Daniel flushed, noticing the nice-looking blonde who'd appeared. She looked to be about his dad's age but had kept herself very well. So well, in fact, had Daniel been older, he might even have considered her hot.

"My handle's Velma now," his grandma continued just a little too loudly. "You down with that?"

Daniel scanned the room, figuring his grandma was up to something. She typically was. "Yeah, sure. Cool."

"Zach," Velma said by way of introduction, "I'd like you to meet my grandson, Daniel." Daniel shook hands with the laid-back-looking guy, then turned his gaze on the blonde, thinking she must be his partner.

"And this is Beth Moore," Velma said, casting the woman an appreciative eye. "An *old friend* of your father's."

Daniel blinked hard. It was all sinking in. Hey, whoa. This Beth wasn't here with the hippie dude. Hippie dude was here with his grandmother! And Beth was here for what...? He eyed his matchmaking grandmother, who'd been bent on his dad getting remarried for some time now. With Paul's plans to close the inn, maybe she figured things were in a state of emergency. She didn't want her Pauly leaving Maine any more than Daniel did. Daniel hoped he hadn't done the wrong thing in advising his grandma of his dad's plans. He'd expected her to be upset, try to talk his dad out of it, maybe. He never guessed she'd show up here with some hot babe in tow!

Suddenly, a huge commotion erupted outside. There was a screeching sound, the squealing of brakes, and then the horrific noise made by metal crunching.

"What was *that*?" Beth cried with alarm.

Paul grabbed his coat off the rack. "I'd better go and see."

Paul trudged through the snow toward the large SUV turned sideways in a parking space. Twisted metal protruded from beneath its front bumper.

A pretty brunette lowered her window with a worried look. "What did I hit?" she asked with a grimace. Despite her downcast expression, Paul couldn't help but be struck by her beauty. She had large dark eyes and long dark lashes to match.

"Only my dog sled," he said in an effort to reassure her. Rather than relieved, she appeared horrified, her lightly flushed cheeks taking on a brighter hue.

"Oh my God, I killed your dog!" she cried with a gasp. She gaped at him in horror. "I'm so, so sorry. I didn't see—"

"Not my dog, lady. I just had a couple of—"

"Two? I hit *two*?" She hunkered forward over the wheel. "I think I'm going to vomit."

Beyond her, Paul spied two kids in the SUV. The boy beside her seemed to be in his early teenage years; the girl in the back was a bit younger. "Whoa, now, just calm down. It's not nearly as bad as you think!"

The kids exchanged glances, then sprang from the vehicle to survey the scene, while the woman tried to stop them. The boy stood, arms akimbo, goggling at the mutilated mess. His sister was beside him. "Wow, what was it?"

"Kids! Don't look!" the woman cried, also leaping from the SUV.

"Was it a moose?" the girl asked Paul with alarm. She looked identical to her mother, only pint-size, with two neatly braided pigtails poking out of her cap. Her panicked gaze locked on his. "She killed our Christmas moose!"

Paul heaved a breath and took in their expectant faces. "You must be the Baker family."

They stared at him numbly as the SUV's "door ajar" alarm sounded. The snow drove down harder, quickly coating the family's winter clothing.

"I'm glad you all made it here safely," he said. "But I don't want you to worry one bit. Why, you didn't hit any dogs of mine at all!" He gave what he hoped was an affable laugh, then addressed the woman, who still seemed out of sorts. "You only plowed into my beat-up old dog sled. Heck, I'd already put it out in the trash."

Relief flooded her face. "Honestly? Oh, thank"— she cast her son a sideways glance—"G!"

That was a new one to him, but he supposed she was being cautious because of the kids. He found this charming somehow. Paul extended his hand. "Paul Love, nice to meet you."

"Carol Baker."

She took his grip and froze a beat. For the first time in the midst of all the commotion, Carol noticed what an incredibly handsome man he was. He was older than she was, but not by much. Probably late thirties, with a rugged face and a smile that could melt the snow in all of Maine. Warm brown eyes danced, apparently amused—and entranced—by her.

Carol felt her face flush, and she rushed to put the conversation on safer ground. She hadn't been looked at like that by a man in a while. Or perhaps he hadn't been looking at all, and she'd simply imagined it. "And these are my kids, Will and Ashley."

"Welcome aboard, all of you," he said through the whistling winds and snow that swirled around them. "I think we'd best get inside!"

Chapter Three

Paul sent Daniel to help the others settle in upstairs while he checked Carol in at the front desk. Her kids had been all too happy to make their way to their separate quarters. From the looks of their mom, it had been a long trip. Her finely drawn features were etched with the worries of a hard day. It was no wonder too. Driving through the North Woods in a snowstorm could tax anyone. More so, someone from a southern state with less winter weather experience than a New Englander.

Carol had just signed her credit card receipt when Ashley bounded down the stairs.

"Mom! There are bears in my room!"

Carol sighed apologetically. "She's got a wild imagination."

"No! I mean it," the child persisted.

Just then, Will appeared, bounding down the steps behind his sister. "And there are foxes in mine! Seriously, Mom. It's way cool."

She turned toward Paul with a puzzled look, as he suppressed a grin. "Perhaps we should go and see?"

Ashley darted into her room as Carol trailed her, then stopped in her tracks. For once, her daughter hadn't been exaggerating. This was the most spectacular display Carol had ever seen. The room's décor was all *Black Bear*, complete with a wildlife painting over the fireplace and a huge four-poster bed with each of its posts carved into enormous claws and a bear's head sculpted into the headboard.

"Wow, this is something," Carol said, agape. She ran a hand down the exquisitely tapered frame of the bed. "Who's the artist?" she asked, turning to Paul.

He folded his arms across his chest and grinned. "Local guy. Did every room in the place."

"You mean they're all animal themed?" Carol asked, intrigued. This part hadn't been included in the brochure, which had shown just a photo of the inn from outdoors along with a shot of its large, inviting living room.

Paul nodded, then motioned for her to follow. They popped into Will's room next, which was equally grand, only in a foxy, hunt-country style.

"Let's go see Mom's!" Will said, excited.

"Is it all moose?" Ashley asked with hopeful eyes.

"Uh-uh," Paul replied with a smile. "Only *one* room in the inn sports a moose theme, and none of the guests get to see it."

Carol felt herself flush at envisioning the very handsome innkeeper's lair. She bet it was as rugged as he was, yet built for comfort like his big, sturdy arms. She blinked, wondering where that last thought had come from. A man his age was certainly married. Besides, she'd had the impression that his older teenage assistant might be his son. They had the same coloring and seemed to carry themselves in the same way, much as a father and son might do. Her kids scurried off, eager to unpack in their separate spaces. "I've got to hand it to you, Mr.—"

"Please, call me Paul."

"Paul," Carol repeated, catching her breath on the word. She couldn't tell him that her very first crush had been on the Beatle Paul McCartney, and that name always had a special effect on her.

A gorgeous blonde appeared in the doorway, holding a large bath towel. "Going to shower before dinner," she told him with a sweet look. He nodded; then his gaze trailed after her with what Carol assumed to be admiring affection. Suddenly consumed by heat, she unzipped her parka. *Naturally, the name Paul has an effect! It clearly has an effect on his wife too,* Carol thought, feeling a fool. She focused hard on the décor, hoping to give the impression that was all she'd been studying. Fantasies involving the innkeeper weren't included in the Holiday Hills package. She'd do well to get a grip and remember that. This was what she got for ignoring the teacher-workroom chatter that told her she should get back out on the dating scene just like her ex had. Truth was, she hadn't been able to imagine a way. Not with looking after little Ashley and Will and managing her job and the household besides. And anyhow, her heart hadn't been ready. It still hadn't recovered from the beating Jim had handed down, and felt the need to remind her of that time and time again. "I've never seen anything quite like this," she said, removing her scarf. "You and your wife must have had a great time decorating."

"Oh, my wife didn't..." he said with a start. "What I mean is, I did all decorating."

Carol caught herself massaging her empty ring finger and stopped, shoving her hands in her parka pockets. "So, what's in my room?" she asked looking up. The White Album began playing through her mind. "Some *Rocky Rac-coo-hoons*?" she sang before snorting a laugh. She'd tried to mimic the lines from the song but instantly realized how idiotic she'd sounded. If these polished wooden floorboards could open up and swallow her whole, now would be a good time. She folded her face in her hands, then dared to peek between splayed fingers.

Paul leaned toward her with a whisper as she inched back. He was devilishly handsome with those deep dark eyes, especially when he stood so close. "I'm afraid that room's already been taken." He twisted his lips in a wry smile. "By a die-hard Beatle's fan."

Carol's heart thumped as her throat swelled shut. He couldn't possibly know she had a fetish for all things Beatles, especially when those things were called Paul. *Paul, the very married innkeeper*, she reminded herself with a start. "Right," she squeaked. "Thought so."

Seconds later, he'd delivered her to her rabbit's den and left her standing with her suitcase by the door. She rushed inside and banged it shut, slamming her back against it. *Oh Gawd,* she thought, biting into her knuckles. *What am I? Fourteen?*

Something rapped soundly at the door. "Just so you know," Paul called from the other side, "dinner's at seven! I'll see you and the kids downstairs."

"Thanks!" Carol cried with a gulp. Now all that remained was forcing herself not to act like one of them. Or to drown her awkwardness in one too many glasses of Chablis and come out spouting "Yellow Submarine." She yanked off her hat, determined to pull herself together. She was here for the kids, after all. A wonderful family vacation. And this place was turning out to be every bit as grand as she thought it might be. The fact that Paul was drop-dead gorgeous was clearly no fault of his own. He didn't seem the stuck-up sort and probably never even thought about it. He was just a good, old-fashioned down-to-earth guy. *Which is why his lovely blonde wife loves him so much*, Carol reminded herself resolutely.

Paul strode away from Carol's room, puzzling at their exchange. She was an unusual yet enchanting woman, engaging in a way that was disarming and funny at once. Sure, she'd been acting a bit punchy, especially about the raccoon thing. But hey, she'd had a long day. Besides, he'd heard that joke before. Running a fanciful place like this one, he'd come to expect lots of animal jokes. Besides, he himself was partial to the Beatles. Though he hadn't played any of their music in years. He and Nancy had met at a Beatles Bash, in fact. It was a themed party the girls in her sorority had put together. They'd danced to some upbeat songs and then to some of the sweeter, early ballads. He'd fallen in love with her nearly at once.

Zach passed him in the hall, headed for the bath at the east end. The main drawback to this place, but one that guests had learned to live with, was the fact that there were only two upstairs bathrooms. The guests had to share, European style. Though, given the rest of the inn's grand accoutrements, none of them seemed to mind. "I think Beth's in that one," Paul said, causing Zach to stop short.

"Thanks, man," he said, turning. "Other one's…?"

"Last door on the left," Paul directed.

He descended the stairs with a spring in his step, thinking this Christmas vacation was turning out to be more interesting than he could have imagined. He hadn't considered becoming involved with a woman in ages, and now two terribly attractive—and single ones—had appeared on his doorstep. Not that Carol Baker was any kind of option. He'd never yet hit on a guest, and it would be highly unprofessional of him to start now. Of course, Beth was a guest in a way too, but in a larger respect, she really wasn't. She was more of an old friend he was helping out in difficult circumstances. That clearly meant he shouldn't be taking advantage of her situation either. Paul heaved a breath, thinking he needed to get his head in order. He had things to organize for the evening meal and other preparations to make as well. For everyone who came to the Love Inn at Christmastime arrived with one primary expectation: to have a memorable, fun-filled holiday. That was something Paul felt comfortable in ensuring. He'd do well to leave thoughts of shoring up his beaten-down heart out of it. Heck, he'd be moving to Montreal by this time next year, anyway.

Beth lathered her hair, pondering this gift of the fates. While her cancelled flight to O'Hare was anticipated, given the weather, running into Velma and Zach at the gate had been a genuine surprise. Getting invited to come back here had been even more unexpected. Paul had been her first, wonderful love. Naturally, she'd thought of him from time to time over the years. Especially after things ran cold with Jack, she couldn't help but wonder if she'd made a mistake. While they'd all been friends in high school, somehow, going away to their separate universities had changed things. Goofball Jack had become more confident, morphing from a gangly teenager into a disarming and dashing young man. Ready to sweep her off her feet with his charm and good looks. Having been a high school beauty, Beth had become unsure of herself in her new coed world. Ever-stable Paul was really the only one of them who hadn't seen the rush to reinvent himself in college. He'd always been focused and mature, maybe more mature than she'd been ready for or had completely understood at the time.

To her, Paul had appeared so predictable, unwilling to take chances and spread his wings. Jack wanted to get away and start over, far from their families and homegrown expectations. That had proved extra appealing to Beth, who couldn't imagine going home again after her four years at Wellesley. Always having been good with his hands, Paul had long ago set his sights on this place, here. It had been foreclosed on when they were still kids, but he'd made a vow to restore and reopen it, even if he had to do most of the grunt work himself—which he apparently had, shortly after saving up funds from his student jobs and majoring in business. His new girlfriend, Nancy, had wholeheartedly supported his dreams. She'd been his partner and his helpmate, until a car accident had taken her unexpectedly shortly after the two of them had opened the inn they'd worked for years to lovingly craft together.

Beth shut off the water, thinking she'd heard something. She was quite sure she'd locked the door, but the way the latch went seemed backwards to her, so perhaps she hadn't set it right. She'd tried the other bathroom first, but the door had either been locked from the inside or set so snugly in its frame she couldn't budge it open, no matter how hard she tugged. Giving up, she'd opted to try this bathroom here, where the door opened much more easily. Too easily, she thought with a start, as a cool blast of air invaded her warm space. She heard bright whistling and lunged for a towel as a ponytailed man pulled back the curtain with a jerk.

"Ack!" he shouted, falling back in shock as Beth shrieked at the top of her lungs. Seconds later, the other inn guests flooded the hall.

Beyond the open door at Zach's back, Velma stood clutching a container of Ageless Skin Cream, her jaw dropping.

Zach sat on the bed with Velma, his arm around her shoulder. She still clutched her open jar of face cream in shock.

"You're getting way too keyed up about this," he told her. "It was nothing, I swear."

"Of course, I know you're right. It's just that... Zach!" She capped her cold cream, turning toward him. "She was right there with you—in a towel!"

"It was more like a washcloth, really. Pretty tiny, actually," he teased.

"Enough!" She fell back on the bed with a moan.

He smiled sympathetically and patted her thigh through her bell-bottom jeans. "You're not jealous?"

She raised her head to look at him. "Who me? Of a woman thirty years younger, half naked in a bathroom with you?"

He scooted down on the bed beside her, taking her hand. "You, Mama Bear, have nothing to worry about."

"No?" she asked, lines creasing her face.

"Do you know who I fell in love with?" he asked,

turning toward her.

"A cougar?" she asked, dark eyes widening.

Zach gave a low chuckle, then brushed his lips to hers. "I fell in love with the woman in here," he said, laying a hand on her heart. "And that woman," he said with another kiss, "is the best-looking babe in all of Maine. I'm talking about at any age."

She sighed and smiled up at him. "You really are the cat's pajamas, you know that?"

"Meow," he said, closing in for another kiss.

"Zach?" she asked a moment later. "How do you think things are going with Beth and Paul?"

"She just got here!"

"I know, but still… Do you think there's a chance?"

"I think there's a good one," he said with a wink.

She playfully tugged him toward her. "It's a shame Pauly put us in separate rooms."

"Probably because there are kids here."

"No, it's because my son's an old stick-in-the-mud."

He thumbed her nose. "Be nice now, and get dressed for dinner."

Carol exited the Rabbit Room all freshened up. Unsure of the protocol in a place like this, she'd worn a short black dress, leather boots, and a suede jacket. Something a little dressed up, but casual just the same. She shut her door firmly, then turned, nearly colliding with Paul. He was dapperly handsome, well turned-out in a sports coat and tie. It was hard to say which way he looked best, like this, the preppie sophisticate, or like he had earlier this evening, dressed down in a flannel shirt and jeans. He quickly shut the door behind him, but not in time to conceal his room's marvelous moose theme. When she'd checked in, Carol hadn't realized her room was straight across the hall from his. All at once she felt like she'd shacked up with the Huntsman in some wild wilderness tale. He was so rugged and easily in charge, in a faraway land like this one. She found herself wondering briefly if she should have worn a red hooded cape. Then she realized with a jolt she was already bathed in that color from head to toe from blushing so hard.

He smiled warmly, brown eyes twinkling.

"After you," he said, motioning for her to move ahead.

"I uh…" *Very…married,* she told herself, counting to three. And an innkeeper merely looking after his guests, besides. His pretty wife was likely in their Moose Room, still getting ready. "I'm just going to check on the kids! We'll see you downstairs." Carol made a vow to investigate online dating the moment she and the kids got home. Things really had gotten out of hand if she couldn't take a simple New England holiday without crushing on the first handsome face she came across. Maybe her coworkers were right and enough time *had* gone by for her to stick her big toe in the dating waters. She didn't have to get into anything heavy. She might even find a friend to enjoy some casual outings with. But even that seemed scary when she couldn't be certain what kind of *friend* that person might be. Maybe a lunatic or a psychopath, or some sort of sick predator after her children! Carol drew a breath, deciding Internet dating didn't sound right for her. Maybe she should wait until the kids were grown and had gone off to college before she started thinking about herself.

She was just outside Ashley's room when another door opened down the hall, and Paul walked by. "Don't you look lovely," he said to the beautiful blonde who—wait a minute—was staying in another room? Carol hoped they hadn't caught her glancing their way as they exchanged amiable chatter and headed down the stairs together. If the blonde was a guest rather than Paul's wife, they still seemed awfully familiar with each other. Perhaps she was a regular here, and maybe Paul wasn't married at all. But what did that matter to Carol? She had more immediate things to think about, like corralling her kids and getting them to dinner on time.

Daniel ran a thumb down Amy's damp cheek, then threaded his fingers through her short, raven hair. Her nearly black eyes welled with tears as she and Daniel stood in the pantry where they'd gone to collect dinner supplies.

"How can you say that, Danny?" she said, her voice cracking. "Can't you see there's no point?"

Daniel took her in his arms, cradling her up against him. "Hey, hey… That's not true. Listen up, Amy I already told you I have a plan. Grandma's in on it too."

"Velma?" she asked with a sniff. She wore smart black slacks with a matching man's tie, draping down a crisp, white, button-down shirt.

He centered his gaze on hers. "You've got to know she doesn't want Dad leaving here any more than we do."

"Does this have to do with the old flame?"

"It might."

"I thought the airport was a coincidence."

"It was. And so much better than Grandma's plan A."

"What was plan A?"

"Introducing Dad to Zach's little sister."

"Ew! How old is Zach's little sister?"

"Not *that* young. In her thirties, I think." He jostled her in his arms. "The great part is, this way's so much better. It's like fate was helping us along."

"I suppose."

"Why do you sound so doubtful?"

"Are you sure you should go meddling in your dad's love life, Danny? He's bound not to like it if he finds out."

"Who says he has to? Besides, getting a girlfriend will be good for the old man."

"Good, how?"

"It will distract him, you know. Make him feel young again, not like some old guy putting himself out to pasture."

"I thought he was buying a condo in Montreal?"

"You're missing my point."

"Which is?"

"Once my dad has a life again, he won't go chasing greener pastures in Canada. He'll be happy staying right here!"

"But whether he's here or there, it's all the same. You'll be gone eight months out of the year."

He held her tighter, pressing his forehead to hers. "Seven months, three weeks, and two days, exactly."

She sighed in his arms. "You counted?"

He looked at her deeply, lost in her beautiful dark eyes. "Of course, I counted. Listen up, Amy Littleton.

This thing is going to work out for us, okay? One way or another, it's working out."

"This isn't just about me—or your dad—is it?" she asked astutely.

"What do you mean?"

"You don't want your dad selling the inn because it doesn't just belong to him and you; it was your mom's place too."

"Yeah, and she loved it. Wanted to see me grow up and get married here."

"Married?"

"Not any time soon," he stammered. "I mean, some day."

She gave him a soft smile. "Yeah, some day."

"I love you," he whispered, leaning forward.

"I love you too."

Chapter Four

When Carol and her kids entered the dining room, she was struck at once by their setting's beauty. Intimate tables adorned the room; each afforded a view through the magnificent bay window. Towering pines and rolling mountaintops surrounded frozen Moosehead Lake, ringed by a fairy-tale-like string of winter lanterns skimming its perimeter. An empty skating rink by a big, brown barn only added to the scene's magical appeal.

Daniel seated them at a table set for three in the corner while the pretty blonde dined solo nearby. Carol was certain now she must be a guest. She wouldn't be seated in here otherwise. Will's cell buzzed, and he took it from his pocket.

Carol narrowed her eyes at her son. "Not *here.*"

He grumpily tucked the cell away, causing Carol to flinch inside. He was perpetually on that phone, but she thought she'd taught him better than to use it at the table.

"Your server, Amy, will be with you in a moment," Daniel said, handing them each a menu.

Carol accepted hers just as Paul entered the room. Suddenly, her world went all woozy, as if she'd had too much wine. He approached them as she sat there dumbstruck, wishing to goodness he wouldn't smile. For when he did, it sent all sorts of wild butterflies fluttering inside her, just like some crushed-out high school kid.

"Miss?" Daniel asked, apparently having offered her some drink choices.

"Might I suggest the Crestwood chardonnay?" Paul offered helpfully. "Or, if you prefer red, the Millhouse merlot?"

Carol focused on her menu but couldn't make out a bit of it. "I… um…"

Paul's face warmed in a smile as he gently took the menu from her hands, then righted it. Carol was mortified. She'd been reading it upside down. Her kids exchanged startled glances as she stared red-faced at Paul. In his effort to correct her menu, he'd revealed something else. He didn't wear a wedding band. Carol swallowed hard, thinking maybe she shouldn't have any wine at all. She was apparently drunk enough on the mountain air. "The merlot sounds great, thanks."

Daniel disappeared to get the wine as Paul's dark eyes twinkled. "Excellent choice."

Carol smiled tightly, hoping she wouldn't need to make too many other choices tonight. She wasn't sure she could handle it. Especially with Paul standing this near. She needed him to back away—just slightly—so she could decide on the chicken or the veal.

"Mom? All you all right?" Will asked her.

She realized she'd been furiously fanning her face with her menu and stopped.

"If you're too warm, I can move you to table farther from the fire?"

"Oh no," she said, setting her menu aside, "this is perfect! Just great."

Paul studied them all pleasantly. "Do you have plans for tomorrow? Can I help you arrange something?"

"I thought we'd go skiing," Carol said.

"Great thought. We packed in twenty more

inches of powder today."

"Twenty?" Will asked.

"For real?" Ashley chimed in.

Paul nodded. "Big Moose Mountain is right up the way. I know an instructor who can give you a lift in the morning…?"

Carol beamed. "That would be terrific. Wouldn't it, kids?"

"Yeah, cool," Will said.

"Really super," Ashley added with a smile.

"Perfect, then. Skiing for the Bakers is on the agenda."

A pretty teenage girl arrived with a notepad, and Paul graciously stepped aside. "I'll leave Amy to take your orders," he said. "Enjoy."

Paul straightened his tie, hoping to goodness he'd sounded as professional as he'd intended. While he wasn't supposed to take a personal interest in his guests, he'd found it impossible not to notice Carol's sweet demeanor, or the delightful way with which she'd studied her menu upside-down. He'd had the impression she'd been nervous, but hadn't a clue why. Perhaps the atmosphere seemed a bit stuffier than she was used to, although that hadn't been Paul's intention. He liked to keep things upscale yet casual for his clientele, because that was how they apparently liked it. Dinner was always the most formal occasion of the day, but drinks afterward were decidedly down-home. He'd have to be sure to include her and her kids in his customary invitation to gather by the living room fire for hot cocoa or other libations. Maybe he could enlist Daniel's help in making the kids feel more comfortable too.

He crossed to the small two-top where Beth was seated, caught off guard once again by her beauty. Then again, she'd once turned that beauty against him and run off with his best friend… Paul collected himself, understanding that was years ago and that times and people change. Heck, Beth and he were little more than Amy's and Daniel's ages when they'd split up and gone their separate ways. He couldn't be so harsh as to hold her accountable now for something that happened so long ago. They'd both crossed a lot of bridges since then, some of them terribly sad ones, it seemed.

"I'm happy to arrange for you to sit with some of the other guests," he said. "I'm sure my mom and Zach will be down soon."

She shot him a brave smile. "I've never been afraid to go it alone."

"There's something to be said for independence," Paul agreed.

"Something, indeed." She took a sip of her wine. "Although there's something to be said for partnerships too."

"Two heads can be better than one."

"Sometimes, so are two hearts."

Paul's pulse picked up a notch. *Surely I didn't hear her right.*

"Paul," she said softly. She extended a hand, laying it on his forearm. "I'm really sorry about Nancy. I only recently heard."

"Thanks, Beth. I appreciate that."

"How are you holding up? Doing okay?"

He stared into stunning blue eyes lined with compassion.

"It's been several years. Time moves on."

She withdrew her hand but kept him in her gaze.

"Yes. Yes, it does. I'm just sorry that we lost touch. If I had… I mean, if Jack and I had known—"

"Naturally, you couldn't have," he said, backing away. Paul couldn't bear extended sympathy. It was one thing to offer *I'm sorry*. Quite another to dwell on things until one pressed old hurts back up to the surface.

Beth looked pained but forced a smile.

"It's good seeing you again, Paul."

"Yeah, you too," he said, studying her eyes. It was hard to forget the way they'd been together all those years ago. Inseparable, and so in love, like crazy teenage kids can be in high school.

"I'd really love a chance to talk sometime," she said. "You know, hear about what you've been up to."

"I'd like that."

A little later, Carol polished off her delicious chocolate dessert, thinking what a nice evening it had been. Even her kids had been behaving, at least reasonably well. She'd noticed Paul lingering by the pretty blonde's table for quite a while during dinner. While he, of course, might have just been checking on a guest, their exchange had seemed more personal. Especially the way the woman had appeared to admire him with affection each time he'd turned his handsome face her way.

"I trust everything was to your liking?" Paul asked, startling Carol out of her reverie.

She nearly choked on her wine, and she quickly set it down. "Oh yes, just fine. The dinner was delicious, thank you. My compliments to the chef."

He tilted his chin with a pleased smile. "I thank you very much."

"Wait a minute," Carol said, surprised. "You mean, you're the cook too?"

"That's weird," Will said under his breath.

"Not weird, you throwback," Ashley quipped. "That's modern."

Carol sent them both a silencing look as her cheeks flamed. "I'm sorry," she apologized to Paul.

He chuckled good-naturedly. "Quite all right. The Baker family would not be among the first I've surprised with my culinary skill." He glanced across the way at the blonde who typed on her smart phone, then clapped his hands together, addressing Carol. "We here at the inn have a special tradition. Each evening after dinner, the guests are invited to convene by the fire with the drink of their choice. We have wine, more merlot if you'd like," he said to Carol. "Cocoa..." he continued, looking at the kids.

"With marshmallows?" Ashley asked.

"As many as you'd like!"

Will slunk down in his chair, obviously bored. There were likely a million things a young teenage boy would rather do than hang out with a bunch of old folks around a fire. And Paul, being the wise man he was, knew one of them. "Plus," he said, addressing Will, "Daniel's thrown down the challenge to take anyone on in a game."

Will scooted up in his chair at attention.

Right on cue, Daniel appeared at Paul's side. "Guitar Hero, anyone?" he asked with a grin.

"You're on!" Will said, seeming delighted.

Across the room, the blonde stood and slipped from the room.

"I'll be seeing you later?" Paul asked Carol.

She felt the warmth in her cheeks in spite of herself. "That would be nice. Thank you."

Paul stopped Beth when she was nearly to the stairs. "Leaving so soon? I was hoping you'd join the others by the fire."

She sighed, her face falling. "I'm sorry, Paul. I wish I could stay. The truth is, I'm not feeling so hot."

He studied her with concern. "Is there something I can…?"

"Oh no. No, thanks. It's just a migraine. I get them from time to time."

"I know how debilitating those can be. Nancy used to get them too."

"I just need to take a pill and chill for a while."

He nodded with sympathy. "Feel better."

She brought her hand to his cheek. "You really are a very good man. That part hasn't changed."

"Thanks, Beth," he said hoarsely.

"See you tomorrow?" She looked into his eyes.

His Adam's apple rose in his throat. "I look forward to it."

Paul watched her walk slowly up the stairs, wondering what was becoming of him. Could it be that the old feelings he had for Beth were starting to resurface? Or, was it more that he'd been alone so long that the attentions of any beautiful woman would tug on his heartstrings?

One way or another, it didn't really matter, did it? He was halfway through his life and certainly not in the market for romance. All he needed to focus on now was seeing this inn through its final holiday

season as successfully as he could. Daniel was leaving for college soon, and Paul would be starting his new life in Montreal. Tons of great fishing and lots of peaceful sunsets were coming his way. Those would be plenty to keep him company.

Carol set down her merlot, thinking maybe she shouldn't have accepted the second glass. She felt light-headed enough from their exhausting journey and trying drive through the North Woods.

"What keeps you busy in Virginia?" Velma asked. She wore a flower-patterned blouse with a complementary indigo headband. Carol had just recently gathered that she was Paul's mom, so she had to be in her sixties, though her dress and demeanor indicated otherwise. She certainly had a much younger boyfriend on her arm, but it was clear they were companionable and comfortable in each other's company.

"I'm a schoolteacher," Carol answered. "Ninth grade English."

"That's a tough subject," Zach said.

"And we're grateful to have folks like you out there doing it," Paul added, offering to refill her wine.

She declined with a shake of her head. "I don't think I'd better. Two's my limit."

"It's good to know your limits," Paul said, his dark eyes dancing. Carol's breath caught in her throat. She knew he was just being congenial, but when he sat this close—just on the other end of the sofa—she found it hard to concentrate. She tried to remember the last time she'd even been on a sofa with a man, but somehow couldn't recall. She really had built a more sequestered life for herself than she'd realized.

She leaned toward Ashley, who was contentedly working a jigsaw puzzle on the large coffee table, an empty cocoa mug at her elbow. "Honey, I think it's time you got ready for bed."

The little girl rose reluctantly as strains of Guitar Hero wailed from the next room. "What about Will?"

"He'll be up in a bit," Carol said with a kind smile. "He is a little older, you know."

Ashley politely told everyone good night, then sadly traipsed up the stairs.

"Cute kid," Zach said. "I never had those kinds of manners at her age."

"Yeah, and you're still working on them now," Velma teased.

"Oh, now, Mama Bear." He leaned forward to nuzzle her neck, and Paul blinked hard.

"I'm awfully glad we could fit your family in," he told Carol.

"Me too," she agreed. "It's good we got here when we did. The weather only seems to be getting worse." As if to accentuate her point, winds howled outdoors, shaking the storm shutters.

"Or better!" Paul said. "Depending on how you look at it." There was a twinkle in his eye that caught the firelight. "You are having your first skiing lesson tomorrow."

Ashley surprised them all by dashing down the stairs. "Mom!" she cried, her cheeks bright pink. "I saw it! I actually saw it!"

Carol stood with alarm, taking her daughter in her arms. "Saw what, honey?"

"My moose! My real live Christmas moose!"

Carol ran a hand through her hair with a sigh. "Now, Ashley…"

"I mean it, Mom," the child protested. "It was there!"

"Where?" Paul asked.

"What's going on?" Daniel asked, resurfacing from the back room with Will.

"Ashley saw a Christmas moose," Carol explained calmly.

"O... M..." Will began.

Carol shot him a look.

"But Mom, she's making things up again!"

Ashley's chin trembled. "Why won't anyone believe me?" With that, she turned and dashed up the stairs.

"I'm sorry," Carol told the others. "I'd better go to her."

When Carol entered the Bear Room, Ashley stood weeping by the window.

"What are you doing, baby?" Carol asked, walking to her.

"Watching my moose run away." Ashley sniffed. "You all made fun of him, so he ran away!"

"Oh now, honey. I'm sure you thought you saw something, and maybe it even *was* a real moose—"

"It was a *Christmas moose*. A big one with lanterns!"

Carol studied her doubtfully. "Antlers?"

"I swear, Mom." Ashley's dark eyes were insistent. "It was, like, glowing and everything! Why won't you believe me?"

"I believe that you believe," Carol said kindly.

"That's not the same thing."

Carol pulled her daughter into a hug and held her close.

"Let's try to get some rest now. Tomorrow is another day." She pulled back to look her daughter in the eye. "A very exciting one at that. The Baker family's going skiing!"

Ashley raised her brow. "Yeah, that will be cool."

Carol pulled Ashley's pajamas from a drawer and the girl reluctantly removed her clothes and tugged them on.

She lightly patted her daughter's head. "Now, go on. Hop into bed."

Ashley scurried to the huge bear bed and scooted down under the covers. Carol gave her a kiss and switched off the light, but not before catching the glimmer of something in the window. Something bright beamed from the deep woods for a flash of a second, and then it was gone. Now Carol was extra glad she'd stopped at that second glass of wine. Next, she'd be seeing reindeers!

Carol was halfway to the landing when she ran into Paul. "Everything all right up there?" he asked.

"Oh yes, just fine." She heaved a sigh. "It's just been a long day for all of us. For Ashley too, it seems."

Paul raised his brow, questioning.

"She's had this fixation all along about some kind of Christmas moose…"

"We do have moose here, you know."

"Not the kind she's looking for."

Paul gave her a knowing smile. "She's mixed in a bit of magic?"

"More than a bit," Carol said with a laugh.

Paul's eyes brimmed with understanding. "She's

just a girl."

"Yes, and straddling that line between real and make-believe."

"Some of us never outgrow it." By the way he said it, Carol had the notion he was talking more about himself than Ashley. He looked deep in her eyes as if trying to discern something, and Carol felt weak from his perusal. "It's not so bad to believe in fun stuff, Carol. Once in a while."

They were standing very close now, closer than Carol had realized in the small space on the landing. She was near enough to breathe him in, the manly scent of sawdust and pine. Even in his dinner jacket and tie, the words *rugged outdoorsman* seemed etched in his handsome face.

"Paul?" a soft, feminine voice asked from above them. "Can I trouble you for a soda?"

Carol stared up the steps to find the beautiful blonde dressed in a robe. Paul had told the others she wasn't feeling well, and, judging from the paleness of her skin, she hadn't much improved.

"Beth," he said, turning toward her in surprise. "Of course."

Carol made her way down the stairs in front of him, awkward in her gait. What had she been thinking? That Paul might feel attracted to her too? She grabbed hold of the railing, nearly stumbling.

Paul caught her by the elbow to steady her. "Watch your step!"

Carol collected herself, determining that was just what she would do. Watch her step every step of the way here, lest she make an utter fool of herself in front of the innkeeper.

Chapter Five

Carol's skis splayed out sideways as she fought to stabilize herself on the slick snow. Paul couldn't help but be captivated by her apparent winter sports naiveté. Her kids seemed much more confident on the slopes and were already passing high above her in a chairlift, complete with hoots and hollers. "Hey, Mom!" Will called before his sister added, "Come on up, the weather's fine!"

Carol hunched forward with a death grip on her poles. "I don't know if I can do this," she said, her breath coming out all puffy with morning cold.

Paul smiled encouragingly. "Sure, you can."

Beth adjusted her dark goggles beside him. "Just like riding a bike."

"But I've never skied before," she said, inching forward.

Paul drew closer to help her along. "Always a first time."

Was it his imagination, or did Beth seem to stiffen at his lending Carol assistance? It was clearly his duty as her host, as well as her skiing instructor. Beth, on the other hand, needed no instruction whatsoever. She was practically pro level, exceedingly at home on the slopes.

Beth slid into the chairlift, then seemed disappointed Paul hoped to position Carol between them. Well, he certainly couldn't leave Carol standing out here on her own while he climbed in ahead. Who knew where she'd wind up. Likely at the base of the Bunny Hill.

Paul clambered aboard and brought the gate down in front of them.

"This thing goes up pretty high, huh?" Carol asked with a worried look.

"If I were you, I'd be more concerned about coming down," Beth said in a tone that was slightly… What? Catty? Beth? His Beth? No. That didn't seem right. Beth was somebody who'd always been one hundred percent sure of herself. It wasn't like her to dig at other people. Unless… Paul felt his neck warm as he thought about what a fool he'd been. *Jealous? Beth is jealous? Of a guest?*

Paul's gaze fell on Carol, and she stared back at him. "You'll do just fine."

"Yeah, right," she said, her voice cracking.

Paul's mind reeled. Beth couldn't possibly be jealous of Carol, a woman he barely knew. Never mind that she was smart, spunky, and funny… And had the most beautiful brown eyes he'd ever seen. They were mesmerizing, really, in a way that could hold any man in their spell.

She peered down the slope at two figures whizzing by, laughing and shouting. "Hey, are those my kids?"

"Looks like," Paul said.

"Wow, they're good!"

"When you're a kid, you don't worry about the danger," Beth chimed in.

"Danger?"

Beth adjusted her grip on her poles. "Normal stuff. There are always a few accidents every year. Some are worse than others."

"Thanks, Beth," Paul said tightly.

Carol's eyes widened as they approached the top

of the slope. She obviously wasn't prepared for the fact that she had to ski out of her chair.

"You mean, just like *that*?" she asked with a gasp, surveying the others ahead of them easily dismounting and skiing downhill. Her gaze trailed the empty lift chairs in horror, noting the seats had dropped out of them and dangled freely during their descent to release collected snow. "You're kidding me, right?" Carol asked in a panic. She turned to Paul and then to Beth. "Please tell me that you're kidding me?"

"Take it nice and easy," Paul said, slipping out ahead of her and then pulling off to the side at the top of a steep precipice.

Since she was frozen in place, Beth gave her a little shove. "Take care with your exit!"

Suddenly, Carol's whole life flashed before her, and it was all coated in white. "Oh! Whoa!" She yelped as Beth whizzed past her in a puff of powder, and her skis took on a mind of their own. Carol held on to the sidebar of the chairlift for dear life, not wanting to let go. But the beast was dragging her along, threatening to pull her straight off a cliff!

"Carol!" Paul called. "Look out!"

She pivoted in time to see the next seat full of passengers swinging toward her, its skiers preparing to dismount. "Arghh!" she cried, skis scrambling beneath her. Paul darted toward her as Beth halted quickly and turned their way.

"Let go!" he shouted, seconds before she was dragged off the edge.

Then, with a thunk, Carol's back hit the ice, and she slid under a small brown shack. *Tell me I did not just do that*, she thought, staring up at the slats of the ski-patrol hut.

Paul raced to the building and peered underneath. "Are you all right?" he asked with a worried frown.

Beth's blue-eyed gaze studied her with concern a few seconds later. "What happened?"

Carol covered her face with her hands, believing this scored as one of her most mortifying moments. "I'll live," she said, inchworming her way out into the open.

Paul sent Beth down ahead to check on the kids while he stayed at the top of the slope with Carol. The ski-patrol guy had just checked her out, and she appeared to be okay, merely frightened by her unnerving experience.

"I'm really sorry that happened," Paul said as the other man resumed his post. "Nothing like that has ever—"

"It's okay," Carol said, stopping him. "It wasn't really your fault."

He heaved a breath. "I don't know... Maybe it was. If I'd truly understood how unsteady you were—"

"Wait a minute!" Her eyes flashed. "I'm not unsteady!"

"On the slopes, I meant."

"I think I can handle those too." She drew a deep breath. "It's just that before, I wasn't ready." Carol was so embarrassed by all the trouble she'd caused, she couldn't have things getting worse. The best thing to do would be to forge right ahead with the rest of this day, as if this horrifying episode had never happened.

"Maybe I should go back to the hut and have him arrange a transport down."

Carol straightened herself on her skis. "I wouldn't hear of it."

He stared at her, clearly perplexed.

"I just got off to a false start. That's all. Now I'm ready."

"If you're sure?"

"Sure I'm sure." She beamed at him with what she hoped was a bright, confident smile. The truth was, Carol was tired of people telling her what she couldn't do. Jim had thought it was ridiculous she was taking her kids skiing in Maine, had he? Well, she could show him and his little beach bunny too. Not only that, she could show herself! After all, how hard could it be? She edged toward the top of the steep slope and looked down, praying she wouldn't faint from the altitude.

"How high up are we?" she asked as little lights darted before her eyes.

"I'm calling for backup."

"Oh no, you don't!" she said. And then quite decisively, she thought, she took off. Suddenly, she was going—really going—so much faster than she ever could have imagined. *"Oh my Gawd!"* she wailed in terror as bright flashes of white tore past her along with dark patches of trees and tiny spots she took to be other people.

"Carol!" Paul called, chasing after her. "Hoe plow!"

Hoe plow? She had no clue what that was, but it sounded dirty. How dare Paul think of pole dancing right now when his guest's life—*her life*—was on the line!

He skied up beside her, somehow magically in control of his own rapid descent. "Snow plow, Carol! Push your heels out sideways!"

Snow plow! Of course, she knew all along what he'd meant. She did it at once, and it seemed to work too. At least a tad in slowing her down. But wait! What was that? Paul had somehow gotten past her and was now directly in front of her. What on earth was he doing? He slowed himself further, but she couldn't break her speed any more than she already had.

"Coming through!" she cried with a wail, beelining straight for his back. The next thing she knew, she'd slammed into his broad, solid frame with a *thwunk* and dropped her poles. He reached back to steady her against him with one arm as he continued to stabilize their descent with the other.

"Just hang on to me!" he ordered as wind, snow and nature swirled about them.

Carol looked down to find her skis had nestled inside both of his and that they were now somehow locked together.

"Don't look now," he shouted. "Here comes a mogul!"

"*What?*"

"Hold tight!" he commanded, seconds before they went airborne.

Carol shrieked as her skis left the slope and dangled in midair. In a flash, they were down again and careening toward the base of the hill, her arms laced firmly around him as her heart beat wildly.

Once they were clearly out of harm's way and slowing to a halt at the bottom, he called over his shoulder with a grin. "Having fun yet?"

"Uh-huh," she said lamely, exhilarated yet depleted at once. "Just don't make me do that again."

He gave a hearty laugh, then dragged them to stop, where the crowd that had gathered burst into applause. "Sorry folks," he told them, holding up a pole. "No encores today!"

Chapter Six

Paul brought Carol a mug of coffee as she sat wrapped in a blanket by the fire. "I can't believe it," she said, still a tad ashen. "I was flying! Up in the air, like a bird!"

Beth settled herself in a nearby chair and studied Carol sympathetically. "Some people take longer to get the hang of it than others."

Paul sat beside Carol on the sofa. "It was an adventure," he said with a grin. "Frankly, the best one I've had…in a long time."

"Really?" Carol asked with surprise.

She looked so sweet bundled up that way, Paul had to fight the urge to reach out and hug her. But that would be ridiculous, wouldn't it? Hugging one of the guests? Even if it had been an unexpected treat being linked together on the slopes, there was no indication Carol would be eager to repeat it. And just because it had felt like heaven having her arms around him, that didn't mean he longed for her to do it again. Besides, she'd been in a fit of panic, desperation, and he'd merely been her appointed protector. There clearly had been nothing romantic about their exchange. Not that Paul was courting romance at the moment. Far from it. Beth eyed him in an odd sort of way that made him wonder if she'd guessed what he'd been thinking.

Velma entered, dressed for outdoors. "Did you kids have fun on the slopes?" she asked as Zach trailed her in a heavy down parka and boots.

"Mom only went down once," Ashley

proclaimed, arriving from the kitchen with her cocoa.

Will joined the group with his own steaming mug. "But it was once to remember."

Zach and Velma exchanged puzzled glances.

"Where are you two headed?" Paul asked his mom.

"We thought we'd go into town," Zach offered.

Velma smiled brightly. "Rent a couple of snowmobiles."

"Sounds great," Beth said.

"The lake is really ripe for riding," Paul agreed.

"You two have fun!" Carol called after them.

The next few days passed with more fun, yet less harrowing, family adventures. Carol and her kids explored the small town, taking in its quaint shops and eateries, and they'd even gone ice skating—and built a snowman or two. Little by little, they'd all become more acquainted with the others, especially Paul. He was always around with a helpful tidbit or the offer of some small comfort. He was a kind and considerate man, the sort Carol could find herself getting used to. He was exceedingly competent too, and appeared to have a really good relationship with Daniel. Carol's heart felt heavy from wishing her son could have that sort of relationship with his own dad. Sadly, she realized that was unlikely to happen. Particularly if Jim continued on his course of mostly looking after himself.

She rapped lightly at Will's door, deciding to check on him before dinner. Ashley had been happily engaged in a game of checkers with Velma by the fire, but her boy had been holed up in his room all afternoon. Despite all the fun family times they'd shared, he'd spent an inordinate amount of time in there. Then again, perhaps that was par for the course, given that he was a teenager.

Will told her to come in, and she entered to find him leaning against the fox headboard, cell phone in hand. He appeared to be texting once again.

"You're on that thing all day long."

"Everybody my age does it, Mom." He cocked his head sideways. "It's not like it's something dirty."

His phone buzzed again, and he checked it.

"That's what I mean," she went on. "It's constant."

"I was out of touch all morning," he said. "There's catching up to do."

"With whom?"

He shrugged and tucked away the phone, which buzzed anyway. "Why do you care who I talk to?"

"Because I'm your mother," she said firmly. "And I care about you." She sat beside him, then added more softly. "That's what a good parent does, Will."

He looked pensive a moment, gloomy. "You mean, like Dad?" he asked, meeting her eyes.

Carol's heart sank. "Oh, Will. I'm so sorry about your dad. Really I am. You don't know how much I wish—"

"It's not your fault." He hung his head. "I know he always missed your birthday too."

Tears caught in throat, but she willed her way past them to speak. "How do you know that?"

He looked up, pain streaking his eyes. "Ashley's not old enough to remember, but I am."

"It's all right," she said resolutely. "*I'm* an adult, I can take it, but you—"

He stopped her by touching her arm. "No, Mom. It's not all right. Can't you see? The way that Dad treated all of us wasn't right at all. It doesn't have to be that way. Not all guys are like that."

Carol studied him, holding in her tears. Who was this young man on the scene, and who had taken away her little boy? "You've been thinking about this a lot, haven't you?"

"I'm growing up. I see things."

"Oh? What do you see?"

He studied her for a beat. "I think Mr. Love likes you."

She inhaled in shock. "Me? What makes you say that?"

"Come on, Mom." His lips creased in a subtle smile. "I've seen the way he looks at you."

"How's that?"

"I guess it's a lot like the way I look at Amanda."

"*Amanda?*"

Will's cell buzzed in his pocket, and Carol finally made the connection. No wonder Will was sneaking peeks at his phone all the time. The boy had a girlfriend!

"She's nice, Mom. Really. Don't freak too much about it, okay? We're just friends."

"Sure, right. That's what I thought," she said. But then she couldn't stop herself. "I don't suppose you have a picture?"

Downstairs in the foyer, Daniel approached Paul, who was doing paperwork at the front desk. On the front porch beyond them, wild winds raked the front of the house. It was Christmas Eve, and they were in for yet another storm. "Yes, son?" Paul said, setting his stack of bill receipts aside.

"Weather's picking up out there," Daniel said, peering through the front-door window.

"That it is," Paul said, studying his son, who seemed to be acting slightly suspicious, though Paul couldn't fathom why.

"So bad, in fact, that the roads might be bad driving later."

"Which is why it's good everyone we know has four-wheel drive."

"Yeah, but Amy's car is older. Not so great on the ice."

"Amy?" Paul narrowed his eyes, wondering where this topic was going. "Just what are you getting at, Daniel?"

"Just that, with the weather being dicey and all..." The boy cleared his throat, then squared his shoulders a bit. "I was thinking it might be best if Amy slept over."

Paul raised a hand and mimicked cleaning out his ear. "I'm sure I didn't hear you right."

"It will be after ten by the time we clean up dinner."

Daniel rarely pressed him, so maybe he wasn't prepared for the pushback. "Well then, maybe this year we can handle it without her."

Daniel sighed, his face sagging. "I wasn't even suggesting she stay in my room."

"Let's hope not."

"Please, Dad. I want to spend some time on Christmas Eve with my best girl. If she has to drive home after we clean up dinner, we'll get almost no time together at all. Besides, it really will be dangerous." He pressed his palms together with a pleading look. "Her mom already said yes."

"Her what?" Paul sputtered. He sure didn't like the sound of this, Amy staying over upstairs. Then again, they did have an extra room, and Paul would never forgive himself if something happened to her on her way home. The truth was, Amy had become as much a part of things in their Christmas Eve tradition as their revolving door of colorful guests was. She'd become a fixture here, with her bright and cheery face and happy disposition. She was a nice girl, bright too. Paul could have picked many a worse girlfriend for his son, and he'd frankly come to care for her as well. In some ways, during these rough few years, she'd been the closest thing he'd had to a daughter.

"I'll need to talk to her mom, then. Be sure this is the right thing to do."

Daniel reached across the desk, gripping his father's shoulders. "Thanks, Dad!" he said with a big, bold grin. "You're the best!"

A little while later, Zach entered the kitchen with a stealthy look. "Can I talk to you a minute?" he asked Paul, who was cubing lamb by the stove.

"Sure," Paul replied. "Come on in."

Zach awkwardly took a seat on a barstool.

"Would you like some coffee?" Paul asked. "A beer, maybe?"

"Naw, man," Zach said, lowering his voice. "I need your help."

"Help?" Paul set down his knife and met the other man's gaze.

"With your mom."

"Velma?" Paul asked with concern. "Is something wrong?"

"Not wrong," Zach said in a whisper. "Extra right." He stunned Paul by pulling a ring box from his pocket. "I want to make it official, man. Me and the Mama Bear, we…" He looked dreamy for a moment before turning his eyes back on Paul's. "What I mean to say is, listen, dude, I think we're meant for each other. I really dig that woman, and she digs me."

Paul gulped, then asked tentatively. "Does she know about this yet?" As far as he knew, Velma wasn't the marrying kind. She'd shot down the last three suitors she'd had, but Paul decided against mentioning that to Zach. He seemed such a lovesick puppy dog. Besotted, even. Paul had never seen anything like it.

"I want to surprise her," Zach went on. "At dinner. More like, dessert time. If that's all right by you. I mean, I thought I should ask you first on two counts."

Paul stared at him, agape. What if his mom said yes? That would be great! Crazy, but great! As long as Zach was really the one. "First," Zach continued, "because you're the son, and I know it sounds a little retro and all, but hey, she loves you a lot, so I thought it would be good if I got your blessing."

Paul tried to process the role reversal as quickly as he could, but somehow the wheels kept sticking, coming back around the same proclamation/question. *Velma's getting married?*

"And the second count?" Paul queried.

"Ah yeah. It's because you're the head honcho here, and I wanted to ensure it wasn't a problem having a big event like this one happen at dinner."

Paul loved his mother, but she could honestly be somewhat of a handful. Of course, he suspected Zach must already know that. Heck, maybe that was part of her appeal. "How long have you known?" Paul asked.

Zach sighed looking distant a moment. "I guess it was that time I took your mom hiking in the North Woods. It was late summertime, really pleasant and lovely. Super quiet too. You know what I'm saying?"

With Velma along, that was hard to imagine, but Paul got the gist, so he just nodded.

"We were walking along like kids, and Velma had these wild flowers in her hair. And I thought to myself, I did, *Zach, old buddy, that's who you need to be walking through the woods with. Someone who looks like she just got here from San Francisco.* And then I imagined those woods, all icy and cold like they are now in winter, and thought, *who's going to be there with me, holding my hand and warming my back up then?*

"Warming your back...?"

"It's the way that we sleep when—"

Paul held up his hand, getting it. "Too much information."

"Sorry." He shot Paul a sheepish grin. "I really do love the lady, though. And since you're her only kid..."

"Of course I'll help." Paul warmly gripped Zach's hand. "And best of luck."

Carol tentatively entered the kitchen to find Paul furiously chopping at the center island. As if there wasn't enough to worry about in having things go smoothly around here on Christmas Eve, now he had to hope his mom's engagement would go swimmingly—and that Daniel would stay out of Amy's room. It wasn't that he didn't trust the kids.

They were great kids, world's best. That didn't negate the fact that they were head-over-heels-in-love teenagers. Paul wasn't so old he'd forgotten what that was like. It was particularly hard to forget with his old flame, Beth, staying at the inn.

"Is this a good time?"

"It's a great time," he said, pausing in his work. "Come on in." Carol's unexpected appearance actually came as a relief. When she was around, the world seemed bright and sunny, and any troubles he had not so pressing indeed.

"I was just looking for a cup of coffee."

"Help yourself. Pot's over there." He scooped vegetables into a large cauldron. "I was just getting a start on dinner."

She walked to the pot and poured herself a cup.

"Cream with that?"

She shook her head. "Smells delicious."

Paul lowered his voice in a mysterious tone. "My family's secret lamb stew. It's a holiday tradition."

"Then I'm glad to be a part of it," she said with a warm smile.

Winds howled outdoors, slamming the storm shutters. Paul thought of the great North Woods in the thick of this cold.

"Where did you learn to cook?" she asked, leaning against a counter.

"Oh, I picked it up here and there."

He indicated a tray of maple-leaf cookies. "Have one with your coffee. It's a Maine staple."

She gave a grateful laugh, scooping one off the tray. "I could definitely use the sugar."

He studied her a moment, suspecting something was off. "Are you okay, Carol?"

She stared at him, and he stared back, trapped in the heat of her gaze. All at once, he felt as hot as the most blazing wildfire.

"Yes, fine," she said with a flush, though she didn't look it.

Paul dropped his gaze to his work and kept on chopping—onion, garlic, potatoes— in a very practiced rhythm. "That's good, because, to tell you the truth, you don't look so hot."

She gasped, apparently affronted. "I beg your…?"

He looked up with a start. "No, I meant… That's not what I meant at all! You are perfectly hot. Very nice to look at, in fact."

She bloomed bright red like a Christmas poinsettia.

"That came out badly," he said, still furiously chopping.

She widened her eyes in terror. "Watch it!"

Paul looked down to see he'd nearly added his index finger to the stew.

"Wow," he said, setting down the knife in a sweat. Why was he so darn nervous? Was it the fact that his mom was getting hitched? Possibly hitched? She might even say no, he reminded himself.

He met Carol's concerned gaze and understood immediately that his being on edge had much less to do with his mom and a lot more to do with the woman in front of him. Her deep dark eyes were centered on his, her lovely face lined with concern.

"Where was I?" he asked, feeling as if he'd completely lost his place in the world.

"Asking me if I was all right." Her gaze traveled to the knife on the chopping block, then back up to his again. "But maybe the question should be reversed?"

"You're right. I'm sorry." He leaned into the counter, releasing a breath.

"I'm not totally myself this afternoon. I've just had a bit of a surprise, that's all." In truth, it was more than *a bit*. Not only had the news from Zach come as a shock, Paul had just admitted to himself he was attracted, seriously attracted, to one certain single mom from Virginia. He'd been fighting it ever since she got here and totally trashed his new dog sled. He hadn't put it out in the garbage at all and had said so only to make her feel better. And making Carol Baker feel better was definitely a good thing. While her skiing trip had proved initially harrowing, once she'd lived through it, she'd seemed to perk right up. Totally upbeat and sunny, running all over town exploring things with her cute kids. And when she turned her chocolate-colored eyes on him and smiled, it was all Paul could do to recall theirs was supposed to be a client-innkeeper relationship.

"What's the matter?" she asked sincerely.

"It wouldn't be professional sharing my personal problems with you."

"Then why don't you think of me as someone else?"

"Like who?"

"I don't know. Maybe a concerned neighbor? Someone who dropped by for a cup of sugar."

I could show you some sugar, all right, Paul thought, before mentally slapping himself with a jolt. What was he thinking? That he'd make a move on her, right here and now? It was only four in the afternoon, but you'd think he'd dipped into the eggnog already. Heavy on the bourbon. *And here I am worrying about Daniel! Could it be because that apple didn't fall far from this tree?*

The back of Paul's neck flashed hot. "You first."

"Me?" she asked with surprise.

"Fair's fair, Carol. You tell me what's troubling you, then maybe…just maybe I'll dish about what's eating me."

She narrowed her eyes, then shook her head. "All right, but you promise not to think I'm silly?"

"Nothing you could tell me would be silly."

"I…" she began, her voice cracking. She pulled a tissue from a box on the counter and dabbed the corner of one eye. "I had a talk with Will…"

Maybe this was worse than he thought, something he was unprepared to deal with. "And?"

Carol broke down in a sob. He yanked more tissues from the box and handed them over. "Carol? What is it?"

She met his gaze, bleary-eyed. "May baby's growing up!" she cried.

Paul laid a comforting hand on her shoulder. "There, there. It happens to all of them."

"Who?"

"Kids."

She sniffed, balling the tissues in her hand. "It's true. One minute you're changing their diapers. The next, they're chasing you out the door, telling you to get a life."

"Have you been talking to Daniel?" Paul asked with alarm.

She shot him a puzzled look. "Daniel? No, why?"

"It's nothing, really," he said, passing her more tissues. "Carol?"

"Huh?"

"You've got really great kids."

"Thanks." She gave a trembling smile. "You too."

She broke down sobbing again, and Paul placed his arms around her. "It's all right. Everything will be all right."

She threw her head back and cried. "You're such a nice man!"

He pulled her to him, lightly patting her back. "I like you too."

She collected herself and pushed back. "Really? But I'm such a mess!"

He shot her a tilted smile, knowing when he said it, it was true. "I like your kind of mess."

She dabbed her cheeks with more tissues. "I really have been the worst sort of guest, haven't I?"

"Actually, you've been the best guest. Certainly the most memorable—and entertaining—one I've had in a long time."

"Oh gosh, Paul. I apologize. I don't know why I got so emotional."

"That was emotional?" he asked, lightly teasing.

"I've just been working so hard to keep everything together for such a long time…"

"Listen, Carol, no one is made of steel. Nobody can be expected to keep everything together at all times."

Dark lashes fanned wide as she stared at him, more beautiful and bewitching than ever. Paul couldn't bear to see tears in her eyes and knew just the right remedy for her sadness. All she needed was a little fresh air.

"Carol," he said, "I'd like to show you something

this afternoon."

"What?"

"The town."

"But the kids and I have seen it."

"Not my way, you haven't."

"What's your way?"

He found himself beaming from ear to ear. "I'd like to surprise you."

"Just me?"

"If you don't mind." By the way she gazed at him, his heart hoped that she didn't.

"What time?" she asked, a little breathless.

"Meet me on the porch at five?"

The kitchen door swung open, and Beth entered. She caught a glimpse of Carol in Paul's arms and started to back away. "It seems now's not a good time."

"No, wait!" he called as Carol quickly collected herself and broke away.

"I'm just going to go upstairs and clean up," Carol said with a shy smile. "I guess I'll be seeing you later?"

"Right," he said, looking from one woman to another. Paul ran a hand through his hair, feeling in the middle of a big mess. Beth's blue eyes were opened wide, taking in the situation. Who knew what she thought, walking in on them? Paul hadn't even had enough time to process his and Carol's interaction himself. All he'd known was that when he'd put his arms around her, it had seemed the right thing to do. He'd been so driven to help her, he wasn't sure he could have stopped himself if he'd tried. And when she'd looked at him with those trusting dark eyes, he'd longed to find ways to comfort her further. He had the perfect outing in mind, one that would make her feel special, because special was what she was. Quirks and all, he thought, eyeing the empty tissue box beside him.

Beth held the door back for Carol as she exited the kitchen, then stared at Paul. "I was hoping we could talk," she said softly.

"Of course," Paul said with a nod. "Pull up a stool. Can I get you some coffee? Wine?"

"Wine sounds good," she said, coming over and settling in at the counter.

"I think I'll join you," he said, pouring them each a hearty glass. What a day this had been. First, he'd had the confrontation with Daniel. Zach had surprised him with his wedding plans next. Then, suddenly, before he could stop it, his heart had apparently jumped all over itself, flip-flopping like a wild fish on a line, just at the thought of holding Carol. Paul only hoped things weren't about to get more complicated. From the look in Beth's pale blue eyes, he wasn't sure.

"I was just looking for an excuse to talk," she said. "It's always so busy around here, it's hard to catch you alone."

As if to punctuate that, Daniel breezed in the side door, toting grocery bags. Amy wasn't far behind him and shut the door firmly against the brisk winds and flurries that drifted inside.

"Thanks, guys," Paul said. "You can just leave the things by the sink over there."

"Want us to put this stuff away?" Amy asked helpfully.

Paul glanced at Beth, knowing she was right. It

really was nearly impossible to get a moment's peace around here. Particularly today—in this kitchen. "Thanks, Amy. I'll get it in a minute. Why don't you and Daniel go and relax for a bit. Take a breather before things get busy for dinner."

Daniel caught Amy's eye and nodded toward the kitchen door. She smiled and followed after him as Beth watched the exchange. "Young love," she said with a sigh after they had gone.

"Hmm," Paul said, stroking his chin. "If you'll excuse me a second…" He stood and walked to the kitchen door, swinging it open—just in time to spy Daniel and Amy, hand in hand, sneaking up the stairs. "I meant relax down here!"

They halted in their tracks, then eased back down the steps.

Beth stared at him with amazement. "Wow, you're good," she said when he came and sat beside her.

"I was young once."

She raised an eyebrow. "I recall."

Paul combated a rash of heat with a swig of wine. "Yeah, me too," he said, surveying her with a tender melancholy.

"What is it?" she asked, seeming to note his wistful look.

"I was just remembering," he said with a laugh, "when we got caught necking in your old man's barn."

"Oh God!" She giggled. "I thought I was going to be grounded for the rest of my life!"

"Back then, three weeks felt like the rest of our lives."

She studied him sweetly then clinked his glass.

"Good times."

"Yeah."

She studied him a beat, then set down her wine. "Paul, I'm not quite sure how to say this. But I want you to know that good times are possible again."

"I'm sorry?" he asked with a cough.

"For you," she said kindly. "Now, I know things have seemed glum, but there's always a rainbow after every storm."

"Beth? What on earth are you talking about?"

She lowered her voice and leaned forward. "Your mother told me about your...*depression.*"

"My what?"

"It's all right. You don't have to pretend with me." She reached forward and took his hand. "I want you to know you have someone to talk to. I mean, I know it's been a while, and things between us ended kind of badly—"

"Kind of...?" Paul withdrew his hand. "You left me for my best friend!"

She dropped her chin. "I know, and I feel terrible about that. But Jack was just so...hot!"

Paul blinked hard, wondering how this was helping things.

"It was high school, Paul."

"Our freshman year in college, actually."

"A million years ago and a billion miles away... A lot has changed since then. *I've* changed."

"Yes, I'm sure you have. Time does that to us all. But"—he crooked a finger in her direction—"I have to tell you something." She leaned toward him; then he said in a whisper, "I am...not...depressed."

"What?" she asked with alarm.

"In fact, I have no idea why my mom would say

that."

"But she said you weren't in your right mind! Were about to do something drastic!"

"Drastic?"

The kitchen door swung open, and Daniel looked from his dad to Beth, then back at his dad again. "I was just coming to grab some eggnog for me and Amy."

"Daniel," Paul said, lowering his voice. "Would you happen to have any clue how Velma got the notion I was down in the dumps?"

Daniel thumbed his chest with a blank look. "Dumps, Dad? No, sir. Not at all. Frankly, you're looking pretty chipper to me!"

Paul narrowed his eyes at the boy, scrutinizing. "You didn't mention anything to her? Nothing at all?"

Daniel scratched the back of his head, then spouted out with a squeak, "I might have said some little, tiny thing about you possibly selling the inn." He swallowed hard. "And moving to Montreal."

"Montreal?" Beth said as Daniel scooted off, apparently having forgotten all about his mission for eggnog.

Paul slowly stroked his chin, a bigger picture coming together. "I'm afraid I need to apologize for my mom. It appears we've been set up."

"What do you mean?"

"Daniel spilled the beans to her about me leaving to retire in Canada. She obviously doesn't want that happening any more than the kids do."

"So when she saw me at the airport, she thought that I, somehow, was the solution?"

"Who knows what my mom thought. I am guessing, though, that she figured your being here might help me change my mind."

"Because we have a history?"

He raised his brow. "Maybe because she thought we'd have a future."

Beth caught her breath. "I have an admission to make."

He looked at her.

"I still have feelings for Jack"

Paul paused a beat. "Does he know?"

Her shoulders sagged. "We've been talking. Texting back and forth. All this uncertainty has had me really on edge. I apologize if I've been crabby."

"When do you plan to speak with him again?"

"He's promised to call on Christmas Eve."

"That's great."

All at once, she seemed fragile. "I hope so," she said, wrapping her hands around her wine.

"I hope so too," he said quietly. "Beth?" She raised her chin to look at him. "You're still one terrific catch for the right guy. I'm sure Jack will see that."

"Thanks, Paul. You're still quite a catch yourself.

The tips of his ears flashed hot. "Oh yeah?" he said with a laugh.

"Something tells me Carol Baker thinks so."

"Carol Baker's one of my guests."

"Oh, Paul," she said, swatting his arm. "Don't be such an old fuddy-duddy. Some chances only come around once, you know."

Chapter Seven

Carol stood on the inn's front porch, bundled in her coat, hat, and mittens. All around her, snow lightly fell, dotting the scenic landscape. The weather was predicted to get worse later, but right now, as dusk settled over the mountains, the setting seemed perfect. Almost like something from an old-fashioned Christmas card, complete with a…horse-drawn sleigh? The horses turned and headed up the hill in her direction. Their driver sat upright in the front seat, dressed in an old-timey winter coat and snow-dusted top hat. But wait! Was that Paul seated in back behind him?

Carol grinned with childlike delight as the sleigh, decorated in winter greenery and jingle bells, pulled up to the porch and Paul hopped out. He held out a hand to help her aboard. "I needed some fresh air too."

"Oh, Paul, it's wonderful," she said, settling in. He opened a large woolen blanket to cover her, then sat beside her, tucking his legs under the blanket as well.

"Where to?" the driver asked them.

"Let's take a pass through town and around the lake. Okay by you?" he asked Carol.

She felt her face warm. "Sounds like a dream." She'd never had anyone do anything like this for her before. Something so nice and unexpected.

The driver snapped his reins, and they took off in a trot down the snowy slope. Paul pulled two insulated tumblers of hot chocolate from a basket on the floor and handed one to Carol. She took a sip, delighting in its rich, creamy warmth.

"Why are you being so nice to me?" she asked with a grin.

He cocked his chin, studying her. "Well, I can't have you suing me for landing you under the ski patrol hut, now can I?"

Carol laughed out loud. "That wasn't your fault."

"Maybe not," he said, leaning close to talk through the chilly winds, "but that doesn't mean I don't feel guilty about it."

"Well, don't! Klutzing out was my doing entirely. I take full responsibility. I'll even sign a waiver if you'd like."

Paul chuckled and toasted her tumbler with his. "Something tells me that won't be necessary."

As they approached town, the winds picked up, and she shivered a little under the blanket. "A bit colder than you're used to in Virginia?"

"More than a bit," she said with a laugh.

"Ah," he said, scooting a tad closer. "Maybe this will help." He placed his sturdy arm around her, snuggling her close. Carol's heart thumped wildly as she gazed up at this wonderful man. Down below, the town was strung with Christmas lights, the frozen lake in its center catching their magical glow. "I hope you don't mind?" he asked her.

"No," she said, a little breathless. "This feels nice."

"I don't normally take my guests sleigh riding, you know."

She looked up into his dark brown eyes. "I didn't figure you did."

"I hope that you don't feel that it's wrong,

unprofessional of me, to want to spend time with you this way."

Nothing had ever felt more *right* in her entire life. Being here with Paul in this wonderful place was more fantastic than she ever could have imagined. "I don't think it's wrong for us to be together as friends."

"Or make-believe neighbors?" he asked with a grin.

"Or that either." Her chin was tilted up toward his, and Carol found herself wishing he would kiss her. It was a deep longing inside, and one she hadn't felt for anyone in such a long while, she'd almost forgotten what this yearning was like.

"I hope you're having a good time, Carol," he said, his eyes dancing. "You and your kids too."

"We're having the best time," she said. "In a way, it's a miracle we came here, but I'm so glad we did after all."

"What do you mean?"

"In truth? Maine wasn't my first choice."

He blinked in disbelief. "But why not? Just look around," he said, sweeping his arm across their surroundings. "It's a winter wonderland!"

"Yes, it is," she said softly. "It's just that, initially, I had our sights set on a vacation locale a little closer to home."

"Oh? Where was that?"

"Asheville."

"North Carolina? How far is that from where you live?"

"Only a couple of hours. A short drive. And," she said with a sigh, "an economical one."

"I don't get it. What made you come here?"

The last person Carol wanted to think about on such a romantic afternoon was Jim. He'd been so cruel to her in so many ways, and there were too many hurts she was still getting past. Tears welled within her in spite of herself. She blinked, turning away.

"Carol?" Paul asked softly.

She turned back toward him and tried to keep her voice from breaking. It betrayed her by cracking pitifully anyway. "He found another girl, Paul," she said as tears streaked from her eyes. "Someone younger and prettier, than me."

Paul lightly stroked her cheek and gazed at her, his voice growing husky. "No one," he said surely, "could be younger...or prettier...than you." He stared at her deeply, and his perusal warmed her through and through. She'd never had a man look at her that way, like she was someone special, just as she was.

He settled back in his seat and tugged her up against him, making her feel safe and comforted in the wintery winds. As they paraded around the lake and through the town, they sat in silence, with only the steady *clip-clop, clip-clop* of the horses to keep them company. It was the perfect rhythm to accompany the beating of Carol's heart. She'd never felt so removed from reality and yet so completely at home at the same time. It made her life in Virginia seem far away, and this world here very appealing. She settled her head on Paul's shoulder, giving in to his comfort and strength, knowing this couldn't last forever. She was just grateful to have experienced it once. Being treated so grandly by a marvelous man.

Later that evening, guests sat at elegant candlelit

tables, enjoying their Christmas Eve meal. Amy cleared Zach's and Velma's dinner plates with a pleasant smile.

"I'll be right back with dessert."

"No dessert for me," Velma proclaimed. "Pauly's stew is always delicious. I couldn't eat another bite!"

Amy shot a perplexed look at Zach, who immediately jumped in. "Come now, Mama Bear, surely you've got room for one more little thing?"

"Huh?"

"You really should try the trifle," Daniel said, breezing by on his way into the kitchen for more coffee.

"Yes, the trifle is good," Amy agreed.

"I'm partial to the chocolate mousse myself!" Beth called from across the way.

"Hmm, and the pumpkin pie is delicious," Carol said.

"Very tasty," Will chimed in.

"Extra good!" Ashley added.

Velma set down her napkin and eyed them all suspiciously. "Is something going on?" she asked slowly, turning her eyes back on Zach. He shrugged with the utmost look of innocence.

Everybody else just stared at her. "Well, okay!" she finally conceded. "I guess I'll have dessert."

There was a communal sigh of relief as everyone went back to their business. Seconds later, Paul arrived from the kitchen with something under a silver dome on a tray. "House special," he said, setting it before her. "Compliments of the gentleman."

Velma stared at Zach, agape. "You didn't?"

He nodded smugly.

"You made me a coconut cream pie?"

"Huh?"

Her face warmed into a bright, beautiful grin, causing her to look several years younger. "I'm just teasing, you big hunk!"

All eyes were on them as Zach stood and lifted the dome's lid. Underneath, a dark ring box sat open, exposing a pretty solitaire offset by emeralds. "The green reminded me of your eyes.

"Velma," he said, taking her hand. She brought her other to her heart. "I don't want to walk through the North Woods without you."

The hush in the room was palpable as candles flickered and snow pinged against the windowpanes. Velma stared at Paul. "You were in on this?" He nodded. "Well, I suppose you told him I generally say no."

Zach's face fell as everyone's heart broke for him.

"Except for this time!" she said, leaping up out of her chair and into his arms.

Carol tucked Ashley in, feeling giddy from the celebratory champagne. What a fun day it had been, right down to that wonderful surprise proposal at dinner. Though she hadn't known them long, she felt so happy for Velma and Zach. They were clearly suited to each other and would serve each other well as partners and friends in the years to come. Carol wistfully thought of Paul carting that ring box out on a tray. For a moment, when she'd gazed at him, she'd imagined foolishly that he'd been bringing it for her. She'd known in advance it was for Velma. Paul had advised them all of the plan and enlisted their support.

It was just hard not to pretend for one split second that a man might feel that forever way about her, then actually stick around to prove it. She even thought Paul had glimpsed her staring at him, and reddened, turning away. How silly he would think her for having such thoughts. Not that she'd ever, in a million years, share them.

"Get your rest now, sweetie," Carol said. "Santa comes tonight!"

"There's no Santa. I know that."

"No one's ever too old to believe in the Christmas spirit. I still do."

Ashley scrunched up her face. "Then why won't you believe in my Christmas moose?"

"What's so special about this moose anyway?"

Ashley shrugged under the covers. "You never believe in good stuff anymore."

"I believe in you," Carol said with a smile. "And you're pretty special."

She scooted down under the covers, pulling them up to her chin. "That's not the same thing."

Carol kissed her on the head and said nighty-night before switching off the light. Once again, she saw it. Some sort of bright light streaming in a tiny beam through the thick woods. She tiptoed toward the window and peered out.

Ashley sat up partway in bed. "What are you doing?"

"Just watching that snow pound down. Weather's really picked up out there."

Down on the ground floor, Carol decided she should investigate. What on earth could it have been? This was the second time she'd seen it. She hunted around the house but couldn't find any of the others. Locating a large flashlight in the kitchen, she took it to the front hall, where she tugged on her overcoat and boots. Carol walked out the back door and trudged through the snow, which was nearly to her knees by now. The beam of her flashlight dissected the forest, drawing her closer and closer to the faraway light. Something rustled in the bushes, and she turned her beam on a dark shadow skirting away. "Oh!" she cried a second later as a red fox skittered across her path. She held up a forearm to shield her face from the blistering winds. Eventually, she could make out a structure. It was a small brown barn set deep in the trees, with its door slightly ajar. She was nearly to it when a growl came from the woods. Carol swung the beam of her flashlight over her left shoulder to encounter a huge, black bear. "Ack!" she croaked, beelining for the barn. She leapt through the snow, bounding over drifts, then threw herself inside the barn, slamming its door behind her.

"Carol?" Paul asked, looking up from where he stood waxing a vintage automobile.

"It was a bear!" she cried, still huffing and puffing. "A huge, black beast, with huge white teeth!"

"Where?" he asked, walking to her.

"Out there! In the woods! It was after me... I—" She felt dizzy, fearing she'd pass out.

He stepped forward to steady her. "I'll let you in on a little secret," he said, looking in her eyes. "That big, old bear was likely more afraid of you than you were of him."

"I doubt that," she said, feeling the blood rush back into her face.

"What were you doing outside anyway?"

"I saw a light…in the woods. Through Ashley's window."

Paul motioned to the single bulb hanging from a rafter above them.

In the backseat of the old Mustang and under the part of the car still covered by a tarp, Daniel and Amy huddled in their parkas. "Who's he talking to?" she asked.

"Shh!" he whispered. "They'll hear us."

"This was a great idea, Danny. Really great," she hissed back.

He held her by the chin. "Amy, do you love me? I mean *really* love me?"

"You know I do."

"Then puleeze stop talking!"

"That's funny," Paul said to Carol. "Did you hear something?"

"Only the thump-thump-thumping of my heart."

Paul patted Carol's arm, then released her. Now that she was safely out of the wild, she was looking better already. "No harm done, there. You're okay. The bear's okay." He grinned reassuringly. "We'll all survive together."

He eyed the back of the car, which appeared to bounce.

"She's a beaut," Carol said, admiring the hood. "Sure don't make 'em like this anymore."

"Nope, they don't." Paul oiled up his rag and put the finishing touches on his wax job, giving it some muscle. "She was my first. Bought her after saving up from my first few jobs in high school."

"It's wonderful you kept her all this time. She

appears in mint condition."

"Almost. But not yet. I'll get her there, though, by April twenty-ninth."

"What's April twenty-ninth?"

"Daniel's eighteenth birthday. The boy doesn't know it yet, but this is going to be his present."

Inside the car, Daniel beamed from ear to ear. He gave Amy a silent high five. Despite her efforts to control it, she giggled.

"Now I *know* I heard something," Paul's voice boomed from outside.

There was a yanking noise, then the sound of cloth sliding across the surface of the car. Little by little, light invaded their dark space.

"Let me see that flashlight," Paul said, shining its bright beam into their hideaway.

"Well, I'll be," Paul went on. "It seems we have some stowaways."

Amy gulped.

"What?" Carol asked with surprise.

She peered into the backseat to spy the two teens nervously huddled together.

"Hi, Dad," Daniel said between clenched teeth.

Paul huffed. "Out of the car. Both of you. *Now.*"

Carol sat on the sofa under a big throw blanket, the lights of the Christmas tree twinkling merrily nearby. The fire before her had burned down to a soft glow, and all was nice and cozy in this warm space. Paul had asked her to accompany Amy back to the house so he could have a father-and-son chat with Daniel. Carol hoped he hadn't been too hard on the boy. It was tough being young and trying to find alone-time with your girlfriend, especially in a place as bustling as this one. Amy had headed straight up to bed, apparently embarrassed by the whole ordeal. But Carol had told her not to worry. Things would work out in the end. After all, it was the holidays.

Carol eased back in her seat, enjoying the peaceful low crackling of the fire. Her kids had long since gone to bed, and Beth had made her excuses to leave a while ago. Zach and Velma had disappeared upstairs shortly after dinner, and no one had heard from them since.

The back door creaked open, and Daniel entered with a glum look, shaking off his boots. He told Carol a quick good night, then headed up to bed himself.

"Kids," Paul said, coming in behind him and shutting the door. He shook his head at Carol, then carefully removed his snow-encrusted parka.

"Everything go all right?" Carol asked with concern.

"As well as it could go," Paul said, sitting down to unlace his boots.

"You're a good dad. I hope you know that."

He looked up. "I try, but thanks for saying so."

He tugged off his boots and set them by the back door. "This has been quite a day!"

"You can say that again," she said, recalling their magical sleigh ride.

"I think I'll have a drink. Can I fix you some eggnog?"

"Eggnog would be great."

The minute he'd gone, Carol leapt off the sofa and rushed to the small mirror hanging by the desk in the front hall. "Oh Gawd," she mouthed, studying her complexion in the mirror. "I look as white as the snow, and not in a good way." She quickly pinched her cheeks, first one and then the other, until they bloomed bright pink. She bit into her top and bottom lips too, until each felt plump and moist. Then she gaped at her hair, which was in a tangled mass around her ponytail holder. Yanking out the rubber band, she hung her head upside down. She heard Paul whistling in the kitchen and raked her fingers through her hair in a panic. She flipped her hair right-side up, admiring the sultry way it fanned about her face in the mirror. "Much better," she told her reflection with a smile before darting back to the sofa. Her bottom met the cushion seconds before Paul entered the room, two eggnogs in hand.

He stopped walking and cocked his head. "You look very lovely."

"Why, thanks!" she said under the blanket.

He twisted his lips in concentration, then handed her a glass. "Did you...do something different with your hair?"

She casually fingered her tresses. "Just took it down," she said in a manner she hoped sounded matter of fact.

"Hmm, yes. I see." He took a seat beside her, and Carol remembered that moment from this afternoon when he'd wiped her tears away. Actually, he'd done that twice. Once in the kitchen, then again during their sleigh ride. Carol wasn't sure what Paul seemed to like so much about her, but he clearly found something. It was written in his eyes each time he looked at her and smiled. Exactly like he was doing now.

"How's the eggnog?" he asked.

She took a sip and was overpowered by the

bourbon. "Wow! Strong! Strong but good."

"If you'd like me to add more...?" he offered, reaching for her glass.

She pulled it back. "No, it's perfect." She took another sip. "Really good."

"What are your kids getting for Christmas?" he asked.

"Ashley asked for a sports game, and Will's getting a new iPod. How about Daniel?"

"I got him a laptop to take off to school with him next year."

"Great idea."

"What about you?"

"Me?"

"Isn't there something you wanted for Christmas, just for yourself?"

"Oh no, I never really..."

"Come now, there must be something you wanted?"

"Well, I wanted to come here. Have a white Christmas with the kids."

He chuckled warmly. "That's too easy. You're already getting that."

She studied him, unsure of what he wanted her to say. "I'm not sure I understand."

He set down his glass and leaned toward her. "Other than skiing. Was there anything else you wanted to do here? While you're in Maine?"

"Well," she began tentatively, "the kids were really bent on dog sledding. I mean, I thought it looked cool too." She sighed. "That was until I checked out the price."

"It is a little steep for a group," he agreed.

"Doesn't matter," she said, smiling happily. "The

important part is we've had plenty of good fun. All of us, together."

"Yes." He checked the clock on the mantel. "Looks like it's getting late. I guess it's best we get some shut-eye."

"Good plan," she said as casually as she could. Carol couldn't help but feel slightly disappointed. There they'd been, all alone by the glowing fire. Just the two of them, and she'd secretly hoped for another romantic moment that apparently wasn't destined to be.

Paul got to his feet, then helped her off the sofa. "After all, Santa comes tonight." He shot her a mysterious grin that made her feel all mixed up inside. She liked him so much and desperately hoped he liked her too. All indications were that he did. But now here he was, forcing them to say good night.

"Yes, yes, he does," she said, barely able to stand it. He was close enough to take her in his arms. Close enough to kiss her. But some inner instinct told her he wouldn't. "Santa and that Christmas moose!"

Paul laughed, dark eyes dancing. "We can't forget Ashley's moose."

"I wonder what she means by that?" she asked, looking up at him.

"Maybe that she's hopeful," he said softly. "Hopeful of a little Christmas magic." He stepped closer, and Carol's heart stilled. "Are you?"

The seconds ticked by like hours as he stared at her with soulful eyes and firelight lapped against them.

"I still believe in Christmas magic," she finally whispered.

"That makes two of us." He leaned forward,

brushing his lips to hers, and she feared she would faint from the warmth of his mouth covering hers. He was so manly and sexy, and smelled of the great outdoors. "Good night, Carol," he said, stepping back. "Sleep well."

She would try, though she didn't know how. Her silly heart did cartwheels all the way upstairs and danced a jig all over her room before she collapsed in a heap on the bed. She tugged a huge feather pillow over her face and squealed with delight, kicking her feet in the air. She'd never known what it was like to kiss a man. A real man, someone so kind, steady, and caring as Paul. It had been a chaste kiss but something so tender and wonderful that she never could have imagined it happening to her. But it had! And right here at Christmas! In beautiful, unforgettable Maine! Carol sighed, pulling the pillow against her chest and rolling happily onto her side. What a wild, wonderful day this had been. As long as she lived, she would never, *ever* forget it.

Chapter Eight

Carol awoke to the sound of yapping. She sat up with a start, frightened by the bunny ears all around her. Then she remembered where she was. She reached over to the nightstand and checked her cell for the time. Five thirty a.m.?

"Mom! Mom!" Ashley called, bursting through her door and into her room. "They're here! They're really here!"

"Who?" Carol groggily looked around as the commotion continued.

Will came in next. "A whole bunch of dogs," he said, dashing to the window. "Look outside!"

Carol clambered to her feet and padded over to the window beside her two kids. To her delight, five dogsleds with teams were parked outdoors in the dark.

Velma poked her head into the room with a bright grin. "Guess who's going dog sledding?"

"All of us!" Zach said, appearing beside her.

Daniel and Amy emerged from separate rooms, then held hands, grinning in the hall.

Beth arrived next in a fluffy white robe. "Santa left a note," she said with a smile.

A few minutes later, the group had scrambled into their clothes and suited up for the snow, which drifted lightly. Carol watched in awe as two team managers gave directions and Paul helped the group split up in pairs.

"Can I have my own?" Will asked with a hopeful

look.

"I don't see why not," Paul said. "Beth can ride with Ashley."

"Sure!" Beth kindly agreed.

"That is…" Paul turned to Carol. "If it's all right with your mom?"

"Are you sure he'll be okay?" Carol asked uncertainly.

"I manned one of these at his age," Daniel interjected.

"He'll do just fine," Paul said with a reassuring look.

Will beamed at Paul and Daniel, then took up his post. Paul seated Velma and Zach in their sled next, then helped Beth and Ashley into theirs.

"How was your talk?" Paul questioned as Beth settled in.

"Better than good." She smiled sweetly. "Jack and I have decided to give it another go."

"I'm glad to hear it."

"Thanks for this. Very nice."

He looked at Ashley and smiled. "Maybe you'll see your moose."

The child drew an expectant breath. "Really?"

"Keep your eyes peeled," he said with a wink.

Amy and Daniel needed no assistance. There were already in place and raring to go.

"Carol," Paul said, encouraging her to climb aboard the last vacant sled. He hadn't even asked if she'd ride with him, because he would have been devastated if she'd said no. Though, given the look in her eyes, he didn't imagine she would have.

"Everyone clear on what to do?" the lead team manager asked.

"We're clear!" Beth called.

"Ditto," said Zach.

Amy and Daniel both gave a thumbs-up.

Carol turned to Paul with a blush. "I can't believe you did this for all of us."

"I didn't do a thing." Paul settled into his seat. "It was Santa."

One of the team managers cracked a whip and called, "*Mush!*" And then they were off—snaking between trees and gliding down hills through the majestic beauty of the deep woods. "It's spectacular," Carol said, captivated.

Paul gave her shoulder a tight hug. "I'm glad you like it."

They passed rabbits and white-tailed deer, and even caught a raccoon creeping along. Suddenly, Paul gave a sharp whistle, signaling the lead driver, and all teams dragged to a halt.

"What is it?" Carol asked. "Is something…?"

Paul leaned toward her with a husky whisper. "I think Ashley found her moose."

Carol saw movement through a tall stand of trees, and then her jaw dropped. Paul pointed, and all heads swung in the direction of the enormous seven-foot-tall creature turning its broad, antlered head toward them in the shadows. Carol's face came alive with excitement and wonder. "Paul, it's…"

"Just watch," he said. At once, the horizon exploded in a bright burst of color, grenadine hues streaking the sky. The moose seemed to glow in its aura, shimmering all around in bright bands of color.

"The aurora borealis," Paul whispered in Carol's ear.

"It's beautiful," she said, catching her breath.

Paul took her hand on the seat between them. "It's magic."

Before Carol knew it, their vacation had ended and they were all standing in the parking lot, packed up to go. Christmas Day had begun with a bang, then eased into a nice, relaxing day of the group playing charades by the fire, then sharing a holiday meal. This time, they'd all gathered to eat in unison by pushing the smaller tables together. Even Paul had decided to join them, abandoning his role as host for one afternoon, at everyone else's insistence. After his wonderful dog-sledding surprise, the separation of innkeeper versus guests didn't seem fitting. They were more like one big happy family. And, they were, in a way. Paul, Daniel, Paul's mom, and Zach were all really related, and—by extension—Amy was too. Beth was Paul's old friend, and Carol and her kids had become new ones.

Carol stared at the others, her heart heavy at the thought it was time to leave. The others appeared downcast, as well. It was like they'd all been caught up in this magical holiday spell, and none of them wanted the magic to end. But it had to, and Carol needed to get her family back to Virginia. She'd hoped Paul would kiss her again as he had on Christmas Eve, or even that he might take her hand as they sat with the others around the fire. But perhaps he'd thought better of making any sort of display in front of the children. Upon reflection, Carol had understood that had been the appropriate decision. What was the point in involving others in their fleeting Christmas flirtation and getting expectations and feelings all mixed up?

Zach and Velma stood in their antlered hats, hugging each of the others good-bye. For the first time in days, the snow had truly stopped and the clouds had opened up, revealing a bright blue sky. "We're going to miss you guys," Zach said, emotion catching in his throat.

"Yes," Velma said, hugging her son. "It's been really great, Pauly."

"I couldn't have thought of a nicer group to host for the holidays," Paul told them all.

"You know you can count on us for next year," Zach said.

Velma grinned slyly. "Only we'll demand the honeymoon suite!"

Everyone laughed companionably.

Daniel nudged his father and whispered in his ear, "You're not closing the inn?"

"I've not yet signed the papers," he said mysteriously.

Daniel shot Amy a jubilant grin.

Ashley raced over, surprising Paul with a hug. "Thanks for the dog sledding!"

"My pleasure. Any time."

Beth gave Paul a happy perusal, looking younger and prettier than ever. "It was awfully good seeing you again," she said. "Almost like old times."

"You haven't changed a bit. Jack's a lucky guy."

"Thanks, Paul. I wish you the best."

Carol turned toward Daniel. "Good luck at Brown. I know you'll wow them all."

He tucked his arm around Amy. "Thanks, Carol. Thanks a lot."

Amy smiled sweetly. "You all have a safe flight."

Ashley hugged the teens good-bye.

"See ya, short stuff," Daniel said. "I'm glad you finally saw your Christmas moose."

Ashley triumphantly looked around. "I told you guys I wasn't fooling!"

There was an awkward beat as the rest of the group watched Paul and Carol interact. He so badly wanted to take her in his arms but couldn't trust himself not to reveal his feelings for her if he did. She'd been all he'd thought about since she'd smashed into him, skiing down that hill. And when she'd melted in his arms in the kitchen, he hadn't wanted to let her go. Seeing her beautiful brown eyes brim with tears during their sleigh ride had nearly broken his heart. He'd felt driven to fill her world with good times and take away that sadness. Then yesterday, when she'd looked like an angel beside him on the sled, her gaze filled with wonder, every expense he'd undertaken to ensure her happy smile had been totally worthwhile.

"It's really hard to say good-bye," he told her.

"I want to thank you," she said softly. "Thank you for everything. You gave us a very happy Christmas."

Unable to stop himself, he stepped forward and embraced her—for what his heart hoped wasn't the last time. "So long, Carol," he said, fighting the ache in his throat. "I hope that all your Christmases will be happy ones."

As he stood at the top of the drive watching them pull away, Paul's heart thumped in his chest. If letting her go was the right thing to do, then why did this feel so wrong? As his gaze trailed after the bright red

SUV, he noted movement inside. Little Ashley turned slowly in the backseat, her sad dark eyes staring back up the hill.

That was all the encouragement he needed.

Paul broke into a sprint as Carol caught a view of him in her rearview mirror.

Brake lights beamed red as she brought the SUV to a stop.

Paul raced to the driver's window, then stood there panting as she lowered the glass. "I couldn't let you leave," he said between breaths, "without asking you...something...important."

She turned her questioning eyes on his.

"What are you doing for spring break?"

"Spring break?" she asked, surprised.

"Don't you teachers have a week off in April or something?"

"Yeah, she does!" Ashley piped in from the back.

Will brought his hand to his chin and smiled.

"What I mean is," Paul went on, "I'd really like to see you again." He looked around the SUV. "I'd like to see all of you again." He turned his eyes back on Carol's. "And I don't want to wait until next Christmas."

Her face colored warmly. "I don't either."

"Is that a yes?"

"Why, Paul Love, are you asking us on a date?"

"Why, yes. Yes, I suppose I am."

She shot him a bright, beautiful grin.

"I was hoping you were."

Epilogue

Three years later, Carol and Paul stood kissing under the mistletoe in Maine.

"If you keep kissing me like that," she said, catching her breath, "you might have to cart me upstairs—and into the Moose Room."

"Good thing the kids are in bed," he said with a sexy grin.

Carol stared into dancing dark eyes, thinking she couldn't possibly love this man any more than she did. He'd help heal her heart and had brought her a beautiful, new, blended family. "I'm awfully glad Daniel's coming home tomorrow. The kids will be happy to see him."

Paul held her tightly up against him. "So will Amy."

"It's hard to believe that Will is heading to college soon."

"I think he's tough enough to handle it."

"He's going to leave lots of brokenhearted girls behind."

Paul gave a chuckle. "Now even Ashley has a boyfriend!"

"Well, after all…" She tilted her chin. "This *is* the Love Inn."

"And I couldn't love you any more than I do," he said with husky rasp.

"You going to prove it?"

"Yes, Mrs. Love, I think that I will." Then he swept her off her feet and carried her upstairs.

As he carted her over the threshold, she gave a

saucy smile. "Did I ever tell you I have a thing for guys named Paul?"

He shut the door behind them and strode toward their bountiful bed. "At this point, sweetheart, there'd better be just one."

She laughed happily in his arms, her heart light. "I like your kind of Christmas magic."

He kissed her sweetly and turned off the light. "And I like yours."

THE END

Holiday Brides Book 4

BEACH BLANKET SANTA

Chapter One

"You know what you need?"

Matt Salvatore stared into his brother's deep blue eyes. They looked so much alike, people sometimes mistook them for twins. In fact, Robert was two years older and an inch shorter than Matt. Why then, did Matt get the feeling he wasn't measuring up? "No, but I suppose you're going to tell me."

Robert pushed back in his leather chair. They shared a lot of things between them, like a law practice in DC and the same dark hair and broad shoulders. From the frown on Robert's face, he was growing weary of bearing Matt's weight. "You need some time away, man. A break from this scene."

"How's that supposed to make things better?"

"Every girl you see reminds you of her. If she's blonde, she looks just like Katya. If she's a brunette, she looks just like Katya might have been had she decided to dye her—"

Matt flagged a palm at his brother. "Slow down there, pal. A man is dying, and all you can do is dance on his grave."

"I'm not dancing. I'm trying to help!"

"By bringing up Katya at every turn?"

Robert sighed. "It's been six months, buddy. She left you before your birthday in June."

"Yeah, and that was awesome, wasn't it?"

"It was…less than nice." His lips twisted in a wry smile. "Never can trust those Russians."

"She was a foreign correspondent. Not a spy."

"Seemed to slip in and out of those shadows

pretty easily."

Matt ran a hand through his short, wavy hair, knowing Robert was right. Katya had been nothing if not slippery—with the truth more than anything else. She'd spent countless nights chasing after hot stories in Washington. It was only by mistake that Matt had learned of her questionable research tactics.

"What was that last guy's name? Carl Benton? Wasn't he running for Congress or something?"

"He lost."

"Well, at least that's some consolation." He leaned forward across his mahogany desk. "Bro, I've got to tell you, I'm starting to worry. This Katya thing has got you all eaten up. And for what? She's just not worth it."

"I apologize if I haven't been at the top of my game."

Robert lifted his brow.

"But things will get better. I swear. I'll turn this ship around."

"Sure you will." Robert's face brightened. "All you need is a little shore leave."

"Where's this going?"

Robert massaged his square jaw and studied him. "Straight to the Outer Banks, I hope."

"Your beach house?"

"You didn't graduate magna cum laude for nothing."

"What about it?"

"I think you should go there, take a breather."

"Who goes to the beach in December?"

"Nobody. That's what's great. You'll have no one to bring down with your sour mood."

"Thanks."

Robert laughed good-naturedly. "You know what I'm saying. It'll be good to have some time away. Read some of those dirty spy novels you're so crazy about."

"What is it with the espionage?"

"Okay, okay. Cast your reel out, then. Whatever floats your boat. Just get your tail out of Dodge for a while. It'll do you good."

Matt understood his brother was trying to help, but everyone knew depression loomed large around the holidays. With him already feeling down, was being even more alone really the answer? "You want me to spend Christmas by myself?"

Robert's expression softened. "That's not what I meant at all. I just want you to go regroup for a week, then join us in Maryland. Margaret and I want you to spend Christmas and New Year's with us."

"And your new baby," Matt reminded him.

"Well, yeah. Sure. Why not?"

Because babies screamed all night, as far as Matt recalled. They also needed diaper changing. This was sounding less and less like the dream bachelor vacation. "That's really good of you," Matt said, standing. "But I've already made plans."

Robert pinned him in place with his gaze. "Name them."

"Well, I was thinking of…" Suddenly it dawned on him that he didn't need to make excuses. Matt couldn't go to the beach. Christmas was always Elaine's week there. Elaine was Robert's first wife, and the one asset neither could bear to liquidate had been their beach house. Besides, with the real estate market having tanked, their oceanfront property was practically under water. So they'd opted to keep it awhile, carefully orchestrating a calendar of his-and-hers usage dates, so both could enjoy it without having to run into each other. "I thought Elaine always took Christmas week?"

"Usually, she does. But this year, she's getting married. Remember? She'll be on her honeymoon. The place is all yours!"

Matt started to think about that. The gentle melancholy of the seashore... A few six-packs of beer. Surf fishing in the waves. Letting his beard stubble grow for a week. Skipping out on the suit and tie routine... And finally—*finally*—forgetting about Katya. After a full week of that, he'd probably feel fine handling Christmas at the beach solo. Or, even heading back to Maryland if that was what he decided to do. Neither he nor Robert were going to Chicago this year. They and their siblings had pooled together to send his folks on a forty-year-anniversary trip to Tuscany's lake region. It would be one of the first seasons in memory the greater Salvatore clan hadn't gathered together to ring in the New Year, a plethora of grandchildren bustling about and blowing plastic horns. Of course, everyone had agreed it was worth it. There'd been tears in his mom's eyes at Thanksgiving when Robert, as the eldest, had handed over the airline tickets and broken the news. Everyone deserved the kind of happiness their parents shared. They'd stuck together through all kinds of weather and seemed to care for each other even more now than Matt had recalled as a kid.

"What about the Barnes case?" he asked his brother.

"I've put our team of interns on it. They'll be busy pulling documentation together until after the first." He shot Matt an encouraging grin. "There's really not much left for you to do here…other than pout."

"Hey!" Matt didn't pout. Did he? Scowl a little, perhaps. Take on the brooding look of an artist. Appear mysteriously morose… But pout? Not on your life he didn't. If this was what Katya had reduced him to, it was way past time to change it. So, yeah, maybe he'd been deluded into believing she was the love of his life. What with that sexy accent and sharp wit, she'd had him practically from hello. But now she was gone. Long gone, and it was time he stopped rehashing the past. It was ironic that the one woman he'd really fallen for had been the one to walk out on him. While Matt had never purposely hurt anybody, he did have a history of the being the *guy who was good with good-byes.* He'd become really adept at sensing when a woman was getting in deep and knew it was kinder to cut things off early rather than unfairly lead somebody on. Matt wasn't sure what he was looking for, but he believed he would know it when he saw it. With Katya, he'd just been vision impaired. Not that he'd ever let *that* happen again. "Give me that key."

Robert blinked in surprise. "Just like that? You're leaving already?"

Matt held out his hand, and Robert slid open his desk drawer, extracting a key chain with a dangling fake sand dollar attached. "Merry Christmas, brother," he said, slapping it into Matt's palm.

"Thanks. And Happy New Year to you."

"Wait a minute. You're not coming back to…?"

"I'll call you," Matt said with a wink.

Robert eyed him suspiciously. "You got another

girl stashed away somewhere I don't know about? Someone you're taking there with you?"

"You wish," Matt said. *I wish*, he thought. But this year, he'd have no such luck. Matt had grown weary of the dating game. That fiasco with Katya had been the final blow. He'd already taken her home to meet the family. His big Italian family, grandmother and all. And she'd apparently bedded the congressional hopeful less than a week later. Matt was supposed to be smart, primed to see things. His work as a corporate attorney demanded keen mental acumen. But every single bit of his brainpower had let him down when Katya had batted her pretty green eyes. *Well, no more of that,* Matt thought, clutching the key. He was done with women for the next little bit. After this breather at the beach, he'd return refreshed to focus on his career. Robert really had been doing more than his share lately. And with a new baby at home, it simply wasn't fair. By all accounts, Matt was the one who should be picking up any extra slack. And he planned to see to it post haste.

Sarah Anderson refilled Elaine's slender sherry glass, then lightly fluffed her veil. "You look gorgeous," she said. "Really you do."

Elaine studied her reflection in the mirror. Her blonde hair was in a perfect updo with loose tendrils spilling forth. Though they were best friends, they couldn't have looked any more different. Sarah's curly brown hair spilled past her shoulders, its color matching her eyes. "I'm going to look gorgeous and drunk if you pour me another glass." Elaine took a sip and giggled.

Sarah adjusted the wedding gown at the

shoulders and smiled. "You'll do just fine."

Elaine surveyed her maid of honor in the mirror. "Not drinking today, are we?"

Sarah caught her breath, recalling the last time she'd indulged at one of Elaine's weddings. "I think it's safer this way."

"Well, I wouldn't worry," Elaine said. "The groomsmen here aren't nearly as dishy as the first time around."

"Elaine! You're talking about Richard's brothers!"

"Oh, come on, Sarah. I may be engaged, but I still have eyes. Charlie and Hank are hot enough, but neither one is eye candy like—"

Sarah felt her cheeks flame. "Please don't remind me." It was all Sarah could do to forget waking up in the gorgeous Matt Salvatore's arms. He'd been the best man, and she the maid of honor. After one too many glasses of champagne and a lot of incredibly sexy slow dancing, they'd somehow wound up back at her place after the reception. She'd had a secret crush on Matt ever since first laying eyes on him at one of Elaine's pre-wedding parties. And when he'd kissed her on the dance floor, her knees had melted like butter. Sarah had never had a man kiss her that way. No one before, and nobody since.

"Those Salvatore men are pretty hard to resist," Elaine said with a knowing look.

"You divorced one of them."

"It's true. But it was for the best. Just look at how things have worked out. Robert met Margaret, and I've found"—she sighed longingly—"Hank."

Sarah took away her sherry. "Richard. You mean, Richard."

"That's right!" she said brightly.

Uh-oh, Sarah thought, wondering if maybe she'd poured one too many glass for the bride.

Someone knocked on the dressing room door. It was Janet, Richard's younger sister. "They want us upstairs in ten!"

Elaine hiccupped.

"Thanks, Janet," Sarah called, reaching for the water on the dresser. She gave Elaine the glass, urging her to take a long swallow. This sherry-drinking-before-the-wedding thing had been a tradition with their circle of girlfriends ever since Elaine's first time at it three years before. They'd all opened two bottles about an hour ago and toasted to Elaine's newfound happiness with Richard. While the other girls finished getting ready in the next room, Elaine had requested some time alone with her maid of honor.

Elaine drained the glass, then met Sarah's eyes. "Can I ask you something?"

"Anything. Ask."

"Do you find it perverse I only fall in love with R guys?"

"R guys?"

"Richard, Robert, Rodney, Rafael… What do you think it means?"

"I think you're thinking too much about it. It's a coincidence."

"Hmm." Elaine reached for the sherry bottle, but Sarah stopped her.

"They're almost ready for us upstairs."

"Right!" Elaine straightened herself on her stool. "Which is why I need you to make a promise."

Sarah pursed her lips a moment, eying her friend.

"What kind of promise?"

"Come on, Sarah. Just say that you'll promise! It's my wedding day, okay?"

"Okay, okay. I promise."

Elaine beamed. "That a girl."

"What-a-girl?"

"You've just agreed to catch my bouquet!"

Sarah swallowed hard. The last thing she needed to do right now was go catching anybody's bouquet. Especially Elaine's. Given Elaine's wedding was today, that would put Sarah in line to marry next. Like that was destined to happen. Of course, that was just a silly superstition.

Elaine shot her a stern look. "You can't drop it. That would be bad luck."

"Maybe one of the other girls will elbow in," Sarah added hopefully. "Jennifer's been trying to nail down Louis for a while."

"Forget about Jennifer and Louis. I'm talking about you!"

"But I don't even have a boyfriend."

"No, Sarah. You don't. You never have a boyfriend, because when a guy asks you on a third date, you always run away."

"That's not true."

"What *is it* about that third date?"

Elaine picked up the sherry, despite Sarah's effort to stop her, and drank anyway. "Oh, I get it." She nodded in slow understanding, studying Sarah in the mirror. "That's like…getting-physical time, huh? You're afraid."

"I most certainly am not afraid," Sarah said, affronted. "I can…party with the best of them."

"I wasn't talking party. I was talking dancing."

She wiggled her eyebrows. "Dirty dancing. You know, the two-to-tango kind. Lovers between the covers?"

A picture of her and Matt under the huge down comforter flashed through her mind. She flushed, pushing the murky memory aside.

"You have too much honeymoon on your mind," she told Elaine.

Elaine set down her glass, misty-eyed. "Yeah, maybe I do. Richard is *such* a tiger in the sack."

"Okay, up with you!" Sarah said, taking her friend by the elbow. "It's almost time to march."

"Ooh, I love this part, don't you?"

"It's special," Sarah said with a warm smile.

Elaine pulled her into her arms, and crinoline crunched. "You're special." She stifled a sob. "You've always been here for me. You're such a good friend."

Sarah patted her back. "I love you too."

"I wish I could give you something for Christmas."

"You have. That beautiful bracelet."

Elaine pulled back from their embrace. "I gave one of those to all the girls. And you're my maid of honor. I should have done something more."

"Just being here with you is enough."

"No, it's not. What do you want?"

"Want?"

"Go on. Name it."

"Elaine, you're getting married in eight minutes, I don't think now is the—"

"How about a vacation?" Elaine asked suddenly.

"What do you mean?"

"You love the beach."

"Like Hawaii?"

"That's a little hard to arrange last minute."

"I wasn't asking you to!"

Elaine's face became alive with excitement. "Bring me my purse," she said, pointing across the room.

Sarah crossed to the small love seat that held it and returned with it to Elaine, perplexed.

Elaine opened its clasp and extracted her key ring.

"What are you doing?" Sarah asked.

"Giving you my beach house," Elaine said with a grin. "For the week."

Sarah loved the beach and adored Elaine's cozy oceanfront cottage, but she couldn't possibly accept it so last minute. She had family to see in Bethesda and other arrangements to take care of besides. "Oh, Elaine, that's lovely, but—"

Elaine removed one key from her ring, the one with the dangling fake sand dollar hanging on a chain. "You simply can't refuse a gift from the bride. Especially on her wedding day."

Sarah thought of long walks on the beach…warm nights of reading by the fire… Elaine's cottage was the perfect getaway. And after the hubbub involved in helping arrange this massive wedding, a peaceful retreat sounded good. Better than good, almost like heaven.

"You don't have to stay there for Christmas, silly. Just use it as long as you'd like. It's my week, anyway. Otherwise it will go to waste."

Four hours later, Sarah saw the bridal bouquet hurtling in her direction like a rocket. Only this rocket had tiny jingling bells attached to its beautiful bright red ribbon. It had actually been Sarah's idea to add this extra holiday touch to the already festive candlelit wedding. It was one week before Christmas, and the entire church had been bedecked in lush greenery, boughs of holly draped from the arm of every pew. Sarah met Elaine's eyes in a panic as the flowers careened toward her. This was really happening. Elaine hadn't even bothered with the pretense of tossing the thing over her shoulder. She'd just grinned and lobbed it straight at Sarah.

Sarah swallowed hard as the musical menace closed in. Elaine's earlier words rang in her ears. *"You can't drop it. That would be bad luck".* Sarah caught a glimpse of Jennifer standing in the wings and a sea of waving female arms outstretched. It was nearer now, just overhead and arching toward her. No! It was nose-diving to the floor! She had a split second to react and avert catastrophe. Sarah leapt skyward, and the weight of the flowers settled in her hands. There was a collective sigh from the guests, and then, after a split second of silence, a loud round of applause.

Sarah's cheeks burned. How she hated being the center of attention, particularly at moments like this. It was common knowledge she wasn't seeing anyone, and folks would wonder why she'd stolen the stage from Jennifer.

Louis surprised her with his approach and jovially patted her arm. "Nice catch," he said under his breath. Across the room, Jennifer narrowed her gaze and walked away. Sarah couldn't have felt any more awkward.

Then Elaine drew near with a stealthy thumbs-up.

"I knew you wouldn't let me down."

Sarah lifted white roses to her nose, inhaling their sweet scent. "Why did you make me do that?" she asked in a whisper, disguised by the fanning bouquet.

"Because, hon. I want you to be as happy as I am. And, after a while"—she nudged the bouquet still clasped in Sarah's hands—"the right guy will come along. You'll see."

"Sure," Sarah said, not believing it. She was thirty-one-years old and hadn't met anyone with marriage potential yet. Not that it bothered her most days. She kept plenty busy with her work as an interior designer and truly loved what she did. It was hard to look for a mate in her field, which wasn't populated with many eligible men. And because Sarah wasn't into the bar or singles scene, she wasn't expressly searching anyhow. Who knew if the right guy for her was even out there? Even if he was, history had taught her that he'd be awfully hard to find.

"There's someone for everyone," Elaine said, smiling sweetly. "And somewhere out there is the perfect guy for you. You've just got to walk through the right door."

Chapter Two

Sarah let herself into Elaine's beach house and called out loudly, "Hello? *Hello?* Is somebody in here?" There was nothing but silence in return. Not that this surprised her. Renters at the cottage next door perpetually parked in Elaine and Robert's drive. She had to admit the landscape was confusing. You had to nearly be a native here to discern the obscure gravel road overgrown with sea ferns that included the neighboring cottage's drive. No matter. She'd stop by later and politely ask the renters to move their car. At the moment, neither was blocking the other in, so there was no real emergency.

Sarah set her suitcases in the kitchen and looked around the bright open space. Sporadic sunlight poured through the sliding glass doors adjoining a broad inviting deck beyond the living area. One side of the room held a rugged pine dining table with a matching bench and chairs. The other had a cozy stone fireplace surrounded by a large, comfy sofa, teak coffee table, and two reading chairs. A fire had been laid in the hearth with extra wood and kindling sticks stacked in a holder nearby. Although, it was hard to imagine building a fire on a day like today. The weather was unseasonably warm, in the sixties with partly cloudy skies and a mixture of light and dark clouds dotting the horizon. She'd heard a hard rain was coming and even that the weather might get dicey for a couple of days. But she'd brought enough supplies to last her, and for now, the beach appeared inviting enough. Sarah smiled as the ocean beyond the plate-glass windows heaved and sighed, white-tipped waves crashing onto an empty stretch of sand. As soon as she brought in her groceries, she'd kick off her shoes and go for a walk.

Down below the house and tucked in a corner behind the storage room, Matt finished his outdoor shower. Since the weather was predicated to change later with a cold front moving in, he'd decided to take advantage of bathing outside while he could. It might prove a tad chilly for some folks, who weren't as toughened to the elements as he was. But Matt, who'd engaged in rugged camping trips since he was a teen near Chicago, was well accustomed to some bite in the air. Compared to the Midwest in December, being in southern North Carolina felt almost like summertime.

There was something very freeing about being *au natural* outdoors, just a rustic wooden barrier between him and the path over the dunes. He'd had quite a catch today. Ten bluefish and nearly a dozen mackerel. Matt scrubbed his hands with extra care using the fisherman's soap he'd brought along to expunge any scent from the cleaning he'd done while still on the beach. He found it easier to take care of the messy work as soon as the need arose and had a simple fisherman's knife that had served him well for years. Matt planned to eat some of his haul while he was here, but most of it he planned to freeze and take back home. There were lots of recipes he could concoct, including a mighty delicious homemade gumbo.

Matt shut off the water, thinking he'd heard a car door slam shut. But that didn't make any sense. Not unless the cottage next door was rented for Christmas, which would be unusual since the house didn't even have a fireplace. And a fireplace at the beach in winter was something renters insisted on, no matter the weather. Matt squinted up at the sun lowering itself behind the dunes and grabbed his towel off a nearby hook. He'd head upstairs, freezer-bag the fish, and pop himself a brewski. *Yessirree*, he thought, winding the towel around his waist and cinching it. He was feeling better already. He hadn't thought about women all day.

Matt hoisted his heavy cooler in one hand while gripping his fishing tackle in the other. He'd just climbed the third wooden step to the side door when a screen door creaked open. Matt stopped in his tracks, thinking he'd heard footsteps. The next thing he knew, some pretty brunette was bounding down the stairs. She stared at him and fell back in fright.

"Oh!" she cried, dropping the flip-flops in her hand. One somersaulted down the steps, landing on Matt's bare foot. He quickly set down his stuff to grip the towel that was sliding south.

"Uh, hello," he said, securing the towel around him.

She stared at his waist, then quickly met his gaze. Matt caught his breath. He'd know those eyes anywhere. "Sarah?"

Her cheeks colored brightly as she swallowed hard. "Matt?" she asked with a squeak. "What are you doing here?"

He picked up her flip-flops and handed them to her, taking care with his towel the whole time. She wore snug jeans rolled up at the ankles and a fitted long-sleeve T-shirt. She was every bit as pretty as she'd been three years ago. Somehow, she looked even better. "Robert gave me the house for the week."

"Robert? But this is Elaine's week, isn't it?"

"Yes, but she's supposed to be on her honeymoon."

"She is."

"Then how…?"

"Elaine gave me the house for the week too. She said nobody would be using it."

Matt had worked hard to push memories of Sarah out his mind, but they all came flooding back now. She'd been so much fun at Elaine and Robert's wedding. He thought they'd really hit it off. Maybe even could start something. But then when the next morning came, she'd pushed him away. Naturally, he got over it. Matt knew better than to knock on doors where he wasn't wanted. And he'd met Katya shortly afterward besides. Matt felt a pang in his chest when the raw truth hit. Katya wasn't the first woman to let him down. It had really started with Sarah. "Then we're in a predicament, aren't we?"

"Well, yes. No," she said, backing up a step. "I should be the one to go. After all, you got here first."

"I don't see how that's fair. This really *is* Elaine's week, not Robert's."

He stared at her, and she stared back, her head and heart still grappling with the situation. Of all people to run into! *Matt Salvatore* with those unnerving blue eyes and that to-die-for statue-of-David body. It was bad enough that he had it; far worse that it was on such vivid display. The winds kicked up with a whistle, riffling his towel.

"If you don't mind," he said, lifting an eyebrow,

"I think we should continue this conversation inside. It's getting a bit breezy out here."

"Of course," she said, quickly turning away and heading upstairs. She held the screen door open so he could make his way through with his collected gear. It was all she could do to avert her eyes from his solidly muscled shoulders and stop herself from thinking about what might have been. He hadn't changed at all. In some ways, he'd seemed to age in a way that made him appear even more handsome. And it was hard to top what he'd been before, which was absolutely devastating.

She closed the door behind them, pressing it shut against the building winds. "Feels like that cold front's coming."

Matt set down his gear by the center island in the kitchen. "Precisely why I should get dressed."

She blinked and bit her tongue to keep herself from saying something idiotic. Like, *no, please, stay half naked for me.* The sad truth was, this was the most action she'd had in months. In fact, it was the most action she'd had since Matt.

He cocked his chin sideways and grinned. "I already put my things in the conch room, but we can work all that out later after we talk."

"Good plan."

He excused himself, and Sarah face-palmed, sinking onto a bar stool at the center island. Matt Salvatore. Unbelievable. She never thought she'd see him again. Certainly not as much of him as *that.*

Matt shut the door behind him and slowly shook his head. Sarah Anderson, all after this time. She was the one person he never thought he'd see again. She'd certainly given him the boot sternly enough, and once things got rocky between Elaine and Robert, there wasn't really any occasion to see her. The newlywed couple stopped having folks over shortly after their wedding. Come to think of it, they hadn't entertained much at all. It seemed they were too busy biting each other's heads off to consider serving up dinner to outsiders. It wasn't that Elaine and Robert didn't like each other. In fact, they'd been madly in love. The trouble was both were headstrong individuals, each used to getting his or her own way. This made for some heavy fireworks when even a discussion of which placemats to set on the table sparked an altercation.

Matt extracted his clothes from the dresser, knowing Elaine and Robert's parting had been for the best. The moment they'd split up, they'd seemed like old friends again, not that they wanted to spend much time around each other. Too many unhappy memories of what their tainted married life had been like. Still, neither harbored ill will toward the other, and each was happy to let the other go on with his or her life. The only real thing that bound them together was this beach house at the Outer Banks.

Matt stepped into his jeans, considering the situation. He supposed he should offer to go. That was the gentlemanly thing to do. After all, this was supposed to be Elaine's week here, not Robert's. And what a shame that was too. The fishing today had been mighty fine. Matt even thought he felt that first hint of beard stubble poking through. He'd nearly forgotten how peaceful this place could be, gulls calling and darting above white-capped waves. Matt stared out the window at the tumultuous ocean suddenly shrouded in dark clouds. Seeing Sarah again had turned him inside out in a way he couldn't have expected. He'd nearly forgotten about her completely until he'd looked in those big brown eyes. And, when he had, every inch of him remembered holding her close as they'd swayed to that sultry ballad by a small jazz band. He could even recall the scent of her, fresh and womanly, like daisies after the rain. And those skies had opened up and poured on him all right, sending him packing during the cloudburst. He tugged on his sweatshirt, thinking that this time he'd be more prepared. Sarah wouldn't need to tell him to leave. He was volunteering.

Sarah peered into her cooler, wondering if she should reload it with the cold stuff she'd already stowed in the refrigerator. But her cold packs had melted, so she'd need to stop by the store on the mainland and secure some ice on her way home. It would be rude for her to deplete this place of the one premade bucketful it had. Listen to her! Thinking of being rude to the one man she'd met on the planet who'd proved himself to have no manners. The morning after the wedding, he'd made a quick exit without caring to explain what went wrong. Only one picture bloomed crystal clear in her mind, that of the irresistible best man leaning forward to lift her bridesmaid's dress over her shoulders. How could he when she wasn't even in her right mind? Well, maybe he hadn't been in his either. They'd both *did* have quite a bit of champagne.

The door cracked open to the right-hand master bedroom. There were two large ones in this house, one on either side of the central living area, and each was decorated in its own ocean theme. One sported sand dollars, while the other, the one in which Matt was staying, was adorned in conch shells. He emerged, and Sarah caught her breath on the impossible. He looked just as good fully dressed as he had standing near naked in a towel. She felt her face redden, fearing he could read those thoughts.

As Matt approached, she noticed a backpack casually slung over his shoulder.

There was a small tug at her heart, something akin to pain. Maybe the thought of him walking out conjured up some mysterious sense of déjà vu. But that was silly. Shouldn't she be grateful at his efforts to make things easy?

He set down the backpack and started gathering his fishing gear. "I think it would be simpler if I just went."

"I thought we were going to discuss it?"

He met her gaze with a placating smile. "I'm not sure what's left to discuss. This place was apparently double-booked. Since this wasn't Robert's week to begin with, I'm the one who should go."

Thunder boomed outside and lightning crackled, sending splinters of light throughout the kitchen. Matt packed his cooler. "Sounds like that storm's moving in even sooner than expected."

Sarah peered through the kitchen window at dark clouds rolling over the horizon. In the past few minutes alone, the weather had changed dramatically, though that often happened out here on this little-known barrier island that lay in close proximity to a broad expanse of others. The house sat on a narrow stretch of sand between the ocean and the sound and was accessible only by four-wheel-drive vehicles carried over on a ferry. No roads came out this far, and the rough-hewn trails worn flat by tire tracks were often washed over during heavy rains. A double booking was one thing, but she couldn't have Matt braving the precarious trek back to the boat during a storm. "Maybe it's not safe to drive." As if to accentuate that point, the wind picked up, rattling the screen door.

He strode to the sink beside her and peeked out the window as well. "It's even darker over the sound." Just then the sky opened up, releasing a broad curtain of rain.

"Looks like you came back from fishing just in time," Sarah said.

"Seems like aborting your walk was a good idea."

She stared into mesmerizing blue eyes, and her heart skipped a beat. Did this mean he would stay? At least for a little while?

"I do think I should wait to get on the road. At least until this blows over."

Thunder boomed and rain drove down harder, smacking against the tin roof. "Conditions could be worse later."

"Then again, they could improve."

She didn't know how driving in the dark would make things any better. That wasn't really safe to do around here, even on a clear night. Surely Matt knew that too. "I don't see how," she said, her voice catching in her throat.

He smiled, giving that sexy tilt to his lips.

She reached out a hand to steady herself against the counter.

"Since you're stuck with me awhile, we might as

well eat something." He cocked his chin in the direction of her grocery sacks. "Bring any wine in those bags?"

"A few bottles of white." She reached in a bag and produced the evidence. "And, oh yes. A nice big bottle of Chianti."

He grinned, and Sarah's foolish heart went all aflutter. "You pour, and I'll cook dinner."

At the moment, a glass of wine sounded good. If she didn't fear Matt would be counting, she might even have two. But her plus Matt Salvatore—plus alcohol—equaled trouble. She hadn't quite forgotten that. This time, Sarah would have to keep her wits about her and watch every step. For there was really no way around it. Unless there was a dramatic break in the weather soon, the handsome heartbreaker was staying the night.

Chapter Three

Sarah set down her fork and dabbed her pretty mouth with a napkin. "That was absolutely delicious. The best fish I've tasted in ages."

"I just hope I didn't use up too many of our rations in preparing the wine sauce." He lifted the bottle of chardonnay between them, offering to pour her another glass. She declined with a shake of her head.

"I don't think I'd better, thanks."

The deluge continued outdoors, slamming the house with fierce winds that howled in from the ocean and ripped in torrents across the sound. Their small refuge was a battering ram in the eye of the storm but fortunately had been built sturdy enough to withstand it. Over dinner, Matt had learned that Sarah now worked as an interior designer. It was an ambition she'd held since she was a little girl who'd meticulously stylized her dolls' houses. The last time he'd seen her, she'd been considering leaving her stint as a receptionist for a political magazine and finally realizing her dream. She'd found a paid internship at a small design company in Northern Virginia and had eventually worked her way up. Sarah was glad to now have clients all over the District and in parts of Maryland as well, and Matt was proud of her for achieving her goal.

While she was just as beautiful as before, in some ways she seemed more mature, like she'd gained inner confidence. And Matt found that self-assurance intoxicating. He started to pour himself another glass of wine but then thought better of it. With Sarah sitting across from him in the candlelight, her dark eyes catching their glow, he was already feeling light-headed. No sense mixing his emotions up further by stirring in alcohol.

She stood to clear the table, then turned toward the oceanfront window, which was streaked by heavy slogs of rain. "I doubt that they're running the ferry."

"I'll bet that ferry stopped running hours ago," he said, standing and scooping up some plates as well. How he wished he had a clue as to what went wrong all that time ago. Perhaps if he got up the nerve tonight, he'd ask her. He clearly wasn't going anywhere in this weather. Not only was the ferry bound to be cancelled, the beach road that led to the dock was sure to be knee-deep in water right now. Even if the squall magically stopped at this moment, it would take several hours for the storm surge to subside.

Sarah walked to the kitchen and set some dishes in the sink. "It's fine with me if you stay here," she said, color dusting her cheeks.

Matt set his plates on the counter and touched her arm.

She turned toward him.

"I really don't have any other place to go."

She flushed more brilliantly now, slightly catching her breath. "Of course, I know that. I mean, it's silly to think… What I mean is, naturally you should stay. There really are no two ways about it."

"No."

She nervously turned on the water and began scrubbing dishes with a furor, her dish brush circling around and around again in exactly the same spot.

Water streamed from the tap, growing hotter, steaming her face, and adding spring to her tight curls.

"Sarah?"

"Huh?" She lifted her brow, appearing surprisingly domestic, standing there by the sink very nearly about to scald herself.

Matt leaned forward and shut off the tap. "I think that one's done."

She stared into the shiny white plate, vaguely spying her reflection. "Uh, yup."

"Tell you what," he said kindly. "Why don't you leave the rest of them for me."

"Really?" she asked, appearing relieved.

He motioned to the plate she'd just finished drying. "After all, you've already done your share."

Sarah was glad to have the opportunity to move to the living area and get out of the kitchen. *If you can't stand the heat, indeed...* Sitting across the table from Matt had proved dangerous enough. What with his easy demeanor and good-natured laughter, it was simple to recall why she'd developed that raging crush on him.

"Can I fix you some tea?"

"Tea would be great," she said, settling on the sofa.

"How about peppermint, in honor of the season?"

"Perfect!" She didn't know what it was about Matt being near that made her such a ball of nerves, but somehow, when he stood close, her heart pounded faster and all reason seemed to evaporate like a wafting soap bubble. Thank goodness he'd sent her out of the kitchen before she'd done some serious damage to herself or the tableware.

Sarah tried to relax and tell herself she was getting all worked up over nothing. So what if she and Matt had a past and he was spending the night? They were two adults and certainly could handle it. It wasn't like there weren't two master bedrooms here.

Sarah nabbed a magazine off the coffee table and casually tried to survey its contents, but her gaze kept traveling away from the copy and homing in on Matt's muscled back. Even through his cable-knit sweater, she could make out its contours, broad shoulders holding steady as he went about his work. He opened a cabinet and stretched tall to grab a teapot off a high shelf, jeans taut across his athletic backside. Sarah recalled that same derriere rising from their cozy bed, clad in nothing but checkered boxers, and felt her temperature rise.

"Doing all right?" he asked, turning toward her as she fanned herself with the magazine.

"Just a little warm in here."

"Warm? I was about to say that it's getting chilly. Suggest we build a fire."

"Great idea," Sarah said, tugging off her too-warm sweater.

Matt set the kettle on the stove, wondering what she was so hellfire nervous about. Okay, so maybe they'd had a bit of a history. But that was years ago. Surely she was over it by now. He was, wasn't he? When they'd tumbled into bed, Matt had thought of nothing more than taking Sarah in his arms. Kissing her soundly. Making love to her... Matt's neck flashed hot at the memory. There'd been something almost hypnotic about her, and the way their bodies had molded together on the dance floor had held the promise of something more. He'd secretly liked her since that first wedding party held on Elaine's outdoor patio. Elaine and Robert had just gotten engaged and wanted to share their newfound joy with a close circle of friends. As it turned out, the dinner guests were also top picks for the wedding party, with Sarah selected as the maid of honor and Matt designated as the best man. He'd taken Sarah a beer, spouting some stupid line about how that meant they'd be working together. She'd narrowed her eyes with a laugh and said, *"Don't bet on us working together too closely."* From that moment, he'd been desperate to hold her and learn more about what made her beautiful brain tick. Sarah wasn't just the best-looking woman in the place, she was also funny and fiery, a bright mischief burning behind those pretty brown eyes. He'd flirted with her all evening and at every prenuptial event after. It wasn't until the wedding reception that she'd finally caved just a little, indicating that all along she'd equally been interested in him.

"You going to get that?"

Matt blinked hard at the kettle squealing on the stovetop before him. He'd been so lost in his reverie, he hadn't heard it go off. "Yeah, sure," he replied as casually as he could. "Just waiting on things to get nice and hot."

Sarah's eyes flashed. "It… I meant, the water… Yeah."

He shot her a tight smile, then turned his back on her to make tea. Hang on, this wasn't right. All this while he'd been thinking she was the skittish one, but just look at him. *Let's build a fire… Let things get nice and hot.* If he was going to come on to her, he could at least man up and do it directly. Not that this was in his plan. It hadn't been his idea to walk out last time. Sarah had been the one to tell him to hit the road. And, given that the roads around here were certainly washed over, Matt decided that now wasn't the time to bring up any touchy-feely subjects.

He strode across the living room with two steaming mugs of tea and sat down beside her, handing one over. Nearly imperceptibly, she rearranged herself on the sofa, scooting just the tiniest bit away from him. This was it, then. No sign could be clearer than that. Sarah wasn't any more interested in Matt getting close than she'd been three years ago. Fine. He could deal with that. He was just here for one night, anyway.

Sarah took a sip of peppermint tea as the rain beat down harder and the winds wailed. "It's delicious. Thank you."

"I'm sorry?" he said beneath the commotion slamming their cottage from every direction.

Sarah raised her voice just a tad. "I said thanks for the tea! It's delicious."

"Glad that you like it," Matt called back. The lights flickered, and they both stared at each other.

"You don't think we'll lose power, do you?"

"Robert put in a generator," Matt said in an effort to reassure her. But all Sarah could think of was being alone here. With Matt. In the dark. It was hard enough to resist him with all the lights blazing, Sarah thought, feeling overheated again. She inched away from him on the sofa, then laughed when he gave her a quizzical look.

"Just getting comfortable, that's all." As if to prove it, she stuffed a large throw pillow behind her back. "Ah. Much better!"

Matt drank from his tea, then set it down. "Hmm. Yes."

"When do you think they'll reopen the ferry?"

"I suppose as soon as the water calms down."

Outside the large glass door, the ocean tumbled about furiously, giving no indication that would be anytime soon. "Sarah," Matt said, studying her sincerely. "I don't want you to worry. Don't think anything will happen here just because you and I—"

"No, of course not," she rushed in, feeling idiotic.

"I mean, we do have separate bedrooms, after all."

"I know," she answered, wishing with all her might he hadn't said that. Bedrooms plus Matt Salvatore in her mind led to one terribly embarrassing memory. Not that she totally blamed her formerly drunken self. She'd been a little younger and a whole less wiser back then. These days she understood what keeping her distance meant. It meant steering clear of unnecessary temptation. She picked up her tea, standing. "I think I'd better carry this back to the bedroom. Start unpacking."

Matt's brow creased with concern. "Did I say something…?"

"Oh no, it's nothing like that. It's just been a long day."

She stared into deep blue eyes, consumed by them. He was one good-looking man, maybe the best-looking one she'd ever seen. It was impossible not to remember what it was like to kiss him and how his mouth had moved over hers with obviously practiced skill.

He held her gaze, and her heart stilled. "I hear you," he said below the tumult of the storm. "Sleep well."

When she spoke, she found her voice a little breathless. "Will this place be in one piece tomorrow?" But the truth was, she was more worried about her heart than the house getting lost in the squall.

"I'm sure we'll be fine. This house has withstood far worse and lived to tell the tale."

It was impossible for Sarah to sleep with the winds wailing outdoors. Each time the house shook, she feared for their security, imagining their tiny cottage being swept out to sea in a swell. But that was ludicrous. Matt was right. This place had been built to withstand the winds. And this wasn't some huge hurricane anyway. It was nothing more than a fierce winter storm tearing its way down the east coast. Winds howled again, sending the window casings rattling in her room, and Sarah sat up with a start. An eerie light illuminated the room, emanating from the solar-powered nightlight placed in a low wall outlet. No way could she settle down now. Maybe some more of that herb tea would help.

Sarah slid out from under the covers and tugged a sweatshirt over her head. It had grown chilly in the midst of the storm, a damp cold seeping indoors. She'd be warmer sleeping with someone else but wasn't about to consider it. Falling into bed at the drop of a hat wasn't her style. This was one reason her escapade with Matt had proved so jarring. While she wasn't precisely chaste, she'd slept only with the few guys with whom she'd had committed relationships. Bedding the best man had been an outlier. So far outside her realm of normal behavior, in fact, that it had caused her to question her priorities. And when she examined those, she saw that what she longed for most of all wasn't some guy who was in it for a one-night stand. She wanted a guy who would stick around forever, in sickness and in health. Someone who wouldn't turn tail and run the moment he learned more about her.

Sarah sighed, wishing so much that Matt had proved himself to be different. But he'd been like all the rest. Eager to take advantage and then ride off into the sunrise at the first crack of dawn. Of course, she understood she was equally to blame for their night of debauchery. It was just a pity that—after all the trouble it had caused—she couldn't recall the details.

Matt rummaged through the cabinets in search of something to eat. He didn't know why he was so incredibly hungry, but his stomach had been growling so loudly he hadn't been able to sleep. Perhaps he hadn't had enough dinner, or maybe it was nerves. Growing up in a big Italian family had taught him that the best way to settle any insecurity was with a hearty dose of food. But why should Matt feel unsettled at all? It wasn't like he had to worry about becoming involved with Sarah. She clearly had no greater interest in him now than she'd had previously. And that was a shame too. The truth was she'd never given him a chance. *Never given us a chance…to see what might be.* He couldn't imagine what he'd done wrong, but she hadn't even wanted to talk about it. At least she'd been upfront in saying good-bye. Conniving

Katya would have kept him coming back for more, as long as he'd failed to discover her duplicity.

He set a box of crackers on the counter and opened the refrigerator in search of some cheese, believing he'd think better after a snack. He didn't know what it was about Sarah that still got to him after all this time. For all intents and purposes, she was a small part of his past. A long-lost flirtation he should have written off over the years. But seeing her again had proved something different. Matt had an odd inner instinct that maybe there was a reason... Some convoluted explanation for why they'd wound up here together. He wondered vaguely if she was sensing this too. Or whether he'd only imagined Sarah's warm brown eyes registering interest as she'd held his gaze, saying good night.

Sarah padded toward the kitchen in her slippers thinking she'd heard noises there. But it was after two in the morning. Surely Matt couldn't be up? She rounded the corner, then stopped in her tracks. It was Matt standing nude on the far side of the open refrigerator door! All she could spy from her position was the top of his gloriously muscled chest, bare shoulders, and his deep blue eyes peering in her direction.

"Sarah?" he asked with surprise. "What are you doing up?"

She took a giant step back, hands to her cheeks, which felt as hot as coals. "I...uh..." She dropped her hands with a questioning look. "What are *you* doing up?"

He glanced downward as if checking something, then once again met her eyes. It was pretty hard to tell in the dim light of the kitchen, but Sarah could almost swear his face had colored as well. "I'm just getting a snack."

"Do you always eat naked?" she blurted out, the words racing off her tongue.

A slow, sly grin worked its way across his sexy face. "Not usually," he said, shutting the refrigerator door.

Sarah gasped and shut her eyes. "Ah!"

She'd hoped she would hear him making his retreat. Or at least, goodness knows, grabbing a dishtowel. Instead she just heard silence, coupled with competing winds.

"Well, they may be a little ratty, but I don't think my camp shorts look that bad."

Sarah peeked between splayed fingers to see he was right. In fact, what he wore—something akin to boxers—made him look absolutely terrific. He smiled and held out some cheese. "I was just sitting down for a bite. Want to join me?"

"Will there be wine involved?" she asked, thinking she needed it badly. Not a whole lot, just a small glass. Enough to calm her nerves—and erase the picture she'd just envisioned.

"There could be."

"Do you think you could put a few more clothes on?"

He laughed warmly. "Anything you'd like. Do you prefer jeans or sweatpants?"

"Doesn't matter," she said, feeling her cheeks warm again.

"Why don't you pick the wine while I go change?"

Sarah found the corkscrew with unsteady fingers. Staying here alone with Matt wasn't nearly as easy as she'd imagined. Every time he centered those gorgeous blue eyes on hers, the memories came racing back. Most of them, anyhow.

"Still don't have it open yet?" Matt asked, resurfacing in record time. He wore jeans and an old gray sweatshirt. Only his feet were bare as before.

Sarah grimaced, wrestling with the bottle. "Cork seems to be stuck."

"Here, let me help with that."

He stepped forward to take the bottle, and Sarah's heart beat faster. It was hard to forget what being in his arms had been like. More impossible still to erase the memory of his kiss.

Matt easily opened the wine and poured them each a glass. Once he'd set some cheese and crackers on a platter, they each settled down on one of the barstools abutting the center island.

"I'm sorry I walked in on you that way," Sarah began.

"Don't be. It wasn't your fault. You had no way to know I was out here."

"No."

It niggled at Sarah that neither of them had brought up their previous night together. Her practical side longed to finally clear the air, but her more emotional self wasn't sure she could take it. Being told by a guy why you weren't appealing to him was never a joy. Although she'd guessed her besotted behavior had something to do with it, she'd always had a feeling there'd been something more. Something else about that evening she hadn't completely understood.

They sat for a moment in awkward silence, both nibbling on cheese and crackers as the storm continued to rage outdoors. At this pace, there'd be no getting out of here tomorrow, or maybe even the day after that. Though it was hard to focus on leaving with the soft light from the kitchen surrounding Sarah in its homey glow. She looked so sweet sitting there in her pajama pants and sweatshirt, just like a vision from a dream. He'd watched her dreaming once before.

"Sarah?" he asked, then sipped from his wine. "Can I ask you a question?"

"I don't see why not."

"Why did you tell me to go?"

She glanced at him, taken aback, as if she hadn't expected the question. "Me?"

"Yes. You. And that was after a whole night of you begging me to—"

"Matt, I don't see why you…" She set down her wine, seeming to grow uncomfortable. "What I mean is, that's all ancient history."

He set down his wine as well and laid his hand on top of hers. "Is it?"

Her cheeks colored slightly. "I'm not sure what you want me to say. That wasn't me. I'm normally not like that."

"Let's hope not!" he said with a laugh.

She withdrew her hand, affronted. "What do you mean?"

"All sick and pukey? Most girls wouldn't want to live through that twice."

"Sick and…?" Her voice fell off with the shock.

"Yes, Sarah. You were deathly ill. All over your bridesmaid's dress, in fact. I had to take it off to clean it."

"I what?"

"That's probably why you repeatedly begged me to *please forget this in the morning.*"

"I said that?"

"Well, yeah, between, you know…" He motioned with his hands, and she got the picture. "Not that I totally blamed you. I wasn't up for remembering certain parts of it myself. Hang on, are you saying you don't remember?"

She shook her head, her cheeks blazing brightly.

"Not even the part about making me swear I'd leave, just get out of your life, and never breathe a word about it to anybody?"

She pursed her lips, struggling with a murky memory. "I remember making you swear, swear…something." Big brown eyes met his. "But to be honest with you, Matt, most of the night is a great big blur."

"Then it's a good thing nothing happened between us," he said, lightly teasing. "For most men, that admission could be a killer."

Her eyes lit with understanding. "So…we didn't?"

"No." He cocked his chin to the side. "We didn't. Not that I didn't want to, mind you. Especially when we first got back to your place, and you kissed me like a house on fire. Heck, I'm only human. But, I wouldn't have. Never like that. Not once I realize your condition."

"And all this time I thought…" She heaved a sigh of relief. "But, no?"

"Is that why you told me to leave?" he asked, his

voice growing husky with the truth. "Because you thought I'd taken advantage of you?"

"I never blamed you. I thought it was both of us."

"Oh, it was both of us, all right. Just not in the way that you imagined."

She stared at him deeply, apology in her eyes. "I'm so sorry. I had no idea."

"I had no idea either," he said softly. "No clue why you gave me the boot. While you'd told me to go throughout the night, I'd taken that to be the liquor—and possibly embarrassment—talking. I thought for sure once you woke up and saw things straight, we'd talk things out, maybe even laugh about them. But instead, you just handed me my coat and said—"

"I think you should go." She hung her head, seeming to relive the moment.

"The truth is, I thought that we'd been getting along. Maybe had started something."

She raised her eyes to his. In the ensuing quiet, Matt thought he could hear every drop of rain pinging on the tin roof. When she finally spoke, her lips trembled, and it was all Matt could do not to lean forward and kiss them. "I thought we'd started something too. But sometimes life has other plans, you know?"

He nodded like he understood, but the truth of the matter was he didn't. "Was there somebody else at the time?"

She shook her head. "How about you?"

"Not then, for me either." He studied her for a long beat. "And now?"

"I'm not seeing anyone, if that's what you mean."

He captured her in his gaze, wondering if there

was a way they could start over. There had clearly been an attraction between them in the beginning. "Me either."

"Matt," she said sincerely, "I really apologize for what happened that night, and also for the way I judged you afterward. It wasn't fair. None of it was fair. I see that now."

"We all make mistakes."

One of the biggest he'd made was failing to pursue things with Sarah. He might have called the next day. Attempted to see her. Instead, he'd just up and walked away from what could have been the best thing in his life. Then, within the next few weeks, he'd met Katya.

"Thank you for saying that. That's really gracious, considering the trouble I put you through."

"No trouble. I'm sure you would have done the same," he said, knowing that would have proved logistically difficult. Matt tried to imagine the petite Sarah hoisting his large frame across the room and depositing it in bed, and chuckled out loud.

"I know," she said, smiling softly. "Pretty hard to imagine, huh?"

"Yeah."

"How do you think the roads will look tomorrow?"

"I'll check at first light."

Chapter Four

The next morning, Matt bent toward the washed-out road, wearing his rain slicker. Water streamed from the front of his hood, cascading down his nose. It was still pouring. Somehow it seemed twice as hard as yesterday. Nobody could get traction on this stretch of beach now. Not even a ranger's four-wheel drive could do it. He was here for the duration. Another day or two at least. He supposed he'd have to break the news to Sarah but hoped she wouldn't take it badly. She'd seemed more at ease in his company this morning, after they'd cleared the air about Elaine's wedding last night. Perhaps her appearing on edge before had to do with her misunderstanding what had really happened. Matt felt a whole lot better fully knowing what had happened as well.

He glanced back toward the house through a curtain of rain as thunder rumbled above. Bright light burned through each window, like warming lanterns speckling the storm. If things looked this bad here, they could be even worse down at the docks. He'd need to call and check on the status of the ferry. He figured Sarah would want to make it home for Christmas Day with her family, and he'd more or less promised Robert he'd share it with him and his wife. For the moment, though, he'd just need to make his way indoors to keep from getting further drenched.

"How does it look?" she asked when Matt stepped inside.

Matt removed his dripping coat and held it

outside the door, shaking it hard. "Not good. That road won't be passable today."

"Oh." Sarah tried to frame her response as mild disappointment, but inwardly her mood lightened. All night long, she'd relived Matt's words telling her he wasn't taken, as if he'd been hinting he wanted to give things with her another go. It was possible she'd misread his signals. There was an equal chance that, even if she hadn't, she wasn't fully ready. Ready to take the risk of telling the truth to yet another man.

Matt picked up the landline mounted on the kitchen wall and started to dial. "I think I'd better call the ferry and see what the status of things is there."

While Sarah couldn't hear the other side of the conversation, she could imagine as Matt creased his brow and said, "Uh-huh. Um-hmm. I see.

"I'm sorry, Sarah," he told her, hanging up the phone. "It seems the docks took quite a beating. They don't think the boat will be running again before the end of the week."

"End of the week? But that means—"

"Looks like we're stuck here for Christmas." He shrugged apologetically. "I'm sure that's the last thing you had in mind."

Actually, the only plans that she had involved spending another uncomfortable holiday with her mom and her mom's new boyfriend. Not that they *tried* to make her feel in the way. It was just that it was pretty clear they enjoyed spending time alone, making Sarah feel like a third wheel. A lovely fantasy began unfolding before her... Just her and Matt, and a big, wonderful Christmas tree, dotted with shiny lights... Then reality sank in, and Sarah realized they had no tree or presents or stockings to hang from the mantel. And here she was acting like she'd already had three hits of eggnog. With bourbon! "Are you sure?" she asked, trying not to sound overly hopeful.

Matt studied her with a frown. "You're pretty disappointed. I can understand that. You probably have family plans."

Her mom didn't even decorate for Christmas and had never really believed in the holiday for myriad reasons. So, they typically ordered take-out Chinese and watched a movie in front of the fake fire. That was the only sort of family holiday Sarah was used to.

"My family's plans will likely go on without me," she answered truthfully. "But what about yours?"

Matt laughed, stepping out of his drenched boots. "Oh, I think Robert, Margaret, and their new baby will manage just fine."

"You weren't planning to go to Chicago?" she asked, remembering the large, happy family she'd met at Elaine's first wedding.

"My brother and sisters and I sent our folks on an anniversary trip to Tuscany this year. It's their fortieth anniversary."

"Oh, how sweet!" she said, meaning it absolutely. Sarah tried but couldn't imagine what that would be like. Being a part of such a warm, loving family and having parents who'd stayed together for that many years. She didn't even remember her father, and her mom refused to say much about him. The men she remembered growing up with were a series of short-term boyfriends for her mom, none of whom ever stuck around. Sarah had liked one of the early ones when she'd been a kid. His name had been Joey, and he'd a few daughters of his own. He was a kind man who'd seemed to take an interest in Sarah from the start. He took her out for ice cream with his own girls and had even taught her how to ride a bike. He'd been a good guy but somehow not good enough for her mom. She'd thrown him over for Fred just about the time Sarah got off her training wheels.

"Don't you think Robert and Margaret will miss you?"

"With that new little bundle to keep them busy?" he said with a smile. "Not a chance."

Lightning crackled, and Sarah stared out the rain-streaked window. "So, what do we do?"

Matt carted his backpack toward his bedroom with a wink. "Make the best of it."

After a soup and sandwich lunch, Sarah found herself chatting easily with Matt before a roaring fire. She'd made them coffee while he'd gotten the fire started, and now they sat discussing their afternoon plans. They'd already had a great time sorting through the house's stash of holiday movies and board games, so they had a sense of what type of entertainment was in store. Being stuck here with Matt wasn't going to prove uncomfortable at all. In fact, Sarah decided it could be a whole lot of fun. Just as long as she could keep her heart in check, she thought with a sigh.

"So, what's on the agenda?"

"Well, I don't think we'll be swimming today," he said with a teasing smile.

"No. You're probably right about that. I think it's cold enough to snow out there."

"Now that would be something, wouldn't it?"

"Snow at the beach? It happens."

"Yeah, it happens. But around here, it's rare."

She smiled above the rim of her cup, enjoying their light banter. They'd both phoned their families to explain neither would be coming home, and incredibly, everyone seemed happy with the situation. As long as they were safe and had enough provisions to weather the storm, everybody understood. In fact, they were glad that Matt and Sarah had serendipitously wound up there together. How much nicer for the two of them that each wouldn't have to spend Christmas alone. "So maybe we'll have a white Christmas?"

"Ha! You'll have to ask Santa for that." He mischievously cocked one eyebrow and studied her. "Don't tell me you're too old to believe in Santa?"

Sarah thumbed her chest. "Me? No. It's just that I've never had the pleasure."

"Of what?"

"Meeting Santa. Knowing him, whatever."

He stared at her aghast. "Are you telling me, not even as a kid?"

Sarah shook her head. "Cheryl doesn't believe in such."

"Cheryl?"

"My mom. She wanted me to start calling her Cheryl when I was, oh…about eleven."

"Really? Why?"

"Once I hit puberty…" She felt her face flush. "Well, I guess the thought of having a daughter my age made her feel old."

"Ouch."

"It's okay. I got over it."

"Not having a mom?"

"Oh, I had a mom. She was just…different. You know?"

He nodded like he was trying to understand, but Sarah didn't see how he could completely. Not coming from the background he did, which was so diametrically different. "So, what about Christmas, then? If there was no Santa, how did you celebrate?"

"Generally with moo shu pork and gas logs."

"Were you happy that way?"

"It was the only way I knew. I mean, sure. I heard the other kids in school bragging about what they got for Christmas and stuff, but after a while I learned not to worry about it. My mom always got me what I needed and didn't want to fill my head with bubble-headed fantasies anyway."

"Like the notion of Santa Claus and make-believe and dreaming impossible dreams?"

"Yes."

Matt's gaze was lined with compassion. He was trying to read her, and Sarah felt as open as a book. "I see."

"It wasn't so bad, really," she said, trying to lighten the moment.

Matt smiled at her, his face brightening. "No, I'm sure it wasn't. Who's to say which way is better? One person's childhood or another? I had a big brother to beat up on me."

"Robert?"

"Yeah, but he did so in a loving way." He shot her a wry smile. "And I still have the scars to prove it."

"Oh!" Sarah replied, not knowing whether he was kidding.

"So, come on," he said. "Let's decide what's next. Between the two of us, we've clearly brought enough provisions to get by. But did either of us plan for anything fun?"

"Fun?"

"Yeah, you know. Something to get us in the holiday spirit?"

"Well," Sarah began tentatively, "I had planned to make Christmas cookies while I was here. Take them home for the holiday."

"Perfect!" Matt said with a grin. "I'm in."

A little while later, Sarah found herself standing at the kitchen counter with Matt. He'd located Robert's CD collection and put on some music. With it turned up loud, they could scarcely hear the howling winds below the sultry collection labeled *Rainy Day Blues.* Nothing could have been more appropriate. Waves crashed outdoors and windy gusts slammed the house, though inside they were safe and warm.

"Well, go on," he said. "Lay it on me."

She looked up at him, and her knees went weak. All this light chatter with Matt had gone right to her head just like a million champagne bubbles. He was so easy to be with. Fun and lighthearted too. Was it any wonder she'd crushed on him so badly three years ago? But now she was getting to know him better— which made things worse. If only she could believe that certain things wouldn't matter to him.

"The supplies?" he said, reading her dumbstruck look. "What did you bring?"

"Oh, that," she said, feeling she sounded a bit dopey. This was crazy, and she knew it. All they were doing here was making Christmas cookies. It wasn't like they were slathering each other all over with icing. Her face flamed hot as she feared he'd read her

thoughts. Of course she wouldn't be coating Matt with icing. *That* was to be reserved for the cookies. But wasn't he a dish? *Yummy.*

"Sarah?"

She swallowed hard, collecting herself. Before they'd started to cook, Matt had offered to serve some wine. After all, they still had that open bottle from their late-night snacking... At the time, she'd been feeling so good and confident in her abilities to resist him that this had sounded fine. Now Sarah wondered if that had been such a great idea.

"Ah, yeah," she said, opening the refrigerator to retrieve the limp tube of sugar-cookie dough. She absolutely, positively, had to get herself under control.

Matt looked down at the dough, then right in her eyes. "Slice and bake?"

"I brought icing," she said lamely, hoping he couldn't read between the lines.

Matt took the cookie dough from her and set it on the counter, shutting the refrigerator door. "Do you mean to tell me you've never made sugar cookies from scratch?"

"Well, no," she said feeling her face warm with embarrassment. "No, actually I haven't. Is that a problem?"

He slowly stroked his chin and studied her. "No, darling, it's not a problem at all. I was just wondering..." His lips creased in a subtle smile. "If you'd like to learn?"

"What do you mean?" she asked, taken aback.

"I have confession to make," he said. His voice was low and raspy. "I'm one helluva baker."

She sputtered a laugh. "Go on!"

"I'm also a dynamite teacher."

Was it sheer coincidence that in the background a song about giving love lessons started to play? Matt could teach her all right, probably a lot of things. A man like him was sure to have had his share of the ladies.

"Are you now?" she said, backing up a step.

He'd be damned if she didn't look enticing, just standing there with that little pout on her lips. Matt took another sip of wine, tuned in to the music. "You're not afraid?"

"Of learning something new?" She pulled herself up a little straighter and squared her shoulders. "Of course not."

That was all the encouragement he needed to grab an apron off a nearby hook and tie it on. "Did you bring any sugar?"

"I brought a small container, enough for what I use in my coffee."

She produced the square Tupperware, and he whistled. "Got quite a sweet tooth, have you?"

Her cute face reddened all over. "I brought extra."

"Well, that's good, extra good. And, I'm betting we both brought butter." He grinned, his enthusiasm building. He was going to do this. Teach Sarah to bake cookies from scratch. Even if forcing himself to keep his hands off her sumptuous body killed him. Man, didn't she look sexy offering up her sugar that way? "I brought eggs and a bag of flour for coating fried fish."

She gasped as he set it on the counter. "A whole five-pound bag? Got quite an appetite, do you?"

He shook a finger at her and grinned. "Got me there. Now, all we need is vanilla."

"Think there's any in the house?"

He turned to check supplies in the pantry, figuring he could replace anything they used later. After a few seconds passed, he held up a small dark bottle.

"Bingo."

Sarah didn't know how Matt made it all look so easy. They didn't even have cookie cutters, but he'd fashioned some makeshift from various-sized drinking glasses turned upside-down to use their rims as cutting surfaces. "It's incredible how you figured all that out," she told him, duly impressed.

"And you thought I'd only studied law at Georgetown."

"You didn't learn this in law school," she said astutely. "You learned this at home."

"Guilty," he said, not looking culpable in the least. "It was all about food at the Salvatore house, especially with my folks running the restaurant."

"That must have been something," she said a bit wistfully. "Growing up with a big happy family and so many siblings."

"We managed," he said with a grin. "Managed to get into a lot of trouble and drive our parents crazy. Though I understand I'll have this coming back at me one day."

"What do you mean?"

"What goes around comes around. I have no illusions about my own kids not giving me grief, in one way or another, when the time comes. I'll more or less accept it as my due."

It was easy to guess that Matt would make a terrific dad. His life experience had primed him for it. Naturally, he wanted kids. Not five children perhaps, but at least one or two.

"Your turn," he said, handing over the rolling pin. "Why don't you try?"

Sarah took the weighty implement in her hand, not knowing quite what to do with it. Naturally she understood she was to press it to that little ball of dough and flatten it out, but she wasn't so certain her results would come out as stellar at Matt's. The truth was, Sarah had never been instructed much in the way of cooking at all. And, for one reason or another had never felt much inclined to learn. Her mom was a restaurant kind of girl who considered prepackaged dinners sold in the frozen section as good as homemade. She'd probably passed that gene on to Sarah. Nearly everything Sarah ate came out of some sort of box. Not that she was prepared to tell Mr. I'm-Italian-and-Cook-Everything-from-Scratch at the moment. He probably thought she'd only packed frozen foods for her trip to the beach.

"Go on," he said kindly. "Just put your weight into it evenly and give it a go."

Sarah smiled uncertainly over her shoulder. "All right," she said, determined to try. She centered her gaze on the big mound of glop on the counter, wondering how she was going to press that into a perfect one-quarter-inch slab the way he had. She grabbed each handle on the rolling pin and gingerly pressed forward. The blob squished slightly, but the rolling pin stuck. Not much else happened.

"Put your back into it," Matt prodded.

She glanced at him cheering her on from the

sidelines and then gave it her all, heaving her might into that little wooden spindle in her hands. Dough splatted out like an egg cracked fresh from its shell, transparently thin on the cutting surface. "Oh no!" she cried with dismay. Even *she* knew there was no way to bake cookies from *that*.

"Here, let me help." He sidled up behind her and calmly collected the mess, transforming it into a new ball. "It's all in the technique," he said, his voice a light tickle at the side of her neck. He drew nearer still, enveloping her in his warmth, and every inch of her came alive. He smelled so good and manly standing so close, the sleeves of his sweatshirt just brushing hers as he positioned himself around her.

He stepped a fraction of an inch closer, and Sarah feared she might faint from his proximity. It was intoxicating being enveloped in his arms, his solid chest pressing into her back as he steadied his hands around hers on the rolling pin. The "Love Lessons" song had ended, and a more provocative one had started to play. "Just like this," he said, swaying forward. She moved with him, letting him lead as dough glided into a flat plane. "And like this…" he whispered in her ear, lifting the rolling pin and repeating the process again as the sexy music played on.

Sarah felt breathless, as if she might faint at any moment, lost in the rhythm of Matt's embrace.

He held her more tightly in his arms and whispered, his voice husky. "What do you think of home cooking?"

In many ways, this felt more intimate than dancing, almost as if they were in bed. But Sarah had never been with a man who moved with such grace and care for her comfort.

"I think I like it," she said, barely breathing the words.

He stopped rolling, wrapping his fingers around hers.

"These are going to be damn good cookies."

"Yes," she agreed.

The seconds ticked by like hours as Sarah's heart beat furiously. Was it her imagination, or could she feel Matt's heart beating in his chest behind her as well? All she could think of was Matt turning her in his arms and kissing her, just as wonderfully as he had on that dance floor all that time ago. But then the kitchen timer went off, indicating the previous batch of cookies had baked.

Matt nestled his chin on her shoulder. "I think we're done."

"What?" she asked, her knees on the verge of collapse. The timer beeped louder, intruding once more on their moment. He lightly squeezed her hands in his.

"The dough, Sarah. It looks like it's perfect."

And it did, a perfect quarter-inch slab. They were ready to cut.

Matt broke his embrace and headed for the oven, which couldn't have burned any hotter than she felt right now.

Sarah excused herself for a moment and strode quickly to her bathroom, where she splashed cold water on her face. Then, she dampened a washcloth to dab the front, sides, and back of her neck. That Matt Salvatore was one hot man in the kitchen. Look at the mess she was in, and all from one teeny little glass of wine. But inwardly Sarah knew it hadn't just been the alcohol that had sent her head spinning and her heart racing. That had more to do with being deliciously wrapped up in the sexy Italian's arms while moving to that sultry music. When he captured her in his deep blue gaze, liquor was beside the point. She was drunk on him, Matt Salvatore the man, and all the wonderful things he was.

And one of those, Sarah reminded herself sternly, was someone who wanted to be a father. She swallowed hard, gathering her nerve to go back out there and face him. She needed to nix the wine and find a way to get through the rest of this day on more even footing. Perhaps she could offer to fix dinner and shoo Matt out of the kitchen for the next little while. There was clearly too much combustible heat in the room for the two of them. Then after dinner, maybe they could do something harmless like watch a holiday movie. One of those funny family films. Romance, right now, was a no-go. It was simple to see how quickly she could fall for Matt. The scary thing was, Sarah worried that she'd started falling already. She needed to stop herself before she got in deeper, in order to avoid a most certain and devastating outcome. Walking away from Matt with a broken heart.

The second Sarah had cleared the room, Matt set the cookie tray on the stovetop and pulled an ice cube from the freezer, pressing it to the back of his flaming neck. It melted on contact, sending little dribbles racing down the line of his back. Sarah had set him virtually on fire. She'd been so subtle and giving in his arms, yielding to his every move. No wonder he'd wanted to take her to bed before. It wasn't just the way she kissed, it was in the sexy way she carried herself, seemed to have complete control of her body. Well…except for that sickness thing. She was definitely out of control then. But everyone's allowed a slipup now and again. He'd had his fair share of his own, particularly in his younger days.

Matt rocked the open freezer door back and forth, rapidly fanning his face with puffs of icy air. It was working already. He was feeling better. Next best thing to a cold shower, he supposed, hoping Sarah hadn't noticed his level of excitement before she'd raced out of here. Or maybe she had, and that was why she'd bolted like a scared rabbit. Matt felt suddenly consumed by guilt, wondering if he'd done something wrong by laying it on so thick. It wasn't exactly like he'd planned their cooking lesson to turn extra hot. It just serendipitously had. Of course, once it had headed in that direction, he'd done nothing overt to stop it. He surely would have if Sarah had protested. Yet she seemed to be enjoying their joint venture into the culinary arts just as much as he had. Matt hoped he hadn't imagined that. He would feel awful if she felt he'd come on too strong and that had put her off. For Matt was growing attracted to Sarah, way attracted. And in his heart of hearts, he couldn't believe he'd gotten her signals that wrong. She was growing attracted to him as well. But Matt needed to be careful not to push it. Maybe the best thing to do would be force himself to back off a bit and let Sarah take the lead. If she was truly as interested as his instinct said, within the next couple of days she definitely would.

Sarah returned looking all fresh-faced with her hair pulled up in a ponytail. By this time, Matt had already washed the baking dishes and was busy putting them away. "I was going to help you with that," she protested, a little after the fact.

"It's all right. I didn't mind it. Besides, the kitchen needed to be tidied before I start dinner."

"Oh no, you don't." Sarah bossily entered the kitchen and took him by the elbow. He set down his dishtowel with surprise. "You've done all the cooking you're going to for the next little while."

He was mildly disappointed by that. Mostly, he'd been hoping they'd do some more cooking together. The good thing was that Sarah appeared bright and cheery, not like she was upset about anything. Perhaps she had enjoyed being close to him but was just too conservative to say so. She handed him his glass of wine and steered him toward the sofa. "Why don't you sit, and I'll refill that for you? I'm doing the cooking tonight."

That sounded super to Matt. He could relax in front of the fire and briefly check the score on the game. "Mind if I turn on some football? Just for a moment."

"Watch it as long as you'd like," she called from the kitchen with a smile. She pulled two frozen pizzas from the freezer, and Matt chuckled to himself, wondering if back in Maryland she did any home cooking at all. Not that it mattered to him. He was sure the dinner would taste just as delicious as if she'd made the pizza dough herself. All he had to do was look in Sarah's eyes and everything seemed better. Even being trapped at the beach in a storm was starting to seem pretty awesome.

Chapter Five

The next day was just as enjoyable. It was still too nasty to go outdoors, with very high winds and lightning. But inside, they found plenty to do. They'd watched a movie together, read companionably by the fire, and had taken turns cooking. Now they were settled at the dining room table, sharing milk and cookies over Holiday Scrabble.

"Not fair!" he challenged with a laugh as she chalked up another triple word score. "You never told me that you were a Scrabble shark."

"It's how you play the game." She playfully met his eyes. "No mercy." She didn't show any either, beating him in a close match. Afterward, they were both tired and ready to call it a day. It had been such a good one, Sarah found herself really looking forward to another with Matt. And what was special about tomorrow was it was Christmas Eve.

"Thanks for another fun day," she said after they'd put away the game.

"Thanks for scorching me in Scrabble. Something tells me I could learn a thing or two from you."

She laughed, feeling lighthearted. The fact was that Matt made her happier than anyone ever had. It was a fantastic feeling, almost like having a partner and friend who was also very easy on the eyes. Sarah cautioned herself against thinking of partnerships with Matt. Once he knew the truth about her, he wouldn't be able to think of her in that way, just as her last serious boyfriend hadn't. "Oh yeah?"

"Yeah." They stood in close proximity now, only inches apart. He stepped forward, closing the small space between them. It was silly to think he might kiss her, but she secretly wished for it just the same. He'd been so gentlemanly in keeping his distance since their cooking lesson, Sarah had started wondering what she'd been doing wrong. Then she reminded herself that things were playing out just the way she'd wanted them to. But if this was the case, why did the outcome leave her feeling sad and conflicted? If only there was a way to make things work, she would find it. But at the moment, everything seemed impossible.

"Sleep tight. I hope you have pleasant dreams."

She held his gaze, knowing her dreams would include him. "You too."

"The storm's supposed to let up tomorrow," he said, his voice raspy.

Sarah's heart skipped a beat. She certainly hoped not. Not if it meant that Matt would be leaving. She was still wrestling with so much in her heart and head, trying to sort everything out. And that was so hard to do with him standing close enough to hold her.

"Of course, even if the roads clear," he continued, "that ferry won't be up and running until late in the week."

Sarah breathed a sigh of relief, remembering. "That's right, the ferry," she said, backing up a step. "Can't go anywhere without the big boat." Wow, didn't he look gorgeous just standing there in all of his studly beauty, a few days of beard stubble lightly framing his face? Never had a man appealed to her so much.

He raised his brow, watching her with amusement.

"You might want to turn around. You might bump into something."

She held up her hand in agreement and whirled on her heels. Quickly enough, she hoped, to disguise her rabid blush. She'd been so intent on ogling Matt she hadn't wanted to take her eyes off of him. Him and that beautiful body and his gorgeous blue eyes. It must have been a subconscious desire, because she hadn't even realized she was doing it.

Sarah ducked behind her bedroom door, closing it with a gasp. Christmas Day was fast approaching, and she could think of only one thing she wanted. Having Matt take her once again in his arms.

Matt approached Sarah as she stood sipping her coffee by the oceanside sliding glass door. She looked beautiful this morning in a pretty pink sweater and slightly worn jeans, her long, loose hair damp from her morning shower.

"Looks like it's still coming down out there," he said, referencing the rain.

"Yeah, but not as hard as before." She smiled sweetly over the rim of her cup, and Matt had the crazy notion that hers was a smile he wouldn't mind seeing at eight in the morning any old time of the year. He was just glad he was getting this unexpected chance to spend the holiday with her. It was way better than intruding on Robert and Margaret's first Christmas as parents. The view was a lot nicer too. And Matt wasn't thinking about the drenched stretch of sand ahead of them.

"Thanks for making the coffee," she said. "It was

a treat finding it ready when I got up."

"It's no problem, really. I set it to brew before getting dressed and right after phoning the ferry."

Her delicate brow rose as she turned toward him. "What's the word?" She didn't say it, but Matt could tell she wasn't any more interested in that boat taking off today than he was.

"Still down for the duration." Even though the winds had abated, storm damage to the docks would take some time to repair. Some of it wouldn't even get started until the rain had fully stopped.

"That's too bad," she said, faking her disappointment badly.

"Hmm, yes. A total shame."

He studied her a long while, lost in the heat of her stare. While it didn't seem possible, each time he looked in those dark brown eyes, they appeared even more enticing.

Her pretty mouth drew up at the corners. "You know, I was thinking... I'm feeling a little cage crazy in here."

"Seriously? I was just thinking the same thing." In fact, he'd awakened this morning feeling a dire need to stretch his legs. Get out on the beach for a long walk. Only he hadn't wanted to inconvenience Sarah by suggesting she join him during the still-bad weather. He equally hadn't wished to cut out on her and leave her in the cottage all alone.

"Want to go for a walk?"

"I'd love that. Anything to get some fresh air. How about if we go right after lunch?" He paused a beat. "Only..."

"What?"

"Did you come prepared for rain? Bring any

gear?"

She reached over to a side cabinet and lifted a bright red, compact umbrella.

In spite of himself, Matt spurted a laugh. "I meant *real* rain gear. A slicker or something?"

She shook her head, loose tendrils spiraling. Matt recalled the feel of his fingers in her luscious hair as he'd cradled her head in his hands and kissed that glorious mouth. He found himself aching to kiss her again but knew he wouldn't until she was ready.

"Even though the rain's let up, it's still coming down hard enough that I don't think you should go out with *that*. Not with those ocean winds at play. Tell you what," he said with a smile. "Why don't you borrow a slicker of mine? I brought two."

"Two?"

"I like to fish here, and I'm never sure what the weather will be. I learned some time ago it's good to bring a backup supply of clothing. Helps ensure I don't miss any opportunities."

She met his gaze. "That's really nice of you, thanks. I think I'll take you up on it."

By early afternoon they were laughing companionably about the oversized fit of Matt's slicker on Sarah's small frame. "I feel like the Incredible Hulk or something," she said with a giggle. "Something lumbering and large that's about to make its way down the beach. Do you think I'll scare the sand crabs?"

"You're far better looking than the Hulk." Blue eyes crinkled at the corners. "Besides, for the next day or two, I don't think we'll be running into much of anything out there, apart from maybe a few hungry gulls."

Sarah's heart warmed at the thought of spending a few more days in Matt's company. She'd never felt so comfortable around a man. He was alluring and attractive but had never once used his charms to try to seduce her. Instead, he'd played the perfect gentleman, keeping his distance just enough to drive her wild.

"Shall we bring the umbrella?" she asked as they headed for the door.

"Only if you want to watch it flip inside out and risk lifting off into the sky like Mary Poppins."

She grinned and tossed the umbrella across the room and onto the sofa. Sarah recalled a lot of Christmas Eves but certainly couldn't remember any of them being like this. Despite the gloomy weather, this one was off to a great start.

Matt offered Sarah a hand as she made her way down the slick steps. She settled her glove in his grip, the wind whipping her hair wildly about her face. Hers was the face of a Madonna, tinged pink from the nip in the air, her dark eyes warming him even in spite of the chill. He was glad he'd encouraged her to layer up. Thanks to the cold front that had rolled in, temperatures were now in the thirties, icy rain pinging against them like tiny sharp needles. "Are you okay?" he asked with concern. "If it's too rough for you, we can turn back."

She stepped off the last wooden stair, releasing his hand. "Not on your life," she said as the winds blew. He loved that she was feisty, undaunted by the challenge. Some girls might have whimpered and begged to hole up by the fire. Not Sarah in her puffed out Incredible Hulk outfit, he thought with a smile. "Then you might want to tighten your hood a bit to keep your hair from getting wet."

She nodded and fumbled with drawstrings but couldn't seem to work them in her gloves. Matt hadn't worn any. Then again, he was a lot more toughened to the elements than Sarah.

"Here, let me do that," he said, reaching forward to adjust them until they fit right. "Perfect," he said, patting her shoulder. "Ready to roll?"

"I think I'm ready to run!" she said, her teeth chattering slightly. "Standing still lets the damp sink in."

Matt twisted his lips in a smile. "You want to run down the beach through the rain?"

"No," she said, her dark eyes daring. "I want you to see if you can catch me."

Before he knew it, she'd taken off, dashing way ahead of him. Matt chuckled, racing after her, trailing her as she tore along the beach beside the crashing waves. He was closing in and she knew it, giggling like a kid trying to keep her distance. But it was useless. In no time at all, he'd reached her and caught her from behind in his arms. "Ha!" he cried with delight. "Think you could get away from me, did you, lassie?"

She laughed out loud, apparently taken with his pirate talk.

He spun her toward him in his arms, the rain coming down in icy prickles all around them.

She looked up at him through the wind and the rain, her eyes a soulful invitation. He'd be damned if he didn't want to kiss her. And he was nearly damned sure that she wanted him too. Nearly, but not one hundred percent. The last thing he wanted to do was have her run away from him again or to tell him to get packing. Matt didn't know why, but he wasn't sure his heart could take that. Just in these few days together, Sarah had gotten to him in a way he didn't believe possible. And, if she could do this much damage after just a few days, he wasn't sure what kind of shape he'd be in at the end of the week. The first time they'd been together, Matt had blown it badly by not following through. If he'd heeded his instincts three years ago, when Sarah had told him to go, he would have asked why and tried to talk it out. Instead, he'd turned like a chastised puppy dog with his tail between his legs and had rushed off, never fully understanding what had gone wrong. Matt wasn't prepared to risk that again. Not with someone like Sarah. Not when just looking in her eyes made his head swim and his pulse race faster.

Sarah stared up at Matt as the elements raged around them. In spite of the storm, she felt sheltered in his arms, as if she'd found her safe harbor. Something about being with Matt felt so right. How she wished this feeling could go on forever. But there were things about her Matt didn't know. A deep secret that would likely alter his opinion of her and cause him to question becoming involved on more than a casual basis.

"Sarah," he said, his lips hovering above hers. "I'm glad that it worked out this way. That the fates, karma, whatever...somehow put us here together."

"I'm glad too."

"Promise me something." He looked deep in her eyes. Sarah's breath caught in her throat. "Promise you won't run away again without giving me a chance, really taking the time to know me."

But she couldn't promise him that. Couldn't promise absolutely. Just look at what had happened in the past. Of course, neither of her former boyfriends had been halfway as terrific as Matt, which made things all the harder. More than anything, she wanted to open her heart up to this new opportunity. But, when push came to shove, would she be able to? "I can promise I'll try," she said, barely breathing the words.

He steadied her chin in his hand. "There's a rainbow after every storm. You just need to believe it."

She nodded still holding his gaze. The next thing she knew, Matt was pulling her close, bringing his mouth to hers in the rain. "Sarah," he said. He kissed her sweetly, first once, then again and again. "My sweet Sarah, all we need is time." How she wished that were true. The trouble was, she didn't know how much time they really had. But instead of saying so, she let him kiss her over and over, until his soft kisses became deeper ones, and her knees melted like butter.

Chapter Six

Later that evening, Matt and Sarah warmed themselves by the fire. They'd come in soaked but happy from their adventures on the beach, and ravenously hungry besides. The prefab frozen lasagna dinner Sarah had prepared actually wasn't bad. Pairing it with the nice Chianti she'd brought proved a plus, and both had totally enjoyed Matt's homemade garlic bread. Now they sat with two goblets of wine, listening to blues music and the haunting melody of the rain.

It was the most romantic Christmas Eve Matt could remember. If only he had a way to do something special for Sarah and make her really feel the spirit of the holiday. "It's too bad we don't have stockings to hang from the mantel."

"We could always hang up our socks," she said with a grin.

"I don't think you want mine anywhere near a heat source. Especially the ones I went fishing in."

She laughed, seeming to guess that was true. "There *is* a washer in this house, you know."

"Yes. I plan to take advantage of it." He clinked his glass to hers. "Tomorrow."

"It's so hard to believe tomorrow's Christmas," she said with a sigh.

Matt shot her a wink. "We'll have to tuck in early so Santa can come."

"Sure," she said, smiling. "Santa and all his reindeer too."

Matt had pondered the problem all evening. Even

given the limited resources at his disposal, he had to come up with some sort of gift. Nothing fancy. Just something to show he'd thought of her. The question was what? Matt had a feeling the answer was right at the tips of his fingers, but he couldn't quite grasp it. "If you could have anything in the world you want, what would you ask for?"

"Anything? That leaves the field wide open."

"I suppose it does."

"You first."

"Me?"

"Fair's fair, Matt. I'm not telling if you won't."

He shared a thoughtful gaze. "Well... If I'm being really honest, I guess what I want... We're talking some day..." He held her hand and smiled, sending wild butterflies fluttering inside her. "Is what my parents have. That kind of life." Naturally he would. Theirs was such a lovely example to follow, Sarah thought with a touch of melancholy.

"That makes perfect sense," she said softly.

"Now you," he urged, giving her hand a light squeeze.

She considered this a moment, watching the flames dance and leap in the hearth. After a beat she turned her face to his, her cheeks warm from the fire. "If I really could have anything..."

"*Anything*," he said for emphasis.

"Well," she said truthfully, "I've always wanted to visit Tasmania. See the Southern Cross."

"Tasmania, huh?" he said with surprise. "That's quite a wish!"

She nudged him with her elbow. "You did say *anything*."

"Tasmania's a nice dream. Nothing at all the matter with that." He wrapped his arm around her and tucked her in close. "It's just a little tough to fit under a tree."

"That's the other thing," she said, looking up at him.

"What is?"

"A tree. I've always thought it would be really lovely to have a tree. A real live Christmas tree."

Matt knew she'd said her mom hadn't ever celebrated, but he was a tad surprised she'd never bought a tree of her own. "You've never had one?"

"I did break down and buy a small Christmas tree prism. It hangs from the rearview mirror of my SUV."

"I meant, for your apartment?"

"It hardly seemed practical with no ornaments to put on it."

"You can buy those."

She looked at him sincerely. "That's not the same. Tree ornaments were meant to be homemade."

"And why is that?"

"Because," she said with certainty, "it means they were made with love. And that's really what the season's about in so many ways."

"You never made any yourself?"

She hung her head, averting his gaze. "I'm about as crafty as I am a Betty Crocker."

He chuckled lightly, tightening his embrace around her shoulders. "You're a wonderful Betty Crocker. The best cook I've ever met, in fact."

She slowly met his eyes, the firelight catching in hers. "Honestly?"

"Honey, there's no one I'd rather bake cookies with."

She beamed at him. How he loved it when she smiled. In fact, her smile was quickly becoming one of Matt's favorite things. "Thanks for saying that, even if it's not true."

"But it is true," he protested with a laugh. It was too. There was no other woman he wanted in his arms when giving instructions on the rolling pin.

"In any case," she continued, "I'm sure I'll get one someday. A Christmas tree, I mean. I'd really like to, anyhow."

Matt held her close, the most brilliant idea occurring. It wouldn't be exact, but it might work well enough. If only he could find that box Robert kept below the house.

A little while later, Matt had kissed her sweetly and said they should rest up for Christmas Day. Sarah went to bed, but her restless emotions had kept her tossing and turning for hours. On one hand, she was elated that a man as incredible as Matt would take an interest in her. He was dynamite to be around and every bit the fantastic kisser she'd remembered. Conversely, she felt down knowing what she kept from him. Could she really hope he'd still want to see her if he knew the truth? Sarah still wasn't done dealing with it, and it had caused her untold hours of anguish. She hadn't even dared to tell her best friend. Somehow, by sharing bad news, you made it that much more real. As long as she dealt with this alone, she could handle it. Then again, handling things alone meant that *alone* was how she'd always be.

Sarah rolled onto her side and hugged her pillow, a tear sliding down her cheek. In the soft glow of the nightlight, she could make out the contours of her room and its huge windows framing the sea. Though she couldn't view it due to the darkness, she could still hear the pounding of the waves against the shore. The rain must have let up; before, its fierce ruckus had overtaken the ocean's roar.

Sarah sat up under the covers, thinking she'd heard the screen door creak open. But how could that be? She studied the clock on the nightstand. It was nearly four a.m. She slid into her slippers, determined to check, and hoping that Matt had heard it too. Even if it had just been the wind knocking the screen door ajar, she'd feel much safer checking it with big, strapping Matt around. Spying her cell on the dresser, she got an idea. She'd call Matt and ask if he'd heard something too. No, that was silly. She couldn't possibly wake him for an unlikely reason. For all intents and purposes, they were marooned on this island together. Who knew how close their nearest neighbor was? She'd initially assumed the house next door was occupied, but as it turned out, that high-end hybrid SUV that had been parked in the drive belonged to Matt. It probably *was* just the wind, Sarah told herself, trying to settle back down. She sat on the bed, but a split second later heard the same noise again. She sprang to her feet, grabbing the nearest weapon she could find, her bright red umbrella. With a shaky hand, she opened the door to the living area, hoping to goodness this was all in her mind. Surely she'd check the house and find everything clear. Otherwise, she aimed to beeline it into Matt's room just as quickly as she could, propriety be damned.

The second she stepped over the threshold, a bright beam of light pierced her vision.

"Sarah!" Matt called from the doorway,

steadying his flashlight in her direction.

"Matt!" she cried, equally in shock. "What are you doing?" He wore a damp rain slicker and appeared to be carting some sort of box indoors.

He set down the box and lowered the beam of his flashlight. When he spoke again, he sounded slightly out of breath. "Fishing."

"Fishing?"

"Yeah, I…" He smiled tightly. "Though you'd appreciate a nice Christmas dinner. Catch of the Day?" he said with a shrug.

Sarah thought something smelled fishy, all right. Since when did people catch fish at four a.m.? And who in their right mind would pack them in cardboard?

He stared at the umbrella angled high in her hand. "Where were you going with *that*?"

"To beat the living daylights out of whoever was breaking in here."

"What if it had been Santa? Since when have you taken to clubbing geriatric citizens?"

Sarah lowered the umbrella and narrowed her gaze. "Hmm, yes," she said, growing suspicious. "What's in the box?"

Matt scratched his head, his eyes darting toward the door, then back toward hers again. "Can't say."

"Can't or won't?"

"Can't/won't. There's a slash in there."

"Matt…" she began. "I'm sure you weren't fishing."

"Got me there," he said brightly. "Doesn't mean I'm not about to!"

"You mean you're going down on the beach now?"

"Down on the beach. Into the waves. Knee-deep if I have to. Yup."

"Then what?"

"Then, I'm headed straight back up here and hitting the hay. Precisely as you ought to." He went about his work as he spoke, hoisting the mysterious box and sliding it into his bedroom, then reemerging with a tackle box and his fishing pole and its holder. My, he was acting strange. Odder than she'd ever seen him.

"Are you sure you should be fishing at this hour?"

"Sarah, I'm a man of the wild. Nature and I? We're like this." He set down his gear to lace his hands together in a tug. "Why don't you go back to bed? I'll be back before long and will see you in the morning."

"All right. If you're sure?"

"Megapositive," he said, picking up his gear and flashing her a grin.

Matt left his gear under the house, then headed for the beach, the beam of his flashlight leading. Whew! That had been close. He wasn't sure whether Sarah had believed his fishing story, but one way or another, he was confident things would come out fine. Now, if he could just locate that huge piece of driftwood he'd spotted when he and Sarah had been here earlier today…

Matt trudged through the sludgy sand, his heart light. So yeah, the beach roads were crappy. Impassable, in fact. In many ways, that was the best Christmas gift he'd ever had. Out of the blue, life had delivered him a second chance with Sarah. A woman from his past who could very well become a permanent fixture in his future. Sarah was beautiful and funny and kind, just the sort of person he'd always imagined himself winding up with. Him and a big bustling passel of kids.

Matt stopped walking, shocked at his own thoughts. Had he just considered making babies with Sarah? Yeah, he had, he thought, feeling his lips tug into a broad grin. Not that he was accustomed to getting ahead of himself, but Matt couldn't help but wonder what that might be like. Just him and Sarah— and their big happy brood— all adorning the family Christmas tree with homemade decorations. Matt recalled how much fun it had been sitting around the kitchen table, making those crafts with his sisters and brother Robert. He'd even enjoyed working with his nieces last Christmas when they'd taught him how to fashion Christmas stars from pieces of tinfoil with little holes poked in them to let through the light. While he didn't have ornament hooks from which to hang them, he had fishing wire to use as a handy substitution. Yes sir, his plan was going to work out fine. All he had to hope was that the tide hadn't washed out his special surprise.

Chapter Seven

Sarah awakened early and stretched in bed. She didn't know what had caused her to rise before seven o'clock. Generally, she slept until eight. Then suddenly she remembered. Of course! Today was Christmas Day! But what did that matter, really? How much could she expect at a beach house on the rugged North Carolina coast? She'd never partaken much in Christmas, anyway. And here she was, stuck with a man who'd never even expected her to be here. And was much less prepared to make the holiday special for her, besides. Sarah unfolded the simple poem she'd composed for Matt, hoping it wasn't desperately inane. All she'd longed to do was give him something of her heart. She'd wanted to say thank you and had thought for a brief moment that this was a good way to start. Now, looking down at her uneven scrawl, she doubted her instincts. What if he thought her a fool, or worse yet—questioned her iambic pentameter? Sarah's poetry had never been in perfect rhythm, but at least it was concise and summarized what she wanted to say.

After Matt had sent her to bed, she'd stayed up an extra hour trying hard to fashion its lines. He'd been so kind, and all she meant to say was thank you. *Thanks for being the kind of guy I'd always believed was in this world.* Since Sarah had been a little girl, she'd been putting words together. Sometimes clumsily; at others, in a neatly arrayed fashion. Her English teachers had told her she had talent, though she'd refused in many ways to believe it. What was important to her more than anything was reaching the people she felt driven to write for. Since coming here, Matt had become one of those people.

Sarah folded over the page, deciding that she'd have to give it to him. Most especially because what they had might not last. And, in the end, she thought with a heavy heart, it was destined not to.

Matt put on the finishing touches, feeling exhausted. He'd work hard all night to ensure everything would come off right. Since he was committed to protecting the environment, he hadn't been about to insult a flourishing pine. Instead, he'd selected found driftwood as the perfect stand-in "Charlie Brown" yuletide tree. With the summer deck lights strung around it, it looked almost festive. The tinfoil ornaments he'd fashioned thanks to his nieces' help had been a boon. Just last season, he'd sat with the three little girls around his mom's kitchen table. They'd taught him a trick they'd learned in Brownie Scouts. How to create shiny star ornaments from cutout pieces of aluminum foil, dotted with pinprick holes to let through the light. They were somewhat reminiscent of Mexican lanterns, only hung from the branches of this wayward tree. Matt felt lucky that, in lieu of ornament hooks, he'd had fishing wire with which to secure them. He hoped with all his heart that Sarah would enjoy it. It certainly looked regal enough, standing nearly five feet tall and spreading its spindling braches wide on all sides.

Matt thought he heard stirring from Sarah's room and debated whether to flee or to stay and wish her a merry Christmas. Before he'd fully processed that thought, she opened her bedroom door and suddenly appeared.

"Oh my." She brought her palms to her perfectly pink cheeks. "What's this?"

"Merry Christmas," he said, his tone husky.

She stopped in her tracks and met his gaze, her voice wavering. "Is this what I think it is?"

He turned to her, his heart pounding. Of all the mornings he'd ever experienced, this was the one he hoped would go off right. "Your very own Christmas tree."

She approached it slowly, then gingerly touched one of its branches. "Driftwood?" she asked, amazement in her eyes.

"I had to get creative," he answered honestly.

"Oh, Matt," she said, her voice cracking. She'd never had anyone do something like this for her before. How he'd done it or where he'd found the lights and decorations, she had no idea. But one thing was clear, the look in his eyes said he'd done it all for her. So this was what he'd been up to late last night with that box and why he'd snuck down on the beach. She gingerly touched one of the stars, and it pivoted on its thin wire, tiny arrays of light streaking through its pattern of holes. "Did you make this?"

He smiled, and the tears that had been aching to break through poured from her eyes. "I can't believe you did this... Did this all for me."

"I wanted to do something for you. Something to show you you're special."

How she wanted to show him he was special too. Sarah debated about giving him the poem but decided to put it off until later. She wasn't sure how he might take it, and, given how well things were going now, she didn't want to put a damper on them. "Thank you. It's wonderful. Probably the most wonderful Christmas gift I've ever received."

He took her in his arms. "I was hoping to make this day great for you."

"It couldn't be any more perfect," she said, looking up in his eyes. And it was true. Sarah was feeling so bright and hopeful this morning. So positive, in fact, that she didn't want any sort of negativity to get in the way. Ever since that first late-night conversation with Matt, she'd struggled with her attraction to him and been conflicted about becoming involved. But he was so warm and wonderful, it was hard not to be tempted to let those doubts slide. Just once, Sarah wanted to feel good about things and bask in this dynamite man's attentions. Would it really be so wrong for them to have one ideal day where she could let herself go and live in the moment?

Matt glanced sideways, then sexily cocked an eyebrow. "Not even…if it's snowing?"

She stared in delight out the large glass door to see a billion little white flakes driving down in droves to coat the deck framing the ocean. The scene was lovely, magical in its unexpected beauty. Matt took her hand and led her toward the door. "Come on!"

"We can't go out there like this!" she said, referring to their sleeping attire.

"You're right." He nabbed a throw blanket from the sofa. "We'll use this to keep us warm."

But when he led her outdoors, Sarah realized she wouldn't need the blanket at all. Matt scooped her in his arms, wrapping the blanket around them as snow beat down on the deck. She looked up at him as a

smile worked its way across his handsome face.
"There really is a Santa," she said. Snow drove down
harder, coating their hair with tiny white flakes. He
brushed his lips to hers, and her world went all warm
and fuzzy, in spite of the freezing cold. "I'm looking
at him."

"You're all I want for Christmas. I'm so happy
you're here."

He kissed her harder then, his deep passion
sweeping her away while the wind and the snow
swirled around them and the pounding ocean echoed
the rhythm of their hearts.

A little while later, they sat wrapped up in a fresh
blanket on the sofa before a cozy fire, both sipping
from mugs of hot cocoa. "I've never had a holiday
like this," she told Matt honestly. "This one's been
like a dream."

"And it's not over yet." He gave her shoulder a
tight hug. "I was thinking of making us some gumbo
for Christmas dinner. How does that sound?"

"Delicious. Do you have everything you need?"

"Catch of the Day," he said with a grin.

Sarah gasped at his revelation. "Are you saying
you really went fishing last night?"

"It was more like early this morning, but yeah."

"I thought you were sneaking outdoors, preparing
all this." She motioned to the makeshift Christmas
tree beside them, sharing its homey glow.

"I was," he told her. "But once I'd set the
driftwood under the house to dry out a bit, I came
back and got my fishing gear. You'll really like the
gumbo, I think. It's not exactly turkey and stuffing,
but—"

"It sounds great. Just let me know what I can do to help."

He wriggled his eyebrows. "Are you making a play to start cooking with me again?"

She laughed. "Might be."

"You won't have to offer twice." He smiled softly. "Though I've got to admit making a roux won't be nearly as sexy as baking cookies."

Her lips took a downward turn. "Darn."

He took her hand in his. "How did I get so lucky? One day I'm all over women, and the next, there you are."

"All over women?"

"It doesn't matter, really. I'm just happy my brother insisted I come here to get away."

"So it was Robert's idea, was it?"

"Uh-huh. Was it yours or Elaine's?"

"Elaine's, actually."

He gave a hearty laugh. "Well, God bless them both. We'll have to drink a toast to them later."

Sarah had fun helping Matt with the gumbo. Though he'd been right, making a roux wasn't nearly as sexy as baking cookies. It required devoted attention to hot oil and flour, and careful timing with tossing in chopped onions and celery. After a delicious dinner filled with easy conversation and laughter, Sarah helped Matt with the cleanup, which was minimal.

"What would you like to do now?" he asked her. "Shall we look for a movie?"

But Sarah was having so much fun talking with Matt, she didn't want to find them caught up in something like that. "Maybe we could turn on some music and just visit awhile?"

"Sounds great to me." He went to the living area to survey the CDs, neatly alphabetized on some built-in shelves. "What will it be? Christmas music or the Beach Boys?"

"Hmm. Tough decision. Why don't we go with Beach Boys. I mean, given where we are."

He grinned and loaded the CD. When *Little St. Nick* began to play, Sarah laughed. "Looks like we're getting both! The Beach Boys *and* Christmas."

"At least with this song," he said with a chuckle.

She carried her wine to the sofa, but before she could get there, Matt approached.

"Care to dance?"

"Sure," she said, setting her glass aside. The music was catchy and upbeat as he took her in his arms and they bounced happily to its tune. He twirled her under his arm, then whirled her back toward him, tucking her up against him. She laughed heartily. "Where did you learn to dance like this?"

"In North Carolina, they call this shag dancing. It's big in the beach areas."

When the song ended, a slower one started. Sarah turned to head back to the sofa, but Matt stopped her by taking her hand.

"Don't go."

She gazed up at him, and blue eyes sparkled, warm in the firelight's glow. "I need you to stay with me," he said, his voice gone husky, as *Don't Worry, Baby* began. "Stay in my arms."

He pulled her to him, and they embraced her pulse fluttering wildly. "This is all I want," he whispered into her hair as he held her close. "Just to be with you. Right here and now."

It was all she wanted too. Everything she wanted and had always longed for was right here in front of her. Sarah held on tight as they swayed to the music and the embers of the fire crackled softly. When the brief snow shower had let up, a deep fog had moved in. From faraway on the sound, the mournful cry of a tugboat wafted across the waters. They'd been through all kinds of weather, but with Matt, she'd felt safe, secure in the knowledge that he would care for and comfort her.

She would remember this Christmas forever.

Chapter Eight

The next morning, they sat at the kitchen island with their coffees.

"I can't believe we got a white Christmas," she said. "I can't remember the last time I had one. I had to have been a kid."

"A light dusting was more like it," he said with a laugh. "But, you're right. It was special."

She studied him with affection, thinking how much she'd come to care for him these past few days. No matter what happened later, she would always recall her time here with him in a fond way. "I want to thank you. Thank you for helping make yesterday the best Christmas ever." She shifted in her seat to pull the poem from her jeans pocket. She'd debated about giving it to him at all but then had decided she needed to let him know that she'd thought of him.

She handed it over, apologizing. "I considered giving this to you yesterday but decided to wait. I hope you don't mind."

"Of course I don't mind." He appeared genuinely touched by the gesture.

He unfolded the page and looked down at the carefully crafted lines. "This is wonderful," he said, meeting her gaze. "I've never had anyone do anything like this for me before."

"I've never had anyone make me a Christmas tree out of driftwood."

He smiled at her warmly, then lowered his head and began to read.

Between the earth and sky,
You and I
Are caught up
In this moment,
Where waves crash,
And lightning strikes
The shore.
You're deep
In my soul,
Warming
The cold
Of my heart.

After a lingering moment, he looked up. "It's beautiful," he said, the words catching in his throat. "But also a little sad, don't you think?"

"I thought it was hopeful."

"Then I'll take it as that way too." He stared through the plate glass door, studying the horizon. "Looks like the storm has lifted. How about you and I take a stroll?"

Matt led her onto the beach, where soft winds blew and gulls called. The sky was cloudy yet calm, the ocean roiling peacefully below it. They walked a long way down the shore, neither one talking. There was an unspoken melancholy between them, as if each sensed their time together was drawing to a close.

"I want to thank you for the poem," he said finally. "It means a lot to me that you'd write it."

"It was nothing."

He stopped walking to look at her. "No, it was something. Something really beautiful that came from your heart."

Sarah felt herself flush. Oh, how she wished she could give him that heart, wholly and unconditionally. But there'd been conditions imposed on her she couldn't help or change.

Matt took her gently by the shoulders and gazed in her eyes. "But Sarah, I want… Need you to understand. This is more than a *brief moment* for me. I mean, I want it to be more than that for both of us."

Emotion swirled within her. "Just what are you saying?"

"That I don't believe we both wound up here by accident. That maybe there was something else at play. Something bigger than the two of us, and maybe even more magical than…Santa."

"It's been really wonderful, but—"

"I'm not talking about anything drastic. Rather that we take this incredible serendipity as some sort of sign. A sign that maybe we weren't meant to walk away from each other three years ago. Then again, maybe we were, because things can be that much better between us now.

"All I'm asking is that when the ferry reopens, things between us won't end. Let me take you out to dinner back in Bethesda. Maybe even a movie. We don't have to rush things. There's nothing wrong with taking our time."

She pressed her lips together for a beat, studying him. When she finally spoke, her chin trembled. "I can't give you what you want."

"You don't even *know* what I want," he said, his voice etched with pain.

Sarah dropped her eyes to hide the fact that they were watering.

"I'm not the girl for you. Not long-term."

"Is it…" he began tentatively, appearing stung by the thought. "Is it that you don't feel the same way?"

"It doesn't matter how I feel."

"Sarah, please. Talk to me."

She gathered her resolve and met his eyes, knowing this was for the best. Sometimes when you really cared for someone, you had to do what was right for that person. Not selfishly only consider yourself. Matt deserved to have the sort of life he was destined to lead. And that life couldn't include her.

"I'm not interested. Not interested in any more than we've had here."

Matt sucked in a breath and stared at her in disbelief.

"I guess that's all I needed to hear," he said hoarsely.

The telephone rang loudly as they reentered the house from their walk. Matt walked in a daze to answer it. So she didn't feel the same. Had no interest in continuing things further. He'd done nothing more than make one big fool of himself his whole time here. He lifted the receiver with a heavy heart as gulls sailed beyond the kitchen window. "Hello?"

It was the ferryman, advising all residents on the island that the boat docks were nearly repaired. With the bad weather ended, the ferry would be up and running again the first thing tomorrow. Well, that was something, anyway. He and Sarah would no longer be trapped here together. Given the conversation they'd just had, that was obviously for the best.

"Who was that?" she asked from the living area.

"The ferry will back in business tomorrow. I

guess I should start packing."

"No, don't," she said suddenly. "You can stay. I'll go."

And, for the first time since she'd arrived here, Matt didn't feel any inclination to stop her.

The next day, Matt sat at the table, watching the waves through the window. The skies had mostly cleared, except for a few dark clouds rumbling above. Scattered showers were predicted, but there were heavier rains raging inside him. He felt all turned inside out, as if someone had extracted his heart and laid it on this very table. And someone had. Her name was Sarah.

"I'm leaving," she said, standing by the kitchen door.

Matt glanced her way and set down his coffee. She'd already loaded her SUV and now held nothing but her small purse and a travel water bottle. "I see."

"Matt…" Her cheeks were flushed. "If there was any way to work things out, I'd stay." Like hell she would. She hadn't even given them a chance, wouldn't even tell him what was wrong. She was just playing herself again, calling the shots, and getting to be the one who decided when it was over. "You're going to miss the boat."

She sucked in a breath, and it sounded like she was crying. Matt didn't dare turn to look at her. He studied the shore instead, watching it take a relentless beating from the waves. His heart knew just how that felt.

He heard the door creak open as she spoke, her voice shaky. "It was good seeing you again."

In a different world, he might have felt the same.

At the moment, though, all Matt wanted was for her to go away so that the pain would end.

Chapter Nine

Sarah waited in line for the ferry, queued up behind two other SUVs and a couple of pickups. These were the greatest signs of life she'd seen in days, and still they were paltry. Few folks ventured to the island this time of year, and those who did were die-hards. Rugged outdoorsmen or property owners, the types not easily put off by a ten-foot storm surge or the occasional nor'easter. She peered through her windshield at the darkening sky. More bad weather was coming, but it could nowhere compete with the storm in her soul. Her parting from Matt had been heartbreaking, yet necessary. Wasn't it so much better to say good-bye now, when becoming even more involved would only make separating worse? He'd told her just what he wanted: the same thing his parents had. She knew what that was because she'd seen it firsthand. A warm, wonderful family with lots of offspring, and having children was not in Sarah's future.

She steeled her heart, worried that she'd always be alone. After rupturing her appendix in college, she'd developed pelvic inflammatory disease, a horrible infection. Its outcome had left her sterile, completely unable to bear children. It was a bitter pill to swallow at age twenty-one and apparently had been too much for her college boyfriend to deal with. They'd talked about graduating and moving to work in the same city. Eventually getting married and raising a family of their own. While he hadn't left her immediately, receiving news of her medical condition had seemed to change the way he felt about her. Though he denied it, afterward things started breaking apart. They began fighting more frequently, then finally split up the second semester of their senior year.

Later, Sarah had chalked up her college boyfriend's reaction to youth and inexperience. Surely a mature man who loved her deeply wouldn't react the same way. She'd learned differently with her first adult relationship in Maryland. It wasn't that he hadn't loved her; it was more that he'd seen a different sort of future for them going forward. Naturally, adoption was an option, but he'd been the only son in his family and had always thought he'd carry on the family line. When he'd also gone away, the breakup had ripped Sarah's heart to shreds with its haunting déjà vu. Consequently, it had become harder for her to become intimate with a man. She'd surprised herself by falling into bed with Matt at Elaine's wedding.

Now that she knew the truth, she could more clearly piece together what had happened. She'd not only been desperately attracted to him, she'd also seen him as someone with potential. Serious potential. He was intelligent, witty, and unbearably handsome, just the sort of guy she'd always known she'd fall for. The more champagne she'd had, the better he'd looked. And the better he'd looked, the more devastated she was by her secret. Here he was, this super terrific guy, and their mutual attraction was powerful. So powerful, Sarah wasn't sure if she could fight it. Part of her wanted to totally give in, see if things would follow through and they might begin a relationship. But most of her was utterly terrified that what had happened in the past would occur again. In her fits and starts between wanting him and wanting to flee from him in order to protect her still fragile heart, she'd drunk herself silly.

If only she'd believed it wouldn't have made a difference to Matt, she would have told him the truth. But he was so clearly into his family and the concept of a big, happy brood. After spending time with him this week at the beach, she believed that more than ever. His background was not just Italian but also Catholic. Sarah recalled all the toasts and jokes that were made at Elaine and Robert's wedding about making tons of babies, and quickly. Creating lots of little Salvatores was clearly a family expectation, one that she'd be unable to fulfill.

Needing to distract herself from her pain, Sarah switched on her satellite radio. It was set to a blues station, and the song *Stormy Weather* began to play. As if on cue, light rain began to ping against the windshield, flecking it with little dots of moisture that ran in sad streaks down the glass. She shut her eyes as Etta James crooned on, and the memories from the week flooded back. Catching Matt by surprise as he emerged in a towel from the outdoor shower... Enjoying movies and board games together... Matt wrapping his arms around her during that very sexy baking lesson... Kissing him in the rain and in the snow... And finally, that truly magical Christmas tree he'd so lovingly crafted for her on Christmas morning.

A horn blared, and Sarah opened her eyes to see the queue ahead of her was moving, the ferryman motioning vehicles onto the broad deck of the boat. She wiped her tears with her coat sleeve and set her vehicle in gear, her hands trembling. Despite the damp cold, her heart was on fire, burning like a forest blaze consuming its final pine. There was nothing much left of her; she had nothing left to give. Why, then, had Matt seemed to trust that she did? Sarah rolled onto the ferry, her SUV rising and falling over the loading ramp with a jolt, as Etta James begged to see the sun... Just then, a beam of sunlight streaked in through her windshield from behind a faraway cloud.

The Christmas-tree-shaped crystal dangling from Sarah's rearview mirror pivoted in its glow, dazzling her with an astounding array of color. Matt's words came back to her in a husky whisper. *"There's a rainbow after every storm,"* he'd said, looking into her eyes. *"You just need to believe it."*

Sarah's heart beat faster as she knew suddenly what she must do. She could no longer run from her life. She had to confront it head-on. She needed to start by gathering her courage to explain things to Matt. Even if he didn't want her after what she had to say, he deserved to hear the truth. He'd been nothing but good and kind to her. So thoughtful and romantic too. It was wrong of her to leave without any explanation at all, leaving him to wonder if he'd somehow been at fault. How could she do that to someone as great as him when the blame was hers and hers alone? It was time for her to stand up and own it, letting the cards fall where they may. But oh, didn't her heart hope that would land her in Matt's arms.

She glanced in her rearview mirror and gasped. Another car was getting loaded onto the ferry behind her. Then another...and yet another still. "Wait!" she shouted, throwing up her hands. The ferryman continued his work, unable to hear her. She couldn't let this happen. Not here, not today. The year was coming to an end, so maybe it was time to consider new beginnings. Sarah laid on her horn and opened her driver's side door, leaping from the SUV. "Stop!" she yelled at the stunned ferryman, who stared at her beneath his tartan-plaid tam. "Off! I've got to get off," she continued, a bit breathless. "Off of this boat!"

"I'm afraid that's impossible, lady. We're already halfway loaded."

Sarah glanced at the line of nearly a dozen vehicles behind her, then met the ferryman's gaze. "What if I ask them all to back up?"

"What?"

"I'll do it! I'll go car to car if I have to!"

"What is this? Some sort of emergency?"

It most certainly was. In fact, it was the greatest state of emergency Sarah Anderson had ever had. For the first time in her life, she was falling for the perfect man, *a good man, a wonderful man,* and she was being foolish enough to let him get away. It was time she learned to fight for her life, work for the future she wanted. Even if it proved painful. Even if she might fail. The hard truth was she'd never forgive herself if she didn't try. "Yes."

The ferryman removed his tam and slowly shook his head before looking up. "What kind of an emergency?"

"It's…" Sarah felt her voice warble and pursed her lips a beat to steady herself. "…my heart."

His faced creased with concern, and he took a step forward. She held up a hand to stop him.

"Two hearts, really. There's a very big risk of

someone getting hurt. Of both hearts being broken."

The ferryman heaved a sigh, his expression lighting with understanding. "And you think that by getting off this boat, you can fix it?"

She stared at him, feeling her confidence surge. "I have to try."

Back at the cottage, Matt morosely disassembled his makeshift Christmas tree. Sarah had looked just like some delighted kid when she'd happened upon it Christmas morning. He'd really thought he'd done everything right, but apparently his efforts had been a major fail. What a fiasco this trip had been. He'd come to beach to forget about one woman and had been unexpectedly raked over the coals by another one. Maybe what Matt needed to do was take a break from women altogether. A long break.

He was just coiling up the deck lights when he thought he heard a car in the drive, screeching to a halt. Seconds later, a door popped open, then slammed shut. Could that be Sarah? Coming back to retrieve something she'd forgotten?

His answer came in the sound of her footfalls racing up the front steps. "Matt!" she said, bursting through the kitchen door. "We have to talk!" She was out of breath, her coat unzipped and her sweatshirt and hair speckled by the light rain that had been falling.

"I thought you were catching the ferry?"

"I was," she said, stepping forward and shutting the door behind her. "But I got off."

"Off?" he questioned, trying to imagine that feat, particularly if she'd already been loaded. "Sarah, what's going on?"

She crossed to where he stood, and looked up, her brown eyes brimming with moisture. "I haven't been completely honest. There's something. Something that I need to tell you."

Matt swallowed hard, not knowing what to expect. "And what is that?"

"I can't…" She stopped, seeming to gather her nerve.

"Are you changing your mind? About the two of us?"

"I've never wanted anything but the two of us."

"Then why…?"

"I can't have children," she said in a whimper. "A long time ago, I had an infection, and—"

He brought his fingers to her lips. "Is that why you left? Why you said we couldn't have a future? Because you believed that was a deal breaker for me?"

She held his gaze through bleary eyes. "Isn't it?"

While he'd never had occasion to consider it, the truth was he wasn't about to let someone as amazing as Sarah get away due to a medical condition beyond her control. What kind of man would that make him? Not the one he understood himself to be. It must have taken tremendous courage for Sarah to come back and tell him the truth, particularly as she had no guarantee what his reaction might be. "No. It isn't," he said, knowing when he said it that answer felt right.

"But you said… You told me that you want what your parents have."

"I meant *their relationship*. The way they are with each other and are there for one another, even after all these years." He took her in his arms, damp clothing and all. "Sweetheart, listen to me. I want *you*.

Do you hear me? You're the person I'm falling in love with and can't bear to see walk away. Please promise me you won't do that again. Twice was bad enough. I'm not sure my heart can take a third time."

She shared a shaky smile, tears streaming from her eyes. "I promise."

"Besides…" He lightly stroked her cheeks. "Some say that kids are overrated."

"They do not," she said with a sniff. "Especially in your family."

"There are options, you know. Life is full of options." He grinned warmly. "I like dogs."

She laughed through her tears. "You're such a great guy."

"Hmm, yes. I'm glad you can finally see that. Only from this point out, I'm going to insist on one thing." He pressed his forehead to hers and looked deeply in her eyes. "That you call me Santa."

"What?" she asked with surprise.

"I thought it was kind of sexy when you said I was like him."

"You *are* him," she said, tugging him close.

He threaded his fingers in her luscious hair and drew her in for a kiss. After an intensely passionate moment, he pulled back. "Can I convince you to stay for New Year's?"

"Why, Santa," she said softly, "we don't even have champagne."

He laughed out loud, snuggling her in his arms. "We'll improvise."

He kissed her deeply then, again and again, only finding himself hungry for more. She molded herself to him, her legs appearing to give way. But he shored her up and held her close, determined now—more than ever—never to let her go.

Epilogue

The following December, Matt took Sarah's hand and led her onto the big, broad deck. The ocean bellowed and tumbled before them, gulls darting in and out of the waves under a darkening sky. Matt wrapped his arms around her from behind as they studied the seascape.

"Looks like a storm's brewing."

She glanced over her shoulder thinking he was the most handsome man she'd seen in *anything*—a tuxedo or a towel. "Hmm, yes. We could be stuck here indefinitely."

"Now, that would be a shame." He leaned forward and nuzzled her neck, causing her to shiver slightly.

"Chilly?"

The wind kicked up ruffling the layers of her billowy white gown. "Just a bit."

Matt removed his jacket and draped it over her shoulders before turning her toward him in an embrace. "I'm glad we bought this place."

"I couldn't think of a better spot to spend our honeymoon," she said, smiling up at him.

He shot her a sexy grin. "And this time we brought champagne."

"What will we toast to?"

Her face warmed under his perusal. "Santa?"

"Yes. To him and Christmastime."

Matt brushed his lips to hers. "Spending Christmas with you is the best."

"Something tells me it's about to get even

better," she said, nearly breathless.

"Shall I carry you back to the sleigh?"

"I'll go anywhere with you," she said, meaning it absolutely.

"How about a trip around the world?"

"*What?*"

"You did say you wanted to see the Southern Cross? Travel to Tasmania?"

"You can't mean…?".

"Sarah, sweetheart," he said with a loving look. "I've arranged some time off, and we've got plenty of money."

"But I thought this was our honeymoon?"

"Beach baby of mine, *the honeymoon* has just begun."

THE END

A Note from the Author

Thanks for reading *The Holiday Brides Collection (Books 1 – 4)*. I hope you enjoyed it. If you did, please help other people find this book.

1. This book is lendable, so share it with a friend who you think might like it so that she (or he) can discover me, too.

2. Help other people find this book: write a review.

3. Sign up for my newsletter so that that you can learn about the next book as soon as it's available. Write to GinnyBairdRomance@gmail.com with "newsletter" in the subject heading.

4. Come like my Facebook page: http://www.facebook.com/GinnyBairdRomance.

5. Follow me on Twitter @GinnyBaird https://twitter.com/GinnyBaird.

6. Visit my website: http://www.ginnybairdromance.com for details on other books available at multiple outlets now.

Did you know there's another book in the *Holiday Brides Series*? Keep reading here for an excerpt from Holiday Brides Book 5 *Baby, Be Mine*.

Holiday Brides Book 5

BABY, BE MINE

Chapter One

Nikki Constantino dabbed the corner of her eye with a tissue. There was so much dust in the room, her allergies were going wild. It caked on the fake flowers in the blue vase and hung heavy in the musty air. No one must have cleaned this study in years.

The stout little man studied her kindly through horn-rimmed glasses. "I know this is hard. You and your aunt must have been close." Snow slapped the windowpanes behind him, painting icy streaks down the glass.

"Actually, I barely knew her." She sniffed, and Jack draped his arm around her. He gave her shoulder a light squeeze, the silent signal between them that everything would be all right. She didn't have to look at him to know his dark brown eyes were focused on the attorney in a way that said, *Don't sugarcoat this. Give it to us straight.*

"Nikki hasn't seen her Great-Aunt Mallory in years."

"Not since I was little. Ten, I think."

The attorney studied the papers before him and licked his plump lips. "Uh-huh," he said, thumbing through them. "Uh-huh, uh-huh, uh-huh."

Jack loudly cleared his throat. "Isn't there something you're supposed to read?"

The lawyer stared at Jack. "To Miss Constantino, yes. Frankly, not understanding your relation to the deceased, I'm not certain you should be here."

Nikki defensively took Jack's hand. "He's my best friend!"

"Friend, huh?" the other man asked, appearing amused. "I was hoping you might say fiancé."

Nikki glanced quickly at Jack, noting his neck had deepened a shade. "Why on earth would you say that?"

"Might make things less complicated."

Nikki would like to see how they could get *more* complicated. Here she sat, summoned to some tiny Midwestern town in the thick of winter, at her late great-aunt's behest. And, she hadn't a clue why. Her memories of Aunt Mallory were less than flattering and concerned an overbearing woman tottering on tiny heels. Her face was pasty pale from too much pressed powder; her lips were fire-engine red. She never seemed to get the color within the lines. And when she opened her mouth to speak, even her portly beagle, Duke, took refuge under the bed. Whether the meatloaf was overcooked or the thermostat set too low, Aunt Mallory could deliver a tongue-lashing bent in the direction of anyone careless enough to get in her way.

For the first few years after Nikki's grandma died, her mom, Emma, felt sorry for her late mother's spinster sister and invited her to join them for holidays. The invitations abruptly stopped after Mallory threatened to stuff poor Duke and pop him in the oven as a replacement for the *too dry* Thanksgiving turkey. Emma surreptitiously placed Duke with an animal rescue and sent Aunt Mallory packing. It was a transgression Aunt Mallory would never forgive. Not, apparently, until her dying day. She left her niece, Emma, nothing, and she didn't even know about Nikki's baby brother since he'd been born after she'd broken family ties. As far as

Aunt Mallory was concerned, her only other remaining heir was her grand-niece, Nikki.

The attorney addressed Nikki as winds howled outside. Or maybe those were the cows crying. Could cows cry from relief, Nikki wondered? They were on Aunt Mallory's dairy farm, all fifty acres of it. Nikki certainly hoped her aunt didn't leave her *that*. She didn't know the first thing about farming. Plus, she was lactose intolerant. "Do I have your permission to proceed?"

She squeezed Jack's hand, then released it and patted his knee. She must have patted one too many times, because Jack suddenly pinned her palm in place right against his pants leg. Nikki sometimes had a nervous habit of doing something over and over, but only when she was stressed. "Whatever you have to say to me, you can say in front of Jack."

"Very well." He shuffled some papers. "I'll read what she said in her handwritten note."

"Handwritten?" Jack interceded. "Isn't a will supposed to be typed or something? Notarized?"

"She had one of those. This was written after. It supersedes the other."

Jack sat back in his chair. "I see."

She was glad he'd come along. When things crowded in on Nikki, she sometimes felt driven to react quickly, and not always in the best-thought-out ways. Like when her knee-jerk reaction was to refuse Mallory's *invite from the grave* to come here. Jack said she shouldn't look a gift horse in the mouth until she at least knew its breed. He was right, of course. There'd be no sense in refusing an inheritance sight unseen. It was just the fact it came from Aunt Mallory that made it seem unpromising. Jack was good for things like that: helping her stay charted in the right direction. She teasingly called him her compass. He didn't seem to mind the moniker. He'd had it since the tenth grade.

"*I, Mallory Gertrude Greene...*"

"Gertrude?" Jack quipped quietly beside her. She slapped his hand with her free one. He still firmly held the other. She tried to tug it away, but he resisted.

"*Being of sound mind and body,*" the attorney continued, "*do hereby bequeath my entire estate—*"

"Entire estate?" Nikki asked him. "What's that mean?"

"I'm getting to that part. *To the one relative on earth who never insulted me...*"

"That's because I was terrified," Nikki whispered to Jack.

"*My great-niece, Nicola Carina Constantino...*"

Nikki swallowed hard.

"*Under the following conditions...*"

"I didn't think the deceased could set conditions," Jack said.

"They can do anything that they want," the attorney answered. "Before I proceed, I need to read this stipulation."

"That's different from a condition?" Nikki wanted to know.

"It's a footnote." He turned the paper sideways to read something scrawled along its edge. "It says here... *Important! In order to inherit, Nicola must be over the age of twenty-five. Otherwise—*"

"Yes." Jack pumped his fist in the air, and the attorney lowered his glasses.

"This will go a lot faster without the

commentary."

"Sorry." He glanced apologetically at Nikki. "It just seemed like that was a score." She'd recently turned twenty-eight, so that wasn't a problem.

The man rolled his eyes and resumed reading. *"Otherwise, the estate will be held in trust until such time Nicola reaches the age of twenty-five and is therefore is suitably mature to meet the aforesaid conditions. Assuming she does, she'll be at liberty to dispense of her inheritance as she chooses."*

Nikki's head was spinning already.

"That means you can sell the farm."

"Good." She didn't know much about real estate, but Jack was business minded. He could help her. *But wait! What if I can't sell quickly enough? What will become of the cows? I don't know a thing about milking! Yikes! What if Aunt Mallory didn't leave instructions? Will the poor cows explode? Would that make me guilty of—gasp—uddercide?*

Jack tightened his grip on her hand, sensing she was growing tense. "Breathe," he told her quietly. He demonstrated by sucking in air.

She inhaled a deep breath then let it go, feeling better. Thank goodness Jack was here. They both turned toward the attorney, who gaped at them.

"How much is it worth?" Jack asked.

The attorney raised his wrinkled brow. Nikki noticed it was flecked with age spots. "You don't know?"

She and Jack shook their heads. "This dairy has an arrangement with all the major distributors: grocery chains, restaurants… Biscuit Barrel…"

"Biscuit Barrel?" Nikki asked in surprise. She and Jack had stopped at one of those on the way here from the airport. Who knew Jack's patty melt was secretly connected?

"That sounds big," Jack said.

"It is big," the attorney answered.

"How big is *big*?" Nikki wanted to know.

"Estimated value of this farm and all your aunt's investments? Just over two million dollars."

Jack choked on the words. "Did you say two...*million*?"

"That's right. With an M."

Bright flares of light blasted before her, and Nikki wondered if she was growing faint. It was like the Fourth of July had come in December. The attorney and Jack were still talking, but she could barely hear them for all the commotion going on in her head. This was what it must feel like to win the lottery. Crazy, exhilarating... Totally surreal! She could quit her day job! Help her mom! No wait, without working, she'd probably be bored. She could become a professional playgirl, maybe. One of those jetsetters she'd heard of. Maybe even take Jack on a vacation with her. She owed him one good trip at least, after all he'd done. And to think, just last week, she'd worried over paying her heating bill.

"Nikki," Jack said, "didn't you hear any of that?"

"What?"

He clenched his jaw before speaking. "Condition one."

"No," she said breezily, mentally sketching out an itinerary. The Bahamas? Bermuda? Maybe the Caymans? Yes. Jack would probably like that. "What's condition one?"

The attorney stared at her flatly. "That you marry by Valentine's Day."

"Ma...marry?" she stammered. Impossible! Nikki didn't even have a boyfriend at the moment.

The attorney righted the hand-scrawled page. *"Tie the knot. Get hitched. Ball and chain. Hook, line, and sinker, yes."*

"She wrote that?" Jack asked in shock.

"Every word, including that next thing about the baby."

"*Baby?*" Nikki squeaked. Now she was certain she would faint.

The attorney shook out the page and flipped it over. "That's condition two."

"Your Aunt Mallory apparently thought she could dictate not just your marriage but your entire life," Jack said, growing indignant.

"She does give you an extra year for the child. To produce one, I mean."

"Great!" Nikki chirped cheerily. "Mallory's just the one to give family advice!"

"Maybe she wants you to have what she didn't," the attorney noted astutely.

"What makes you say that?" Jack asked.

"It's in her PS here. And this is to Nicola. *PS: Just in case you're wondering why I'm doing this, dear child, it's for your own good. Life is too short to die embittered and alone. It might take a while, but you'll understand this yourself one day. You'll be thanking me until the cows come home.*"

"Until the cows come home?" Nikki asked weakly.

"It's an expression," the lawyer said.

Jack translated. "For a really long time."

"Huh?"

"Cows are very slow creatures," the lawyer

explained. "I think she meant forever."

"Oh."

"This is crazy," Jack said to the lawyer. "You know it is."

He held up his hands. "I didn't make the rules here. I'm just the referee."

The fog in Nikki's brain lifted. "Can we contest it?"

"Sure you can." He sat back in his chair and crossed his arms. "Just as long as you think you can move things through the courts before that February fourteenth deadline."

"But that's less than eight weeks away!"

"What if we can't?" Jack asked.

"It's a risk. You'll have to prove that Mallory was unstable when she wrote this. I mean, more so than in her previous days. You'll also have to find a judge who will hear your case. We're not talking weeks now. We're talking months. Years, more than likely. But you're young. You've got plenty of time."

Yeah, maybe she did, but her mother didn't. Nikki would have to talk to Jack about that. Talk to him seriously. "What becomes of the farm in that case?"

"It gets stuck in probate."

"And the cows?"

The attorney stroked his chin. "The people your aunt hired to work this farm can continue for a while but not indefinitely. Certainly not without being paid. Mallory left behind enough money to keep them on through the end of February. At that point, I think she assumed you'd either take over running the business or sell it off."

Nikki's voice rose in panic. "But I don't *own* the

business."

"You will by February fourteenth—if you marry."

Jack finally released her hand and leaned forward on his elbows. "And if she doesn't?"

"Everything will be liquidated and absorbed by the state."

"What do you mean liquidated?" Nikki asked. "They won't hurt the cows?"

"I can't say what will become of the cows. Perhaps another dairy will take them, or they'll be farmed out to different ones. There are other options too. But you may not want to hear about them."

Nikki gasped. She *was* about to become responsible for uddercide. How horrifying!

"Holy cow," Jack said. "This is a mess."

The attorney handed Nikki a weighty portfolio. "I'd encourage you not to make any rash decisions until you've read this. In spite of what you think of it, your Aunt Mallory's bequest to you was really quite generous."

Nikki nodded numbly, seeming to have lost all sense of time. "What day is it?"

"December twenty-fifth," Jack said.

The attorney dismissed them with a smile. "Merry Christmas."

Jack stopped Nikki as she was about to lay her hand on the latch that opened the barn door. "Are you sure you want to do this?"

Winds whistled around them, riffling through her layered brown hair. It fell in waves past her shoulders above her puffy white coat and was now dotted with flakes from the driving snow. She met Jack's gaze with pretty blue eyes that had his caused his heart to skip a beat ever since high school. Not that she'd ever know he still felt that way. That was Jack's little secret. "Positive," she told him. "One hundred percent." But when she shoved at the latch, it appeared to be frozen.

Jack had to muscle in beside her to get it unstuck. "Here, let me."

Her hand-knit mittens with the funky patterned stitch slid out of the way just as loud mooing erupted. Nikki jumped back with a start. "What was that?"

"Your cow babies," Jack said with a smile. "To be."

Nikki dusted the snow from her hair and shoulders, then stepped past him when he opened the door. "Ew!" She covered her mouth against the stench. "Really!"

"They've got to go somewhere," he told her, jimmying the door shut.

She stared up and down rows of stalls as huge brown eyes turned in her direction. "Mooo!" one cow bellowed. Nikki surveyed a large one that appeared to be nearly twice the size of the others. "Jack, look!" She pointed to a metal plaque that hung above the cow's head. "Mallory named them."

Jack read the lettering. This one had been named *Mama*. "I think she forgot the *Big* in front of that."

Mama craned her neck forward, and Nikki tentatively patted her head.

Jack spoke from behind her. "Hey there, Ma. How's it going?"

"Stop it," Nikki scolded. "You're making fun of her." The cow met her gaze in agreement and tried to nuzzle closer, but a stall crossbar stopped her. Nikki studied the host of equipment protruding from the far wall. "That's ghastly. Do they hook her up to that?"

"I'm guessing they do."

Nikki frowned. "Doesn't seem like a very good life."

"Maybe it's all she knows?" He gave the cow a pat, and they kept walking. Jack was impressed by the size of the operation. From the outside of the barn, he'd had no idea. No wonder Nikki's aunt raked in a fortune in Cheez Whiz. They passed stall after stall, each of them labeled with an individual name.

Nikki paused before one, her jaw dropping. "She didn't."

Jack surveyed the name plaque with amusement. "Maybe she meant it as a compliment?" He reached toward the cow. "Here, Nikki, Nikk… Nikk—"

Nikki slapped his hand away. "Very funny." But her lips twisted up slightly at the corners, and Jack knew she saw the humor in the situation as well.

"Could have been worse," he said, glancing back at Mama.

Nikki started to say something smart, but then her face fell in sadness. "Jack," she said, slowly meeting his eyes. "They *will* be okay? All of them?"

Hoo boy, he'd known this was a bad idea from the moment she suggested it. The last thing someone as caring as Nikki needed to do was go involving her emotions in what was already primed to be a highly charged situation. "I'm sure your aunt wouldn't really have left them without some sort of plan."

Big Mama mooed.

"She's right," Nikki said. "You didn't know her."

She set her chin and glanced around the crowded barn.

"You seen enough?"

Nikki paused a long while before answering. Finally, she said, "We've got to find a way to fix this, Jack. A way to make it work for everyone."

"I know you have a soft spot for animals, Nikki, but—"

"For *everyone*, Jack. Not just them."

She dove into his soul with a stare, and Jack knew that whatever was coming next was serious. "I haven't told you about my mom. But I will."

"When?"

"Tonight, when we get back to our motel. But first…" She wiped back a tear with her mitten. "I need to get out of here."

Nikki sat across from Jack as he munched on his Philly cheese steak sandwich. He'd insisted they grab a bite before heading back to their motel, and he'd been right. They'd done delivery pizza the night before and had spent half an hour arguing over ingredients. Jack took another bite, and melted cheese oozed out the side of his sub.

Nikki set down her salad fork. "I wish you hadn't done that."

Jack stared at her with utmost innocence. "What?"

"Ordered *that*."

"Hey, look." Jack wiped his mouth with a napkin. "Just because you've gone all vegan on me doesn't mean I can't enjoy a bit of beef."

"Bad time to order cow, Jack. Not to mention provolone."

"Well, Ms. Cream-of-Mushroom-Soup—but oh! Can you hold the cream? What would you have suggested instead?"

Nikki frowned at the nasty cup of soup she'd pushed aside. She really should have known better at a place called the Royal Corral. When she made her request, the server looked at her like she'd arrived from Mars. Everything on the menu involved either meat or dairy, except for the meager side salad, which Nikki eagerly dug into now. "I'm just saying you could have showed a bit of sensitivity."

"Sorry." Jack picked his sandwich back up. "My sensitivity doesn't extend all the way down to my stomach."

They finished their food in silence, and Jack could tell Nikki was growing grumpy, like she did when her blood sugar got low. Maybe they could find something on the dessert menu to perk her up, assuming the pie a la mode could be served without the ice cream. "Hey, look," he told her. "It's really not that bad. It's not like the world's coming to an end or anything like that."

"Tell that to Big Mama."

"We really shouldn't have gone in that barn."

"Of course we should have." Her pretty blue eyes flashed with determination. "I needed to see for myself what I was getting into."

"Or out of, Nikki. There's still time to get out of it." She stared at him. "Your aunt's ridiculous condition, I mean."

"Conditions," she corrected. "With an S."

"Yeah, both of them. I can call my cousin Dave. He's a lawyer. Maybe he knows someone up here."

"I appreciate what you're trying to do, but—"

"But what?"

She inhaled deeply, then let it out. "I could really use that money, Jack."

"Yeah." He laughed lightly. "We could all use a couple of million. But not all of us are willing to sell ourselves for it."

"You make it sound so cold."

"Blame Mallory, not me." He studied her a beat, noting her expression had grown cloudy. "Is there something else going on that I don't know about?"

"My mom's not getting any better."

"That neck thing?"

"Her slipped disk, yeah."

"I thought she was going to have surgery?"

Nikki looked at him sadly. "She can't afford it."

"What about the diner? Don't they provide insurance?"

"It's a crappy plan, barely covers half the cost." Her brow creased with worry. "It hurts her every day to go to work. Even getting up in the morning is painful."

"She said that?"

"She didn't have to. I've seen how she moves."

"Well, maybe she can get a loan, talk to the doctors? Hospitals sometimes have repayment plans."

"We've looked into that. I even offered to help."

Jack understood that was generous, but he also knew Nikki didn't make a lot of money herself on her department store tailor's salary.

"But she's too proud. She'd never take me up on it, knowing I barely scrape by myself. Besides, she says if I'm going to help anyone out, it should be Tony."

"Tony?"

"He graduates high school this year, and really

has his heart set on going to college."

"That's expensive these days."

"Way costly. Even in state."

"What about scholarships? He's a good student, right?"

"State assistance was cut back with the recent budget cuts. He says he may have to put off going. Work a few years first."

Jack studied her with sympathy. "Sounds rough."

"Some days Ma can't even make it in to work. They dock her pay in that case. And she's got a mortgage to meet and bills to pay for Tony."

Jack stared at her with incredulity. "Just what are you saying? That you're considering meeting your Aunt Mallory's conditions?"

"Maybe it won't be so bad? In the short term."

He leaned forward and touched her arm. "But in the long term? Over time?"

"I'm not saying it has to last forever. Me and the prospective"—she appeared to nearly choke on the word—"*groom* can cut a deal."

Jack massaged his brow. "Who are you planning to marry, Nikki? You're not even seeing Dean anymore."

"That's true." She licked her lips and sat up a little straighter. "But I'll find someone, don't you think? I'm not such a bad a catch. Especially not for half a million dollars."

"I thought it was two?"

"That's the amount I'm willing to share with someone who'll go through with it. I guess if they insist, I could negotiate up to half the total."

"Now you're talking crazy."

"No, I'm being reasonable." And when she said

it, for a lunatic instant, it looked like she believed it.

"So you're going to go out there and find someone to marry. Just like that! By February fourteenth."

"Yes."

"Who?"

"I don't know. I guess I'd better start looking."

Although he suspected the outcome, Jack decided to chance it anyway. "You could always marry me...?"

"Oh, Jack, please be serious!"

He affected a chuckle to make it seem like he'd been kidding. "Well, someone's got to lighten the mood around here."

"Yeah, right. You're a very funny guy. But most importantly, you're my best friend. Which is why you've got to help me."

Jack adored Nikki, would move heaven and earth for her. But help her find another man to marry? He wasn't sure he could do that.

"Come on, Jack, *puleeze?*" She batted those eyes, and Jack knew he was a goner. He'd never been able to refuse Nikki anything in his entire life. And now his life, and all the secret hopes and dreams he'd harbored, were about to be harpooned by her ludicrous request. "I've always wanted a baby."

"There are places you can go for that without signing the rest of your life away."

"It's not the rest of my life. I don't even have to stay married. Just long enough to get pregnant."

Jack willed his mind not to go there. There was nothing worse than thinking of Nikki with another guy. When she was with a boyfriend, it was easy enough for him to push those thoughts away completely. It was when she was *between them* that Jack's hopes became renewed. Time and time again. When would he ever learn? Hadn't Nikki made things clear enough the night of their senior prom?

She appeared to be thinking, those mental wheels turning in some sort of diabolical plan. When she set her gaze back on his, she seemed buoyed, as if she'd convinced herself this entire wacky scheme could work.

"We'll have the kid call you Uncle Jack," she continued brightly. "In the end, you'll probably be closer to him than his own dad. It's not like *Dad* will be much in the picture. That will be part of the deal."

Jack felt the burn in his eyes but smiled tightly to disguise his feelings. "What if *Dad* doesn't agree?"

She brushed aside his concerns with a wave of her hand. "Aren't you the one who's fond of saying there's always a way to work things out?"

Now she was twisting his words to serve them back at him. "Nikki—"

"Don't *Nikki* me. You know we can do this, you and me. If anyone can pull it off, we can." She reached across the table to take his hands. "Please tell me you'll help. Help Ma. Help Tony, and…" She hesitated, then said with a desperate look, "Big Mama."

Jack pursed his lips, knowing there was no way he could do it. But in a stronger sense, he knew he couldn't deny helping the one person on earth he loved. Nikki'd had his heart forever, and now— without even being aware—she was going to stomp all over it. And Jack was going to help her, damn it. Help her because he understood that if he couldn't be hers, he'd better damn well ensure that the guy who was deserved her. For Nikki wasn't just beautiful. She was smart and funny, and such great company to be around. The fact was, he'd rather hang out with her than any of his buddies. She was way more entertaining and very easy to be with. Nikki had that eclectic blend of streetwise and sophisticated, with her own unique quirkiness mixed in. And Jack found that headily intoxicating. Now he was about to help someone else get drunk on her. Once they did, and discovered what is was like living with her day after day, Jack was certain no man in his right mind would be willing to give up Nikki. Worst-case scenario, she might even start falling for him… This was turning out to be a very un-merry Christmas for sure.

Jack fought the lump in his throat and squeezed Nikki's hands. "What are best friends for?"

Chapter Two

Nikki sat cross-legged on one double bed while Jack propped himself up against some pillows on the other. They'd been too cheap to get separate rooms. Besides, what did she have to worry about with Jack? Nikki reached into her large corduroy bag and withdrew Jack's present. She'd nearly forgotten what day it was until the attorney reminded them. Christmas. Who would have thought she'd be spending it in some budget motel with Jack?

"Here," she said, handing him the gift. "I got you something."

He looked up from where he'd been busily typing a message into his smartphone. "You what?" he asked, setting his phone on the nightstand.

"For Christmas, you big monkey. Go on," she urged. "Take it."

He reached across the narrow space between them and accepted the package, visibly touched. "Geez, Nikki. You didn't have to. Especially with this sudden trip... How did you...?"

"Got it a while ago. On sale," she lied. The truth was this holiday gesture had cost her a fortune. Nearly a week's wages, in fact. But if anyone deserved it, Jack did. Nobody had stood by her the way Jack had, not even any of her girlfriends over the years.

He tore back the wrapping and extracted the gift CD. Then his face fell.

"What's wrong?" she asked. "Don't tell me you already have it?" It was a new Christmas album release of Jack's favorite jazz artist. It had only been available since Thanksgiving.

"I love it." He met her eyes, and his own registered sadness. "It's the best. You're the best. The only thing is…" He hesitated a moment, holding the CD in his hands. "I didn't bring your present with me."

"Is that all?" she asked, relieved. "Gosh, Jack, you had me worried there I'd really flubbed something up."

"You never mess things up," he told her, his fingers apparently skimming the tickets taped to the back of the case. He flipped it over in awe. "You didn't." Though their surroundings were dreary, Jack's smile lit up the whole shabby room. Nikki couldn't help but think how good-looking he was. Tall, dark, and handsome, and a totally great guy too. What was wrong with the women out there?

He leapt off his bed to give her a hug. "I can't believe you did this! This is amazing, Nikki. *You're* amazing. Thanks so much."

She hugged him back, laughing. "Hey, it's only tickets and not a backstage pass."

"Doesn't matter." He settled down on the bed beside her, studying the tickets like they were some sort of holy grail. "I see you got me two," he said, fanning them in the air.

"I was hoping you might get lucky."

"Thanks for your vote of confidence."

"No, seriously. How long has it been?"

"Since?"

"Don't play cute with me. I know you've been seeing Veronica."

"Well, maybe it's none of your business."

"You know all of mine."

"That's because you've got a great big blabbermouth."

"I do not!"

"Um-hmm," he said smugly. "But, no worries. Your secrets are safe with me. All of them."

She nabbed a pillow and bopped him over the head.

"Ow! What was that for?"

"For being such a smartie. And for forgetting my gift!"

He grabbed a pillow and slammed her back, whacking her across the shoulder. "And that's for not giving me the benefit of the doubt!"

"Hey!" She hit him again, harder this time, clean across the chest, then fell back with a giggle.

"Oh no, you don't…" he said, clobbering her again.

She raised her eyebrows, and he tackled her by the shoulders, tumbling forward. Nikki stopped laughing as he lay on top of her on the bed, his torso pinning hers to the mattress. She could feel the solidity of his frame, the lean muscles in his thighs and chest, the power of his masculinity above her. Jack looked down at her with deep brown eyes, and she could swear she could hear every measure of his breathing. Or maybe it was her own breath that was coming out in rapid puffs as her heart hammered hard between them. "Nikki, I…"

She felt fire in her cheeks as her heart careened wildly out of control. "Jack… What are you doing?"

He blinked hard, then pushed back, rolling off her and onto the mattress. She hoped he would say something, but even she couldn't explain what had just happened. It was as if in that split-second he'd gone from being just Jack to some sexy, desirable...

The pillow crashed down on her crown with a thwunk! "*That*," he teased, "is a lesson in what happens when you tempt fate."

Nikki grabbed another pillow away from him before he could nail her again. "Oh, so you're *fate* now?" she asked, clutching the pillow against her.

Jack rolled onto his side and stared at her, dark eyes dancing. "One day, some woman will call me her destiny."

Nikki's breath caught in her throat, because she knew that was true. Jack wouldn't be single forever. Someone out there was bound to snap him up, and then what would become of their friendship? Another woman might not be as understanding as Jack had been of Nikki having boyfriends. "I'm sure that's true."

His brow rose in amusement. "What? No snarky comebacks? No contest?"

But Nikki didn't want to banter anymore with Jack, not even if it was play arguing. She was having a difficult enough time getting the feel of his rock-hard body out of her mind. She handed him the pillow she'd been holding and sat up. "I'm going to grab a shower."

He appraised her as if he was trying to discern whether something was wrong. "All right."

"And when I'm done, we need to talk about wardrobe for the funeral tomorrow."

"I thought we were talking about finding the guy you're going to marry?" he called after her as she strode toward the bathroom.

"That too!" she answered, shutting the bathroom

door. Then she ran the shower water until it came out icy cold and stepped inside.

Nikki stood beside Jack under the green canvas tent. The sky beyond them was gray, with big, dark clouds hovering above. The snow had stopped, but that didn't take the edge off the bitter winds. Nikki gathered her arms around her, gripping her elbows for warmth. She and Jack hadn't discussed wardrobe last night. In fact, they hadn't discussed anything at all. When she'd emerged from the bathroom, he'd fallen dead asleep. On her bed no less. She'd had to take the other one. She cast a furtive glance his way, noting he'd dressed in a dark suit and tie, his charcoal-colored overcoat appropriately morose. She, on the other hand, wore white. Not that she could help the color of her down jacket, or the fact that her handmade scarf, hat, and mittens were brightly patterned in oranges and blues. Their base color was neutral, though: a soft beige shade, somewhere between off-white and tan. While her sweater was baby blue, her skirt, tights, and boots were jet black. So at least she was dressed right from the waist down.

Jack elbowed her, and she realized the minister had just finished his prayer. She added her "*Amen*" just in time, so as not to sound out of step with the others. Not that there were many others present. There was the attorney from yesterday, somebody from the bank, she had learned, plus some sort of investment portfolio manager. Money people, every last one. Did her Aunt Mallory leave no personal connections behind? As the minister said his final words, she viewed the urn before them that contained Aunt Mallory's ashes. It was simple but tasteful in marbled black. Nikki had taken care to lay some flowers before it. She and Jack picked them up at a small grocery store on the way over. Now she was glad they had. They were the only things that leant a bit of warmth to this perfunctory service. Though she hadn't seen her in years, and really hadn't liked her when she'd known her, Nikki couldn't help but feel sad for her late great-aunt. What a depressing way to die. Truly all alone.

The minister finished up, and she thanked him for his time. Jack slipped him some cash, and Nikki was glad he'd thought of it. Compensating the clergy hadn't been on her mind. There'd been so much to do and arrange during their hurry to get here. She'd only received the call on Christmas Eve, and the interment was to occur just two days later. If she could get there in time, the attorney said he'd prefer to read Aunt Mallory's will prior to the funeral. He had other commitments afterward that couldn't be rearranged. Nikki had agreed to fly right up and meet with him the next day. The whole thing had taken her by surprise, and she was eager to get things done with. She never could have guessed the reading of the will would leave her with a whole new problem.

After they said their good-byes to the others, Jack turned to her.

"You want to stay until it's finished?"

Nikki eyed the two grave workers appointed by the cemetery to lower the urn in the ground. She felt an unexpected lump in her throat, thinking about how lost and lonely her Aunt Mallory must have felt. She had to have been pretty desperate to write that kind of crazy will. Desperate enough to want to ensure that her grand-niece wouldn't suffer the same fate.

"Yeah," she said softly. "I think we'd better."

Jack nodded and stood by her, not bothering to offer further condolences or make unnecessary small talk. He knew her well enough to read her mood and could likely see she wasn't interested in conversation. Just by being there he said a lot. And, at that precise heartbreaking moment, that was all Nikki needed to hear.

Later, Jack steered their rental car toward the airport as Nikki stared out the window. She'd been really down since the funeral and had barely spoken during the time they'd packed up and checked out of their motel. "It was good of you to want to stay," he told her. "Until the end, I mean."

"It seemed like the right thing to do."

"Yeah." After a beat, he asked, "You doing okay?"

"I'll probably feel better once we're on the plane."

"And you order a scotch and soda?" Jack knew Nikki didn't drink much and rarely imbibed hard liquor. Except when circumstances were extreme. This seemed like one of those times.

She laughed lightly, her dark mood brightening. "You really do know me."

"I've had a few years on the job," he quipped back.

"Oh, so I'm *work* now, am I?"

His lips twitched in a smile. "You can be."

"Fine, you can think that." She adjusted her shoulder harness and repositioned herself in her seat. "Just don't tell that to Dean."

"Dean?" He was Nikki's last boyfriend. They'd

broken up eight months ago. "What's he got to do with anything?"

"That's where we're starting. My most recent mistake makes the most sense."

He stared at her, then set his gaze back on the road. "I wish you could hear yourself talking."

"I am hearing myself, and I think I'm making perfect sense. Dean's the logical choice. He's my most recent…involvement. He's smart, hot, and just a little bit sexy."

Jack blinked.

"Okay. Sexy enough. I could have his baby, I think."

He couldn't believe she was actually going to do this. Cave to her aunt's ridiculous request. "So, you're going to what? Just walk right up and ask him?"

"No. I'm going to suggest we meet in the park."

He knew that Nikki and Dean had met in Boston Common. She'd been pet sitting for a neighbor, and he'd been out walking his dog. Their leashes had gotten tangled just like in some silly romantic comedy. "You're going to get nostalgia working for you?"

"That and a little bit of cash. I'll explain the whole thing to him."

"But Dean doesn't need the money. He does well enough in business."

"Everybody can use an extra million."

Yeah, even me. Although, if Jack were to marry Nikki, it certainly wouldn't be for the money. He glanced her way, spying her jaw set in that determined fashion that said she believed she'd come up with a great idea and was prepared to act on it.

"It won't be so bad," she told him. "I actually

liked Dean."

"Yeah, but like and love are two separate things."

"Yes, like I *love* my mother and my baby brother, and have developed a deep…affection for a barn full of cows, including Big Mama."

"You're determined to do this, aren't you? What if Dean doesn't work out?"

"Gosh, Jack." She sounded mildly offended. "It's not like I don't have options."

He knew that much was true. If "options" was a code word for exes, Nikki had plenty.

"If Dean's not interested, I'll talk to Jeremy. And then Gordon."

"Kurt?

"Even Peter."

"Geez, Nikki. Are you sure about this?"

"In the past twenty-four hours, I've thought a lot about it. Yes. Tons of places in the world have arranged marriages. People marry for lots of reasons, including benefiting their families. In a way, it's nothing new. I'll just be upholding a centuries-old tradition that still plays out in many parts of the planet today."

"But this is *America*. The US of A."

"That means I get to make my own choices, doesn't it? Do whatever I decide is right for me?"

If only he could believe it *was* right. But everything about this whole twisted scheme screamed wrong, wrong, *wrong*! "I thought the deal was you were only getting married for a year. Just long enough conceive."

"Maybe we'll grow to love each other," she said a bit wistfully.

He stared at her in disbelief.

"Really! It happens all the time."

"Most often, I've seen it happen the other way. People start out head-over—"

"Will you stop being such a pessimist, for just one second? I mean, once we have a child between us, it only makes sense to give it a go."

Jack massaged his forehead with one hand while keeping the other firmly on the wheel. Maybe he was the one who needed a scotch and soda. Heavy on the scotch. *Better make mine a double.*

Chapter Three

A few days later, Jack huddled under an umbrella and sipped from his coffee. Tiny icicles rained down from the sky in spiky jabs, prickling his neck and bare knuckles. He'd been in such a rush to get here, he'd forgotten to bring his leather gloves. She'd only given him an hour's notice about the meeting. That was just like Nikki. She was impetuous and emotional, and so last minute. Undeniably, he found those things charming. But Jack also knew Nikki well enough to guess she wanted to barrel through this first attempt before she lost her nerve. Jack clutched his paper cup as she approached. She wore a luminous raincoat that matched the bright red polka dots on her umbrella. Waves of luscious brown hair spilled out from beneath her knit cap as her blue eyes sparkled. She strode past him and whispered, "Wish me luck…"

"Luck!" he called after her, but he didn't mean it. The last thing he wanted was for Nikki to go marrying another guy. At the far end of the park, he spied Dean standing by a hedge abutting the lake, his tall, lean form framed by Boston's highest buildings. They stood like gloomy towers in the fog, but nothing could feel more dismal than the ache in Jack's heart. He'd scarcely slept last night, tossing and turning over this whole ordeal. In the end, he'd decided the best thing he could do was play along. Nikki was headstrong enough to forge her own path, and any resistance she encountered would only lend that much more zeal to her quest. If Jack took it easy—even acted supportive—Nikki was sure to see the error of her ways.

Dean spotted Nikki, and his expression brightened. They embraced briefly, umbrellas tilting backward as an icy stream of rain shimmied down between them. Both laughed and wiped their clothing, appearing to chat easily over small talk. He was probably asking her how she'd been, and she was likely suggesting he help her make a baby. Jack felt his neck flash hot and his temples pound at that last thought. It was hard to forget what had transpired in their motel room when he and Nikki had been kidding around. From one moment to the next, they'd morphed from long-time friends into potential lovers. It had lasted only a second, but Jack had felt that fire down to his very core. He wondered if Nikki had sensed it too.

Suddenly, Dean seemed taken aback. He thrust his hands to the side, setting his umbrella askew and letting his head get drenched in the process. He didn't seem to notice the rain as he stared agape at Nikki. Then he began speaking rapidly, righting his umbrella in one hand, then pulling something from his coat pocket with the other. It was a wallet. He flipped it open. *What on earth? Did she require identification? Or a sperm count?*

Nikki took the billfold and studied something inside it, her face falling. *I see,* she appeared to be telling him. *Who knew?* Then she flipped the thing shut with a shrug.

Dean tucked the wallet in his pocket and shook his head. The next thing Jack knew, Dean was shaking his finger at Nikki. Scolding her, he supposed, for the very idea as she backed away. Nikki cast a tight grin in Jack's direction, knowing he was waiting. Dean wheeled toward him. *Wait a minute,* he seemed to think. *Jack's been watching?* Dean's voice was harsh, cracking in the morning air as she retreated quickly toward Jack and he barked after her, "That's rich, Nikki! Just rich!" He shook the heavy moisture from his umbrella, then straightened it and strode away. Nikki scurried toward Jack.

"Didn't go so well, I take it?"

She was out of breath, little puffs of air appearing between hot-pink lips. "It was awful. *He* was awful. And to think I might have married him!"

"Hmm, yes."

"After all this time, I thought he still might care."

"You were together three years."

"That's what I told him. Exactly."

"What was in the wallet?"

"A picture of Mary Ann, and—get this—her three kids!"

"Who's Mary Ann?"

"His wife!"

"Guess you're a little late."

"Here's the horrible thing. Dean used to say he'd never have kids."

"Then, why did you—?"

"He said not at least until he turned thirty. Which would have been perfect, since he's twenty-nine and a half."

She gazed at him, desperation in her eyes. "And now he's gone and gotten the package deal!"

"Well, you *have* been apart a while."

"Eight months? That's more than a kid a quarter!"

"But they're not *his*—biologically, I mean. Right?"

"Mary Ann's his old college girlfriend. They broke up after school, and she married someone else."

"It apparently didn't last."

"She told Dean she'd never forgotten him. That he was the only guy she'd ever loved. I guess he decided the feeling was mutual."

"Ouch. He said that?"

"Said what?"

"That Mary Ann was the only woman he'd ever loved?"

"Thanks for rubbing it in, Jack. I didn't even think about it that way."

The wind picked up, rustling her raincoat and billowing their umbrellas.

"I'm sorry, Nikki. Really, I am." In a strange sort of way, he saw it was true. He hated seeing that disappointed little pout. Besides, he was mad at Dean for being crass. He could have said a polite *no, thanks* without shoving it in Nikki's face that he'd never loved her. At least not as much as Mary Ann. He must not have wasted any time in saying *I do* once the two of them hooked up again.

She met his gaze. "You wouldn't believe what he said about you."

"*Me?*"

"Yeah, and that was before he knew you were in the park."

Jack leaned toward her. "What did he say?"

She blinked hard. "Just that it would be impossible for me to form a real relationship with *any* man as long as Jack was along."

"Hey!" He didn't know why, but he didn't like the sound of that. Then, secretly, he wondered if it was true. If the roles were reversed, he wasn't sure he'd be so understanding.

"Ludicrous, right? What an inane thing to say."

"Totally stupid."

"Then, when he saw you were here, he really flipped out."

"I caught that part."

She heaved a sigh and shivered.

"We need to get you out of the rain."

"Yeah, and you've got to go to work." The truth was, he did. He was already an hour late, but he knew the boss would cut him slack. His boss was not just his dad, he was also one of Nikki's biggest fans. Plus, he was a huge proponent of helping out distressing damsels. Yeah, he said it that way because he knew Nikki was the one who gave Jack the biggest headaches. He also thought she was funny and sweet and *"just as cute as a button."* He'd known her since she was a kid, when she and Jack had first started hanging out.

"When do you go in today?"

"Four o'clock."

"Night shift?"

"Yeah."

"Stop by later for some fish and chips? I'll even toss in a draft beer." Jack helped his dad run a restaurant by the water. His dad managed the place while Jack kept the books. One day, his dad hoped to turn the operation over to Jack completely, and Jack wouldn't be opposed. He loved chatting with the customers at The Wharf and had a great time shooting the breeze with the fishermen who brought in their daily catches.

"Girl can't refuse an offer like that." She flashed him a smile, and his whole world seemed warmer.

"Besides, we've got to plan our next move."

"Move?"

"Jeremy," she answered, like that was so logical he should have thought of it.

"Oh right," he said, his heart sinking a bit. "Jeremy."

"Ow! Watch it, will ya?"

Nikki pulled back the straight pin, realizing she'd just poked the poor man's shoulder. She was taking the jacket in to adjust for the slope in his shoulders, as well as for the fact that one of his arms was longer than the other.

"I'm sorry, sir. I'll try to be more careful."

He studied her in the mirror with cool, gray eyes. "Yes, do that, won't you?"

Nikki's face heated under his stern gaze. She couldn't afford to mess this up. She'd already had two customers complain to her boss today.

She nodded and continued marking the seam, taking extra care with her work. She finally finished, then adjusted the jacket. "Better?"

He turned to study his own reflection, pivoting from side to side. "I think it's an improvement. Don't you?"

"You look exceptional," she said in her best, polished tone.

He eyed her skeptically.

"No, seriously. The cut is perfect on you now."

He shook out his arms, then turned to get a rear view, glancing over his shoulder. "You're right!" He surprised her with a smile. "It works."

Nikki smiled in return, sighing inwardly with relief.

"How soon can you have this ready?"

"Tuesday?"

He twisted his lips, then pulled a billfold from his pocket and extracted some cash. He pressed a large bill into her hand. "Can I convince you to have it ready by tomorrow?"

Nikki looked down in shock to see it was a hundred. "Sir, I can't—" She tried to hand it back to him, but he nodded her off.

"Nonsense. I know it's extra work: a rush job."

She attempted to return the money again. "I really can't accept tips."

"It's not a tip. It's an incentive."

She met his eyes. "Incentives either."

"That's too bad." He plucked the bill from her fingers. "Then I'll have to take my business elsewhere." He removed the jacket and handed it to her as she stood there dumbstruck.

"Wait!" she called as he turned to go. "I can have it ready tomorrow. No extra incentives necessary."

He studied her. "By noon?"

Nikki felt sweat bead at her temples. Noon would mean either staying late or coming in very early. She already had three other orders to finish and had fallen behind due to her time away. If she lost another customer today, her boss would have her head. Marilynn had been less than enthusiastic about her taking time off for her aunt's funeral. The day after Christmas was big for sales, and the other tailor they employed, Roger, was on a cruise in the Caribbean that he'd booked months in advance. Nikki had promised to hold down the fort during the holidays, but she couldn't have foreseen her family emergency. She equally couldn't have known she'd return from the Midwest such a mess.

It was hard to focus on her job with Mallory's deadline looming overhead. If she got that inheritance, she might not need this job at all. But at the moment, the prospect of two million dollars seemed like pie in the sky, and Nikki needed to keep her feet on the ground. Her mom's supervisors were even less understanding than Marilynn, and that spoke volumes. They'd said that if Emma had to keep taking days off due to her health, perhaps it would be best for her to think of not coming back at all. Times were tough, and plenty of others needed employment. Others who could be relied on to come in to work day after day.

No matter how independent her mom tried to be, Nikki knew that if push came to shove—and she really did lose her job—Emma couldn't support herself and Tony on unemployment, even with him keeping his part-time job. Nikki would have to step in and help out. And she'd be glad to. She'd take on added work if that was what her mom and Tony needed to make ends meet. But the best way to earn extra cash involved working overtime here. That would prove impossible if she lost this job. Nikki swallowed hard, then met the customer's gaze. "Tomorrow at noon will be fine."

Once he'd gone, Marilynn leaned her head into the fitting room. She wore a short, blonde bob and little tiny glasses that set severe dark lines against her steely gaze. "At least you didn't mess that last one up. He actually *complimented you* on the way out."

Nikki blinked and smiled politely, holding her tongue. While she'd gotten on famously with the old boss who had hired her, Marilynn had been on her case since day one. Nikki didn't even know why. She worked hard and was generally good at her job.

"Oh, and since you'll be coming in early tomorrow anyway…"

Nikki held her breath and waited, expecting the ambush. When Marilynn began a sentence with "Oh…" it typically meant one was coming. "You might want to take a second look at those gabardine slacks you hemmed."

"But they're all done. Set for pickup."

"Not quite." Marilyn wagged her index finger. "I took a look at the stitching, and frankly…" She shared a twisted smile. "I found it a bit uneven."

"But, I—"

"No *buts* about it," Marilyn scolded sternly, as if Nikki were some wayward preschool child. "You know how we feel about quality control at Stanley's." Her voice took on a sing-songy tone. "I wouldn't want to have to mention anything to the higher-ups about someone getting sloppy."

Nikki met Marilynn's gaze. "I'll look at the slacks," she told her. "First thing."

Later that evening, Nikki sat at the bar with Jack. He'd poured them both draft beers before putting in her order. The place was closing up, with just a few scattered diners lingering at their tables. Nikki could understand the patrons' reluctance to leave. The view of the harbor was stunning from here, particularly at night with lights dotting the docks and twinkling from nearby establishments. She took a swig from her mug, then set it down. "Marilynn was extra feisty today."

"Uh-oh, don't tell me she used the 'O' word."

"As in *Oh, Nikki…*?" Nikki took another sip of

beer. "Yeah, she did."

"What've you done now?"

"Oh, Jack—"

"Now you're using the 'O' word on me."

She burst out laughing. "Not like she does, and you know it."

"Right." He quaffed his own drink. "So tell me. What's the infraction?"

"Gabardine slacks."

"Sounds serious."

"More serious than I knew."

He stroked his chin. "Too long in the crotch?"

She swatted him.

His brow shot up. "Too short?"

"Stop it!" But she was giggling just the same.

"You can't let her get to you. Just think of her as an unpleasant aspect of your job. Necessary but unpleasant."

"I wouldn't call her necessary."

"What would you call her, then?"

"Resident evil."

Jack chuckled behind his mug just as his dad, Greg, appeared. "Nikki!" he said, holding his arms out for a hug. "Aren't you a sight for sore eyes?" Greg looked just like Jack only about thirty years older, plus about twenty pounds heavier. His brow was wrinkled and his hair was thinning, but he was one of the kindest men Nikki knew. He embraced her sweetly, then pulled back with a frown, his face etched with concern. "I'm sorry for your loss, kiddo."

"Thanks, Greg."

"How was the trip? Jack here says it was a whirlwind."

"We were pretty much up and back."

"And the service?"

"A little lonely."

"Lonely, huh? I'm sorry to hear that."

"Her Aunt Mallory didn't have many friends," Jack said.

Greg gave Nikki's arm a pat. "Well, at least she left good family behind her. And family, as we all know, means everything."

Nikki smiled sadly. "Yeah."

Greg glanced at their beers. "All taken care of? Got something to eat?"

"It's coming, thanks," Nikki answered.

"Well, you let me know if there's anything I can do for you, kiddo. Anything at all." He glanced at his son. "Meanwhile, I'll leave things in Jack's capable hands." He met Nikki's eyes. "You know he has your back."

"I know that, and I'm very grateful."

Another middle-aged man approached Greg and held out his hand with a loud hello. Greg turned toward him, smiling brightly. "Well, I'll be a monkey's uncle!"

"See you later!" Nikki said as he left them.

Greg shot her a wink before walking away with his long-lost chum. "Hope so."

Just then, Nikki's cell rang. "It's my mom," she said, checking the number.

Jack nodded as she took the call.

"Hey, Ma. How are you feeling?"

"Good, Nikki. I'm good. I was just calling to see how things went at Aunt Mallory's."

"It…was a busy trip."

"Jack went with you?"

She eyed him sitting beside her at the bar. "Yes."

"That's good. I'm glad you had company for the road." There was a brief pause on the line before her mom continued. "I'd like to hear more about it. I was thinking that maybe you could come to dinner. You can bring Jack if you'd like."

Nikki covered her cell with her hand. "She wants you to come to dinner."

"Just me?"

Nikki glared at him because he never stopped teasing, but he knew her ire was pretend.

"Fine. Yes. I'll go... When?"

"When were you thinking, Ma?"

"Friday."

Nikki glanced at Jack. "It's New Year's Eve," she whispered. "Maybe you have plans?"

"No plans I can't cancel."

"Seriously?" she asked, her cell still covered.

"Nikki," he told her firmly. "I'm not sending you in there to spill to your mom alone."

"Who says I'm spilling to my mom?"

"You're not planning to tell her?"

"Not planning to tell me what?"

Nikki looked down to see her hand had slipped off the mouthpiece. "It's nothing," she answered quickly, "nothing at all." Then she said her good-byes and stared at Jack. "I don't want Emma knowing anything."

"About the will?"

She shook her head.

"But why not?"

"She'll say it's crazy, just one more way Aunt Mallory is trying to manipulate things from the grave."

"And she'd be right!"

Nikki's fish and chips arrived, and boy did they smell heavenly. "Jack, I don't want my mom knowing anything, including anything about what happened in the park today. Because she'd tell me to stop, try to talk me out of it."

"Selling yourself off for cold, hard cash?"

Nikki's temperature spiked. "Hey, listen. I do not sell out, okay?" she said, remembering her earlier client. "At least not in the way you're thinking. You believe this is all about me, don't you? That I'm somehow being selfish." Moisture built in her eyes, but she fought back her tears. "Sometimes Jack, there's a nobler cause, you know. Something that is bigger than ourselves."

He met her gaze. "It's not up to you to set the world right."

"Not your world, maybe. But in my little universe? Yeah. I'm taking control." She picked up a bottle of malt and sprinkled it liberally on her fried fish.

"Hey," Jack said softly. "I'm not the enemy."

She stopped what she was doing to look at him.

"I'm the one who's here for you, remember? The one who has your back?"

Nikki knew it was true. There was nobody else she could count on. No one else she'd trust with her deepest secrets, especially the ones she was harboring now.

"I won't say a word to your mom about the whole Mallory thing. I promise."

"I couldn't wish for a better friend."

Jack's eyes glistened slightly in the dim light. "Neither could I." He surprised Nikki by reaching into his jeans pocket and pulling out a small, wrapped package. He set it on the bar in front of her beside her steaming plate. "A few days late, but...Merry Christmas."

Nikki was overwhelmed by emotion, and embarrassed for having snapped at him. "You didn't."

"I have to get you back somehow." He shot her a tilted smile. "For those amazing concert tickets."

She lifted the tiny box in her hand. It was professionally wrapped like it had come from a jeweler's. "I hope you didn't break our pact."

"By getting you anything too expensive or personal?"

She stared into his deep brown eyes and slowly nodded.

"Nope."

"Well, good."

"Nothing's too expensive—or too personal—for a best friend."

"Jack!"

"Okay, okay. The truth is I might have stretched the limits just a bit. But it was for very good reasons."

"I'm listening."

"Remember last spring when we were talking about relationships? About what makes them perfect?"

"Romantic relationships, you mean?"

"Yeah. It was just after you broke up with Dean."

"He dumped me."

"His loss."

"Thanks."

"Both times."

"Can we cut to the chase here?" She rattled the present, ready to open it. There was nothing Nikki loved more than gifts, and she rarely received any.

Usually she was the one making stuff for other people. Handmade stuff, but still. It really *was* the thought that counted.

"We both laid out our criteria. Yours were a little more picky than mine."

"Precise, Jack. I believe the word is *precise*. You said that setting expectations didn't really matter. When you found the one, you knew it somehow. It was like fate, karma…destiny. And I said there's more to it than that. The two people should be compatible in three important ways. A melding of mind, body, and—"

"Spirit," he finished for her.

She studied his face for clues but couldn't find any answers. "What's this about?"

"Open it."

She carefully slid off the silky ribbon, then peeled back the shiny red paper. It was a jewelry box. Nikki's heart pounded. He couldn't have… Shouldn't have… She lifted the lid to find a lovely necklace nestled inside. "Oh Jack, it's beautiful."

"It's an infinity charm," he told her.

Nikki held the charm up by its silver chain, seeing three thin metal bands braided around each other and coiled into a circle.

"That's white gold, yellow gold, and silver."

"Mind, body, and…" Nikki choked back a sob, overcome by the moment.

"I was thinking if you wore it, it might bring you luck. In finding the right guy."

"And right now, I need all the luck I can get."

"No, you don't." He looked at her with compassion. "All you've got to do is be yourself."

"Do you really think I can do it? Find that sort of

person between now and February?"

"You may have to lower your standards a little."

"What?"

"I bought you the necklace before Christmas, Nikki. Before I realized you were on a deadline."

Her head wrestled with her heart, but her head ultimately won. "Two out of three's not bad."

Jack studied her pretty profile, wishing he could find a way to convince Nikki not to settle. But when Nikki was determined, there was no convincing her of anything.

"Which two are you going for?"

"The two I can get, I guess."

He watched her a moment, then said quietly, "Your food's getting cold."

"Oh yeah." She dropped the necklace back in the box and replaced its lid. "Thanks for the necklace, Jack. I really love it. I love it a lot."

She took a bite of her cod and it crunched, steam escaping. "So, what did you get Veronica?" she asked, referring to his girlfriend.

"A digital camera, like she wanted."

"That was nice."

"Yeah." *Especially now that she's out of the picture*, Jack thought but didn't say. They'd had a big fight the night he returned from Mallory's funeral. Veronica hadn't liked him going away, and he wouldn't give in to her demands for him to stop seeing his best friend. What's more, Jack understood he'd emerged from the trip conflicted. He couldn't keep seeing Veronica when he felt so mixed up about Nikki. As if her caving in to her aunt's demands for her to marry another guy wasn't bad enough, their exchange in that motel room had jumbled his emotions. He had to sort out his own head before getting involved with any female—ever again.

"How are you going to explain New Year's to her? Won't she be upset about it?"

"No more than she is already."

Her face registered understanding. "You didn't. Right before Christmas?"

"It was after, actually. She took it okay." He shrugged. "Maybe all she wanted was that camera anyway."

"Come on."

"I spoke with Dave," he said, changing the subject.

"Your cousin the lawyer?"

"Yeah."

"When?"

"Today, after the park."

"And?"

"He says maybe there's a way out of it. We... You can contest, just like your aunt's counsel said."

"How long will that take?"

"At least a couple of months. Maybe more."

"That's cutting things awfully close."

"Yeah, but it could work. You could still get the money and not have to go through with any of this."

"That sounds like a pretty big *if* from this stool."

"I think it's an angle worth pursuing."

"How much will it cost?"

"I can get him to cut you a deal."

"I doubt I can afford it."

"I'll talk to him."

"I don't know." But she looked like she was considering it. "What if I miss the boat, and the whole wad goes to the state?"

"It's a risk, I know. But—"

She looked him square in the eye. "I'm not willing to take a risk."

"Nikki, listen to me. One week ago, you didn't even know about the money. Now that you do, you're whole life's gone crazy."

"No. Now that I do, my life's got potential. Potential beyond what I ever dreamed possible. I can *do something* for my mom and brother, Jack. Finally give back."

"And sacrifice yourself in the process?"

"It won't be a sacrifice."

"How do you know?"

She laid her hand on the present he'd given her. "If I don't at least feel a full two out of three, I won't do it."

"You mean there has to be something there besides the money?"

"I mean I have to believe I can actually *love* the guy. I'm not a robot, you know. I have a heart beating in here." She thumped her chest with her fist. "All I'm saying is, there are people I've loved in the past. What's so wrong about believing I could maybe love them again? It happened to Dean with Mary Ann, didn't it?"

There was nothing Jack could say to that. In a very strange way, Nikki was almost starting to make sense.

"It could all work out. Can't you see? Maybe I and one of my exes didn't make it for a reason. That reason could be as simple as timing."

"And who knows?" Jack interceded. "Maybe you haven't even found him yet. Your soul mate. You still could run into him. There's time."

"You're right." Nikki reopened the gift box and took out the necklace. "Here," she said, handing it to him. "Help me put this on."

Nikki lifted her hair, and he draped the delicate chain around her neck, clicking its latch in place. The eternity charm dipped toward her cleavage as it hung in the opening of her V-neck sweater. She looked up at him with big, blue eyes and smiled. Jack had always found her pretty, but she seemed extra beautiful in this moment.

"I like it. I think it's going to bring me luck."

He smiled back at her, thinking this was going to be one hell of a ride. "What time should I come to get you on Friday?"

"I'll probably have to go straight there from work. Still got lots of catching up to do."

"Pick you up a six o'clock?"

"Better make it seven."

~ * ~

End Excerpt from
Baby, Be Mine